A LEGACY OF LIGHT

A LEGACY OF LIGHT

THE DRAGON WAR, BOOK ONE

DANIEL ARENSON

Copyright © 2013 by Daniel Arenson

ISBN: 978-1-927601-06-8

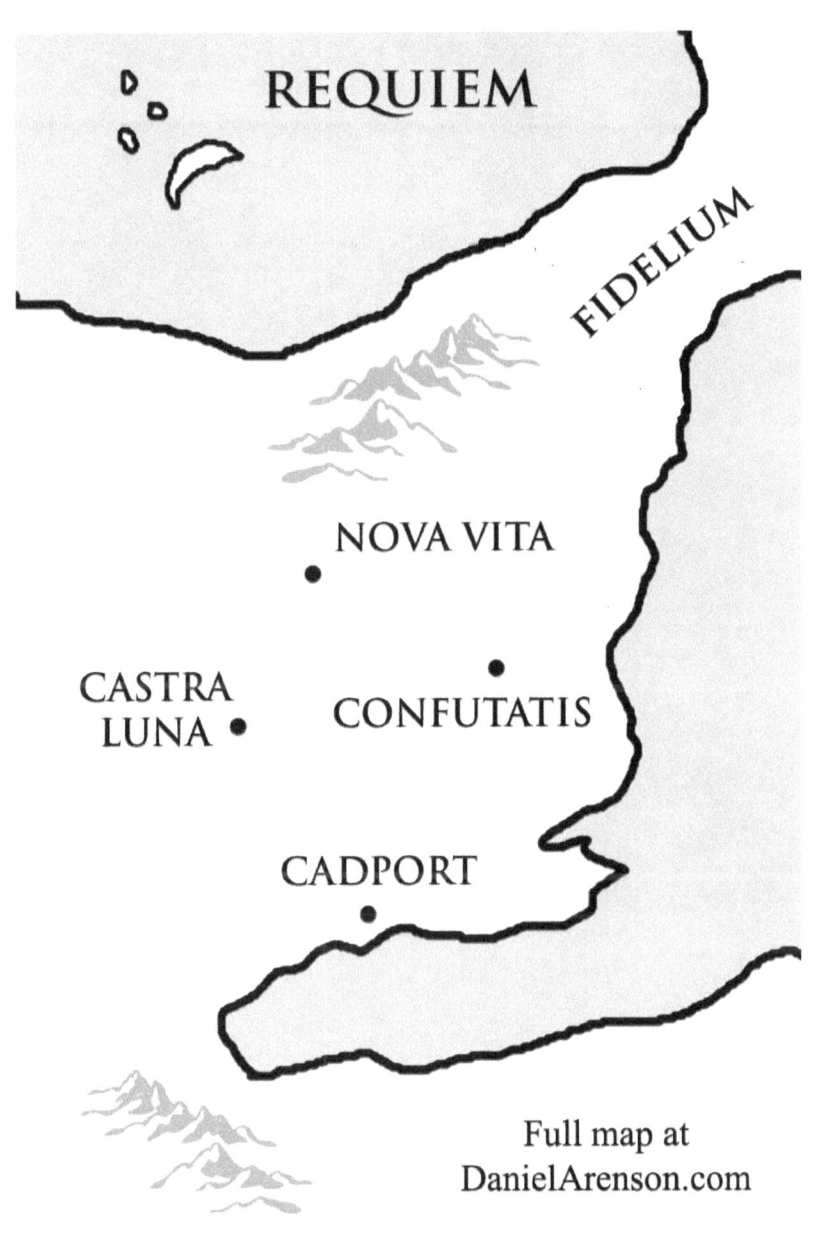

REQUIEM

FIDELIUM

NOVA VITA

CASTRA
LUNA

CONFUTATIS

CADPORT

Full map at
DanielArenson.com

KAELYN

Kaelyn ran through the forest, clutching her bow, as above her the dragons shrieked and gave chase.

The night was dark; the treetops hid the moon and stars. Kaelyn could barely see. Her foot slammed into an oak's root and she tumbled, cursed, and leaped back up. She kept running. Her quiver of arrows bounced across her back. When she looked up, she saw them there, shades of black above the canopy.

Damn it.

Five or more flew above, and they had picked up her scent. Kaelyn snarled and ran on. Branches slapped her face. Her ankle twisted atop a rock, and she cursed and nearly fell again.

Just keep moving, Kaelyn, she told herself. *They can't see you through the trees. The cave is near. There is safety there. Just don't stop running.*

Dirt and fallen leaves flew from under her boots. Even in the cold night, sweat soaked her leggings and tunic, and her long golden hair clung damply to her neck and cheeks. A stream of fire blazed above. Kaelyn ducked and rolled. The flames roared, lighting the night, and for an instant Kaelyn saw a thousand black trees, mossy boulders, and a fleeing deer.

"I see the girl!" rose a shriek above. "Right below. I want her alive!"

Then the fire was gone. Wings thudded and air blasted Kaelyn. Claws longer than swords tore at the trees. Wood cracked and branches flew. Two red eyes blazed, their light shining on fangs and black scales.

Kaelyn leaped to her feet. She nocked an arrow. She fired.

The arrow whistled and slammed into the dragon. The beast reared and howled and clawed the sky. Kaelyn turned and ran.

The trees blurred at her sides. Fire blazed behind her. The dragons swooped and claws uprooted trees. A bole slammed down before Kaelyn, showering splinters and broken branches, and she yelped and fell back. A dragon landed upon the fallen oak. Its maw opened, a smelter of molten fire, and light bathed Kaelyn, and heat blasted her.

She fired another arrow, hitting the dragon's chest. The beast bucked and roared, spewing a fountain of fire. Kaelyn leaped, rolled down a rocky hill, and crashed into a tree. Pain exploded. She yelped, sprang back up, and fired a third arrow. She hit another dragon, then spun and kept running.

Damn it! she thought as she raced between the trees. Her heart thudded and her lungs ached. Her bruises blazed so badly that she ran with a limp.

They weren't supposed to be here.

But somehow these beasts knew about the boy in the city. Somehow they knew Kaelyn would try to reach him. She cursed as she sprang between more collapsing trees. If these dragons reached Cadport first, and if they found the boy before she did...

"Then we are lost," she whispered as she ran. "Then all hope is dead. Then the world will fall."

She snarled and ran up a hill thick with oaks and maples.

So I will have to kill these dragons. And I will have to reach the boy before he's found.

A howl tore the air above her.

"Kaelyn!" one dragon cried and laughed, a throaty sound like boulders tumbling. "Kaelyn, you little whore. Haven't you learned you can never hide from me?"

Ice encased Kaelyn's heart.

So the spies were right, she thought. Kaelyn had not wanted to believe, but now she saw the beast above her. *It's her. She knows. She's here.*

Flames roared. Blasting fire, a blue dragon swooped down before her, claws tearing trees and shattering boulders. Flames howled in an inferno. Red eyes burned. The beast's maw opened wide, and it shot a stream of flame across the forest. Kaelyn ducked and screamed, and the fire blazed over her head.

There was no doubt now. It was her.

My sister.

Kaelyn fired an arrow.

The shard whistled, slammed against the blue dragon, and snapped. The beast only laughed, nostrils flaring and leaking smoke.

Kaelyn had not wanted to use her magic. Not today. If she had learned anything during the long years of resistance, it was this: As a human girl, she was sneaky and silent and could hide in shadows. Dragons were burly, their scales clattered, and their maws leaked fire that could be seen for leagues. Humans survived in the wild; dragons were hunted and died.

And yet no arrows or shadows would help her now. This was no ordinary dragon facing her, a mindless soldier with weak scales. Here before her, atop a pile of charred trees, roared Shari Cadigus herself.

My older sister. Princess of the empire. The most dangerous woman I know.

Kaelyn tightened her lips, narrowed her eyes, and summoned her magic.

Wings burst out from her back with a thud. Green scales flowed across her, clanking like armor. Her body ballooned. Her fingernails grew into claws, fangs sprouted from her mouth, and a tail flailed behind her. As her sister howled, a blue beast roaring fire, Kaelyn flapped her wings and took flight as a green dragon.

She crashed through the treetops. She burst into a burning sky. Three other dragons circled under the clouds; they saw her, roared fire, and dived her way. Below, her sister Shari burst from the trees, smoke wreathing her blue scales.

Oh bloody stars, Kaelyn thought.

She spewed her flames, raining them down upon Shari. The blue dragon howled as the fire crashed into her. The beast kept rising through the inferno. With a curse, Kaelyn began to fly higher, shooting up in a straight line. Beneath her, her sister and the others blew fire and soared in pursuit.

Kaelyn shot into the clouds. For a moment she could see nothing but the gray mist; she was hidden here.

A pillar of flame rose before her, piercing the sky and nearly roasting her. Kaelyn cursed and spun the other way. Another flaming jet rose there. She ducked and nearly fell from the cloud cover.

"There!" Shari cried below. Her voice rang across the sky, high-pitched and demonic. "I want her alive—grab her."

Kaelyn flapped her wings. She rose a few feet, then leveled off and began flying south. At least, she thought she was heading south; she could barely tell within these clouds.

Stars save me, she thought. *None of this should have happened. Oh, stars, none of this should have happened at all. They'll be heading to Cadport now. They'll find the boy. They'll kill him. And it will be over.*

Dragons shrieked before her. Jets of flame pierced the clouds like spears. Kaelyn bit down on a yelp. She kept flying, daring not blow her own fire.

They can't see me, she thought. *I'll reach the boy before them. He's our only hope.*

She snarled and flew harder.

She had not thought more bad luck possible. As if the world itself conspired against her, the clouds began to thin.

Kaelyn dived and darted from wisp to wisp, trying to remain in cover. But it was no use. She was too close to the sea now. She could smell the salt on the wind. That salty air would lead her to Cadport and the boy who hid there.

It also dispersed the clouds, leaving her green scales to shimmer in the moonlight.

She looked over her shoulder.

She saw them there, the blue dragon and her three servants. A jet of fire blazed her way and Kaelyn ducked, barely dodging it. The heat blasted her. Claws reached out and grabbed her back leg, and Kaelyn yowled. She blew fire over her shoulder, hit the dragon who grabbed her, and tore herself free. She dived low. They followed.

A slim green dragon, she raced across wild grasslands, heading toward the sea. The grass bent under the flap of her wings, sending mice fleeing. The great blue dragon, a furnace of flame, and the three smaller black ones followed. Their fires blazed, and Kaelyn knew that she would die this night, and that with her the Resistance too would fall.

But no. Not yet. There! She saw it ahead—the hill and the cave. Hope bloomed inside Kaelyn like a flower from snow. She let out a cry, swooped, and flew toward the shelter.

Jets of fire blazed around her. Kaelyn darted like a bee, dodging them, until the cave loomed close. A blast of flame seared her tail, and she yowled but kept flying. With a roar, the green dragon shot toward the cave. It rose only as tall as a door, too small for a dragon to enter. Feet away from crashing against the hillside, Kaelyn released her magic.

Her wings and scales vanished. She shrank. She returned to human form. She rolled into the cave as a woman, sprang up, and ran into darkness.

A tunnel stretched before her.

Fire blasted behind.

Kaelyn raced around a bend in the tunnel and spun backward. The dragonfire crashed before her, hitting the stone walls and showering. Kaelyn took a few steps back. The heat bathed her, and she brushed sparks off her tunic and leggings. The flames kept roaring for a moment, then died.

Her sister's shriek rose outside like a storm.

"Get in there, maggots! Bring her out alive, or by the Abyss, I'll make a cloak from your skin. Go! Bring me the little trollop. I will break her."

Her clothes smoldered, and her leg throbbed with pain, but Kaelyn drew an arrow. Her fingers shook so badly she could barely nock it.

The fires died. Outside the cave, Kaelyn heard the clank of scales become the clatter of armor. The four dragons had released their magic.

"Now we will fight as humans," Kaelyn whispered. The tunnel walls closed in around her, too small for two to enter abreast. "One by one, I will slay you."

She stood, waiting around the bend, fingers shaking and lungs burning with smoke.

Boots thumped into the cave. Steel hissed—swords being drawn from sheaths. Kaelyn snarled and tugged her bowstring back.

The first man emerged around the bend—one of Shari's brutes. He towered above Kaelyn, a burly man clad in black steel. A red spiral blazed across his dark breastplate, and he clutched his dragonclaw sword. This one was a common soldier, no more than a thug.

Kaelyn's arrow slammed into his breastplate, drove through the steel, and crashed into his chest.

The man fell, and Kaelyn reached into her quiver for another arrow. Before she could draw it, a second man raced around the bend.

This one too wore black armor, and a helm of steel bars shadowed his face. His sword swung, and Kaelyn leaped back. The blade whistled before her, missing her belly by an inch. She nocked her arrow and fired. The arrow scraped the man's helmet, then slammed against the wall. The soldier cackled and swung his blade down.

Kaelyn scurried back and fell down hard. The man's blade hit the floor between her legs, raising sparks. With a snarl, she drew her own sword, a silvery blade named Lemuria after the drowned isle of ancient gods. She leaped up and thrust her steel.

Lemuria scraped against the man's breastplate, denting it. The brute grunted, spat, and swung his sword. He bore a longsword, thick and heavy, a blade for two hands; her sword was smaller and lighter, a single-handed weapon of thin steel. The blades clashed, spraying sparks, and Kaelyn growled.

No. I will not die here. The boy needs me. The Resistance needs me. She snarled. *I will live.*

She pulled her blade back, screamed, and fell to one knee. She drove Lemuria up. The blade crashed into the man's armpit where his armor's plates met.

Blood spurted. Snarling, Kaelyn drove her blade deeper, shoving it through the man's armpit and into his chest. Blood dripped down her arm. She pulled her blade free, and the man crashed down dead.

With a thin smile, her blade red, Kaelyn walked around the bend to see the third man there.

She charged toward him, their blades clanged, and Kaelyn swung Lemuria low. She swept the man's legs out from under him. He fell to his knees. With a shout, she drove her blade between the bars of his visor. Blood seeped out. The man gurgled, then fell silent.

Kaelyn stood panting. Her head spun and every breath sawed at her lungs.

Languid clapping sounded ahead. Kaelyn looked up.

At the cave's entrance, her sister stood in human form.

"Shari Cadigus," Kaelyn whispered. "Princess of the empire. The Blue Bitch." Her lips twisted. "My sister."

It had been years since Kaelyn had seen Shari, but the woman hadn't changed. Shari was twenty-eight years old, a full decade older than Kaelyn, and the two sisters looked nothing alike. While Kaelyn was short and slim, Shari was tall and muscular. While Kaelyn had golden hair and hazel eyes, Shari sported a mane of brown curls and dark, blazing eyes. While Kaelyn wore gray leggings and a green tunic, the garb of a woodswoman, Shari wore black armor, a crimson cape, and steel-tipped boots.

A rebel and a soldier, Kaelyn thought. *Sisters. Enemies to the death.*

Shari laughed, hands on her hips. "The Blue Bitch! So they still call me that, do they? A reference to my dragon scales, I imagine." She tapped her cheek. "You know, a man once called me that to my face. His skin still hangs somewhere in my closet."

Kaelyn raised her bloodied sword. "Shari, if you take a step closer, I will stick this in your neck."

A crooked smile twisted the older woman's lips. She raised an eyebrow and nodded. "So we will play. Like we did as children. I will enjoy that."

With a long, luxurious hiss, Shari drew her longsword. The blade was black and wisps of flame danced around it. The pommel was shaped as a dragonclaw, the crossguard like wings. Shari's leather glove creaked as she twisted her fingers around the hilt.

Kaelyn snarled and fear flooded her. She remembered the "games" Shari had enjoyed playing when they were young. Kaelyn still bore the scars across her body—the scars of Shari's blades, heated irons, and pincers, the toys of a sadistic youth who delighted in shedding her little sister's blood.

But tonight I will be the one spilling her blood, Kaelyn swore. She snarled and raised Lemuria before her. Her blade was smaller, her arms were shorter, and she wore no armor, but Kaelyn swore this to her stars. *Tonight I kill her.*

Screaming, she ran down the cave toward Shari.

Her sister smirked, swung her sword, and the two blades crashed.

"Yes, scream for me!" Shari said and laughed. She pulled her blade back and thrust, and Kaelyn barely parried. "You always did scream as a child when I cut you. You sounded like a sow in heat; it was the best part."

Kaelyn clenched her jaw and swung. Shari parried lazily, still smirking, her eyes mocking. Kaelyn tightened her lips.

Ignore her, she told herself. *Ignore her taunts. Focus! Be one with the blade. Kill her.*

She thrust her sword. Shari checked the blow.

"My my, you've grown feisty, little one." Shari barked a laugh. "Do you remember that time I caught you trying to eat dinner before me? Do you remember how you screamed when I drove my fork down into your hand? So many tears you shed!"

Kaelyn snarled. "My hand still bears that scar. That hand now holds the blade that will kill you."

With a grunt, she thrust Lemuria. Shari parried with a yawn.

"So far, not much luck there, beloved sister." Shari smirked. "Are you growing tired already, little one? You look a little winded."

Kaelyn swung her blade yet again, but Shari's defenses seemed impenetrable. *Damn it.* Kaelyn was a competent swordswoman, but Shari's skill with the blade dwarfed her own. Screaming now, Kaelyn swung again and again. The swords clanged, crashed against the cave walls, raised sparks, and kept flying. Shari wasn't even attacking, just checking every blow.

She's toying with me, Kaelyn realized.

Fear flooded her. Shari blocked the exit from the cave; fleeing was not an option here, yet how could she kill her sister? Shari hadn't even broken out in a sweat, and Kaelyn was so tired; her clothes clung to her, her throat burned, and she panted.

"My sweet little Kae," Shari said, and mock concern filled her eyes. "You look ready to collapse. Don't you realize, little sister? Did you never know? Of course your silly little... what do you call it? The Resistance? Of course this little *adventure* of yours was doomed to fail." She blocked another thrust and pouted. "Poor Kaelyn. Father will continue to reign. And I will follow him. And you, sweet sister, will wish that I'd killed you tonight. You will weep and beg for death many years from now, as you still hang in my dungeon, as my whips break your skin again and again."

Finally Shari attacked.

Her face changed, all the mockery vanishing, and rage flooded her eyes. With a snarl, she thrust her blade.

Kaelyn screamed as she parried. The blow was a terrible thing, a bolt of lightning, a striking asp. Kaelyn barely deflected it. The two blades crashed together, one long and black, the other slim and silvery.

Shari thrust again, and Kaelyn grunted and raised her sword. Her blade clashed against Shari's, but could not stop its onslaught. Kaelyn ducked and Shari's sword nicked her ear. Pain blazed and Shari laughed.

"Yes, bleed for me, harlot!" She swung her sword downward. "Bleed a little before I drag you home and make you beg."

Kaelyn leaped sideways and hit the cave wall. Shari's blade bit Kaelyn's hip, tearing her legging and drawing blood.

The memories pounded through Kaelyn: memories of a frightened, weeping child in a dark palace, memories of an older sister tying her, cutting her, and laughing as she wept. Tears stung her eyes.

No. Never again. You will never more torment me, Shari. You will never hurt me or anyone else.

The scar on her hand blazed, and Kaelyn screamed and drove Lemuria down in an arc.

Shari raised her sword. Kaelyn's blade slid down Shari's, raining sparks, and slammed into the older woman's pauldron.

Lemuria was perhaps slim and short, but it was northern steel forged in dragonfire, the blade of a princess. It cracked open Shari's armor and blood sprayed.

Shari screamed and fell back a step. Her eyes widened and she clutched her wound. Shock filled her eyes; she had obviously never imagined that Kaelyn could hurt her.

Kaelyn stood panting before her. She raised her blade, nodded, and smiled.

"Let us keep dancing," she said. "Or have you had enough?"

Now the duel truly began.

Now Shari fought with a snarl, all amusement gone from her brown eyes.

Now blades flew like striking lightning, and they danced, and the ringing of steel filled the cave, and Kaelyn snarled and drove her sword forward again and again, all the pain of childhood and war and wounds pulsing through her. In her rage, she struck down her sister's sword, screamed hoarsely, and slammed Lemuria so hard into Shari's breastplate the steel crumpled like tin.

Shari gasped. She stood frozen and her sword clattered to the ground. Her eyes widened and her mouth worked silently, but no breath found her.

Eyes narrowed, Kaelyn swung her blade, prepared to finish the job.

Still gasping, her breastplate caved in, Shari leaped back, and Kaelyn's blade sliced the air. Before Kaelyn could attack again, her sister turned, stumbled outside the cave, and shifted back into a blue dragon. She fled into the night.

For an instant, Kaelyn could not move. She wanted to chase. She wanted to run outside the cave, shift into a dragon too, and blow fire at her retreating sister. Yet for that instant, such pain and weariness filled her that Kaelyn could only stand panting. Her blade felt so heavy; she could barely hold it, and blood dripped down her thigh and cheek.

Be strong now. Pain can wait.

Kaelyn snarled, sucked in her breath, and raced outside the cave.

Shari was already distant, a squealing dragon coiling under the moon. Kaelyn did not know if she could even muster her magic now; she was too weak, too hurt. She ran, leaped into the air, and summoned the old magic with every last bit of will.

Pain exploded. Her magic coiled inside and she clung to it, refusing to release it. Scales flowed across her, and her wings beat, and Kaelyn flew into the night, a slim green dragon.

She could just make out Shari ahead under the stars; the blue dragon was flying north, no doubt to fetch reinforcement. When Kaelyn glanced over her shoulder, she saw the distant sea, the cliffs of Ralora, and the twinkling lights of Cadport, the city where the boy hid.

Stars damn it.

Kaelyn looked north and south, wings beating, breath rattling in her lungs.

Damn it, what do I do? Do I chase my sister? Do I slay the fabled Shari Cadigus, the cruel commander who killed so many of my men, who tortured me so many times? Or do I fly south to save the boy before the might of the Regime falls upon his city?

Kaelyn roared fire in frustration.

After all these years, she lusted to finally slay her sister. But her own vengeance would have to wait.

"Saving the boy is what matters now," she said into the darkness. "If the Regime approaches the city at night, or if they're already there... they will take him. And all hope will fall." Kaelyn snarled at the north where she could still see her sister fleeing. "This is not over, Shari. I will face you again. And next time, my blade will pierce your heart."

Kaelyn spun in the sky.

She flew south.

She flew to that distant port city. To the boy. To Rune Brewer and to hope.

RUNE

It was the last night Rune Brewer would see his best friend. He walked beside her along the beach, not sure how to say goodbye.

The moon glowed full overhead, haloed with winter mist. The light shone upon the sea, drawing a path into the black horizon. The waves whispered, their foam limned with moonlight. With every wave, strings of light glimmered, formed new shapes, and faded upon the sand.

"Do you know why I like the sea?" Tilla said softly, watching the waves.

Rune looked at her. The moonlight fell upon her pale face, illuminating high cheekbones, large dark eyes, and lips that rarely smiled. Her hair blew in the breeze, black and smooth and cut the length of her chin. She wore a white tunic, a silvery cloak, and a string of seashells around her neck. She was tall and thin—too thin, Rune thought. They were all too thin here.

"Because it's always different," Rune answered.

She turned to look at him. "Yes. Have I told you before?"

He smiled thinly. "Only a hundred times."

"Oh." She turned back toward the water. "Tonight the moonlight glows on the foam. Last night the sea was very dark; I couldn't even see it. Sometimes in the mornings there are many seashells, and the waves are shallow and warm and golden in the dawn. Sometimes the water is deep and the sand clear, and the waves near me are gray, and those far away are green. Sometimes there are crabs on the sand and fish in the water; other times life is hidden. Tomorrow there will be a new sea here."

Rune heard what she did not add. *But I will not see it. I will be far away.* He wanted to tell her that he would walk here tomorrow, that he would write to her about the water, that someday she might return and see the waves again. But the words would not come to his lips. Somehow speaking about tomorrow felt wrong, felt too sad, too dangerous.

So they only kept walking. Silent. The waves whispered. The remnants of old battles littered the beach: the rotted hull of a ship, wooden planks rising like whale ribs; a cracked cannon where crabs hid; an anchor overgrown with moss; and the shattered sabers of fallen sailors. Old wars. Old memories. Nothing but rot and rust in the sand.

Finally they saw the cliffs ahead, rising black in the night. As children, Rune and Tilla would often play under these cliffs, imagining the old battles fought here. They said that seven hundred years ago Elethor, the legendary king, had fought the tyrant Solina upon these cliffs. They said that the dead still whispered here, their bodies buried under the waves.

Rune and Tilla kept walking. Finally the cliffs loomed to their left. To their right, the waves whispered and raced across the sand. Here they stopped, turned toward the water, and stood still. A cold wind blew from the sea—it was the first moon of winter—and Rune hugged himself.

He smiled. "Tilla, do you remember how we used to play here as children? I always pretended to be King Elethor, and you were the wicked Queen Solina. Remember how we would fight with wooden swords?"

A thin smile touched her lips, but there was no joy to it. "Of course you always made me play the villain."

He raised his hands in indignation. "You wanted me to play the queen?"

Her smile widened and finally some warmth filled it. "Yes. I did. I think you would have looked nice in a dress."

He gave her a playful push. She fell back a step and sighed.

They sat in the sand. Rune opened his pack and pulled out a skin of ale—he had brewed it himself—and a wheel of cheese. Tilla's eyes widened to see it.

"Rune," she whispered. "Where did you get that?"

He shrugged and winked. "I have my ways."

Cheese was a luxury these days. Years ago, when Rune had been a child, he remembered eating cheese every day. But since the war had begun and trade died, cheese was rare as gold.

But this night was rare.

This was Tilla's last night home.

They shared the cheese silently, sitting side by side, watching the waves. They drank the ale. They had eaten here many times, the cliffs to their backs, the waves ahead. They could always talk here for hours, laugh, tell stories, play with the sand, and whisper of all their dreams.

Tonight they ate silently.

When their meal was done, they sat watching the water. Rune wanted to say so many things. He wanted to tell Tilla to be careful. He wanted to tell her that he'd see her again someday. He wanted to say *goodbye*. But his throat still felt so damn tight, and his lips so frozen, and his chest felt wrong, as if his ribs were suddenly too small.

Just say something, he told himself, staring at the waves. *Just... just make this a good memory for her, tell her stories, or laugh with her, or... stars, don't just be silent!*

He turned toward her, prepared to tell some old joke to break their silence, when he saw a tear on her cheek.

She was not weeping. Her lips did not tremble. Her eyes did not flinch. She only sat there, staring ahead, still and silent like a statue. Only a single tear glimmered on her cheek, not even flowing, just frozen there like part of the sculpture.

"Tilla," he said softly. "It... will be all right. It—"

She turned toward him, her face like marble in the moonlight.

"No, Rune," she said. "None of this is all right. None of this has been all right for years." She looked aside and her fists clenched in her lap. "This stupid, stupid war, and this stupid red spiral, and..." She looked back at him, reached out, and grasped his arm. "It wasn't always like this, Rune. I know. My father told me. Before the Cadigus family took over, there was trade here. Ships sailed this sea—tall ships from distant lands, ships with huge sails like dragon wings, and they brought cheese to Cadport, and fruits, and silks, and jewels, and my father had work then. He sold so many ropes to those ships. He showed me paintings of them, secret ones he keeps in the cellar. Stars, Rune! Those ships had so many ropes on them. It wasn't like today when we sell only a few ropes a year to farmers. And your father too, Rune— so many merchants visited his tavern, and they all wanted to taste his brew, and he was wealthy then. Both our families were wealthy; all of Cadport was. Only it wasn't even called Cadport then. It was called Lynport, and—"

"Tilla!" he said. He placed a finger against her lips. "You know we can't say that word. We—"

She pulled his finger away. Her eyes flashed. "And why not? Why can't we speak the old name of our town? Why can't we look at paintings of ships, but have to hide them? Why can't we ever say, Rune, that things were better then, that maybe the Cadigus family didn't help us, that—"

Rune leaped to his feet. "Tilla! Please."

His heart pounded. Memories flashed through him. Somebody else in Cadport—and stars damn it, it was called Cadport now, like it or not—had once spoken like that. The fool had drunk a few too many ales at the Old Wheel Tavern, which Rune owned with his father. After his tenth drink, the red-faced

loomer had begun to blabber about the old days, the one thing
you were never to speak of.

"Back then, now, I could sell fabrics all over the world," he
had bragged, teetering as he waved about his mug of ale. "Ships
came, picked 'em up, and I got paid silver. That's called trade, it
is. And no bloody fortress rose on the hill." He guffawed and
spat. "No damn soldiers on every street in Lynport. Yeah, you
heard me!" He waved his mug around, spraying ale. "Stand back,
scoundrels, I won't be silent! *Lynport* our town was called then,
named after Queen Lyana Aeternum, not after that bloody
bastard Cadigus or whatever the Abyss his name is."

A crowd gathered around him. Wil Brewer, Rune's father,
tried to pull the drunkard back into his seat. Rune himself begged
him to be silent. All around, the other townsfolk hissed at the
man to sit down.

But the soldiers who drank here did not hiss. They did not
beg. They only stared, then rose, then grabbed the drunkard.

Rune never forgot that evening. He never forgot how the
drunk loomer had screamed in the city square. He never forgot
the *cracks* as the hammers descended. When his bones were
broken, the soldiers slung the loomer's mangled limbs through the
spokes of a wagon wheel. They hung that wheel from the
courthouse and guarded it. The screams sounded all night, and all
the next day, and it was night again before the loomer finally died.

That had been years ago, but tonight Rune still heard those
screams. When he looked at Tilla, he could still hear those bones
crack.

"Tilla, please," he whispered. "Please."

Her chest rose and fell. Her eyes still flashed. But when he
held her hands, she let out a long sigh, and the flames in her eyes
died, and she lowered her head.

"Rune," she whispered.

Her hands were warm in his, calloused from the ropes she wove. She had long, pale fingers that Rune could not imagine gripping a sword. How could this young woman, a mere ropemaker, his best friend, pick up weapons and go to war? They had played with wooden swords here many times, but this was real, and this stung his eyes and squeezed his chest.

"Rune," she whispered again. "Rune, I'm scared."

Tilla had been his friend all his life, and Rune had spent countless hours playing, laughing, and talking with her, yet he had never—not once—embraced her. Today he pulled her into his arms, and he held her, and she was warm against him, and he stroked her hair and marveled at its softness.

"I know, Tilla," he said. "I'm scared too. But it will be fine. I promise you, Tilla. Everything will be fine."

He was lying. She knew he was lying; he was sure of that. But it was what she needed to hear now, and so Rune repeated it, again and again, holding her close as the waves whispered.

"It can't happen twice to one family, right, Rune?" She looked at him with her large dark eyes, and suddenly she was no longer eighteen, a solemn young woman, but a child again. "It's impossible, right?"

He squeezed her hands. "You'll be safe, Tilla. The Resistance is small now; most of the resistors are dead. You won't have to fight. You'll train a lot, and you'll learn how to use a sword, but it will just be training. The war is dying down."

Rune still remembered the funeral. Five years ago, when the rebellion against the Cadigus family had flared, many of Cadport's people had been pulled out of workshops and farms, thrust into the army, and sent off to fight. Tilla's brother had been one of them. They had not heard from him for three years. Then one winter morning, soldiers from the north arrived in Cadport, carrying the young man in a coffin.

Hundreds had come to the funeral, Rune remembered. They had covered the cemetery, weeping and praying, and stars, how Tilla's parents cried. Even Rune cried that day. Only Tilla did not shed tears. She stood silent and still that day, staring at the coffin as they lowered it underground. Since then, she had rarely smiled and perhaps never laughed.

But it won't happen twice in one family, Rune told himself. *Tilla is eighteen now, and she will be a soldier, and she will train in some distant cold fort, but she will live. And someday, even if it's years from now, I will see her again.*

"Rune," she said, "do you think maybe... maybe in a few moons, when you're eighteen too, you might end up in the same fort?" She gave him a crooked smile. "Wouldn't that be something?"

He snorted a laugh. "There are only... what, about a hundred million forts in the empire?"

She shook her head and sighed. "Not that many, Rune. Not that many. Let's pretend, okay? Let's pretend. I would like that. I would like us to be in the same fort. Maybe if you ask them, Rune, maybe they'll let you." She grabbed his hands and squeezed them. "Will you promise me? Promise you'll ask them. They keep records of these things, Rune. They know where every soldier is stationed. Tell them you want to serve with Tilla Roper of Cadport. Tell them. Promise me."

Rune did not like thinking about his own enlistment. He was still a few moons shy of eighteen; tomorrow morning, when soldiers arrived from the capital to take Cadport's newest adults, he would still be too young. But in the summer, when they came again, he would be old enough. And he too would be given a sword. And he too would be sent off to some distant fort to train and to fight the Resistance.

No, Rune did not want to think about summer yet; summer still lay too far away, and this was bad enough, this was all the sadness and fear he could handle this night.

Tilla's eyes were large and damp as she stared at him. Her fingers clutched him desperately. Her breath shook. Tilla had always been somber, quiet, and reflective; she rarely spoke to the other girls in town but called them vapid and silly.

I've always been her only friend, Rune thought. *And she's always been mine.*

"I promise," he said. "I will ask to serve with Tilla Roper of Cadport. I will see you again, Till. I promise you."

She pulled him into an embrace.

The only two embraces of our lives, he thought, *both on one night.*

In the silence he could hear the waves again, and the wind billowed her hair so that it brushed his cheek, and when he tucked it back behind her ears, he found himself kissing her. She trembled against him, and her lips opened, and though they had never kissed before, this felt as familiar as her eyes or the memory of her smile. It was not a kiss of passion. It was not a kiss of fire or love or sex. It was sadness. It was salt and tears. It was goodbye.

"Rune," she whispered, "fly with me. One last flight. Like we used to."

He nodded and whispered, "One last flight."

It was years since the Cadigus family had outlawed the old magic. Only soldiers could shift now, and only when flying to battle. If others were caught using the old magic, they would not be left to die upon a wheel; they would be dragged into a dungeon and tortured for moons, maybe for years, before being allowed to die. But this night, in darkness between cliff and sea, all fear left Rune.

One last flight. Like we used to fly.

They stood up in the sand, walked several paces apart, and faced each other. The wind blew their hair and the waves sprayed them with mist.

Tilla shifted first. She closed her eyes and let the magic fill her. White scales like mother-of-pearl flowed across her, gleaming in the moonlight. Wings unfurled from her back, a tail sprouted behind her, and she grew until she towered above him. She stood in the sand, a pearl dragon with sad eyes.

It had been a long time since Rune had let the old magic fill him, the magic that flowed from the stars. Today he let the warmth fill him like mulled wine. He sucked in his breath, raised his head, and let the dark scales rise and clank across him. His fingernails grew into claws, and he felt his teeth lengthen and wings rise from his back. It felt as familiar and warm as her kiss, and he stood before her in the sand, a black dragon.

He lowered his head and nuzzled her, and she gave him a sad smile, and they took flight.

They were children of Requiem. They were Vir Requis, an ancient race blessed with starlight. For thousands of years, their people had flown as dragons, free and wild over forest and mountain. Today they flew in darkness, alone and afraid under the Draco constellation, stars of their fathers.

Their wings scattered the waves below. They rose higher until they glided over the sea, two dragons, black and white. They rose above the cliffs. Rune could see for miles along the shore and all the distant lights of Cadport.

Years ago, when they would first fly here, they would circle the moon and pretend that they could almost reach the stars. These days too many eyes could be watching the skies, and so they flew low over the water. They watched their shadows scuttle over the moonlight, and the cold salty night filled their lungs.

He looked at her. She looked back with a soft smile. They kept racing over the sea, flying south away from Cadport, away from what awaited her tomorrow, away from a place where no ships sailed, where not enough ropes could be sold, where drunk loomers screamed upon wheels and brothers returned in coffins. They flew over the water, and Rune wished they could keep flying forever, streaming forward until they reached whatever distant lands ships had once sailed from.

And why not? Rune thought. *Why can't we just keep flying? Why can't we see what lands we find?*

He looked ahead into the darkness, and a sigh clanked his scales.

No—those distant lands of ships and merchants had burned long ago. There was no more wonder in the world. Only this empire. Only the iron fist of the Cadigus family. There was no more light in the world, and no matter how far they flew, they could not escape the darkness.

But we can fly together one last night. Like we used to. Me and her.

They flew until the shore and the lights of Cadport disappeared behind them, then turned and flew back, landed upon the beach, and released their magic. They stood on the sand, a boy and girl again, and he held her hand.

"We will fly together again, Tilla Roper," he said.

She touched his cheek. "Remember this night, Rune. No matter what happens, remember how we kissed, and how we flew together, and even if we fight, and we bleed, and we're very alone and afraid, know that we have this memory. Know that we must stay alive so we can fly here again."

He wanted to say more, but could not speak; his eyes stung, and his throat tightened, so he only kissed her again and held her close as the waves lapped at their feet.

They walked back home in darkness, hand in hand.

Nobody knew whether Cadport, with its fifty thousand souls, was a city or a town. It was a common argument among its people; most elders longingly spoke of their rustic town, while youngsters boasted of their modern city. Whatever it was, tonight Cadport's brick walls, cobbled streets, and seaside boardwalks seemed dark and lonely to Rune. It was his hometown, but tomorrow it would feel empty.

When Tilla stepped back into her small home, Rune stood outside for long moments, then turned and walked alone down the silent streets. His throat still felt tight, and his lips were cold.

Instead of returning to his own home, he walked to the old port. He stood on the cobblestones and placed his hand upon an old iron cannon that pointed to the sea. Rune stared into those dark waters. He tried to imagine days long ago when ships sailed here, Tilla's father sold his ropes, his own father served ale to merchants, and life and laughter had filled this city, not soldiers and broken men on wheels and boys returning home in coffins. Rune's eyes stung and he could barely fathom that tomorrow night, he would walk on the beach alone, and Tilla would be gone—maybe for years, maybe forever.

"We were called Lynport then," he whispered. "And ships sailed here. And none of this would have happened."

But that had been long ago. It had been a different world. It was best to forget. Remembering brought pain, danger, and hammers that cracked bones.

Rune turned away from the water. He walked to the tavern that was his home. He stepped into the empty common room, walked upstairs to his chamber, and tried to sleep. But he could only lie awake, thinking of Tilla and her brother and what would happen in summer.

TILLA

She stood in the city square, hands clasped so tightly she thought her fingers would snap.

Be strong, Tilla, she told herself. *Do not show fear now. Even if your heart trembles, and even if your chest feels so tight you can hardly breathe, you must hide it. If you show weakness now, they will crush you.*

The others crowded around her—six hundred youths her age, all just turned eighteen this year. Their faces were pale. Their lips trembled. Tears flowed down one girl's face, and another girl was sobbing into her palms. A few boys huddled together, snickering and speaking of killing rebel men and bedding rebel women, but they too were scared; Tilla saw the sweat on their foreheads and the tremble to their fingers.

They laugh to hide their fear, she knew. *They will stop laughing soon.*

The Regime's soldiers surrounded the square, sealing in the youths of Cadport like wolves surrounding deer. They wore armor of black steel, the breastplates emblazoned with the red spiral, sigil of Emperor Frey Cadigus. Steel spikes tipped their boots, and steel claws grew from their vambraces. Crimson capes fluttered behind them. On their left hips, they bore swords with dragonclaw pommels. On their right hips, they bore their punishers, the tips crackling with lightning.

That last weapon scared Tilla more than the steel claws or blades. Each of these batons, their grips wrapped in leather, ended with a ball of spinning energy. Tilla had once seen soldiers torture a fisherman with their punishers. The man had writhed, wept, and screamed so loudly the whole city heard; his flesh still bore the scars.

They are demons, Tilla thought, looking upon these soldiers of the empire. *They were created to kill, to torture, to destroy.* She gripped her fingers so tightly she winced with pain. *And they will turn me into one of them.*

One soldier, a burly man who stood across the square, met her gaze.

Tilla froze.

The man's eyes were dead; his stare chilled her like a blast of winter through a door. He was easily the largest of the soldiers, probably the largest man Tilla had ever seen. He hunched over as if his arms were so beefy his back bent under their weight. Even so, he towered above the men around him; he must have stood almost seven feet tall. Lines creased his olive skin, and scars rifted his stubbly head. Dark sacks hung under his eyes, and his brow thrust out like a shelf. His armor was crude, all mismatched plates and chainmail cobbled together, and he bore no sword. Instead he carried an axe—not even an elegant battle-axe, but the heavy axe of a lumberjack, forged for felling trees.

This one must be Beras, Tilla thought with a shiver, unable to tear her eyes away. She had heard of him; everyone in this city had. Lowborn, once an outlaw, Beras was infamous for raping and strangling a girl two towns over. The Cadigus family had hunted him down... and employed him.

The brute kept staring at Tilla, his eyes blank, his expression dead. There was no humanity in Beras's eyes, no rage, no hatred, just cold ruthlessness. Tilla forced her eyes away and found that she had held her breath.

"Tilla!" whispered a girl beside her, a short and demure cobbler named Pery. "Tilla, what fort will they send us to?"

Tilla shook her head free of thoughts, blinked, and glanced at the girl. Pery was a pale, mousy thing, barely larger than a child.

Her hair was so pale it was nearly white, and her eyes seemed too large above her gaunt cheeks. Her fingers were slim and quick, accustomed to helping her father make shoes. Could those small fingers ever wield a sword? Pery looked up, a foot shorter than Tilla and trembling like a rabbit cornered by a fox.

"I don't know, Pery," Tilla said softly. "They'll sort us when they're ready."

Pery's eyes swam with tears, and her fingers clutched at Tilla's tunic. "But... I can't go too far. I can't. My father needs my help at the shop. His joints hurt, and his fingers don't move quickly anymore, and..." She sniffed. "Tilla, do you think they'll station me at Castellum Acta here in Cadport—the little fort on the hill—so I can go home at nights to help him?"

"Maybe," Tilla said and patted the shorter girl's arm. "Maybe, Pery. Let's just wait and see."

Pery nodded, bit her lip, and lowered her head.

Dozens of other girls stood around them. Tilla stood tallest among them; she had always thought herself far too tall. Today she found her height useful. She looked over the heads of the others, scanning the crowds that stood behind the soldiers. Parents, siblings, or just curious townsfolk stood in the city streets, peering into the square. A few even stood upon roofs or gazed from tall windows. Many mothers were weeping and waving at their sons and daughters. Some fathers were beaming with pride and speaking about how their sons would slay resistors; most fathers looked as tearful and worried as their wives.

Tilla's own father did not stand here.

I saw my son recruited in this square five years ago, he had told Tilla last night. *He never returned.*

Tears had filled the old ropemaker's eyes, and Tilla had embraced him and whispered her goodbyes. He was not here today, but her father was in her heart; she would carry his love to wherever this war took her.

There was one more man in her life, and this winter morning, Tilla sought him, scanning the crowd of faces.

"Where are you?" she whispered.

Finally she saw him in the crowd, and her heart gave a twist.

Rune Brewer stood in an alley a few hundred feet away. Two soldiers stood before him, separating the new recruits from the crowd of onlookers; Tilla could only glimpse half of Rune's face. He leaned sideways, stood on his tiptoes, and gazed between the soldiers.

Tilla's eyes locked with his.

She wanted to wave to him. She wanted to mouth a goodbye. The youths around her were reaching out to friends and family, waving and weeping. But Tilla could only stand still.

Stars, she thought, fire blazing inside her. She wanted to do *something,* even shed a tear. And yet she could only stand frozen, staring at Rune over the hundreds of youths, and he only stared back, frozen too. Their stare seemed to last an era, and though still and solemn, his eyes cried out to her. They spoke of their lives: of wrestling together as children on the floor of the Old Wheel Tavern; of forbidden flights over the sea at night; of Rune sneaking bread rolls and porridge over to Tilla's house when they could just not sell enough rope; and finally of what had happened last night, their first kiss, a memory Tilla knew would anchor her during the years ahead.

And then soldiers stepped in front of him, severing their gaze, and Tilla thought: *I won't see him again for years. Maybe never again.* Her eyes stung and she blinked. *My brother never came home. He left us from this very square, and we never saw him again. Will I ever return?*

Wings thudded above, interrupting her thoughts.

A roar sounded across the city.

Tilla looked up and clenched her jaw.

A blue dragon flew above, still distant but diving fast toward the square. The dragon was female; her horns were shorter than those of a male dragon, and her was body slimmer but no less powerful. A wake of smoke and flame trailed behind the beast.

Within an instant, the blue dragon was circling above the square. She howled a cry so loud, people across the city covered their ears and grimaced. The dragon's wings blasted Tilla's hair and filled her nostrils with the scents of ash, smoke, and oil. The dragon flew so low her claws nearly toppled the roofs of buildings. With another roar, she blew fire, forming a flaming ring around the square. The flames crackled, blasting Tilla with heat, then descended as a wreath of smoke.

Many youths cowered and whimpered. Since the Cadigus family had taken the throne, only soldiers were allowed shift into dragons; the magic was forbidden to everyone else, and many here had never seen a dragon display its might with flame and roar. At her side, Pery mewled and covered her head, but Tilla only stood tall and stared up at the blue beast.

This one is boastful, she thought and narrowed her eyes. *This one delights in fear. This one I will watch out for.*

Across the square rose Cadport's courthouse, a building of marble columns. Tilla's father would whisper that once, before the Regime, this had been a temple to the Draco constellation, the stars of Requiem. Today the banners of Cadigus hung from the building's balcony, black and long and emblazoned with the red spiral. With a final blast of fire, the blue dragon descended toward the courthouse, shifted into an armored woman, and landed upon the balcony.

The woman stood before the crowd, and Tilla sucked in her breath.

"Stars damn it," she whispered.

She knew this woman who stood on the balcony. She had seen this one in a dozen paintings; by imperial decree, they hung in Cadport's courthouse, guildhalls, and even Rune Brewer's tavern.

The Demon of Requiem. The Princess of Pain. The Blue Bitch.

"Shari Cadigus, the emperor's daughter," Tilla whispered.

Heir to the empire, Shari wore the garb of a soldier. She stood tall in leather boots and clad in black steel. Her breastplate sported the red spiral. Upon her hips hung her weapons: a black longsword and a punisher wrapped in red leather. A mane of brown curls cascaded down her shoulders, and her dark eyes stared upon the crowd in amusement; Tilla could see that amusement even standing a hundred yards away.

What was Shari Cadigus herself doing here? Every winter and summer, Tilla had come to this square to see youths drafted into the Legions. She had stood here seeing her cousins, her brother, and so many other townsfolk taken to distant forts to fight and die. Yet it was always some old, gruff soldier who arrived to lead the youths north. What was Requiem's princess herself doing here, so many leagues away from the glory of the capital?

Shari raised her right fist high, then slammed it against her breastplate.

"Hail the red spiral!" the princess shouted, voice ringing.

All across the square, hundreds of youths, eighteen years old and pale and shaky, repeated the salute. Hundreds of fists thumped simultaneously. Tilla hit her chest so hard, a gasp of pain fled her lips.

I will give the salute, she thought. *But my heart does not belong to the red spiral. It does not serve Emperor Frey or his daughter. My heart belongs to my father and his ropes, to Rune and his tavern, to secret flights above the water and a kiss I will not forget.*

Shari lowered her fist to her hip, nodded, and looked over the crowd. A thin smile played across her lips. Her head moved from side to side, scanning the youths. When her gaze fell upon Tilla, the princess nodded and pointed.

"There!" Shari barked at Beras, the burly soldier with the scarred, stubbly head; he stood below the balcony, axe in hand. "That one, Beras. Bring me that one."

Tilla stood frozen. Her heart thrashed. She could barely even breathe.

Beras's eyes remained dead and shadowed under his brow. With a grunt, he shifted into a dragon.

He was easily the largest dragon Tilla had ever seen, a beast of bronze scales, spikes, and black horns. The creature took flight, grunting and snorting smoke, and swooped toward the crowd.

When Beras flew directly above Tilla, he reached out claws like swords.

Tilla winced, ducked, and a yelp fled her lips.

Beside her, Pery screamed.

The claws closed, wings beat, and the bronze dragon soared. It took Tilla half a moment to realize she still stood in the square, hunched over and drenched in sweat.

Pery no longer stood beside her. Beras now flew with the cobbler's daughter in his claws.

Thank the stars.

Tilla couldn't help it. She breathed out a shaky breath of relief... and hated herself for it.

The bronze dragon howled and beat his wings, blasting the crowd with waves of stench. In his claws, Pery screamed and begged.

"Bring her to me!" Shari commanded, still standing on the balcony in human form. She laughed. "Place that mouse before me."

The youths in the square stood still, faces pale. The crowd behind them, separated from the youths by the soldiers, stirred and whispered. A graying woman reached out her hands—Pery's mother.

Beras flew to the balcony, hovered before it, and tossed Pery down. The girl thudded onto the balcony and mewled. With a grunt, the dragon flew down, landed outside the courthouse, and shifted back into human form. He stood still, clutching his axe.

"Stand up, darling!" Shari said to the fallen girl. "Stand up—you are a daughter of Requiem! Stand before me, child."

Pery rose to her feet and stood before the princess. She looked so small and frail, a good foot shorter than Shari, and wispy in her tunic next to Shari's armor and blades. The girl trembled and whimpered.

Be silent! Tilla thought, watching from the square. Her heart pounded. *Don't show her any weakness, Pery. You must be a soldier today.*

Tilla wanted to shout out to her friend. She wanted to shift into a dragon too, to fly to the balcony, to shake Pery and slap her until she stood strong and silent. And yet she dared not. Danger hung in the air. A wrong movement meant death now. All around the square, the people stood frozen; not a whisper rose.

Upon the balcony, Shari's face softened. Her lips pouted. The princess looked like a woman who saw a mewling, kicked puppy that begged to be hugged. She reached out and, with gloved fingers, caressed Pery's hair.

"Are you frightened, child?" Shari asked.

No! Tilla thought. *No, Pery, no. Tell her that you're brave, tell her you're strong.*

Pery looked around nervously. Her eyes scanned the crowd, and they fell upon Tilla, and the girl whispered something Tilla could not hear.

"My child!" Shari said. She touched Pery's chin and turned her face back toward her. "Don't seek answers there. Simply speak the truth. Are you frightened?"

Pery lowered her eyes, bit her lip, and nodded.

"I thought so," Shari said. She leaned over and kissed Pery's forehead.

A scream fled Pery's lips.

Shari stepped back with a smile.

No. Stars no, stars no. Standing below in the crowd, Tilla shook, and her heart thrashed, and tears filled her eyes. *Oh stars no.*

A dagger, its pommel shaped as a dragonclaw, thrust out of Pery's chest.

Tilla couldn't help it. She cried out.

"Pery!"

Everything seemed to happen at once.

Pery fell, blood gushing. Princess Shari stood above her and laughed. Pery's parents cried out below, reached toward her, and wailed, and soldiers dragged them into an alley. The crowd rustled and whispered. A girl not far from Tilla fainted. One man shouted and tried to run toward the courthouse, but soldiers held him back.

Tilla stood frozen, fingers trembling, and her eyes widened. She had not thought things could get worse. She had not imagined greater terror. She gasped and covered her mouth and her eyes stung.

"No," she whispered. "Oh stars no."

Shari knelt above the body, snarling and laughing. She had pulled the dagger free and thrust it into Pery's neck. More blood gushed. Shari hissed as she sawed back and forth. Finally she lifted Pery's severed head and held it above the crowd.

"See what happens to the weak!" Shari shouted and laughed. Blood splashed her face, and the severed head dangled and dripped in her hand. "See what happens to cowards!"

Some people wailed and tried to flee; soldiers grabbed them. One man—Tilla recognized him as Pery's uncle—began driving through the crowd. Soldiers twisted his arms, and one drove a punisher into his back; the man collapsed and screamed, his flesh smoking. Above the commotion, Shari laughed and tossed the head off the balcony.

It arced through the air and slammed down by Tilla's feet, splattering blood.

Tilla closed her eyes, clenched her fists, and swallowed a lump in her throat. A tear streamed down her cheek.

I'm sorry, Pery. I'm sorry. May your soul find its way to our starlit halls of afterlife.

"Beras, bring me another one!" Shari's voice rang above. "That one—the one who cried out, the tall one beside the head. Bring me her!"

Tilla's eyes snapped open.

The bronze dragon swooped toward her.

Tilla winced and sucked in her breath. Beras's claws closed around her, and the beast lifted her.

They flew above the crowd. Strangely, no fear filled Tilla as the dragon carried her toward the balcony. Perhaps after seeing Pery's death, after flying in the night with Rune, and after losing her brother to the war, no more fear could fill her. The crowd spread below, a gray sea, and Tilla looked back, trying to find Rune. Before she could locate him, the dragon reached the balcony and tossed her down.

Tilla tumbled and landed on the balcony, slamming her knees against the floor. She inhaled sharply, gritted her teeth, and made no sound.

Below the balcony, the crowd hushed. All the whimpers, whispers, and wails faded into tense silence. Jaw clenched with pain, Tilla raised her head to see Shari standing above her.

Kneeling so close, Tilla saw that Shari wore finer armor than a common soldier. Golden filigree covered her steel plates, shaped as dragons aflight. The red spiral upon her breastplate was not just red paint but formed of a hundred rubies. Small golden skulls grinned morbidly upon her boots like spurs. The princess was a soldier, but she was also vain.

"My princess," Tilla said, still kneeling before her. She slammed her fist against her chest. "Hail the red spiral!"

Standing above her, Shari nodded approvingly. "Hail the red spiral! Well spoken, child. Stand. Stand before me."

Barely daring to breathe, Tilla rose to her feet. She raised her chin, thrust out her chest, and squared her shoulders. She stood tense and proud, one fist still against her breast.

This is the stance of a soldier, she thought. She was just the daughter of a roper, of course, but the daughters of ropers and cobblers would die today. Soldiers would live.

I must live, she thought, her throat tight. *My father lost one child already. I must survive.*

Shari scrutinized her, her brown eyes narrowed. Tilla was among the tallest women in Cadport; she stood almost as tall as Rune, who was taller than most men. Her arms were strong from weaving ropes and carrying casks of Rune's ale. And yet she felt short and frail beside Shari; the princess stood several inches taller, and even her armor could not hide her powerful body.

Many call her the greatest warrior in Requiem, Tilla knew. She could see why.

"You stand well," Shari said and nodded. She placed a finger under Tilla's chin and raised her head higher, examining her jawline. "Show me your teeth, child. Open your mouth."

Rage flooded Tilla. Was she a recruit or a horse? She snarled and hissed. If Shari noticed her anger, however, she showed no sign of it. As Tilla snarled, she bared her teeth, and Shari got her look at them.

"Good," the princess said. "White, sharp, straight." She grabbed Tilla's arm and squeezed it. "Strong arms; slim but ropy. What is your profession, child?"

Tilla stared into her princess's eyes. "I was a ropemaker, Commander. I will be a soldier."

The princess barked a laugh. "This one will be a soldier!" she shouted to the crowd.

When she turned back toward Tilla, a dagger gleamed in her hand.

Tilla gasped. Fast as striking lightning, Shari placed the blade against Tilla's neck.

Tilla froze.

Her heart thrashed.

Shari snarled, holding the blade so close Tilla felt it nick her skin.

"You are confident," the princess hissed. She leaned so close to Tilla their faces almost touched. "You are a haughty one, aren't you? Nothing but a ropemaker. Nothing but a pathetic little worm. And you think you can be one of my soldiers."

Tilla froze, daring not speak; if her neck bobbed, the blade would slice it. She only stared back, not averting her eyes from Shari's fiery gaze.

There is madness in those brown eyes, Tilla thought. *There is cruelty. But there is cunning too; there is method to this madness. I must play her game to live.*

She chanced a whisper, allowing the blade to scrape her skin.

"If you teach me, my princess, I will fight for you, and I will kill for you, and I will grow stronger. I am not afraid. I am not weak like the other girls. I will fight for the red spiral until my last drop of blood."

And I will live, she thought. *I will spit upon the red spiral in my dreams every night, but in the days, I must survive. The weak will die. I will be strong, and I will live to return to Rune.*

Shari pulled back her dagger, and Tilla took a quick, hissing breath.

"You are an interesting little worm," Shari said. She narrowed her eyes and scrutinized Tilla, as if trying to peer through curtained windows. "You are either very brave or very cunning. Which one will remain to be seen." She tapped her dagger against her hip. "I will keep an eye on you, Tilla the ropemaker. I will watch you like a poor drunkard watches a tavern's last mug of ale. If you stray one inch... if you make one mistake..." Shari sliced the air with her dagger. "...your head will rot with the other one."

With that, Shari slammed her dagger back into its sheath, turned to the crowd, and shouted.

"All right, you miserable lot! Beras will lead you out. We're heading north to make you soldiers. You will crush the Resistance, or you will die in their fire!"

With that, Shari leaped off the balcony, shifted into a blue dragon, and flew so low over the square the youths had to duck. With a grunt like a beast in heat, the dragon disappeared over the city roofs.

Beras shifted too. The gruff, silent man became the bronze dragon, grabbed Tilla in his claws, and carried her back to the square. He tossed her down among her comrades. Tilla fell again, banging her hip so hard she gasped and saw stars. She forced herself to her feet among hundreds of other recruits.

Around the square, the soldiers drew their punishers; the tips crackled with lightning. They began herding the crowd forward, shouting and cursing.

"Move it, scum!" one soldier shouted. "Move!"

"Go on, maggot!" another said. "Damn you, move, or I'll make you move."

They thrust their punishers. Bolts crackled, youths yowled, and smoke rose from seared flesh. The soldiers laughed and kept goading the crowd forward, cruel dogs herding sheep. Soon all six hundred youths were moving across the square, then following Beras down Cadport's main street. The youths jostled against one another, looking over their shoulders with darting eyes.

Tilla moved among them, limping and wincing with the pain. Her hip and knees throbbed; bruises would cover them tomorrow. As the recruits flowed into the street, Tilla kept looking over her shoulder, trying to see Rune among the crowd of onlookers. She saw parents, grandparents, and siblings, but they were all strangers. Where was Rune? She wanted to give him one last look, to whisper to him, to call out one last goodbye, maybe even reach out and touch his fingertips. But she could not see him, and the faces of the crowd swam around her.

With tears and whispers and the memory of blood, six hundred of Cadport's children, eighteen and old enough to die, swept out of their city walls... and into a wilderness of steel, snow, and fire.

RUNE

For a long time, Rune stood in the empty square, staring at the blood on the cobblestones.

The recruits were gone, Tilla among them, and Rune's heart ached at their loss. The crowd of families and onlookers dispersed slowly, many among them teary, leaving the city square empty. Yet Rune remained standing here, staring at the blood, unable to calm his thrashing heart.

They cut off her head, he thought. *Stars, they cut off her head right here, and we stood in the square and did nothing, and they almost killed Tilla too, and we only stared like sheep frozen before the wolves.*

He clenched his fists. The blood seeped between the cobblestones and ran toward his boots. A priest had lifted Pery's head, chanted a prayer, and placed it into a bag for burial. But Rune could still imagine it—its mouth open in a silent scream, its eyes still wide with fear, blood dripping from its neck.

"I'm sorry, Pery," he whispered. "We should have helped you. We should have done something."

Thousands of people had watched the execution, and each had magic to shift into a dragon, to thrust claws, to roar fire. Only a hundred guards had surrounded the square.

We should have shifted! Rune thought. *We could have saved her! We could have slain the soldiers, and...*

He sighed.

And thousands more soldiers would have streamed here from the capital, he thought. *They would have burned this city to the ground and slaughtered us all.*

He turned and began walking home.

He normally took the wide main road, but today, Rune walked on narrow side streets, seeking solitude. His boots thumped against the cobblestones. Houses and shops rose at his sides, built of wattle and daub; oaken beams formed rough frames, and white clay filled the space between the timbers. Rot darkened these wooden frameworks, and holes dotted many roofs; since the port had closed a few years ago, few could afford to maintain their homes. Only Cadport's largest buildings—like the courthouse, the fort on the hill, and the prison—were built of brick. The Cadigus family now ruled those.

It wasn't always like this, Rune thought. He watched a thin little girl sit outside her home, hugging an equally thin dog. *When I was a child, we'd run playing down these streets, laughing and banging wooden swords together.*

It had been years since he'd heard children laughing; children today did not play, but scavenged and begged for food.

Rune fished through his pocket, found a copper coin, and tossed it toward the skinny girl. Her eyes lit up. She caught the coin and ran off.

"Buy something to eat!" Rune called after her, but she vanished around a corner, and he did not know if she heard.

As he kept walking, again rage filled Rune. He remembered standing at the docks with Tilla years ago; they'd been younger than that thin girl. They'd watch the ships from foreign lands approach, bearing sacks of grain, exotic fruits, strong dry wine, and many other treasures. The ships would leave days later, laden with Requiem's crafts: ropes Tilla's father wove, shoes Pery's family cobbled, ale Rune's father brewed, and many other goods.

Nobody in Cadport was hungry then, Rune thought. It wasn't even called Cadport in those years, of course; it had been Lynport, the jewel of the south.

But then... then the war broke out, the Regime's great war to purify the world of "lesser nations". Then the Cadigus family

burned those distant lands. Then those ships sank, and the port
closed, and Cadport began to rot.

"And now this," Rune whispered. "Silence and hunger and
blood upon stone."

And Tilla torn away from me.

He kept walking until he reached the boardwalk along the
sea. He walked upon the cobblestones, watching the gray waves
beat the sand below. A breakwater thrust into the water like a
stone dragon, and upon it rose the old lighthouse; it hadn't shone
in years. Docks still spread out into the water, but their wood was
rotted, and many planks had fallen and floated away. Rune could
barely remember the ships that would dock here; the only sign of
life now was a stray, thin cat who wandered the beach, seeking
dead fish.

Rune kept walking. To his other side, shops lined the
boardwalk, but their wood too decayed. Most doors were
boarded shut. Years ago, these shops had sold ale, wine, meat
pies, and even women for lonely sailors. When the ships stopped
sailing here, the shops fell to ruin; one now housed a scrawny
orphan girl named Erry, a waif Rune sometimes brought food to,
and the others housed rats.

Only the Old Wheel Tavern remained in business, Rune's
home. When Rune reached it, he stood outside for a moment and
stared. The cold wind whipped his cloak and ruffled his hair.

"Home," he whispered.

The tavern stood three stories tall, built of wattle and daub.
Tiles were missing from its roof, and mold had invaded its
timbers. Only one of the three chimneys pumped smoke.

By summer, I'll be eighteen too, Rune thought. *And I'll be carted
off with hundreds of youths. Who will help Father then?*

He sighed. He knew the answer. Wil Brewer was growing
older, and he depended on his son's help. Without Rune, the

tavern would become another ghost hall like the dozens along this boardwalk.

A gull circled above, cawing a laugh as if the bird could read Rune's mind and was mocking him. Rune smoothed his cloak, opened the tavern's door, and stepped inside.

The shadowy common room greeted him. Scratches covered the hardwood floor like cobwebs. Odds and ends that Rune's father collected bedecked the walls: an old tapestry showing dragons aflight in a starry night, antlers on a plaque, a canvas map of the city, and two fake swords—forged from cheap tin—crossed upon a shield. At the back of the room stood the bar, its surface waxed a thousand times. Mugs hung above it from pegs, and behind the bar, casks of ale and wine stood upon shelves. Ten tables filled the room; all were empty today.

Hands in his pockets, Rune stared up at the ceiling. A wagon wheel hung there, topped with candles, forming a makeshift chandelier. It gave the Old Wheel its name. When Rune had been a babe, the tavern was called *Lyana's*, named after the legendary Queen of Requiem who had fought a battle at Ralora Cliffs outside the city. But of course, Lyana had been an Aeternum, a queen of the old dynasty. Today all memories of that dynasty were forbidden. And so the tavern's name had changed. And so everything had changed.

"Father!" Rune called out. "Father, are you home?"

A shadow scuttled. Paws scratched across the floor. A large black dog came lolloping from the kitchen, leaped onto Rune, and began to lick his face.

"Hello, Scraggles," Rune said and patted the mutt. "Are you alone here? Guarding the place?"

Scraggles panted, a wide smile across his face. Some folk, Rune knew, claimed that dogs couldn't smile, but they had never met Scraggles. He was an old hound now but still acted like a pup, happy and careless. His tail wagged furiously, dusting the floor, and Rune felt a little better.

"At least I still have you, Scrags," he said, but then a lump filled his throat. In summer, when Rune himself was drafted, he would be torn away from his dog too. Scraggles was getting on in years; when Rune returned from his service, the dog would be gone.

Rune blinked his stinging eyes. The tavern seemed too silent, too cold, even with Scraggles jumping against him. Tilla used to visit here most days. They would play dice or mancala, a southern board game a ship had once brought from the desert. They would sweep and polish the tavern while talking about their lives. Sometimes they would just sit by the fireplace, sip ale, and say nothing, but feel warm and safe and close.

Five years, Rune thought. *Five years in the Legions.*

She had been gone for a couple hours, and already Rune wanted to pound the walls, fly toward the capital, slay the emperor, and bring Tilla home.

"Father!" he called out again. He wanted to see the man, the only other soul he now had, aside from his dear dog. Where was the old brewer?

Leaving Scraggles in the common room, Rune trudged upstairs. The second floor of the Old Wheel held the guest rooms for merchants and travelers; those rooms were now empty. He kept climbing to the third floor where his own chambers lay.

He entered his room, and his breath died.

Upon his bed sat the most beautiful woman Rune had ever seen.

He froze and stared.

The beautiful woman stood up. Her clothes were torn and bloody, and she bore a bow and sword.

"Rune," she said, "we must run. They are going to kill you. They are coming."

Rune blinked, looked over his shoulder, then back at her. "Excuse me," he said, "do I...?"

She stepped toward him, grabbed his arm, and narrowed her eyes.

"You don't know me, Rune Brewer," she said. "But I know you very well. And you must trust me today. We leave—now. Or we're both dead." She began tugging him toward the door. "Come."

He stood frozen, squinting at her. She was not from Cadport, that was certain; she spoke with the northern accent of the capital, a great metropolis many leagues away. And surely, Rune would have noticed a young Cadport woman so, well... so perfect.

Rune had seen beautiful women before. As a hot-blooded young man, seeking beautiful women was among his main pursuits. With her pale skin, noble features, and midnight hair, Tilla was beautiful; Rune had always thought so. And he had noticed Mae Baker too, a girl up the road with a strawberry braid, pink cheeks, and shy eyes. Even Erry the waif, who lived sandy and scrawny on the docks, had big brown eyes that Rune liked looking into.

But he had never seen anyone like *this* woman. She seemed to be about his age, maybe a year or two older. Her mane of hair cascaded down her back, a deep golden color like honey. Her eyes were hazel, her features feline; she reminded him of a lioness. Her body too was catlike, slim and lithe, a body made for leaping and running and climbing. She wore deerskin boots over tattered gray leggings, a blue cloak over a green tunic, and a belt with a golden buckle. A sword hung from that belt, and a bow hung across her shoulder. She had obviously seen battle recently; a bloody line ran across her hip.

He squinted, a dim memory pulsing inside him.

She looks familiar, he thought. Had he seen her before after all? He would have remembered a woman so beautiful, yet his memories only flickered, a soft glow he could barely see.

"Come on!" the woman said and tugged him. Her eyes flashed and she bared her teeth. "We're getting out of here."

Rune stood still, not allowing himself to be moved.

"I'm quite sorry," he said, "but if you're going to drag me out of my home, the least you could do is introduce yourself first."

She groaned, released him, and darted toward the window. She peered outside and cursed, then turned back to him.

"Kaelyn," she said and gave a mocking curtsy. "Good? Now *come on.* They're outside. They'll be here soon, and they'll be thirsty for beer."

She grabbed him again and tried to pull him outside, but he yanked himself free.

"Who is out there, Kaelyn?" he said. He walked to the window and peeked outside. "It's only a few northern soldiers. They drink here whenever they're in Cadport. We could use some business, and—"

"You woolhead!" Kaelyn said and pulled him away from the window. She yanked the curtains shut. "You idiotic boy! Stars know why they even *bother* trying to kill you." She grabbed his arm, twisted it, and began manhandling him toward the door. "Move it and be quiet!"

Then, finally, Rune understood.

He sighed.

The young woman was mad. No doubt, she was some wandering halfwit cast away from her northern town, sure that the world was out to kill her. Stars knew how she had ended up in his bed.

He planted both feet firmly on the ground, refusing to budge; he stood a foot taller than this woman, and he weighed a good deal more, and if he didn't want to move, she wouldn't move him.

"Look," he said, "Kaelyn or whatever you're called. Why don't I fetch you a pint of ale and a bowl of soup—on the house—and I'll even give you a bed for the night. In the morning, I can—"

Steel flashed.

She drew a dagger from her boot.

Before Rune could react, she placed the blade's tip against his back.

"That's right," she said. "Be silent. Good. Now move! Out the door and downstairs, or I'll stab you. You'll thank me for this later."

The knife pierced his tunic; he felt the cold tip between his shoulder blades, almost cutting him. He sucked in his breath and winced.

"Kaelyn, are you... kidnapping me?"

Rune had always imagined kidnappers as gruff, scruffy men covered in mud, their blades rusty and chipped, their odor less than pleasing. Kaelyn had the mud part right—her boots and leggings were coated with it—but she was definitely not scruffy, and Rune thought that she smelled rather nice.

But she only shoved him forward, keeping the dagger pressed against his back. "Out the door, boy. And keep your hood *low*. Hide your face or I stab you."

She grabbed his hood and, standing on tiptoes, tugged it low over his face. When he glanced over his shoulder, he saw her do the same with her hood. He noticed that, despite their ragged condition, her cloak and hood were woven of fine fabric. The cloth was a costly blue. Blue dye came from distant isles where mollusks leaked the color; Rune rarely saw blue fabric in Cadport. Kaelyn's cloak had been through rough times—tatters, mud, and burns marred it—but it had once belonged to a noblewoman.

So she's a thief, Rune thought. *She stole her cloak from a lady, then dragged it through the forest. She probably hopes to kidnap me for ransom.* He sighed. If only she knew his father had no ransom money to pay.

"Move!" she said and shoved him. "Go on, good boy— downstairs."

He grumbled under his breath, but he walked. The dagger poked his back; he thought it might have nicked his skin. Kaelyn kept pushing him forward. They left the room, crossed the hallway, and began walking downstairs.

"Kaelyn," he said, "will you please calm down and listen? If you're after money, we have none. If you want a good meal and a bed, I—"

"Keep walking!" she said and kept manhandling him downstairs. "And be silent. Bloody stars, they're almost here."

"Who's alm—"

"Hush!"

A thud filled the tavern—the front door slamming open. Boots thumped and the voices of soldiers cried out, demanding ale and food. Their armor clanked and their cries filled the tavern.

"Bloody stars," Kaelyn cursed. "Is there a backdoor to this place?"

Rune looked over his shoulder at her. Her face was pale. She was chewing her lip and whipping her head from side to side, seeking an exit, even though they still stood in the stairwell.

Rune thought of calling out. If he shouted, the guards would hear and rush onto the stairs.

And... Kaelyn might stab me before they arrive.

"Go on!" Kaelyn said. She pressed the dagger closer, close enough that now Rune was sure she nicked him. "There must be a backdoor for supplies; every tavern has one. Lead me there!" She snarled into his ear. "And if you lead us anywhere near the common room, this dagger goes right into your heart."

She gave his arm a twist, and he groaned.

"All right!" he said. "All right, I'll lead you there. Stop poking me."

He decided to humor her for a while. Sooner or later, she would tire of holding the dagger against his back. When that happened, he'd break free. The girl was just hungry, scared, and probably on the run from the Regime. Once she felt more comfortable and was far from these soldiers, she would let her guard down. He would flee her then. After all, she couldn't keep her dagger pressed against him forever.

"Come on," he said with a grunt. "In here. We'll sneak out through the kitchen."

They walked downstairs, moving close to the common room. Over the stairs' bannister, Rune saw the shadows of the soldiers as they bustled about. A few were banging the tabletops and calling out for ale.

"Rune!" Kaelyn warned. "If they see us..."

"Don't worry," he said. "And stars, loosen your grip. You're ripping my arm off."

The stairs led down to a hallway. To one side, casks of ale stood piled up; the shadows and sounds of the common room leaked from behind them. To the other side, the hallway curved toward the pantry and kitchen. Rune led them there, moving away from the common room and into a chamber stocked with sausages, flour, jars of preserves, bottles of spirits, and dried fruits.

"Where's the backdoor?" Kaelyn demanded.

"Be patient!"

They kept walking. Soon they entered the kitchen, where embers glowed in the hearth. Plates, mugs, and pots lay piled high on shelves. Beyond them a backdoor led into an alley.

Scraggles lay on the floor, gnawing a bone. The black mutt raised his head and stared at Rune, then at Kaelyn. With a growl, the dog leaped to his feet. His tail straightened like a blade, and he began to bark wildly at Kaelyn.

Behind in the common room, the soldiers fell silent and chairs creaked.

"Oh bloody stars!" Kaelyn said. She shoved Rune forward and grunted. "Go, go!"

She manhandled him around the dog, wrenched the door open, and shoved Rune into the alley. She hurried after him, dagger still pointed at his back, and slammed the door shut, sealing Scraggles indoors. She looked from side to side, cursed under her breath, and began pulling Rune down the alley.

"Come on!" she said. "Move quickly and silently. You try to escape me, or you make a sound, and you're dead. Trust me— that's a better fate than what these soldiers would offer you. They'd make you wish you were dead."

They hurried down the alley, cloaks fluttering around them. Cold wind moaned, and behind them Rune could still hear Scraggles barking. The alley walls closed in around them; it was just wide enough for him to walk comfortably. At least, he would be comfortable if Kaelyn weren't twisting his arm and goading him on.

"You do realize," Rune said as they walked, "that Cadport is swarming with hundreds of soldiers? They stand at every street corner—even on days without a recruitment. How are you going to avoid them? Or is your plan to just live in this alley for the rest of our lives?"

They reached the alley's end. Beyond two shops spread a wide road lined with homes.

Kaelyn tugged him back and positioned herself beside him, pressing her dagger against his waist. She gripped his arm and snarled at him.

"All right, listen to me, boy," she said. "You and I are nothing but a couple on a stroll, do you understand? I've hidden my dagger under my cloak's sleeve, but don't you doubt it—it's still pressing against you, and if you try to escape, I'll shove it into you." Her voice softened and she sighed. "I'm doing this to save your life, you know. Well, you don't know, but you will soon enough, Rune. Keep your hood low; these soldiers would kill you on sight."

Rune glared at her. "What's going on here, Kaelyn? Who are you? Why do you think these soldiers want to kill me? I've spent eighteen years around soldiers, and—"

"Not Princess Shari's soldiers. Do you really think Shari herself, the daughter of Emperor Cadigus, would visit this backwater town for a mere recruitment? The recruitment is a facade. She's here to find you, Rune, and to capture you. Her soldiers know your face. They know your name. They know to take you on sight. They weren't just in your tavern for ale; they were there for *you*." She looked at him strangely. "If they catch you, Rune, they will bring you to the capital. And they will torture you. They will break you upon the wheel, or disembowel you alive, or flay you, or quarter you. Do you know what quartering is? That's when they tie bulls to your four limbs, then send each bull running a different direction. And finally, when you've screamed long enough, they will cut off your head and stick it upon the city walls."

Rune felt himself blanch. "Stars," he whispered.

"Am I scaring you?" Kaelyn asked and narrowed her eyes, scrutinizing him. "Good. Because I'm scared too. And I want you to be scared; fear will keep you silent and moving. You might think my dagger cruel; it's nothing compared to what Shari would do to you. I'm taking you into the forest, and I'm going to bring you to the only man who can help you now."

He raised his eyebrows. "And who might that be?"

Behind them, a door slammed open.

The Old Wheel's backdoor.

Soldiers called for an innkeeper.

"Damn it!" Kaelyn said. She pulled Rune out of the alley and onto the wide, cobbled road.

A dozen of Cadport's people walked here. Their faces were pale; they were still shaken after the morning's beheading.

Two men stood outside a butcher shop, clad in black robes and hoods. Rune had never seen such men, and shivers ran down his back.

He could not see their faces; within the shadows of their hoods, they wore iron masks. Around their waists, they wore ropes heavy with knives, needles, and pincers—the tools of torturers. Strangest of all, neither man had a left hand. Their arms ended with axeheads strapped to stumps.

They serve the Axehand Order, Rune realized with a shudder.

He had heard of the Axehand, a religious order of fanatics who worshiped Frey Cadigus as their god. They were assassins, enforcers, and torturers—Frey's personal thugs. Every man of the Axehand Order, they said, completed his training by lifting an axe and severing his hand; the same axe was then strapped to the stub, a reminder of their loyalty to Cadigus. Rune had never seen their kind in Cadport before; many had whispered that the Axehand Order was only a myth.

"Keep walking calmly," Kaelyn whispered, and for the first time, softness filled her voice. "Come on, Rune. This way."

They walked down the road, heading away from the two axehands. Even after they'd left the robed priests behind, the chill lingered along Rune's spine.

Shops and houses rose at their sides, three stories tall, frowning down upon them. Whoever passed them by did not spare them a glance; the people stared at their shoes. As they moved down the street, Rune glanced over at Kaelyn. Her lips were pursed, her eyes darting, and her skin pale.

The whole thing is ridiculous, Rune thought. *If the soldiers were after me, why did they sit in the common room calling for ale? Why didn't they storm upstairs or burn the tavern down?*

He sighed. Kaelyn heard the sigh, glared at him, and pushed her dagger close.

"Keep walking," she whispered.

They moved through Cadport, street by street. They passed by the old amphitheater, a great ring of stone where singers and actors would once perform, and where the Cadigus family now executed the city's criminals. They walked around the granite statue of Emperor Cadigus, twenty feet tall, his fist upon his chest and his hard eyes watching the city. They walked down narrow streets filled with more townsfolk and soldiers, then across the square where Pery had been killed.

Finally they approached the city walls and the northern gates. Five guards stood here, each one bearing a sword, a shield, and a crackling punisher.

"This will be the tricky part," Kaelyn whispered as they walked. "Just act natural. If the guards ask, you and I are simply going into the forest to collect firewood. Do you understand?"

As Rune walked, he thought that he did understand... and it chilled him.

Stars, oh stars, he thought. *How didn't I see this? Kaelyn isn't just some common thief. She's... she's one of them. A member of the Resistance.* He swallowed. *Of course.*

The Resistance lived out in the forests, they said. They hid in trees and holes and secret tunnels, and they fought the Cadigus family, and they hated order and law and life. They stole from good folk to fill their coffers, and they weren't afraid to slaughter the innocent. Rune had heard all about their deeds.

He thought back to that day two years ago, the day they had buried Tilla's brother. Hundreds had come to the funeral. Soldiers whispered that Tilla's brother had fought nobly, slaying

many resistors before they swarmed him. They said Valien
Eleison himself, cruel leader of the Resistance, was the one who'd
landed the killing blow. All joy had left Tilla that day; Rune had
not heard her laugh since.

Every year, Cadport's soldiers—hard men trained in
northern forts—caught a few resistors in the forest. They chained
them outside the city courthouse, disemboweled them alive, and
left them to die. If they caught Rune with a resistor now, he
realized, they'd do the same to him.

His heart pounded and cold sweat trickled down his back,
but he managed to nod.

"I understand," he whispered in reply.

"Good," Kaelyn said. "Beyond those gates is safety.
Follow my lead, and we'll soon be in the forest. There is haven at
my camp. Just be calm and silent."

As they walked toward the guarded gates, Rune's heart
pounded.

Bloody stars, he thought. A forest camp? The woman *was* a
resistor; now there could be no doubt. Rune held no love for the
Cadigus family, but if Kaelyn thought she could involve him in
her war, she was dead wrong. He was only a brewer. He wanted
no trouble, and Kaelyn was made of the stuff.

They reached the gates, hoods pulled low. The guards
stared at them from behind their visors, and their hands clutched
their punishers. Their leather gloves creaked, and the rods' tips
crackled with red lightning.

"Good morning, my dear men," Kaelyn said from the
shadows of her hood. "My brother and I seek to collect firewood
outside the city gates. Would you be so kind as to—"

Rune had heard enough. His heart thrashed against his
ribs. His breath quickened. This was too big for him; outside in
the forest, a thousand of these resistors could be lurking, and stars

knew what they wanted with him. Rune would not wait to find out.

If I want to escape, now's my chance.

While Kaelyn was looking at the guards, Rune gave her a mighty shove.

She fell a few steps backward, gasping. Her dagger left his side and gleamed, suddenly exposed.

"She has a dagger!" Rune shouted to the guards. "I'm not her brother. She's a thief or a resistor. She—"

"Oh merciful stars!" Kaelyn shouted. She cursed, sucked in her breath, and shifted.

Wings burst out from her back. Green scales clanked across her. Rune gasped. He had never seen anyone but soldiers shift in Cadport; if carrying a dagger could land her in the dungeon, shifting was a capital offense. The green dragon soared and blew fire. Rune stumbled backward.

The guards at the gates cursed. They began to shift too, bodies ballooning and armor morphing into scales. Before they could complete their transformation, Kaelyn reached out her claws toward Rune. He leaped back, trying to dodge them, but she moved too quickly.

Kaelyn, an emerald dragon wreathed in flame, scooped him up like an eagle grabbing a mouse. She shot up so fast that Rune's head spun. He shouted, his legs kicked, and the wind whistled around him. The claws were so tight he could barely breathe.

"You bloody fool!" Kaelyn roared, wings beating. She rose so high the houses looked like toys below.

The guards began to fly too, metallic dragons roaring flame. Pillars of fire blazed up toward Kaelyn and Rune.

"Kaelyn, what the Abyss are you doing?" Rune shouted, kicking in her grip.

She banked sharply. Jets of flame blasted at their side, narrowly missing them. The heat baked Rune. The dragons below kept rising, and more fire blasted their way.

"It's the boy!" one of the dragons below shouted. "The brewer's boy Shari wants. Grab him and kill the girl!"

More jets of flame soared. Kaelyn banked again, and the fire screamed only feet away. The heat seared Rune and he shouted out.

What the Abyss was going on? Why did Shari want him? Could Kaelyn have been speaking truth all along?

Kaelyn rose so high the air thinned and Rune could barely breathe. Clouds streamed around them. With a howl, Kaelyn spun and began to swoop.

Wind screamed.

Blackness tugged at Rune and he gagged.

Five metallic dragons, guards of the city, came soaring toward them.

Kaelyn rained her fire.

Flames exploded across the world, and the dragons below howled. Kaelyn crashed between them, and her tail lashed, and her fangs bit, and blood showered. The metallic dragons bit and clawed all around, their fire blasted, and Rune screamed.

Kaelyn shot past the last dragon. She dived so close to the city that Rune—still held in her claws—nearly slammed against the rooftops. She began to rise again, the dragons in pursuit. More soldiers across the city saw the battle, shifted, and began taking flight.

Kaelyn cursed. "You bloody blockhead, Rune! You got us killed!"

She rose and flew above the city walls. The forest streamed below them. When Rune looked behind, he saw a hundred dragons, soldiers of Cadigus, shooting toward them.

He also saw something that chilled him far, far more than all the soldiers in the empire.

At the boardwalk, a building was burning.

The Old Wheel tavern.

Rune gasped and his eyes stung. Kaelyn kept streaming forward, cursing and beating her wings, and the dragons kept pursuing, but Rune could see nothing else.

The rest of the city still stood; only his home blazed.

They were looking for me, Rune realized. *Kaelyn was right.*

A blue dragon took flight from the blazing tavern. The beast screeched and clawed the sky, wings wide and tail flailing.

Shari Cadigus.

"Bring me the boy!" the blue dragon screeched. "Kill my whore of a sister, and bring me the brewer's boy! Bring me Rune Brewer!"

In her claws, Shari held a charred body. With a disgusted howl, she tossed the corpse down, and it crashed onto a nearby roof.

The body was badly burnt, but Rune saw that it wore a red and green cloak.

Rune knew that cloak. It was his father's favorite garment.

Tears filled his eyes, and Rune screamed out, and the world spun around him.

Then Kaelyn flew higher, crashing into the cover of clouds, and the city disappeared. The clouds streamed around them. Rune's eyes stung, his chest tightened, and he couldn't breathe.

The Old Wheel. My father. Stars, they're gone. Shari burned them.

"Father, no," he whispered, clutched in Kaelyn's claws. His voice rose to a howl. "What have you done, Kaelyn? What have you done? I'm a wanted man now, I—"

"You were wanted from the day you were born!" she snapped. "You just didn't know it until today. Thank me for pulling you out of your tavern moments before Shari burned it, or you'd be dead too."

"Kaelyn, what's going on?" he demanded, tears in his eyes. "Where are—"

Fire roared.

A hundred jets of flame pierced the clouds, shooting all around them. Hundreds of howls sounded behind, and Shari's voice pealed across the sky.

"Grab them!" the blue dragon screeched in the distance. "Burn them! Bring me my sister and the boy!"

Kaelyn howled, tightened her claws around Rune, and kept flying.

TILLA

The cart trundled down the road, jostling the recruits against one another. Tilla gasped for breath and clung to the girls around her. They had packed them like cattle, and even in the cold winter day, sweat drenched Tilla and she felt faint.

"Tilla!" whispered the girl beside her. "Tilla, can you see anything? You're tall!"

Tilla frowned down at the girl, the daughter of a baker, her blue eyes wide with fear, her cheeks pink, and her strawberry braid slung across her shoulder. Rune had been infatuated with the girl, Tilla remembered; her bakery stood only a few buildings away from the Old Wheel Tavern. Tilla herself had bought bread there, but could not remember the girl's name. She was a soft, doll-like thing, pretty but too fragile. Tilla could not imagine this one ever wielding a sword.

"What could I possibly see?" Tilla said and gestured around her.

The cart had no windows. It was wide enough to house a dragon... or about a hundred girls cramped so tightly together they couldn't even lift their arms. The shorter girls gasped for breath. At least Tilla was the tallest among them; her head rose above the mass, allowing her to breathe the hot, fetid air. The forest road was paved with rough cobblestones; the cart bumped and tilted with every turn of its wheels. The girls would have fallen were they not packed so close together.

"I don't know!" said the baker's daughter, and tears filled those large blue eyes. She clung to Tilla's hip. "Maybe you can see a crack, or a very small window, or..." The girl sniffed, then began to quietly weep. "I just miss Jem. I love him so much."

Tilla rolled her eyes. She remembered Jem Chandler, the girl's love. He was a useless dolt who spent more time drinking at the Old Wheel than crafting his candles.

They had not seen any of the boys all day, not since leaving Cadport. Outside the city walls, Beras and his soldiers had herded the female recruits into three cramped, rotted carts. The boys had been rustled into their own carts. Beras had driven his punisher into the backs of those too slow to climb in.

Dragons pulled these carts now, dragging them over bumps, ruts, and slopes that left the recruits bruised and whimpering. It had been a long day: a day of sweat, of gasps for breath, of recruits whispering and praying and—like the baker's daughter—weeping incessantly about loved ones.

"What's your name?" Tilla asked, not unkindly, and touched the girl's shoulder.

She sniffed and looked up at Tilla with damp, red-rimmed eyes.

"Mae," she said. "Don't you remember? You bought bread from me once. Mae Baker."

"Well, Mae, as I see it, you have a choice now," Tilla said. "You can cry and weep and mope for your boy. Or you can shut your wobbling lips, stop crying onto my shirt, and maybe act like a soldier. Okay?"

Mae's eyes widened, her jaw unhinged, and for a moment she just stared as if trying to understand if Tilla had truly said those words. Finally fresh tears filled her eyes.

"But I don't *want* to be a soldier!" Mae said. "All I want is my Jem, my sweet Jem who loves me."

Tilla glared at her. "Well, you *are* a soldier now. Or at least you will be when we reach whatever fort they're taking us to. I don't want to be a soldier either, but given that we don't have a choice in the matter, you can either cry yourself to death, or you can toughen up."

But the girl seemed not to hear her. She covered her eyes and began mumbling something about how her father was the richest baker in Cadport, and how he would save her from this place, and how handsome Jem Chandler was going to run away with her, and how Tilla would be so sorry she hadn't joined them.

Tilla heaved a sigh.

I'm not going to make any friends here like this, she thought. She had never been friends with any of these girls back in Cadport. She had always thought them moon-eyed, empty-headed peasants. It was no wonder she had never bothered learning their names. Standing here in a cart of them only confirmed her distaste.

It's little wonder Rune was my only friend in Cadport, she thought. She missed him. Perhaps not with tears and trembles the way Mae missed Jem, but she missed him nonetheless.

Where are you now, Rune? she wondered. *Are you brewing ale for the soldiers, or walking along the beach, or thinking about me?*

Her eyes began to sting and Tilla growled. She tightened her lips, narrowed her eyes, and clenched her fists. No, she could not think of Rune now. She could not cry, especially not after admonishing Mae.

I have three choices now, she thought. *I can try to escape this cart, run into the forest, and live on the run, and if the Legions ever catch me, I will die. Or I can stay here and weep and yearn like Mae and the others.* She raised her chin and grinded her teeth. *Or I can do this properly, and I can become a real soldier, and I can banish this pain from my chest and these tears from my eyes.*

She mulled over each option. Running seemed the worst of the bunch. Tilla had seen deserters caught before; the Cadigus family made sure every citizen in Cadport came to see them quartered by mules. Tilla rather liked having four limbs, so running was out of the question.

As for moping, she did not relish that option either. Thinking about Rune wouldn't get her back to him any sooner. Thinking about home would only weaken her. There was no point missing home now; or at least, she could try to suppress her homesickness. She could push those thoughts deep down where they couldn't hurt her. After all, how would weeping and yearning help her survive?

And so that left only one option.

I will play the game, she thought. *I will become the soldier they want me to be. For now, I will play by their rules. And maybe I can survive the next five years. Maybe I will learn enough to fight and live once they cart us off to fight the Resistance.*

Tilla nodded. Here in this cart, surrounded by the weeping and trembling girls, she vowed that she would *live.* If she had to fight a war, she would be strong and she would survive it, and in five years she could return home. In five years, maybe she could see her father and Rune again.

She looked at Mae, who still wept at her side, and iciness clutched Tilla, for she knew: Once their training was complete, and they were sent to fight, Mae would die.

She would die first.

Tilla closed her eyes and tried to forget Pery's head splattering down at her feet.

The cart kept trundling on and on. Finally whatever sunlight leaked through cracks in the walls faded. Darkness fell over the cart, and even the heat of a hundred bodies pressed together could not warm Tilla. She had not eaten, drunk, or sat down since that morning. Her back, feet, and stomach ached. Wolves howled outside, wind shrieked, and still the cart kept rolling.

"Tilla," Mae said, speaking for the first time in hours, "are we going to keep traveling all night?"

Tilla grumbled at the baker's daughter. "How should I know? Do I look like Beras?"

The girl whimpered and bit her lip. "Don't say his name," she pleaded. "Don't say the name of that man. They say he... he..." She sniffed. "It's horrible, but they said he r-r-... he did something horrible to a little girl. And then he strangled her to death." She shuddered. "Please don't say his name."

Tilla wondered if the stories were true. Had Beras the Brute truly raped a child, then strangled her and buried her body? Had the Cadigus family, impressed with his cruelty and reputation, hired him based on that merit? Tilla did not know, but after seeing Shari Cadigus behead Pery, she was inclined to believe it.

A woman like Shari would find a child-killer her perfect companion, she thought. Tilla looked at her boots and clenched her fists. Yet like it or not, Beras was the one leading this caravan. And Shari Cadigus, the emperor's daughter, was the one who had recruited them.

I might find them repulsive. But if I'm to survive, I must follow them. Tilla gritted her teeth so mightily it hurt. *I will live. I will return home. I will not be another Pery.*

After what seemed like hours of darkness, the cart finally slowed to a halt. It came with both a sigh of relief and a chill of fear.

The girls around Tilla looked at one another, mewling and whispering. Mae grabbed Tilla's arm, squeezing it so hard Tilla grunted and yanked herself free.

"What's happening?" Mae whispered.

"Hush!" Tilla said. "Be quiet, Mae, and be strong. No more tears, okay? If you want to live, you can't cry. Wipe your eyes."

Sniffling, Mae obeyed. After knuckling her eyes dry, she bit her wobbling lip so hard it turned white.

Boots thumped outside, and a voice cried out hoarsely across the convoy, the words muffled. The door of her cart jolted madly, keys rattled in the lock, and a low voice muttered curses.

Mae trembled. The hundred girls in the cart fell silent, and all eyes turned toward the door. Tilla squared her shoulders, straightened her back, and raised her chin. She could easily stare above the shorter girls, and she sucked in her breath and held it.

The door yanked open.

Beras the Brute stood outside in the night, holding keys in one hand, a torch in the other.

The girls inside the cart stared, frozen. Beras stared back, his beady eyes shadowed beneath his thrusting brow. Dark sacks hung under those eyes, tugging them down toward his cheeks. His face was ashen, and though close-shaven, his beard was so dark it left his cheeks in perpetual shadow. He wore no black, polished steel like the other soldiers, but crude plates of iron over patches of mail. Even this suit of metal could not hide his size; he easily weighed twice as much as Tilla, a blend of muscle and fat that pushed at his armor.

For a long moment, he merely glared at the girls. He grumbled, then hawked loudly and spat. A few girls started and Mae whimpered.

For the first time, Tilla heard Beras speak.

"All right, you miserable lot of whores," he rumbled. "If you ask me, you're good for nothing but spreading your legs in a brothel, the lot of you." He spat again. "But since Shari Cadigus thinks she can whip you into soldiers, you're mine for a few days until you reach your barracks." He clutched his groin and tugged it. "Any one of you harlots moves too slowly or disobeys my orders, you'll get a taste of this." His voice rose to a howl. "So move—now! Off the cart!"

For an instant, rage bloomed inside of Tilla. It coursed through her and spun her head. How dared this man threaten them? There were a hundred women in this cart, and each one could turn into a dragon. He was one man, one miserable murderer who—

She gritted her teeth.

He's one miserable murderer who's a darling of the empire, she reminded herself. *Unless you want to shift into a dragon and have that empire hunt you down, obey him.*

The girls began exiting the cart, silent, their eyes darting. Tilla moved among them. When she stepped outside, cold air stung her, so shocking after the stifling cart that she gasped. She found herself on a roadside in a forest clearing. All around the glade, dark trees rose naked to claw at a starless sky. Six carts camped here in a ring, and Cadport's youths were stepping out from each one, faces pale. At every cart, a soldier stood shouting, threatening to flay, whip, or behead anyone who moved too slowly. The shouts rose across the forest.

"Move it, maggots!" howled one soldier.

"Form ranks, worms!" cried another and raised his punisher, its tip crackling.

Tilla had seen soldiers in Castellum Acta, the small hilltop fortress in Cadport; she knew about forming ranks, but did the others? The six hundred recruits stumbled into the center of the clearing. Around them spread the carts and twenty soldiers or more, each holding a crackling punisher.

"Form ranks—move it!" one soldier howled, a gaunt man with one eye. "Or I swear, blood will spill tonight."

The other soldiers all shouted and thrust their punishers, goading the recruits closer together. All around the clearing, the trees creaked and distant wolves howled.

"Come on!" Tilla hissed and grabbed a girl beside her. She pulled her forward and stood her in place. "Stand here. You— Mae. Stand behind her, like this. Go. And stand tall and still, don't slouch!"

The girls glanced around nervously, but they stood where Tilla directed them. She grabbed their shoulders, pulled them straight, and shoved their chins up. Around them, the other recruits saw and followed suit.

"Form lines!" Tilla whispered, moving between the others. "Three soldiers deep; that's the standard form. Go! And stand straight."

Finally the recruits began to form ranks. They stood in three lines, every recruit a foot apart from the others. Tilla took her spot at the front line; Mae stood to her left, trembling and standing so straight her heels did not touch the ground.

Tilla stood frozen, barely daring to breathe. She stretched her own back straight, kept her arms firm at her sides, and raised her chin. She had seen this formation in Cadport before—it seemed the most common one—but she knew there were other formations too. Which one did these soldiers demand? If they formed these ranks wrong, and she was responsible, would they behead her too?

When the ranks were complete, and the recruits stood at attention, Beras began trundling down the lines. He lolloped like a bear, armor clanking and axe clattering against his back. His torch crackled and he grunted as he walked.

"He walks like he got a thorny stick up his arse," whispered a girl beside Tilla, a scrawny little thing with short brown hair, an upturned nose, and fiery eyes. "You reckon he likes to shove sticks up there, Tilla? I knew me a man once who—"

"Shh!" Tilla hushed her.

She remembered this skinny girl—an orphan named Erry Docker, a dockside urchin who slept on the beach and ate whatever she stole. Some whispered that Erry was the daughter of a long-dead prostitute. Others whispered that Erry herself had taken up the profession and already bedded a thousand men.

"I was only—" Erry began, eyes flashing.

"Hush!" Tilla said.

Beras kept lumbering around, indeed moving much like Erry had described. The recruits stood silently.

"I could have bedded two whores by the time you formed ranks!" Beras shouted. "If you cannot form ranks here, in a guarded camp, how will you survive at war? When we send you miserable worms to fight the Resistance, do you think the enemy will wait for you to form the lines?" He spat and shouted hoarsely. "They will butcher you, and skin you alive, and they will rape your flayed bodies as you thrash and beg to die."

Tilla's throat tightened. She had heard many stories of the Resistance. They whispered that these rebels, wild men and women who lurked in the forests, were even crueler than the Cadigus family. They were bloodthirsty.

They killed my brother.

Cold sweat trickled down Tilla's back. Could the Resistance be hiding in *this* forest, waiting to charge with steel and fire?

Beras kept moving down the lines, inspecting each recruit in turn.

"In a few days," he called out, "you will reach your barracks, and they will try to train you, to turn you whelps into soldiers. If you ask me, they'll be wasting their time. I don't see soldiers. I see cannon fodder." He stopped before one boy, leaned close, and sneered. "You're a skinny one; I bet you weigh less than my axe."

The thin, pale youth kept standing still. "Yes, my lord," he whispered.

Beras grunted and walked on. He paused before another girl, licked his lips, and ogled her.

"And you," he said, "you are soft and rounded. You're made for a brothel, not a barracks." He spat at her feet. "I bet two coppers you end up in one. I'll be there to break you in."

He kept moving and stopped before a tall, broad youth with black hair. Tilla recognized him as Jem Chandler, the lazy lout who spent days drunk at the Old Wheel—the youth Mae pined for.

"You!" Beras barked. "You've got some meat on you. Big lad. You think you can be a soldier?"

Jem stood so stiffly it looked like his bones could shatter. He managed to nod.

"Yes, my lord."

Beras spat at his feet. "I'm not a lord, boy. And you're not a soldier and never will be. What did you do back at that cesspool you call a city?"

Jem held his head high, the veins straining in his neck. "I'm a chandler."

"Chandler!" Beras rumbled. "What the Abyss is that—you rolled over in a whorehouse for sailors?"

"I... I made candles, my—" Jem bit his lip. "I just made candles. But I can be a soldier. I can fight. I'm strong."

Beras snorted. "Are you now? We will see. Fight me." He tossed his torch down; it crackled upon the earth. "Come on. Show me how you fight, boy."

Jem looked aside nervously and licked his lips.

"I—"

Beras drove his fist into Jem's belly.

Tilla winced, clenched her jaw, and held her breath.

Jem doubled over, gasping for breath. Standing before the youth, Beras changed—his eyes burned with wildfire, his lips pulled back from his yellow teeth, and drool ran down his chin. He was like a rabid beast. He swung, and his fist *cracked* against Jem's head.

At Tilla's side, Mae whimpered.

"Hush!" Tilla whispered to the girl. Her fists trembled. "Don't make a sound!"

Jem lay on the ground, hacking and coughing blood. Beras laughed and kicked him, again and again, as the youth mewled.

"See the mighty candlemaker!" Beras announced, arms raised and fists bloodied. "See the boy who thought himself a soldier!"

With a laugh, Beras kicked hard. The steel-tipped boot drove into Jem's head. The youth's neck snapped, and Tilla closed her eyes and struggled not to gag, not to faint.

Stars, oh stars. Her eyes stung and the world spun around her. *Another death.*

"You lot are nothing but maggots!" Beras shouted. "You think you can be soldiers? You can be dead! You will be fed to the cannons, and your flesh will rot in the fields. You are nothing! You will be nothing. You are worms and if any of you doubts it, I will crush you."

Tilla opened her eyes and looked at Mae. The girl was trembling. She bit her lip so hard blood trickled down her chin. Tears streamed down her cheeks and she whimpered.

"Hush!" Tilla warned. "Mae, you—"

"What's this?" Beras demanded. His boots thumped. Tilla turned to see him marching toward her, fists at his sides. Blood splashed his boots.

Tilla fell silent and straightened, standing as stiff as she could.

The stench of sweat and blood flared as Beras came to stand before her. Tilla was the tallest girl here, and taller than half the boys, but Beras towered above her; he made her feel small as a child. He thrust his head close, scrutinizing her, and his lips peeled back. His teeth were rotten, and his breath assailed her, scented of corpses.

"Well, well," the brute said. "Look at what we've got here. My, you're a tall one." He reached out. With rough fingers, he grabbed her throat and squeezed. Pain shot through her; it took all her will to suppress a gasp. "I like tall women."

Tilla dared not look into his eyes, but she stared at his forehead with all the strength she had in her. His fingers squeezed her tighter. She could barely wheeze. She managed to whisper through the pain.

"Shari Cadigus liked me too." Her breath rasped, but she kept staring at the spot between his eyes. "You remember. You were there."

Beras kept his hand around her throat, crushing her, and glared. He hissed and his breath blasted her face, and she nearly gagged at its rot. His beady eyes burned.

"Yes," he hissed. "I remember. You're that whore I grabbed in my claws. The Abyss knows what Shari saw in you. You look like nothing but a cheap harlot to me." He spat onto her boot. "Shari isn't here. You remember that. You remember that well. Over here, on this road, you are mine. What's your name?"

"Tilla Roper," she whispered, voice raspy.

He leaned closer. He whispered into her ear. "I'll be watching you, Roper. You are trouble. You make one wrong move, and you will envy that boy whose misery I ended. You I would not kill so quickly."

He released her, turned around, and kept trundling down the lines. Tilla allowed herself to gasp with pain. She sucked in air. Her throat ached and her head spun, and she could still smell his rot.

"Now get to bed!" Beras shouted. "We keep moving at dawn. Get some sleep, and if I see any worms crawl, I crush them."

With that, the brute stepped into a cart and slammed the door shut. One soldier began dragging Jem's body into the woods; the others entered the other carts, leaving the recruits outside in the clearing.

Nobody dared speak. Nobody even dared whimper or cry. Six hundred recruits lay down, glanced around, and huddled together.

Tilla lay on the hard, cold earth. The wind moaned and chilled her, and rain began to fall. She shivered and her belly ached; she had not eaten all day, and she didn't know when she'd eat next. The forest creaked around them, and the wolves kept howling.

Another death, Tilla thought, the blood dancing before her eyes. *Another memory that will haunt me. Oh Rune. If you knew how bad it was, you'd have hid me under your tavern's floor with your old books.*

Mae curled up at her side, and tears streamed down her cheeks. Though she had vowed to be strong, Tilla felt her own eyes dampen. Perhaps it was the death she had seen. Perhaps it was the cold, the hunger, or pain. Perhaps she simply missed home. But her own tears fell, and her own lips trembled. Here, in the dark night, she did not feel like a soldier, only like a young and frightened girl.

"Jem," Mae whispered at her side and shook, sobbing quietly.

Tilla wriggled closer to the girl. The rain fell upon them. Lying in the mud, Tilla embraced the baker's daughter. Mae wept against her shoulder, and Tilla shed her own silent tears. They held each other as rain fell, wolves howled, and the night wrapped around them like claws.

RUNE

They ran through the forest as the sky burned.

Smoke blazed in Rune's lungs. His chest ached from where Kaelyn's claws had clutched him. Branches slapped him and roots snagged at his feet. A green dragon, Kaelyn had crashed through the treetops a mile back; they had been running in human forms since, side by side.

A hundred dragons screamed above, soaring and swooping and tearing at trees. Their flames blazed across the sky in crisscrossing lines. Rain fell and smoke blew above the forest.

"Find them!" rose a shriek above. The blue dragon soared—Shari Cadigus blowing fire. "Bring them to me alive, or bring me their charred corpses, but find them!"

Rune snarled and kept running. His lungs blazed, his knees throbbed, and his chest felt ready to collapse. He looked at Kaelyn, who ran at his side. Sweat dampened her mane of golden hair, and mud covered her clothes. She ran with bared teeth, her eyes narrowed. Her sword clanked at her side, and her bow bounced across her back.

Rune looked up. The forest canopy was thick; he could barely glimpse the dragons between the branches. For now they were hidden, but how long would that last?

"Kaelyn, they will burn down the forest," he said. "You can't possibly outrun a hundred dragons, they—"

She glared at him. "They will not burn their empire. This is Shari Cadigus, and these are her lands; she still loves Requiem in her twisted way." She panted and wiped sweat off her brow, but kept running. "Keep your voice low."

She scuttled over a boulder, climbing as deftly as a squirrel. Rune cursed and scrambled after her; she had to grab his wrist and pull him over. They ran down a hillside bumpy with roots. Vines tangled around Rune's feet, and a dragon swooped so low that he cursed and fell into the mud.

The dragon shrieked and roared fire skyward. Claws uprooted a tree. Rune cursed and ran aside, scurrying under the cover of an oak. Kaelyn ran at his side, and they raced between more trees. Fallen leaves and moss flew from under their boots.

"Tear down the trees!" Shari screamed above. Rune could not see her, but he heard her wings thud, and the trees bent as in a storm. "I can smell them. They cower below."

Rune cursed and panted. Sweat drenched him. He had been running for so long. He could run no longer. Perhaps he should surrender, should explain to Princess Shari that this was all a mistake; surely she was mistaking him for somebody else. He had nothing to do with Kaelyn or the Resistance. He was just Rune Brewer, and Kaelyn had tried to kidnap him, and he just wanted to go home.

Only there is no home anymore, he remembered, and his eyes stung. *Shari burned it down. And she killed my father. And like it or not, I'm stuck with Kaelyn now.*

"Kaelyn," he whispered between pants. "Kaelyn, where are—"

Her eyes lit up and she flashed a grin. "Here!"

She darted toward a mossy, twisting oak. Rune paused from running, and as soon as his legs stilled, pain bolted up them. His head spun and his chest felt full of fire.

Had Kaelyn gone mad? Rune had expected a camp full of warriors, or a hidden castle, or... not just a tree.

"Kaelyn!" he said and glanced skyward. Dragons streamed above the branches, dipping down to uproot trees. One beast grabbed a pine so close, Rune cursed and ducked. The roots yanked up, raining dirt and moss, less than a hundred feet away.

He looked back at Kaelyn. The young woman was scrambling around the tree, muttering curses and kicking the earth. She got down on her knees and began rummaging through the leaves.

"Stars damn it!" she said. "Come on, where are you—"

A dragon swooped fifty yards away. Another tree was uprooted and howls rose. The blue dragon dived above, wings bending the trees, and blew fire across the sky.

"They're near!" Shari howled. "I smell them. They're close! Tear up every tree."

Rune ducked and grasped a rock, as if tossing it could defeat dragons. He snarled and prepared to die.

"There!" Kaelyn whispered in triumph. She straightened, holding a rope that rose from the fallen leaves.

"Kaelyn, we need an army, not a rope—"

Before Rune could finish his sentence, Kaelyn yanked the rope, and a trapdoor opened upon the forest floor. Leaves and grass covered its top; below, a stairway led into darkness.

"Well, go on!" Kaelyn said. "Close your mouth and get down there."

Rune dutifully closed his mouth. Just as another dragon dived, he rushed forward, passed under the trapdoor, and leaped onto the staircase. Kaelyn jumped down beside him and tugged the trapdoor shut.

Before Rune could examine his new surroundings or even take another breath, thuds sounded in the forest above. Even through the trapdoor, Rune knew that sound: dragon claws landing in the forest. Flames crackled outside, wings flapped, and dragons screeched.

"They were here." Shari's shrill voice rose above. "I smell them. I see their prints. They ran here moments ago."

Great nostrils sniffed above, loud as a bellows. Kaelyn cursed and gripped her sword. With her other hand, she drew her dagger from her boot. For an instant, Rune thought she'd threaten him with the blade again. Then he saw that she was holding its hilt outward, offering it to him. Rune took the dagger and gripped it.

Shari screamed above, a sound of fury like storms and mountains cracking.

"Uproot every tree!" she cried. "Spread across this forest and find them. If you cannot, I will decimate you. Spread out! Find the whore and the boy."

With that, wings beat, fire crackled, and Shari's shrieks faded into the distance. The other dragons seemed to follow her.

Rune let out a shaky breath. He lowered his head, breathed raggedly, and tried to calm his thrashing heart. His muscles cramped, his breath sawed at his throat, and his skull felt too tight.

At his side, Kaelyn too breathed in relief. She wiped her brow again, only smearing sweat and mud across it. She released her grip on her sword.

"Come, Rune," she said. "Down the stairs and into the darkness. We're safe—for now." She managed a weak glare. "No thanks to you; you almost got us killed. You're more trouble than you're worth, if you ask me. From now on, you listen to me, and you follow my every order—no questions. Is that clear?"

He grumbled under his breath. "You sure have a way with people. But I'll listen to you for now, at least until I can rest and eat. You do have some food and drink squirreled away down here, right?"

She gave him a withering stare, then turned and began walking downstairs. He followed. The steps were dug into soil and rock, reinforced with planks of wood. Roots thrust out from the walls, and a family of mice huddled in a hole. The air was colder down here, and the place smelled of moss and soil.

After descending twenty steps, Kaelyn reached into an alcove dug into a wall. She produced two candles and a tinderbox.

"Here," she said and passed him a candle. "Hold this and do try not to set yourself on fire."

She opened the tinderbox and rubbed flint against steel. Sparks flew and Kaelyn lit their candles. The orange light flickered, and they kept descending.

The stairway led into a narrow tunnel. A wooden framework held the walls and ceiling; the floor was mere soil. The tunnel was so narrow it pushed against Rune's elbows. Kaelyn walked ahead and he followed silently. He wanted to pester Kaelyn for answers, but her talk of fire reminded him of that morning. The Old Wheel burning. The charred corpse of his father. Rune lowered his head and walked silently, candle in hand.

The tunnel took them to a round chamber; it was roughly the size of Rune's bedroom back at the Old Wheel. Kaelyn moved about the room, lighting more candles in alcoves. The light fell upon casks of wine, shelves of preserves and sausages, a rack of swords and bows, and chests of tunics and cloaks.

"Do you live here?" Rune asked.

"I live nowhere," she replied, not turning to look at him. "This is what we call a gopher hole. Stop—don't go looking around for gophers, you won't find any. It's just what we call these hideouts. They're safe places we can use when traveling."

She rummaged through a chest and produced some bandages. She closed the lid, sat upon it, and peeled back the rents on her legging. Grimacing, she examined the cut along her hip.

Rune knelt before her and reached for the bandages.

"Let me take a look," he said. "I know a bit of healing; I stitched a wound on Scraggles once."

She gave him a sidelong glance. "Scraggles?"

"You met him." He gave her a wan smile. "He barked at you."

She yanked the bandages away from him. "I will tend to my own wound, thank you. You go... go look at the swords or something. I hope you know how to use one." She sighed and rolled her eyes. "Of course you don't know how to use one. You were an innkeeper. I suppose that if Emperor Cadigus ever attacks us with a mug, you'll know how to clean it."

She began to tend to her wound, wincing. Rune grumbled and paced the chamber, this "gopher hole". He felt less like a gopher here and more like a trapped dragon; fire fumed inside him. His boots thumped against the earthen floor.

"You're right," he said. "You're right, Kaelyn, I'm no warrior. I don't know how to use a sword. And I've cleaned a lot of mugs in my day. I *am* an innkeeper and a brewer; that's all I want to be. You're the one who dragged me here at dagger-point. You're the one who got me into this mess." He stomped toward her, grabbed her shoulders, and glared at her. "Why, Kaelyn? Whatever feud you have with the Cadigus family, why did you drag me into it?"

She looked up from her wound and laughed mirthlessly. "Feud with the Cadigus family? Boy, did you not hear Shari call me her sister? I *am* the Cadigus family."

He frowned. He gave her a piercing stare, taking in her golden mane of hair, her feline features, and her sharp hazel eyes. Then he barked a laugh.

"You?" he said. "You are nothing like Shari Cadigus. Shari is... well, first of all, she's much taller than you. And she has dark hair and dark eyes. And, well... she's more of a warrior. You're kind of small and sneaky. Aren't the Cadiguses supposed to be big and tough and scary?"

Kaelyn glared at him. "I didn't say she was my twin sister. I have one twin already, a madman of a brother, and pray you never meet him. And no, I'm not like Shari. I'm not big, or tough, or particularly cruel." She sighed. "Why do you think I ran away?"

Rune stared at her with narrowed eyes.

Stars, he thought, *she's serious.*

He clutched his head.

This is bad.

He had heard of Kaelyn Cadigus, of course—the princess who had escaped the palace and joined the Resistance. But Kaelyn was a popular name, and somehow—with all the fire, running, and blood—Rune had not pieced things together.

His head spun.

"This is bad," he muttered. "Oh stars, this is bad." He pointed at her. "*You* are Kaelyn Cadigus."

She raised her hands to the heavens. "Stars bless us, he can be taught! What gave it away?"

Rune resumed pacing the room, tugging at his hair. He remembered that winter two years ago, the winter Kaelyn Cadigus was said to have escaped the capital, flown into the forest, and joined the rebellion against her father. Soldiers had stormed through every city, town, and farm in Requiem that season, tearing through homes, burning farms, torturing and killing and seeking the girl in every last hovel. They had never found her, but some whispered that Kaelyn Cadigus had risen high in the Resistance, ranking second only to Valien Eleison himself, the uprising's leader.

"Oh bloody stars," Rune said. "I'm here with Kaelyn Cadigus. No wonder they were hunting me. They must have seen you sneak into my tavern. Stars, woman, you're the most wanted soul in Requiem, do you know that?"

She gave him a wry smile. "No, Rune, I'm not the most wanted soul in Requiem—maybe second or third. Most wanted? My dear boy, that honorable distinction goes to you."

It was his turn to raise his hands in frustration. "Me? Merciful stars, Kaelyn, your sister didn't even know I existed until you sneaked into my tavern. Why did you drag me into this?" He shook his head as he paced. "That's it. I have to turn you in. No other choice. I'll fly to Shari, and explain that this was all a mistake, and—"

"And she would break your every bone, and flay your skin, and disembowel you alive, and laugh as you scream and beg," Kaelyn said. "I've seen her do it to others. Rune, come here. Sit down beside me. I have some things to tell you. You'll want to sit down for them."

She wriggled sideways on the chest, making room for him. He glowered down at her, but she only looked up with large, sad eyes, all their mockery and anger gone. Suddenly Rune again realized how beautiful she was, and stars damn it, he was a young man, and a beautiful woman still muddled his mind and dissipated his anger. With a sigh, he sat down beside her.

"Well, it's about damn time you told me what's going on here," he said. "So talk. I'm listening."

She placed a hand on his knee and looked at him softly. Her fingers were slim and warm; her eyes were warmer.

"Rune," she said, "do you know how my father came into power?"

He nodded. "Of course I do. We had to sing his songs every harvest fair. Requiem was weak in the old days; the Aeternum Dynasty had weakened it. Griffins ravaged our kingdom. Phoenixes burned us. Desert warriors rode wyverns to shatter our halls. We were hunted, afraid, dying. And then... Frey Cadigus flew to the capital, a great general leading a host of loyal dragons. They took the throne. They cast aside the weakness of the old dynasty. They hunted and slaughtered the griffins, the phoenixes, and all those who had hurt us. They turned Requiem from a frightened, crumbling kingdom into an empire. Requiem is strong now; Frey Cadigus made her strong." Rune's lips twisted into a grimace. "At least, that's what they taught me as a boy. That's what they forced us to sing. If you ask me, your father is a right bastard."

"That," she said, "he most certainly is. And yes, I too heard the stories of how weak the Aeternum Dynasty was. I grew up hearing horrible stories, Rune. My father would relish in telling them. Stories about how the griffins tore apart our children, spilling entrails and blood; how phoenixes burned our people so that their skin peeled and they ran flaming; how wyverns invaded from the south, how their acid melted flesh and left us deformed and forever screaming." Kaelyn sighed. "Those stories might be true; they are written in books from before my father's rule. But those books grieved for our fallen, for all the wars we fought. My father did not grieve; he *raged*. He blamed the Aeternum Dynasty for weakening Requiem, for allowing our enemies to kill us. He would mock the old dynasty's *compassion* and *righteousness*, spitting out those words like insults. He told me that he delighted in killing them. He told me how he slaughtered the old Aeternum king, his wife, and his children. When telling these stories, his eyes would light up, and he would lick his lips, and he seemed almost in rapture."

Rune nodded. "Like I said—right bastard. But I know all this. Stars, Kaelyn, the whole empire knows that the Cadigus family hated the Aeternums, that they are... how does Frey put it?" Rune puffed out his chest and spoke in a deep, bombastic voice, imitating the speeches he had heard soldiers delivering at Cadport. "We are strong now. We will never fall. We are mighty and powerful and no enemies will threaten us again, and any weakness within us must be crushed." He rolled his eyes. "I've never met your father, but stars, every soldier of his I've seen repeats the same thing. An army of parrots, he has."

"Deadly parrots," Kaelyn said. "Big ones who can blow fire." She smiled and lowered her head. Her hand still held his knee. "Rune, you said I don't look like my sister; that is true. Did you ever wonder why you don't look like Wil Brewer, the man you called father?"

Rune had smiled at her jest about fire-breathing parrots; now his smile vanished, and pain twisted his chest. *My father.* Again Rune saw it: Shari rising from the burning Old Wheel, clutching the charred corpse in her claws. *She killed him. She killed my father.* He clenched his fists and tears burned in his eyes.

All his life—gone. His kindly father. His home. His books. All burnt and gone. He wondered if his dog, at least, had fled the flames; yet even if Scraggles had escaped, would Rune ever see his pet again?

Everything is burnt, he thought and a lump filled his throat. *Everything is lost.*

"Oh, Rune," Kaelyn said, voice soft. "I'm sorry. Truly I am. I didn't mean to... I..." She touched his hair. "I know this is painful. I know this is confusing. But hear me now. There will be time to mourn, but first you must hear everything I say."

He looked at her, silent. His eyes stung, and tears blurred his vision. He nodded, unable to talk.

"Rune," she continued, "this is going to be hard to accept. You might not believe me, but you must hear this. When my father took over the throne, he slaughtered the Aeternum family, every last one—the king, the queen, the princes, the lords and ladies... all but one Aeternum. All but the babe of the family. All but you."

Rune rubbed his eyes and sighed. "I had a feeling you were going to say that." He gave her a sidelong glance. "And damn it, you didn't disappoint. Yes, I've heard of this missing Aeternum babe. I realize he vanished around the time I myself was a baby.

Stars, Kaelyn, every boy in Cadport my age was mocked for being the missing Aeternum."

Kaelyn's eyes narrowed and flashed. "Well, he really is you. Your true name is Relesar Aeternum, son of Ardin, heir of a dynasty four thousand years old. My father hates you—he hates you more than all the griffins and phoenixes that ever flew. He's been hunting you for seventeen years now, since I myself was only a babe. Why do you think Shari showed up in your city?"

"To enlist recruits? To behead a girl and terrify us into obedience? Because she likes the seaside air and the mild southern winters?"

"Because she was looking for you." Kaelyn jabbed him sharply in the arm. "You look like your father, the old king. Damn it, you're the spitting image. I've seen the man's paintings. People noticed. *Soldiers* noticed. You have the same dark hair, the same gray eyes, the same straight nose..."

"Kaelyn, that describes about a million people in Requiem!" He laughed. "So the old king Aeternun had brown hair and gray eyes—stars above, that proves it!"

Kaelyn looked at her feet; she twisted them uncomfortably. "Well, I... might have had something to do with Shari showing up. We've known about you all your life, Rune. Our leader, Valien, is the one who placed you at the Old Wheel Tavern; you were only a few moons old. Since then, the Resistance has been watching you. We'd visit the tavern. We'd drink your ale. We'd make sure you were safe, that the Cadigus family hadn't found you. And, well..." Kaelyn bit her lip. "I'm sorry, but we grew careless. Shari's soldiers saw our movements. They knew we were visiting Cadport. They followed me one day to the Old Wheel, and they saw you there, and they put two and two together." She looked back at him, her eyes rimmed with red. "I had to look after you, Rune. I had to. You understand, right?"

For the first time, Rune realized where he had seen Kaelyn before. Of course!

The young, demure priestess had visited the Old Wheel the last two winters, claiming to be on a pilgrimage to Ralora Cliffs, the place where Requiem had fought a battle hundreds of years ago. The priestess would wear a headdress, heavy robes, and a hood, but Rune remembered her large, hazel eyes.

Kaelyn's eyes.

He rose to his feet so suddenly he nearly knocked the chest—and Kaelyn—over. He rushed toward a wall, grabbed a sword that hung there, and sliced the air. His jaw clenched and anger constricted his throat.

"Shari followed you!" he said, staring at Kaelyn with burning eyes. "I knew it. I knew it! And now my father is dead, and I'm stuck in this hole, and if they catch me, I'm dead too. And... stars, Kaelyn, how could you..."

He let his sword drop; it thumped against the ground. He fell to his knees beside it, covered his eyes, and felt Kaelyn's hands in his hair.

"I'm sorry," she whispered. She knelt before him and embraced him. "I'm so sorry—for everything. But you're safe now."

He lowered his hands and stared at her. Her face was inches from his, soft with concern.

"Am I, Kaelyn? Am I safe?"

"Safer than you were." She touched his cheek. "Believe that, at least. You are safer here."

He let out a long, shaky sigh. He felt too weak to stand up again, to ever leave this hole.

"What now?" he said and lowered his head.

"I will take you to see Valien, our leader. He has known you all your life; he smuggled you out of the palace when my father killed your parents." She nodded. "He is wise, the wisest man I know. He'll know what to do next."

"Valien Eleison," Rune whispered.

Like everyone in the empire, he had heard of Valien—the disgraced knight turned resistor, the silver dragon with one horn. Some called him a hero. Others called him a brute, a drunkard and thief and murderer. And some, Rune knew, said that Valien Eleison himself was the man who slew Tilla's brother.

And I will meet him, Rune thought and swallowed. *I will meet the man who crushed my best friend's soul.*

Kaelyn nodded. "But for now, eat and drink something. There is food and wine here. It will be a long journey, and you'll need your strength." She looked at the fallen blade. "And you'll need that sword."

"I thought you said I wouldn't know how to use one."

Though her eyes were still damp, Kaelyn managed to flash a grin. "You wouldn't, but I'd like a spare, and I'm not carrying two." She stood up, grabbed an apple from a shelf, and tossed it toward him. "Eat this. And kick your boots off. We're staying the night. You're stuck with me in this hole for a while longer."

On any other night, being stuck in a burrow with a beautiful woman—overnight, too!—would have made Rune feel like the luckiest man in Requiem. Today the apple tasted stale, and he missed home, and he missed Tilla and his father.

When his apple was eaten, he lay down by a wall, and Kaelyn lay beside him. She covered herself with her cloak and placed her cheek upon her palm.

"Goodnight, Rune," she said.

"You're not going to stab me in the middle of the night, are you?" He rubbed his side. "Your dagger nicked me back there."

She grinned again, a grin that showed all her teeth. "No, but I do kick when I sleep." She gave him a mock kick. "You're safe from Shari's fire, but no promises that I won't kick you to death."

"Fair enough." He closed his eyes. "Goodnight, Kaelyn."

Goodnight, Tilla, he added silently, wondering where she was now, and whether she too had a dry, safe place to sleep.

Goodnight, Father, he thought. He wondered if the old man's soul had risen to the starlit halls of afterlife... and how crazy Kaelyn was for claiming Wil Brewer hadn't been his father at all.

SHARI

She flew back toward Cadport, shrieking and blowing fire. Her blood pounded in her ears. Her wings beat, bending trees below. Six of her warriors flew around her, metallic dragons blasting fire and howling.

The boy escaped.

Shari screeched and streamed above the city walls.

This backwater will pay.

"I seek Rune Brewer!" Shari screamed to city. She flew above the streets and homes, smoke streaming behind her. "You let the boy escape."

She swooped, reached out her claws, and slashed at a home. Its clay walls collapsed, and the family inside wailed. Shari rose higher, breathing fire.

"You will bring me the boy!" she cried. "You will bring him to me, or this city will burn."

She dived over a square and blew fire at another home. Its roof burst into flame. The family inside screamed and fled into the street.

Shari snarled, rage pounding through her. This foul southern city was conniving against her. This was a hive of resistors; she knew it. How else could Kaelyn have smuggled the boy out?

She turned to look at her warriors, six iron dragons who flew behind her.

"Each of you," she said, "grab two of this city's vermin. I don't care who. I don't care how young they are. Grab a dozen of these filthy maggots and break them upon a dozen wheels."

The six dragons blasted fire, grinned toothily, and swooped.

Claws slammed into homes. Walls collapsed and people ran through the streets, wailing.

Shari beat her wings, flew toward the hill above the boardwalk, and circled around Castellum Acta, citadel of this city. She screeched orders, voice pealing across the sky. A hundred soldiers streamed out of the craggy fortress, shifted into dragons, and streamed above the streets. The city shook and jets of fire crisscrossed the sky. Homes burned.

"Raise twelve wheels!" Shari howled, wings beating back flames across the city. Smoke filled her throat, and she roared hoarsely. "Raise them outside the courthouse!"

As thousands wailed and fled across the city, her soldiers dragged twelve wagon wheels into the city square, that same square where Shari had spoken to the recruits. Dragons dived and grabbed people from the streets—men, women, and children.

"Break their bodies!" Shari shouted, flying above.

Her six dragons returned and rallied around her. Each clutched two people, one in each claw. They dived, tossed the people onto the square, and pinned them down. Soldiers streamed from alleyways to form a ring around the plaza.

Shari landed upon the cobblestones and blasted fire skyward. She roared so the entire city could hear.

"Break them!" she cried. "Shatter their bones and hang them here. I want the city to hear them scream!"

The twelve, selected randomly from the thousands, squirmed and tried to flee, but they could not escape the claws that pinned them down. One of them, a young man with wide eyes, tried to shift into a dragon, to break the law of Cadigus. Scales began to appear across his body, but the dragon above him, one of Shari's soldiers, pressed his claws down. The young man below wailed and his magic left him.

"Break them! Bring hammers!"

Soldiers walked forward in human form, clad in black armor and bearing great hammers. The dozen townsfolk wailed, trapped under the claws.

"Please!" one begged, a young girl no older than ten. "Please..."

Another wailed, an old woman with white hair. "Please, my princess, have mercy—"

The hammers swung.

Bones snapped.

The dozen screamed.

Shari stood, snarling and snorting smoke, and laughed.

The hammers swung again. Again. Snapping limbs. Snapping spines. Shari laughed.

"Sling them onto the wheels!" she commanded.

The soldiers dragged the wailing, broken bodies onto the wagon wheels, slung limbs between spokes, and tied the dozen down.

"Hang them on the courthouse balcony!" she commanded, laughing and blasting smoke.

Her soldiers laughed too. Ropes were slung over the balcony, and Shari smiled; had she not met the ropemaker's daughter at this very place?

The wheels were raised to dangle off the balcony like bloodied wind chimes. Upon each one, a shattered body twitched and wept. Shari stood in the square, still in dragon form. She was tempted to blow her fire, to roast these wailing bodies and taste their flesh. But no, she thought. No. She would let them linger here. She would let them scream a while longer.

She flapped her wings and rose high above the square. The city rolled around her. From up here, she could see Castellum Acta upon the hill, the boardwalk lined with rotting shops, the docks that stretched into the sea, and the abandoned lighthouse upon the breakwater. In the north, beyond the city walls, stretched the forest where the boy had fled.

Shari roared her cry, making sure every soul in Cadport heard.

"I seek Rune Brewer!" she shouted. "You let him flee this city. This is your punishment. These bodies will hang until they rot!" She blew fire down at homes, torching roofs. "You will bring me information about the boy. You will tell me where he fled. Or next moon, I will break a hundred bodies, then a thousand, then ten thousand, until none are left alive." She screamed so loudly her eardrums thrummed. "You will bring me Rune Brewer or you will die!"

People streamed into the square below her, weeping and wailing and reaching out to those dying upon the wheels. They were the families of the broken, Shari realized, and her grin widened.

Good, she thought. *Let them see their beloveds suffer. This city sheltered an Aeternum.* She shrieked and blasted fire. *They will suffer greatly until he's mine.*

She spun and flew away. Once she had crossed the city walls and flew over the forest, a chill claimed her belly, overpowering the fire of her rage.

She had told her father she would return the boy.

She had vowed to drag Relesar Aeternum back to the capital, he a broken wretch and she a glorious ruler. She had promised her father this gift within the moon.

Frey Cadigus, she knew, was not one to take disappointment well.

She howled, thrashed her tail, and blasted fire.

"You will pay for this, Kaelyn!" she roared. "I will break you too, and I will break the boy, and I will break this city, and the world itself will weep until Relesar is mine."

With fire and roars, Shari flew north, heading to the capital, to her father... and to the rage of an empire.

LERESY

He flew on the wind, a red dragon snorting fire, and licked his maw. He saw it below, rising glorious from the forest.

"My birthday present," he hissed, and smoke curled from between his teeth. "It's mine. My own."

He was eighteen today, a grown man, and his first fortress—the first of many he would command—shone below. Obsidian tiles covered its limestone foundations, reflecting the winter sun. Its four corner towers rose like skulls upon scraggly necks, their tops snowy. Their banners flapped in the wind, hiding and revealing the red spiral, sigil of his house. A fifth tower rose above the grand hall, twice as tall as the others. Upon it ticked a great clock, its four dials as large as dragons, the hands shaped as blades.

"Castra Luna," whispered the red dragon. "The oldest standing fortress in Requiem. My birthright."

As he flew over the forest toward the castle, Leresy Cadigus, prince of the empire, grinned and breathed his fire.

The forest streamed below him, pines and oaks bending under the flap of his wings. When Leresy drew closer to the fort, he saw hundreds of soldiers in the courtyard, mere scurrying ants from here. He narrowed his eyes and found himself salivating.

Yes, he thought. *Yes, lots of new recruits here—young, afraid, and female.* He licked drool off his maw. *So much flesh to claim. So much to taste, to savor, to conquer.*

Some in the capital had wondered, Leresy knew, why he had demanded Castra Luna for his birthday gift. His older sister Shari had scoffed.

"You could have any fort in Nova Vita!" she had said.
"You could command knights, seasoned warriors, and garrisons
of legend. And you choose... a training outpost halfway across the
empire?"

She had laughed, and Leresy had only stood before her,
silent, a small smile on his lips. So little she understood. So little
she knew of what lurked here in Castra Luna, this distant southern
pile of stone.

Here lurked real power, more than Shari could imagine in
her small, petty mind, the mind of a warrior.

"You think like a fighter," Leresy whispered into the wind.
"Like a brute. Like the mindless killer that you are. But I want
more than the glory of war, dearest sister. When I am done here,
I will have such power that you will kneel before me."

Flames exploded within him. He clenched his jaw and
blasted fire skyward. Shari thought herself so mighty, so proud,
so powerful. As Leresy circled above the fortress, he roared his
rage, a shriek that could tear through human eardrums.

*You might be heir to the empire, Shari, but soon even you will quake
before me.*

He now flew directly over Castra Luna, the ancient fortress
that had been guarding southern Requiem for seven hundred
years. He dived toward the courtyard and flew so low the soldiers
below—fresh meat just carted in from the backwaters—had to
duck. With a grin and howl, Leresy blasted fire across the
courtyard, then soared again. His wings stirred dust below, and
he shrieked to the sun.

He rose high above the courtyard and blew fire. He had
seen enough of the soldiers below to whet his appetite. Half were
frightened, pale farm boys no older than himself—fools for him
to crush under his heel. The rest were ripe females, and Leresy
snorted and grinned and felt his pulse quicken.

I will savor them, he thought. *This fort is mine, and they are mine. I own these bricks, and I own this flesh.*

He flew toward the command tower, the tallest among them, a great spire of obsidian. It rose hundreds of feet tall, flaring into a capital like a flanged mace. Its clock ticked upon it, a masterwork of black and red gears that clanged the noon hour as Leresy approached.

He flew between towering black spikes, each taller than a dragon, and landed upon the tower roof. He snapped his teeth and grinned. Below him spread the fortress, barracks and armories and courtyards, and beyond them the snowy forests rolled into haze. He blasted fire upward, a beacon of his dominion, and shifted into human form.

Wind whipped him, trying to tear off his cloak. The rooftop spikes towered around him. When he peered off the roof, the height seemed dizzying. For an instant Leresy faltered, and his heart leaped, and he was sure he would fall to the courtyard below. He gritted his teeth, clutched his sword, and trudged across the roof.

A trapdoor lay below him, carved of bronze. Leresy grabbed the knob, pulled the door open, and found a ladder leading into a chamber. He entered, closed the trapdoor above him, and descended the rungs.

Once his feet touched the floor, he cursed.

The room was bare, cold, and utterly distasteful. Disgust washed Leresy, and for a moment, he wondered if he had made a mistake flying here. Only one wall held a tapestry, and even that tapestry was plain, black fabric emblazoned with the red spiral—cheap dye. The furniture was bare pine, and no gold or jewels adorned it. The bed's mattress was stuffed with straw, not feathers; Leresy could tell just by looking. The chamber did sport a stained-glass window, but even its design was simple—it showed a dragon atop a red spiral—compared to the majestic stained glass of northern palaces.

Leresy's lips twisted and he snarled.

"At least they have a proper mirror," he said and stepped toward it.

The mirror rose taller than a man, and Leresy admired his reflection. Whenever he felt sour, his reflection could lift his spirits.

He was remarkably good-looking, he thought. He placed his hands on his hips, raised his chin, and felt his mood improve. His hair was woven of purest gold, short enough to look like a soldier's hair, but long enough to shine. His eyes were blue as sapphires. His cheeks were smooth, his lips full and pouty.

Some said he looked like his twin, the filthy traitor Kaelyn, but of course, Kaelyn would be wearing rags now and crawling through the mud. Lersey's dress was immaculate. Not a scratch spoiled his armor of black steel and gold. Not a single errant thread marred his fine cloak of crimson wool and fur. An apple-sized ruby clasped that cloak, and ancient stones—each one taken from the grave of a great hero—embossed his scabbard.

But his greatest treasure, greater even than his jewels and blades, was his punisher. Leresy's lips peeled back. Delicately, he drew the rod from his belt and held it before him. The finest, softest leather wrapped around its grip. Upon its rounded head, red lightning crackled and flared. Leresy's breath quickened and his eyes narrowed. He could already imagine the flesh he would burn with his tool, the screams he would hear, and the trembling females he would break and tame and invade.

"My birthday gift," he whispered, holding the punisher before him; it throbbed in his hand. "My birthright. My—"

A creak sounded behind him—the trapdoor being opened.

Leresy spun to see a burly old man descending the ladder into the chamber.

The man wore leather armor studded with iron bolts—the crude armor of the outposts. White scruff covered his cheeks, and snow and mud stained the hem of his cloak. A longsword hung at the old man's side, but no jewels adorned it; it could have been taken off a dead mercenary. Leresy's lips curled in disgust.

"Lord Raelor," he said, letting that disgust suffuse his voice. "Look at your garb. I've seen farmers dressed finer. Look at your beard. I've seen cleaner hair on seaside whores. And you call yourself a lord?"

The burly old man sucked in his breath. His eyes widened and he knelt.

"Prince Leresy," he said gruffly, head lowered. "You surprise me with your visit, my lord."

Leresy snarled, stepped forward, and grabbed the man's collar.

"And I suppose you don't like surprises, old man," he said with a sneer. "If you knew I was coming, would you have improved your appearance? Would you have shaved your scruff, or washed that fleabag of a cloak, or prepared this room for a prince?" He spat on the floor. "Castra Luna is the oldest standing fort in the empire. Did you think you could allow it to rot, and the capital would sit by idly? Stand up."

Raelor rose to his feet, his armor and joints creaking. His eyes were small, blue, and cold, the eyes of a hardened warrior, but Leresy saw fear in them too, and that pleased him.

"My prince Leresy," he said. "Aye, it is a gruff life here in the south, far from the northern comforts of the capital. If you are tired from your flight, however, we have strong wine in our cellars, and—"

"Do I look tired?" Leresy narrowed his eyes. "Are you saying I look tired, old man?"

Raelor stiffened. "My apologies, my prince, I merely—"

"But I *will* have some wine." Leresy turned away from the man and stomped toward a table; a jug of wine stood there by a pewter mug. "Have you no servants here to pour your drink? Truly, this is a cesspool of a fort. Things will change around here."

Lips curling, Leresy poured his own wine. It was the first time he'd had to pour his own drink. He sipped, swished the liquid in his mouth, then spat it onto the floor.

"Pig piss!" he said. He spun back toward Raelor and glared. "Do you drink pig piss here in the south, Raelor?"

The old man's eyes hardened; Leresy could see the hatred and fear locking horns behind those eyes.

"If the wine is distasteful to you, my prince, we can order other vintages shipped in. We receive shipments every moon, and—"

"You won't be around for that, Raelor," Leresy said. He pulled the scroll from his belt and tossed it forward. "A letter for you. Read it."

Raelor stared at Leresy for just an instant longer, just a heartbeat, but in that space of a breath, Leresy saw the man's well of hatred... and he grinned.

Good, he thought. *Good—hate me, old man. It will make this all the sweeter.*

The scroll bore the emperor's official seal, a red spiral surrounding the initials F.C. — Frey Cadigus. When Raelor looked at the seal, he sucked in his breath and blanched.

Leresy's grin widened. *A letter from the emperor is rarely good news,* he thought and licked his lips.

With stiff fingers, Raelor broke the seal, unrolled the parchment, and his eyes darted as he read. His skin grew paler, and a drop of sweat rolled down his temple. He rolled the scroll back up and looked at Leresy.

"My lord prince," he said. "If I have failed in my duties, allow me to mend them. My family has ruled Castra Luna for generations. We have served the empire loyally. We—"

"You," said Leresy, "are relieved of command, Lord Raelor. Oh, I'm sorry... but you are not a lord anymore at all, are you?" He *tsk*ed his tongue. "That makes you... nothing. Nothing but an intruder in my fortress."

More sweat rolled down Raelor's face. His fingers began to tremble. "Please, my prince. My family... allow me to..." His lips shook, his throat constricted, and he could speak no more.

Leresy allowed mock concern to soften his eyes. He stepped toward the larger man and placed his hand on his shoulder.

"Your family is safe in the capital!" Leresy said. "Do not worry, my good man. The empire remembers your loyal service. And your family will remain safe; we will not harm them. Not if you relieve yourself of duty honorably. The empire allows you this great, final honor."

Raelor's neck bobbed as he swallowed. He stared at the floor, and his teeth grinded, and his forehead glistened. When he looked back up at Leresy, red rimmed his eyes.

"Why?" he whispered. "Why, my prince? How have I failed?"

Leresy shrugged. "Because it's my birthday. And this is what I wanted." He gestured at the dagger on Raelor's belt. "Go on then. Do it. Just... not on the rug."

Raelor raised his chin. "And my family...?"

"We will make it painless," Leresy said. "Do this now, and they will not suffer. It will be in their sleep." He snorted. "I would have preferred to watch them broken and hear them scream—perhaps the rack or an old-fashioned quartering—but my father is more merciful than I am. Well, go on then! Don't test that mercy."

Tears dampened Raelor's eyes, but he managed to keep his chin raised. He gave a final salute, slamming his fist against his chest.

"Hail the red spiral!" he said, stepped back, and drew his dagger. With a gasp and blinking stare, he shoved his blade into his neck.

Leresy stood above the dying man, watching him writhe and bleed out onto the floor and rug.

Damn it, he thought. *I told him not to stain the rug.*

The blood seeped and ran between the tiles. Leresy sighed. This damn tower—the whole stinking fort—would need to be scrubbed and remodeled before it was fit for a prince.

A voice spoke behind him.

"Same old Leresy... still not killing his own enemies."

Leresy spun around and saw her there.

He grinned.

"Nairi," he said.

A backdoor stood open by the tapestry, revealing a staircase that plunged lower down the tower. Nairi stood in the doorway, hands on her hips. A crooked smile played across her lips.

Leresy felt his blood heat; stars, he had missed her. Her short blond hair had grown a little longer, just long enough to fall across her brow and ears, but her green eyes still shone with the same old mockery. When she walked toward him, the sway of her well-rounded hips still stirred his loins. She too was dressed crudely—she wore tan leggings, a steel breastplate, and muddy boots. She carried a rough sword across her back—it wasn't even jeweled—and a punisher hung at her waist. Only the black rose engraved upon her breastplate, sigil of her house, denoted her nobility.

When she reached him, she placed a finger under his chin and closed his mouth.

"Careful, my prince," she said. "There's blood on the floor, and your tongue nearly rolled that far."

With a snarl, he reached behind her, cupped a handful of her backside, and squeezed.

"Why kill my enemies myself?" he said to her. "My blade is far too fine to dirty with the blood of pigs. And you, Nairi, you too are a pig." He sniffed. "You stink of oil and dirt, and you're dressed like a peasant's daughter. Do you forget who you are? Did life here in this outpost turn you into a commoner?"

Nairi raised an eyebrow and gave him a mocking smile. "It's true. My clothes are dirty and foul; the clothes of a warrior. Why don't you remove them from me? I can see that's what you want." She patted his cheek. "Such a refined prince does not dirty his dagger..." She reached down to his breeches and grabbed him. "...or any of his blades."

He snarled and shoved her back. He walked toward the table, grabbed the wine, and drank deeply, pig piss or not. After slamming the mug down, he walked toward the bed, sat on the mattress, and stared at Nairi. She stood with one hand in her hair, smirking at him.

Stars, the woman drips sex, he thought.

"Well?" he said to her. "Go on. Get those clothes off."

"Somebody's impatient!" she said. She pouted and began unbuckling her breastplate.

Leresy leaned back and breathed deeply. *Perfection,* he thought as he watched her undress. *Exquisite perfection.* Piece by piece, she tossed aside her garments and armor, and Leresy's smile widened. The young woman was sex in boots, and her father...

Leresy licked his lips. *Her father is the most powerful, feared man outside my family.* He couldn't help but snort a laugh. *Once Nairi and I are wed, even my brutish sister will fear my might.*

Nairi pouted, naked before him, and crossed her arms across her breasts. "You laugh at my naked body?"

"No," Leresy said. He stood up, approached her, and grabbed her waist. He dug his fingers into her and snarled. "I claim it. Your body is mine. Today is my birthday, and I take this castle, and I take you."

He shoved her facedown onto the bed. When she tried to flip onto her back, he pressed her down.

"Ler—" she began.

"Lie still. Don't talk." He mounted her. "Scream if you like."

He reached under her torso, grabbed her, and took her roughly, and she screamed. Stars, he made her scream, and Leresy smiled and drooled above her.

"You are mine," he hissed into her ear. "Don't you forget that, Nairi. I am your prince, and you belong to me."

With a grunt, he rolled off her and lay at her side. The mattress creaked beneath him.

I was right, he thought as he stared at the ceiling. *The mattress is stuffed with straw. Raelor, you bloody peasant. I should torture your family after all. I'll start by making them sleep on this mattress.*

He turned to look at Nairi. For once, no mockery shone in her eyes or twisted her lips. She looked almost shy, almost demure. He had hurt her. *Good.* He had made this feel like the first time, and in his bed, she now felt like a newly deflowered maiden.

And in this bed I will deflower many more, Leresy thought. *As soon as I replace the mattress, that is.*

"Soon we will be wed," he told her. "I haven't told my father yet. I will when the time is right; I'll fly to the capital and let him know in person. I will tell your father too."

Fire coiled through his chest, and his fingers trembled. Yes. Nairi's father. He was perhaps an ugly bastard, all bald and lumpy skin—not nearly as intoxicating as his fresh young daughter—but he was powerful, and if Leresy craved anything more than female flesh, it was power.

His lips curled.

Soon you will fear me, Shari, he thought. *When I'm married to Nairi, the son-in-law of the Axehand Order's commander, you will fear me. Once I'm wed into the Axehand, even you will be unable to hurt me. Even you will shiver when I approach, dearest sister. You've tried to kill me so many times. Don't think I don't know this, Shari. But soon, very soon, the tables will turn.*

"I would like that," Nairi said, her voice small. She propped herself up on one elbow. "Would we fly and tell them together? I haven't been to the capital in a year now. I would like to return."

He spun toward her and frowned, disgusted. "The capital?" He snorted. "What do you want to visit the capital for? Nova Vita is a cesspool, all politics and rules and..."

And Shari trying to kill me, he wanted to say, but bit down on the words. No. It was best Nairi did not know about that. In the capital, there was his father, his sister, and motley nobles with daggers forged for stabbing backs. But here... here in the south there were perhaps crude mattresses, bare chambers, and peasant armor, but there was also dominion. Here, Leresy was lord.

Once I'm wed to Nairi, I can return to the capital as a lord as well. Once Shari is killed, I will be heir.

"Never mind that," he finished. "The capital will be ours in time. Get up. Get dressed. Don't you have recruits to train?"

Some of the fire returned to her eyes. "Don't you have a floor to mop of blood?" She rose to her feet, lifted her clothes, and began to dress herself. "To answer your question, yes. There's a new shipment of fresh meat rolling in today—six hundred recruits from a southern backwoods called Cadport." She hopped on one leg, tugging up her leggings. "Cadport! What a ridiculous name. Why does your family insist on naming everything after itself?"

He scoffed. "I'll do the same to you, wench. Nairi Cadigus you'll be when I'm done with you."

And yet his belly tightened. Cadport, Cadport... where had he heard that name? He sucked in his breath, realization hitting him. *Bloody Abyss.* His sister had said something about flying down to Cadport; she had taken that brute Beras with her, a halfwit she had hired a few years back. Were these two events connected?

What are you up to, Shari? She had flown to the southern port, and now hundreds of its youths were arriving here, where Leresy was staking his claim. He grinded his teeth. Stars damn it, his sister was up to her own schemes; he felt it in his gut.

I'll have to marry Nairi soon. I'll have to grow close to her father. He clenched his fists. *And then my sister will die.*

Nairi fastened the last buckle on her breastplate, then slung her sword across her back. She nodded down at Leresy, who still lay abed.

"Come see them roll in, my prince," she said and grinned. "Lots of fresh meat for you to terrify. You should enjoy that."

Oh, but I will enjoy their fresh meat, he thought. *Though not the way you think.*

He had spent his love only moments ago, yet already Leresy felt his blood heat again. Yes, he would break in many of those recruits—with sword, with whip, and here in his bed. He wondered briefly whether Nairi would like to join him in his conquests, then decided against it. It was best not to share this with her; at least, not until after he wed her and killed Shari.

He left the bed and smoothed his robe.

"Are there any servants in this pile of bricks?" He nodded down at the corpse. "The thing stinks already."

She strapped her punisher to her hip; it was clad in the blood-red leather of a phalanx commander.

"Come, my prince," she said, "and don't worry; I'll send up a recruit or two to dispose of the corpse. We have no servants here, but we have thousands of youths to break, to train, and to command. They will do your dirty work. Come, let's go introduce them to the great Prince Leresy Cadigus."

She patted his cheek, winked, and turned to leave the room, hips swaying with reclaimed swagger. Leresy stood a moment, admiring the view, then followed.

They climbed back onto the tower's roof. They stood in the wind, looking down at the fortress. The smaller towers, the courtyard, the grand hall, the armory, the kitchens—they all looked like stone blocks from up here. Around them rolled the forests. A single, cobbled road snaked across the land, leading from the camp's gates down south. Leresy was a child of the north; to him, Castra Luna was as south as he could imagine. But the empire stretched even farther from this outpost, all the way to the Tiran Sea where Cadport lay, and beyond that sea to the endless deserts.

My birthright, he thought. *Once my father and sister are dead, all these lands will be mine.*

Movement caught his eye. A convoy was moving north along the road, heading toward the camp. Leresy counted six carts, each one wide enough to house a phalanx of recruits. A dragon tugged each cart down the road, and smoke plumed from their nostrils.

"Here they are!" Nairi said, standing beside him. The wind ruffled her short blond hair, and she smiled crookedly and clutched her punisher. "The fresh meat rolls in. Let us go greet them."

Her lips peeled back in a hungry grin, and she shifted. Gray wings burst out from her back. Her fangs shone. She took flight as an iron dragon, roared, and blew fire at the sky.

Leresy followed suit. He shifted into the red dragon, roared a spray of fire, and flew after her. They circled above the fort, howling their flames, and waited for the recruits to roll in.

As Leresy flew, he grinned and licked his chops. His chamber perhaps was bare, and the mattress rough, but Leresy thought he would enjoy his eighteenth birthday after all.

TILLA

The cart trundled forward, and they were close now. Dragons shrieked ahead, fire crackled, and Tilla could feel it. After ten days in the wilderness, they were nearing their destination.

What fort will it be? she wondered, standing in the dark cart as a hundred other girls pressed against her. She tried to remember all the forts she knew within ten days of Cadport, but there were too many. It would have to be one for training recruits—seasoned soldiers didn't share forts with recruits—but that only narrowed it down by a couple of forts.

She went over all the names she had heard soldiers speak of. This could be Castra Nova Murus, a great fortress in the east; that would be good fortune, Tilla thought, for soldiers said a benevolent lord commanded Murus. Or it could be Castra Alira, a dilapidated fortress in the west; Tilla remembered soldiers saying the rooms there were rough, but the training light.

Or it could be... Tilla swallowed and twisted her fingers. She did not want to be grim but had to consider the possibility. They could be rolling toward the infamous Castra Luna.

Tilla clenched her jaw, remembering the stories. They whispered that Luna was not only the cruelest fortress in the south, but in the entire empire. They said obsidian tiles covered the old bricks of Castra Luna, as black and cold as the heart of its commanders. They said recruits were broken there—physically and mentally. Tilla had once met a soldier who had, they said, trained in Castra Luna; the man had been a mute, grim killer, a demon in human flesh.

Her own brother had trained at Castra Luna. He had never come home.

Tilla sucked in her breath.

No, she thought, *the odds are against it. It won't be Luna. Please, stars of my fathers, don't let it be Luna.*

She moved through the crowd of girls, heading toward a cart wall. Two days back, the cart had overturned, and a crack now opened in the wall, too high for the other girls to peek through, but just the right height for Tilla. She jostled her way forward. The other girls moved aside, mumbling prayers. Tilla reached the crack, stood on her toes, and peered outside.

Her heart sank.

A snowy forest rolled around her, the trees bare and dark. Above the branches, still about a mile away, Tilla saw black, glimmering walls.

Obsidian. Castra Luna.

A hand tugged at her sleeve.

"Tilla, what do you see?"

Tilla turned to see Mae peering up at her. The baker's daughter bit her trembling lip. Other recruits gathered around and peered at Tilla, all whispering.

"What do you see?"

"I hear dragons flying, are we close?"

"Tilla, where are we?"

In darkness, Tilla thought. *At the gates of pain. In a world we might never escape.*

She raised her hand.

"We've reached a fort," she began.

"Which one?" demanded Erry Docker. The scrawny waif's short, brown hair lay in tangles, her knees were skinned, and her eyes flashed. "Tell us the bloody fort's name, Tilla."

"Are we at Castra Murus?" called another girl. "My brother trained there."

Mae Baker began to weep. "But I want to go home! I don't want to go to *any* fort. I want to go back to Cadport... Please... My father will be so angry, he's going to come save me..."

Tilla had to shout over them all. "Be quiet! Don't make noise or Beras will hear. You know he hates noise. We've reached the fort of Castra Luna." The girls began to whisper and weep, and Tilla raised her hands and spoke louder. "You will be safe here! I promise this to you. I know men who trained at this fortress, and I will protect you."

"How will *you* protect us?" Erry said and spat onto the floor. "You're just a pissant recruit like us. Bloody bollocks, I could take you in a fight, I reckon."

"No you couldn't, Erry!" said Mae, tears in her eyes. "Tilla is stronger than us, and she's about twice your height, so be quiet. And stop cussing; my mother said a girl should never cuss. Princess Shari liked Tilla too, you all saw it, and even Beras was a little afraid of her." She clung to Tilla and her lips wobbled. "Tilla is going to look after us here."

Erry rolled her eyes and groaned.

The shrieks of dragons grew louder, and Tilla peered out the crack again. She cursed under her breath. Two dragons were circling above the fortress, blowing pillars of fire. One was red, male, and long of fang. The other was female, and her scales were an iron gray. Both sported gilded horns; these ones were nobility.

And they are cruel, Tilla thought. *I can see it in their fire. They will try to break us.* She clenched her fists at her sides. *But I will not be broken. Whatever horror awaits here, I will survive it. I will see Cadport and Rune again.*

The cart kept trundling, and the black walls grew closer. Cannons lined their battlements, and soldiers in leather armor manned each gun. Tilla had seen cannons before, long and narrow things along Cadport's boardwalk; not far from the Old Wheel stood the oldest cannon in Requiem, a rusted sentinel watching the sea. But these cannons dwarfed Cadport's like greatswords beside daggers. Each gun was long as a dragon; she could have climbed into the barrels.

She swallowed. These cannons were not built to blast ships, she thought. They were built to slay dragons.

"Tilla, bloody dog dung, what do you s—" Erry began, but Tilla hushed her and kept staring outside.

The gates of Castra Luna rose ahead. From where she stood, Tilla could only see half of one door. That door loomed twenty feet tall, its oak engraved with carvings of the red spiral. The sigil also appeared upon black banners that draped the walls and fluttered from the tower tops.

But Castra Luna hadn't always been a Cadigus stronghold, Tilla knew. She thought back to the old, banned books Rune kept hidden under the Old Wheel's floor. Once this had been a castle of House Aeternum. The great Princess Mori Aeternum had raised this place from a small, southern outpost into a great castle, and many princes and princesses of Aeternum had ruled here, a beacon of southern light. In old drawings, Tilla had seen a castle of bright bricks, of green-and-silver banners sporting Aeternum's two-headed dragon, and of justice and light. Today... today she saw a prison of darkness.

The doors creaked open, revealing lines of soldiers. A chill ran through Tilla. Each soldier stood stiff as a statue, clad in leather armor studded with iron. Each bore a longsword. Helms hid their heads, bowls of black steel. They seemed to her not human, but automatons of metal, leather, and cruelty.

This will be me soon, Tilla thought. *I will no longer be Tilla Roper of Cadport. I will be one in a line, a soul broken and remolded into a killer, nothing but a machine—no more alive than the cannons upon the walls.*

Several carts rolled ahead of her own. They vanished under the archway, and Tilla's cart soon followed.

And so we enter the long, cold night, she thought and her throat tightened. She missed Rune so badly her belly clenched. Perhaps, she dared to hope, when he was drafted in summer, he would be sent to Castra Luna too. Would Tilla still be stationed here then? And if so, would Rune even recognize whatever demon they molded her into?

Six carts rolled into Castra Luna's courtyard. Through the crack, Tilla saw the brutish Beras lumbering about. He was howling, banging on cart walls, and unlocking the doors. Saliva sprayed from his mouth as he shouted.

"Out, vermin!" He growled and spat. "We've carried you maggots for long enough. Out, you miserable lot of bastards and whores!"

When the brute reached Tilla's cart and tugged the door open, the light nearly blinded the recruits inside. A few whimpered and covered their eyes. They had not seen daylight for ten days now, not since leaving Cadport, aside from what little light fell through the cracked wall.

Cadport's youths stumbled out into the courtyard like prisoners from dungeons, pale and blinking and frail in the sun. The sky was white, and the small winter sun reflected off the fort's obsidian walls. Tilla blinked and struggled to steady her limbs. Throughout the journey, they had been fed but scraps—old bread, burnt sausages, and some moldy cheese. Their training had not even begun, and already Tilla felt weaker than she'd ever been.

She looked around her, trying to focus her eyes. The recruits stood in the courtyard, still wearing the same tunics and leggings they had worn when leaving Cadport. A thousand other youths surrounded the square, but these ones were not weak. They did not tremble or blink or whimper. They stood in armor, silent, faces blank.

Tilla looked beyond them to see walls and barracks, all carved of the same obsidian, all bearing banners of the red spiral.

A tower rose above them, the tallest she'd ever seen; it must have stood three hundred feet tall. It sported a great clock as large as a wagon; its hands were shaped as swords, ticking in an eternal battle. A hall stood below the tower, large enough to house a thousand men, and upon its walls perched two dragons, red and gray.

The red dragon stared directly at her, and Tilla felt as if an icy fist punched her.

Lust filled that red dragon's eyes—lust for her flesh, for her blood, and for her very soul. The beast stared into her, licked his chops, and snarled. Smoke rose between his teeth, and Tilla tore her eyes away. Her heart thrashed and her fingers trembled.

"Form ranks!" Beras bellowed, lolloping around the courtyard. "By the Abyss, if you embarrass me now, I'll flay your hides. Form ranks, sons of whores!"

Standing beside Tilla, Erry smirked. "He still walks like he got a stick up his arse. I bet he stick 'em there good himself."

Tilla glared at the skinny ragamuffin. "Don't you ever stop talking? Come on, form ranks; stand behind me."

Cadport's recruits shuffled together, forming ranks as Beras and his fellow soldiers barked orders. They had formed ranks every night for ten days, and they moved faster now. The girls stood in lines to one side, the boys to another. As always, Erry Docker stood to Tilla's right, smirking to herself, and Mae Baker stood to her left, biting her wobbling lip.

When they all stood in three lines, Beras stared at them in disgust.

"Miserable maggots," he said and spat again. "Bloody waste of time, you are. Good riddance to you. I deliver you now to your new masters. My only regret is I won't be here to see you broken."

He marched down the lines, huffing and thumping his boots. When he walked by Tilla, he paused and turned toward her. His beady eyes narrowed and he snarled. His breath wafted between his crooked teeth, scented of rotting meat.

Tilla stood stiff and frozen before him, chin raised. Her heart pounded, but she dared not say a thing, not even breathe.

"Oh, I'll miss you, child," Beras said, voice rough as his face. "I'll be seeing you again, don't you doubt it. You'll spread your legs for me yet." He spat onto her face. "You'll be mine, whore."

With that, he stepped back, shifted into a bronze dragon, and took flight. With a few flaps of his wings he was gone, leaving only a wake of smoke.

Tilla stood, knees weak and nausea rising in her. Belas's foul spit clung to her face, but she dared not wipe it off. The last recruit who'd moved in formation had been dragged off, hung from a tree, and beaten until his ribs snapped. And so she stood, breathing hard and struggling not to gag as the saliva dripped down her cheek.

"Recruits!" rose a female voice above. "Face north!"

Around the courtyard, a thousand soldiers spun upon their heels, slammed their boots down, and faced the grand hall. Fumbling and glancing around, Cadport's recruits followed, a breath late. Tilla and the others stood facing the hall. Upon its walls, the two dragons—red and gray—glared down at them, smoke pluming from their nostrils.

The gray dragon blasted fire skyward, then shifted. She stood upon the walls in human form, hands on her hips and a smirk on her face.

She was a young woman; she looked not much older than Tilla herself. Her yellow hair was just long enough to fall across her brow, and mockery filled her eyes; Tilla could see that even from here. She wore tan leggings, tall boots, and a breastplate engraved with a black rose. A sword hung across her back, and a she held a punisher in one gloved hand. Its tip crackled.

"Welcome to pain!" the young woman shouted. "Welcome to blood, to tears, and to death. Welcome to Castra Luna! I am Lanse Nairi, but to you, I am a goddess, I am a mother, I am a tyrant, and I am your savior." She smirked. "To me you are worms to crush."

Lanse. Tilla had heard that word before. It was a rank, she remembered. Tilla knew little of rank; she did not know how lofty a lanse was.

Lofty enough to command me, she thought. *But then again, that is probably everyone here other than my fellow recruits.*

"Today," Nairi continued, "we have a new lord in Castra Luna. Kneel, servants of the red spiral. Kneel before Prince Leresy Cadigus!"

Nairi gestured toward the red dragon, who snorted fire and shifted into human form.

The recruits below gasped, paled, and knelt.

The red dragon now stood as a young, golden-haired man. A smirk played across his lips. Unlike the others in this fort, Prince Leresy wore no crude leather. The finest steel plates formed his armor, each filigreed with golden dragons. A cloak hung across his shoulders, the crimson fabric lined with fur and probably worth more than all the coins in Cadport. A sword hung at his belt, its pommel shaped as a dragonclaw, its scabbard jeweled. A red spiral, shaped of rubies, shone upon his breastplate.

Shari's younger brother, Tilla thought, glancing up at him as she knelt. *Ten days, and I've met two of the emperor's children, and I don't know which one frightens me more.*

"He's looking right at you," Erry whispered from the corner of her mouth; the urchin knelt beside her. "The prince. Bet he wants to thrust right into you with his royal rod, and I don't mean his punisher. Not bad-looking, he is. Bloody bollocks, Tilla, but all the menfolk stare at you. I also need to grow a pair of big—"

"Shush!" Tilla whispered.

Terror froze her, but it seemed nobody had heard the exchange. She glanced back up at Prince Leresy. He stood on the wall, looking down upon the courtyard, and again he met her eyes.

She shivered. She had heard of Leresy's cruelty; everyone in Requiem had. They said that every week, Prince Leresy walked through the capital, seeking a woman he fancied. They said he favored mothers. When he found one, he would slaughter her family before her eyes, take her to his palace chambers, and force himself upon her. In the morning, they whispered, servants would collect the woman's battered corpse from the courtyard outside Leresy's window.

And now this prince—this monster—stared right at her across the crowd. His smirk grew, and he gave her a wink. He licked his lips—slowly, luxuriously, as if savoring the taste.

Tilla forced her gaze away. Her belly twisted and her heart pounded. She released her breath, only now realizing she had held it.

I must never stare at him again, she thought. *He is the most dangerous man in Requiem.*

"Children of Requiem!" the prince cried. He had the high voice of a youth, but carried it with the arrogance of a man. "I welcome you to my home. Rise."

The recruits rose to their feet, those newly arrived and those already armored.

"Hail the red spiral!" Prince Leresy shouted and slammed his fist against his chest.

"Hail the red spiral!" shouted thousands of recruits below, and thousands of fists thumped against chests.

To her left, Tilla heard Mae whimper. To her right, she heard Erry smirk and whisper something about sneaking into the prince's bed. But Tilla only stood still and silent, and though she had vowed to never look at the prince again, she could not help it. She found herself once more glancing his way.

He met her eyes and stared. The stare seemed to last forever, and in his eyes Tilla saw haughtiness, lust, and unending malice.

Without another word, the prince spun on his heel and stepped away from the battlements. He vanished, leaving Tilla feeling as empty and violated as a ransacked home.

"All right, you miserable lot of filthy maggots!" Nairi shouted above. She shifted back into a gray dragon and took flight. "It's time to sort your useless arses into phalanxes. A bloody waste of time, if you ask me." She blasted a pillar of fire. "Commanders, to the courtyard! Fresh meat!"

With roaring fire and thudding wings, five dragons appeared, rising from behind the grand hall. Fire and smoke filled the air. Scales clanked. Orders rang. Soldiers rushed about the courtyard, goading recruits with crackling punishers. Welts rose on flesh and recruits screamed.

Tilla moved with the crowd, her belly knotting.

Her life in Castra Luna began with fire, smoke, and pain.

RUNE

They climbed the hill, cloaks billowing in the wind, and beheld a landscape of ruin.

Rune stood for a moment, frozen, and softly exhaled. At his side, Kaelyn nodded and took his hand.

"My father's cruelty," she said. "Here it lies below us. Here we hide. Here we fight him."

They had been traveling through the wilderness for ten days now, keeping off the roads. At least, Rune thought it was ten days; it all blurred into one long, confused dream of hiding in holes, scurrying between trees, and living off dwindling supplies of dried meat, rough cheese, and stale bread. He had fled Cadport wearing everyday clothes—old boots, woolen pants and a tunic, and a warm cloak—and the journey had worn them into tatters. He was down one notch in his belt already, and he felt about a day away from losing another notch.

And here... here they reached the end of their journey, and Rune realized: He would miss the long days in the wilderness.

"Why this place?" he said, a chill tingling his spine. He turned to look at Kaelyn. "In the entire empire of Requiem, with all its forests and mountains and swamps and deserts, why hide here?"

She stood watching the ruins. The wind ruffled her golden, wavy hair and pinched her cheeks pink. She held her sword's hilt, and suddenly she seemed so sad to Rune, sadder than he'd ever seen her. Years ago, a wandering bard had traveled to Cadport, entered the Old Wheel, and played a song upon his harp. Men had wept to hear the music of old forests, ancient kings, and starlight upon marble columns. Rune had never forgotten that song, that sadness of longing and beauty; today he saw the same song in Kaelyn's eyes.

"It is safe," she said softly. "Imperial dragons fly here, but they don't land. No one but the Resistance walks among these ruins. We can hide here, survive, arm ourselves... and dream." She turned to look at him, and her eyes glistened with tears. "This place reminds us. Everywhere you look here, you will see my father's evil. It keeps us strong. And one day, his collapse will begin here—in this place that he crushed."

Rune looked back at the fallen city.

Confutatis, he thought. He knew of this place. He had seen its maps and cityscapes in the books hidden under the Old Wheel's floor. Only twenty years ago, this had been the capital of Osanna, a kingdom east of Requiem, a land whose people could not shift into dragons but rode horses, wove silk, studied the stars, and honored ancient alliances with the Vir Requis. In the old pictures, Rune had seen spires scraping the sky, temples with silver domes, thousands of homes and streets, and white walls topped with banners. It had been a place of life, science, and creation.

Today he saw a place of death, ash, and shattered stone.

The white walls lay fallen. The streets and homes lay shattered. The stems of towers rose like broken ribs, barely taller than men. The city spread for miles; a million souls must have lived here. Today Rune saw no life but for crows that circled above.

All who lived here—dead, he thought. *Cadigus killed them all.*

"Why?" he whispered. "Why would your father kill so many, crush an entire city?" He spun toward her, eyes stinging. "These people had no magic; they could not become dragons, could not defend themselves. Why, Kaelyn?"

"Because he is proud," she replied, looking upon the city. The wind billowed her blue cloak. "Because he is cruel. Because he is hurt." She sighed. "My father... when he was younger, he trained to be a priest, did you know?"

Rune frowned. "A priest? Your father? I've met priests; they tend to be meek, humble, and kind. I've seen statues of your father. He doesn't exactly seem the priestly type."

"He isn't," Kaelyn agreed. "But he was born into poverty, the son of a logger. His father beat him, and priesthood was an escape. A temple could give him food, shelter, and most importantly—books. My father had always craved knowledge."

"He doesn't seem the bookish type either," Rune said, remembering the man's statues. Even carved in stone, Frey Cadigus scared him. The emperor was a tall, powerful man—or at least sculpted that way—clad in armor and bearing weapons. Yet the statue's eyes would always frighten Rune the most. Those eyes stared, cold and always watching, from a hard, lined face. Those eyes seemed crueler than the man's sword.

"Books contain knowledge, and knowledge brings power." Kaelyn tightened her cloak around her. "He spent years in temple libraries, reading every book he could find. He especially craved histories of battle; even then he lusted for blood. He read how the people of this land, of Confutatis, enslaved the griffins, rode them to war, and toppled the halls of Requiem. That was a thousand years ago, but to a skinny boy in a dark temple..." She shook her head sadly. "I think those stories stabbed him like griffin talons. He left the priesthood. He became a soldier, an officer, and finally a general powerful enough to take Requiem's throne. And then... then he became a killer." She gestured at the city. "Then he took his vengeance. Deep inside, he was still that boy in candlelit libraries dreaming of slaying Requiem's enemies. But now this boy had an army of dragons. And still this death lies before us." Kaelyn snarled and gripped her sword. "And here,

Rune, here his own death rallies." She began walking downhill. "Come. I will take you to Valien."

Ash swirled around their boots. Charred trees and skeletons, their flesh picked cleaned, littered the hillside. Kaelyn squeezed Rune's hand. Her grip was warm, and when he looked at her, she stared back with huge, somber eyes.

At the foothills, the ruins spread around their feet. The shells of houses stood blackened, roofs gone, walls chipped like teeth in smashed jaws. Bricks, shattered blades, and cloven helms littered the streets, so thick Rune had to wade through them. Inside the homes, skeletons still lingered—soldiers grasping rusted swords, children hiding in corners, and mothers huddling over babes. Dragonfire had burned them; the bones were charred.

Rune could barely breathe. His throat constricted. His fists trembled. He wanted to reel toward Kaelyn, to shake her, to yell at her.

Why didn't the Resistance bury them! he wanted to demand. *How could you just let your father's victims lie dead here?*

Yet when he looked at Kaelyn, prepared to shout, he saw tears on her cheeks. She did not tremble. She did not weep. She walked tall and proud, clutching her sword and bow, a warrior. Yet tears for the fallen, even these strangers of a different kingdom, shone in her eyes. Rune felt his rage ebb, and sadness replaced it.

Requiem was once a noble, peaceful kingdom, he thought, looking around at the destruction. *This is what the Cadigus family has made us. Killers. Monsters. Demons of fire.*

They stepped over a pile of bricks. A doll's hand peeked from between them. A crow sat upon a smashed keystone, pecking at a human jawbone. Half a tower rose to their right, ending with a shattered crown; inside, Rune saw skeletons in rusted armor. Looking upon this death, Rune remembered the

Old Wheel burning and Shari clutching his father's body, and tears stung his eyes.

The Cadigus family had done the same to his home and family. The dead of Confutatis were his brothers now, bonded in grief. His eyes stung and his breath shook.

I don't want any of this, he thought. He climbed over half a child's skeleton; the legs were missing. *I never wanted this! All I wanted was to live quietly, to see Tilla again, to help Cadport cling to hope. Not this death. Not this war.*

He lowered his head. He missed home. He missed his father, his dog, his books, and everything else. The pain filled his belly like ice.

Kaelyn squeezed his hand. He looked up to see her gazing at him softly.

"I'm sorry, Rune," she whispered. "I'm sorry you have to see this." She touched his cheek. "But you need to. You need to see everything Frey Cadigus has done. And you will need to remember this." Her eyes hardened. "You will need these memories when you face him."

He laughed mirthlessly. "Face Frey Cadigus? After seeing these ruins, Frey is the last person I want to confront."

"I know," she said. "Yet you are the heir of Aeternum, and he seeks you. He will find you. He will want to slay you himself. And you will have to fight him. And when you do, remember this place." She looked around her. "Remember why you fight."

Rune sighed, shook his head, and kept walking. He could not get rid of that lump in his throat.

"You're mad, Kaelyn," he said. "Mad! I joined you only because Shari burned my home. But to fight your father? The emperor himself?" He barked another humorless laugh. "I'm only a brewer. Not a warrior."

"You *were* a brewer," she whispered. "A warrior you will become. Valien will teach you. We are near."

They kept walking through the ruins. They walked across a wide, cobbled square strewn with hundreds of skeletons still clad in sooty armor. They passed a shattered temple; its dome was cracked open like an egg, skeletons slung across its shattered rim. They were walking down a street littered with bricks, shattered shields, and bones when a shriek tore the air.

A dragon shriek.

Rune bent low and scurried for cover. Kaelyn leaped at his side. They landed in a ditch, scuttled under a fallen statue, and huddled deep in shadow.

They had run for cover so many times over the past ten days. Rune's knees and elbows were skinned from a hundred dives under logs, brambles, or tangled roots. Yet in the forest, the leafy canopy had offered extra concealment. Here in these ruins, the sky was clear; peering from under the fallen statue, Rune saw the dragon in all its wrath and flame.

The beast had copper scales, white horns, and great black wings like curtains of night. It shrieked to the sky, then swooped and blasted fire across the street. Walls of flame roared before Rune, heat blasted him, and he cursed and grabbed his sword.

"Bloody stars!" he hissed. "I thought you said this place was safe, Kaelyn."

She knelt beside him in the shadows. The fallen statue stretched above them, forming a roof. Kaelyn's face glistened with sweat. She clutched a dagger in her hand, bared her teeth, and breathed sharply.

"Hush!" she whispered. "Keep your voice down. This dragon hasn't seen us. If he had, we'd be dead. They patrol these ruins several times a day."

Rune rolled his eyes. "And you chose your hideout here? Where your father's dragons patrol daily?"

She tightened her cloak around her. "Forests can be uprooted. Towns can be toppled. Forts can be crushed. This place is already dead—lots of places to hide, nothing left to tear down."

Perhaps Kaelyn was right, Rune thought. The forests had seemed to offer no more safety, and as for Cadport, well... Rune's chest still ached to remember Cadport. Perhaps no place was safe anymore from Frey Cadigus. Once this had been a distant kingdom; now it lay ruined. Now there was just this, just the empire, as far as they could go.

And Kaelyn thinks we can topple it!

Rune wondered if he was crazy to even be here. He could grow a beard to disguise his face, he thought. He could take up a false identity, move to a new town, and find work. He didn't have to fight this war. He didn't have to walk through death.

He had thought this many times over the past few days. And yet he had kept following Kaelyn through forest, field, and ruin. Why? Was it Kaelyn's big eyes and her body pressed against his? Or had he simply gone mad?

I can't keep doing this, he thought. *I'll listen to what this Valien has to say. I'll tell him I'm not the man he's looking for. And then I'll leave this place and forget about the whole damn rebellion.*

Finally the dragon shrieks faded into the distance. Kaelyn released her dagger and began crawling back onto the street.

"Come on," she said and looked over her shoulder at him. "Follow me. Another dragon won't be back for hours."

Rune sighed. "So said half the skeletons on this street, I reckon."

Yet as she walked down this street of death, he followed. In the distance, he could see the dragon flying into the southern horizon, a mere speck blowing a thread of fire. Crows replaced it in the sky; a few dipped down to pick at old ribs.

They reached a wide, cobbled boulevard that looked wide enough for a hundred men to walk abreast. This must have been the main street of Confutatis. Along its sides, the iron frames of chariots rusted, and the skeletons of horses lay shattered. The stems of lost columns, the shells of burnt towers, and crumbling walls lined the roadsides in a palisade of destruction. Far ahead, past mist and shadow, the path led to a shattered palace, its pocked walls rising from ash and ending in ruin. Even the crows did not fly above this street, as if they feared it.

"What is this place?" Rune whispered.

"Welcome," she said, "to the Boulevard of Bones. It leads through death. It leads through old fire. It leads to hope."

They began to walk down the street. The skeletons at their sides seemed to stare at Rune. The skull of a horse grinned. Ash carpeted the cobblestones; it muffled their footfalls and stirred around their boots. Rune was looking at the burnt skeleton of a child, a sword piercing its ribcage, when movement caught his eye.

He spun sideways, clutched his sword, and drew a foot of steel.

"Kaelyn!" he hissed.

An archer stood in the broken tower, peering through a crack in the wall. The man wore a gray cloak smeared with ash, and gray paint covered his face; he blended into the tower's bricks. Rune snarled and prepared to dive for cover, but Kaelyn gripped his arm.

"It's fine, Rune!" she said. "He's one of ours."

She pushed Rune's sword back into its scabbard and nodded at the archer. She raised her left hand, holding her index and middle fingers pressed together. Inside the shattered tower, the archer returned the gesture and lowered his bow.

As they kept walking down the boulevard, more movement stirred. Rune looked from side to side and blew out his breath. Dozens of archers hid here, each one cloaked in gray, the color of the ruins. They peeked from broken towers, from behind shattered walls, and from under fallen statues. As Kaelyn walked by, they each raised their hands in salute, index and middle fingers pressed together.

"Welcome, Rune," Kaelyn said softly, "to a voice of hope, to a light in the dark, to courage in an empire of fear." She gave him a sad look that spoke of her childhood, of countless deaths, and of hope almost lost under pain. "Welcome to the Resistance."

They kept walking down the Boulevard of Bones. All around among the broken towers, walls, and halls they hid— warriors of the Resistance. As Rune walked, his head spun. Every year in Cadport, soldiers of the Regime would speak of the resistors' evil and might. Every year, they would draft all those turned eighteen, cart them off to forts, break and mold them into soldiers, then send them off to fight the Resistance. Rune had always imagined hosts of demonic beasts mustering with fire and steel. But this... this was just a rabble. Here were only a few men—Rune doubted he saw more than a hundred—clad in rags and dust, their blades chipped.

This isn't an army.

The Cadigus Regime had been lying to its people, Rune realized. With fiery speeches and military terror, they had turned a toothless pup into a rabid beast. The wars against the phoenixes, the griffins, and the wyverns had ended years ago. With Requiem's external foes defeated, Frey Cadigus needed a new enemy, Rune realized. He needed a new way to terrify his people, to rally them around a threat. How else would a soldier keep his power? How else could Cadigus maintain his iron grip, if not with fear of monsters?

This Resistance is nothing but a ghost of a threat, Rune thought. *They cannot win. Not with me here. Not with ten thousand more men. This is a hopeless war. They only serve to give Frey Cadigus the enemy he so desperately needs.*

They continued down the Boulevard of Bones, this vein of destruction Cadigus had carved. With every step, they drew nearer to the fallen palace of Confutatis. Soon its ruin rose before them.

In one of the books Rune had hidden under his floor planks, he had seen an illustration of this palace. Its dozen towers had risen into the clouds. Banners had streamed upon its walls. Soldiers bearing red, green, and yellow standards had ridden horses through its gates. All of that was gone now. The towers lay broken. A single archway rose in a crumbling wall; its doors had burned away. A few walls still stood, and a few archers still manned their arrowslits, but that was all. If this was the heart of the Resistance, Rune thought, it was barely beating.

"Is Valien in there?" he asked.

Kaelyn tightened her cloak around her; it was flapping in the wind. She nodded and clutched her bow tight to her chest.

"He is in there," she said. "Our leader. Our guiding star. Valien Eleison, leader of the Resistance."

Rune shook his head. *She treats me like a child,* he thought, *yet she speaks of this Valien as a god.* How mighty could this Valien be if he dwelled in ruin? Was this truly a man to speak of in awe? Judging by Valien's home, they were going to see not a great leader, but a ragged outlaw barely better than those who roamed the forests, seeking travelers to rob.

They walked toward the archway. Several haggard men stood alongside it, their cloaks the same gray as the bricks, their faces ashy. When they saw Kaelyn, they lowered their bows and heads.

"My lady Kaelyn," one said.

"Welcome home, my lady," said another.

She nodded at them, the wind in her hair. She stepped through the archway into shadow. With a last look at the skeletons that littered the boulevard, Rune followed into the darkness.

TILLA

Six soldiers surrounded the square, standing on pedestals and shouting names from scrolls.

"Yar Potter!" one soldier shouted, a portly man with a dark beard.

"Sana Tanner!" shouted another soldier, a muscular woman with a thin nose and cold, black eyes. "Sana Tanner!"

Tilla stood in the square with the other youths of Cadport. As every name was called, that recruit moved to join the summoning soldier. As Tilla stood, waiting to be summoned, she squinted at the six soldiers crying out the names. Each wore a black breastplate and pauldrons. Upon each shoulder, they sported a red spiral.

"Lanses," Tilla whispered. "That is their rank."

When speaking from the walls, Nairi—the soldier with the short yellow hair—had called herself a lanse. The young woman now stood upon one of the pedestals, also shouting names from a scroll.

The lanses seemed young—Tilla guessed them little older than herself—but lofty and well groomed. Each displayed a different sigil upon his or her breastplate. Nairi sported a black rose; other lanses displayed red skulls, dragon heads, towers rising from thorns, and other emblems. These were no brutes like Beras; Tilla guessed them the sons and daughters of noble houses, their blood too pure to serve among the unwashed commoners.

She thought back to Cadport. Soldiers there displayed their rank—one or more red stars—upon black armbands; their shoulders bore no red spirals, and their breastplates sported no emblems. Only the lord of Cadport, a gaunt and dower man,

wore red spiral insignia and displayed a sigil—his was a boar—
upon his armor.

The lanses are young officers, Tilla understood. *Noble born. They
wear their house's sigils upon their breasts. The others are the common
soldiers, like I will become once I'm sorted.*

Standing on a pedestal, scroll in hand, Nairi shouted. "Mae
Baker!" The young lanse looked over the crowd with narrowed
eyes. "Mae Baker!"

Tilla looked to her left. Mae stood there, eyes wide and
damp, face chalk-white.

"I..." Mae's lips trembled. "I... I don't..."

Nairi shouted louder and reached for her punisher. "Mae
Baker, damn it, report to me!"

Mae sniffed, feet frozen on the ground. Her body shook.

"Go to her, Mae," Tilla said. She gave the girl a gentle
push. "Go to Lanse Nairi and stand before her. It's okay."

Sniffing and looking around, Mae took hesitant steps
forward. She looked over her shoulder at Tilla, as if unsure
whether to proceed. Tilla gestured her on.

But Nairi was less patient. The officer snarled and leaped
off her pedestal. As she marched forward, she drew her punisher
from her belt. The tip crackled with red lightning.

"Are you Mae Baker?" the lanse demanded, marching
toward Mae. Her every footstep clanked across the square.

Mae stood frozen and nodded, tears in her eyes.

With a snarl, Nairi drove her punisher forward, bringing its
tip hard into Mae's stomach.

Smoke rose.

Lightning crackled across Mae.

The girl screamed, doubled over, and begged. Nairi stood
above her, growling and shoving her punisher against Mae's flesh.

No! Tilla wanted to shout. She took two steps forward.
She froze. She winced. *Please stop!* She wanted to rush forward,

to shove Nairi back, to save her friend... yet she only stood staring, eyes stinging and feet frozen.

Finally—after what seemed like ages—Nairi pulled her punisher back.

Mae collapsed against the cobblestones, legs twitching and the last wisps of lightning racing across her before vanishing in smoke. Tears streaked her cheeks and she whimpered.

"Mewling dog," Nairi said. She spat. "When I call you, you *race* to me like an obedient pup." She raised her voice to a shout. "Do you understand me, you flea-bitten mongrel? Stand up, damn it!"

Mae whimpered, still lying on the ground.

"You better stand up, dog," Nairi said, teeth bared, and raised her punisher. "Do you want some more?"

Finally Tilla could move. She leaped forward, knelt by Mae, and reached under her arms.

"Come on, Mae," she said softly. "Stand up. On your feet. I'll help you."

She pulled the trembling, weeping girl to her feet. Mae stood shaking so wildly Tilla had to hold her up. Burn marks spread across her tunic.

"Well, well," Nairi said. She laughed mirthlessly, tapping her fingers against her thigh. "Seems like you have a guardian, Mae Baker."

"Just a friend," Tilla said quietly.

She stared at the lanse; for the first time, she got a close look at Nairi. Most women were shorter than Tilla, and Nairi was no exception; the young woman had to raise her eyes to meet Tilla's gaze. But Nairi was strong, far stronger than Tilla; she could see that. This young woman had not shaped her muscles from weaving ropes, but from swinging swords. Her stance, her haughty green eyes, and her bared teeth all spoke of a huntress, a thirst for blood and battle. Her yellow hair was short like a boy's, but her lips were full and red and cruel, and they twisted in disdain.

"What is your name, dog?" Nairi hissed.

"Tilla Roper," she answered.

Nairi stared at her, eyes narrowed and burning with green fire. Then she spat again, looked down at her scroll, and smirked.

"Good," she said slowly, as if savoring the word. "Very good. Tilla Roper—you're one of mine." She looked back up at Tilla. "I will enjoy breaking you. Go join the others! Take your pup with you."

Tilla's heart sank.

Stars, oh stars, I've been sorted into Nairi's phalanx. She swallowed. *The one officer here to use her punisher—and she's now my commander, and already I've angered her.*

"Go on, move!" Nairi shouted and snarled. She thrust her punisher, forcing Tilla to leap back.

Clenching her jaw, Tilla began to walk toward the pedestal, helping Mae along; the young baker limped upon shaky legs, and her clothes still smoked. As Nairi kept shouting out names, the two girls reached the pedestal. Several other recruits already stood there. Looking around, Tilla saw Cadport's youths forming six groups.

They're called phalanxes, she thought; she vaguely recalled hearing the term. Looking around, it seemed that each phalanx held a hundred recruits. A lanse commanded each group.

Tilla squinted and tried to understand how each phalanx was formed. Who had written the names on the scrolls? Had they been sorted randomly, or was there some method here— farmers to one phalanx perhaps, tradesmen to another? All Tilla saw was that male lanses led three phalanxes; they took command of Cadport's boys. Women commanded the remaining three; the girls of Cadport were sorted into these.

The lanses continued shouting out names. More and more girls kept joining Nairi's phalanx and crowding around Tilla.

Finally Nairi shouted out the last name. "Erry Docker!"

The slim girl, her short brown hair mussed across her brow, raised her chin and marched to stand among them.

"Well, griffin guts," the waif said and flashed a grin. "Tilla-bloody-Roper. I thought I was rid of you, I did. Looks like I'm stuck with you." She shoved her way among the recruits, giving Mae Baker a particularly strong push. "Shove off! Make room."

Tilla was strangely relieved to see the fiery, foulmouthed girl among them. In Cadport, Erry was known as the city's chief troublemaker. An orphan, she claimed that her father had been a dockhand, and that she would beat bloody anyone who claimed otherwise. Behind her back, many did claim otherwise; they whispered that Erry was born of a dockside prostitute and a penniless, foreign sailor.

Whoever Erry's parents had been, they had died or left Cadport years ago. Until her enlistment, Erry had lived alone upon the docks, as feral as a stray cat. A *dock rat* they called her, an urchin with a filthy mouth, skinned knees, and gaunt belly. Cadport's girls whispered that Erry herself was a prostitute; half the boys bragged that they had bedded her.

Yet I too have always been an outcast, Tilla thought. At least Erry had some fire to her, which was more than Tilla could say about Mae and the others; they all stood here pale and sniffling.

The sorting was complete. From her height, Tilla could see Cadport's youths fully divided into six phalanxes—three for the boys, three for the girls.

"Move it, maggots!" Nairi shouted.

The lanse marched between them, shoving them aside, and leaped onto her pedestal. She raised her punisher high; it crackled above her head, incurring several whimpers from the girls.

"Listen up, you daughters of whores!" Nairi continued, holding the rod above her, a beacon of light and pain. "Form ranks—groups of threes! Triple up—now!—or I'm going to shove this punisher down your throats."

Around the courtyard, the other lanses were shouting similar orders and threats.

Tilla began to move. She grabbed Mae, who was still whimpering, and placed her upon a cobblestone.

"Stand still!" she said. "Form the middle line. Erry, you stand behind her—"

"You will form ranks silently," Nairi shouted, "or I'll cut your tongues from your mouths!"

Tilla bit down on her words. Lips tight, she pulled Erry to stand behind Mae, then moved to stand before the baker's daughter. At her sides, the other recruits scurried into their own ranks, forming three lines before Nairi.

The lanse stood, fists on her hips, and scrutinized the lines with narrowed eyes. Her lips curled in disgust.

"Hail the red spiral!" she shouted.

A hundred fists slammed against a hundred chests. Behind her, Tilla heard Mae sniff and Erry snicker.

Flexing her fingers around her punisher, Nairi marched up and down the front line, snarling and cursing. When she passed by Tilla, she paused, thrust her face forward, and glared.

"Roper," she said, voice dripping disgust. "You open your mouth again when I'm giving orders, and you will taste this punisher." She shouted. "Do you understand me, worm?"

Tilla raised her chin and swallowed her pride.

It's just a game, she told herself. *Just a game. Nairi is just like me, just a girl, just somebody sucked into this war. We must play this game for now.*

"Yes, Nai—"

The lanse drove her punisher forward, shoving its tip against Tilla's chest.

Pain exploded.

Fire raced across Tilla.

She clenched her jaw, but a scream still fled her lips. Sweat drenched her. The fire! The fire burned her, twisting in her teeth, in her fingers, burning her bones—

Nairi pulled the punisher back, leaving Tilla gasping. Tears filled her eyes, and it took every last bit of strength to stay standing.

"You will call me Lanse Nairi," the young woman said, "or you will call me Commander. If you ever call me anything else, I will press this punisher against you all night; by morning you will be begging to die. Do you understand me?"

Tilla could barely stay standing. She trembled. Pain throbbed across her chest.

"Yes, Commander!" she managed in a choked voice.

It's a game. Stars, let this just be a game. I will play by the rules, and I will survive this.

Nairi spat, left her, and kept marching down the lines. Across the courtyard, the other lanses were doing the same, and punishers crackled, and recruits screamed.

When Nairi reached the end of the line, she growled.

Tilla peeked from the corner of her eye.

The formation ended with a single recruit, a redheaded girl whose name Tilla could not remember. While all the others stood in threes, this recruit stood alone.

"You!" barked Nairi. "I said form into threes. Where are your other two?"

"I..." The girl faltered and sniffed. "There aren't enough others, Lanse Nairi. I... all the others formed into threes, but there are a hundred of us, and..."

Nairi snarled, grabbed the girl's throat with a gloved hand, and squeezed.

"Then you are useless," the lanse hissed.

With her other hand, she drew a dagger from her belt and drove it forward.

Tilla started, winced, and looked away. But she was too late. She had seen the blade enter flesh. She had seen the blood.

Behind her, Mae whimpered and even Erry gasped. The red-haired recruit screamed. She thumped to the floor. She wept and begged.

Tilla glanced over again, just long enough to see Nairi thrust the dagger again, this time into the girl's neck. The lanse smirked, pulled the blade back, and licked the blood from it. Her eyes burned with hunger, and she bared bloody teeth.

No, this is no game, Tilla realized. She trembled and her chest still ached. *Only the strongest will survive here. I must survive this place. I must. I will see Cadport and Rune again.*

"The rest of you miserable lot!" Nairi shouted. She cleaned her dagger on the dead girl's cloak before slamming it back into her belt. "Your groups of threes—these are your flight crews. These are your fellow warriors. From now on, you will remain in these same flights! The two worms with you—they will stick to you like boils to a leper throughout your training. Do you understand me, whores?"

"Yes, Commander!" they shouted together.

Nairi smirked. "Welcome! Welcome to my phalanx. You are now worms serving me. You are now miserable slaves. You now live for one purpose: to obey my commands." Nairi drew her dark longsword and raised it. "This is the Black Rose Phalanx. This is your new family. This is your new temple. This is your new life. You have no more parents, no more siblings, no more home. Your life is now the Black Rose! Your life is to obey me, your commander. Do you understand, worms?"

"Yes, Commander!" they shouted.

As much as her chest hurt, and as cold as her fear pounded, Tilla was glad to at least make some sense of things. Leaving Cadport, they had been nothing but a mass of frightened youths carted like cattle. But now Tilla had a phalanx and a commander. Now Tilla had a flight—a group of three. Now she finally had some grounding.

There are thirty-three flights in a phalanx, she thought, vowing to remember the numbers. *And a hundred troops: ninety-nine soldiers and one officer.* She swallowed. *The Black Rose Phalanx had one hundred soldiers. One too many.*

Tilla still had a thousand questions. Did she herself have a rank—the way Nairi was a lanse? Would her flight have a name too, or did just phalanxes get names? Would her flight have a commander, or was she equal to Mae and Erry? The questions kept bubbling inside her, but Tilla dared not ask. She had never had a chance to learn these things. Her brother had served, but he had died in the war. Those soldiers who did return to Cadport never spoke of their service, and Tilla could now understand why.

A lump filled her throat. *If I ever see Rune again, we won't talk about this either.* Her eyes stung. *We'll forget all about this nightmare. We'll walk along the beach, and he'll kiss me again, and we'll just walk there forever and look at the waves.*

"Now march!" Nairi shouted. She turned and began walking toward an archway in the courtyard's wall. "Follow me— three lines! Anyone who breaks formation tastes my blade."

Mae whimpered. Erry rolled her eyes and smirked. But they all followed. A hundred legionaries of the Black Rose Phalanx snaked out of the courtyard, under the archway... and into a nightmare of blood and pain.

SHARI

Shari flew upon the wind, blue scales clanking, and blasted fire. Across field and forest, she saw the distant lights of the capital, and she cursed.

On any other evening, flying toward Nova Vita, the great torch of Requiem, would fill her with pride. Ahead shone the lights of Requiem's center of power, the mighty city that ruled the world. Ahead shone her birthright, a metropolis of a million souls, the heartbeat of her lineage. Ahead shone might, pride, and strength.

Yet today Shari did not fly home as a heroine wreathed in glory. Today she flew in fear. Today she did not fly leading a battalion of dragons all roaring her name, announcing her return. Today she flew alone in the sky, a single blue dragon in the sunset.

I've failed my task, she thought, and fire flickered between her teeth. *Today I will face no glory but the wrath of my father.*

She streamed over the fields. The walls of Nova Vita rose before her.

These walls snaked for miles around the city, thick limestone bedecked with obsidian tiles and lit with torches. Upon the battlements stood hundreds of cannons, each one as long as a dragon, mounted on gears fast enough to spin, aim, and fire within an instant. At each cannon, three men in armor stood vigil. Between the guns perched dragons clad in armor, their great dragonhelms topped with spikes. Thousands of warriors guarded this city, the jewel of the empire.

During the reign of Aeternum, enemies had attacked and destroyed this place—griffins, phoenixes, and wyverns. But Frey

Cadigus swore: Nova Vita would never fall again. All his wrath shone here, a glory of blade and gunpowder and fire.

And tonight, the wrath of this emperor will fall upon me, Shari thought as she flew.

The city sprawled below her, lit with countless lanterns. The streets were arranged like a great wagon wheel, its spokes leading toward the palace of Tarath Imperium, an obsidian edifice whose battlements clawed the sky. Fortresses, amphitheaters, aqueducts—thousands of great structures rose here, monuments to the empire's might, and Tarath Imperium dwarfed them all. The palace rose before Shari, clawing the sky, its windows burning with fire like the eyes of demons.

I should flee, Shari thought. *I should turn around and fly away and—*

She scoffed.

And what, live like my sister? Become a forest wildwoman like Kaelyn, fighting my father in a hopeless war?

She shook her head, scattering sparks and smoke. No. Shari was still a proud daughter of Cadigus, still heir to Requiem, the greatest empire the world had ever known. She would face her father. She would take his punishment. And it would make her stronger.

She flew over the great Cadigus Arena, the largest amphitheater in Requiem, and saw prisoners chained as dragons, their maws muzzled shut, forced to fight packs of tigers and wolves. Past the amphitheater, she flew over the Colossus, a gilded statue three hundred feet tall, depicting her father staring with cold eyes, his fist against his breastplate. She flew over the fortress of Castra Academia, its walls and towers bearing the red spiral upon black banners—the great academy that trained the Legions' officers.

Finally she neared the palace, and fear roiled through her belly like a horde of icy demons.

Four thousand years ago, the stories said, the first king of
Requiem—King Aeternum himself—had raised a column here, a
pillar of marble and starlight. Requiem became a kingdom that
day, and that marble column still stood; ancient magic let no claw,
fang, or tail shatter it. King's Column rose hidden now, a white
spine enclosed in black flesh. Frey Cadigus had extended his
palace, letting it spread like a growth. Today black walls, towers,
spikes, and turrets covered the original marble the Aeternums had
raised. Today this was no longer a place of beauty and peace, but
an edifice of might—Tarath Imperium, terror of the empire.
Dragons in armor perched upon its battlements. Men stood vigil,
ready to fire cannons. Torches crackled and the dragons
screeched and blew fire.

Black stone. Flame. Death. *My home.*

The guards upon the walls recognized her blue scales,
gilded horns, and dragonhelm that bore the red spiral. They
howled in salute. Those in dragon forms blew pillars of fire.
Those who stood in human forms, manning the cannons,
slammed fists against chests.

"Hail Shari Cadigus!" they chanted. "Hail the red spiral!"

Shari ignored them. The palace, its base wide with walls
and barracks, tapered into a great steeple. This tower of obsidian
rose a thousand feet tall, crowned with jagged spikes, a black arm
clutching the sky in its claws.

Shari flew toward the tower top. Its spikes rose before her,
taller than dragons, greater than most homes in this city. Shari
flew between them, descended, and landed upon a stone roof. All
around her rose the battlements of Tarath Imperium, a crown
upon the empire.

The red and black clouds swirled above her, swarming with
dragons. Shari shifted into human form. The wind whipped her,
billowed her hair and cloak, and stung her cheeks. She snarled

and marched across the platform, heading toward a staircase that led into the tower.

Twenty figures stood guarding the staircase, robed in black—men of the Axehand Order. Here were no simple guards; the axehands were elite killers, chosen for their cruelty and strength. Within the shadows of their hoods, they wore iron masks; they were forbidden to ever remove them, not even when they slept. At their waists, they sported the tools of their trade: pincers and blades for torturing their victims. Worst of all, they had no left hands; their arms ended with axeheads strapped to stumps.

They maimed themselves to prove their loyalty, Shari thought and shivered. *They lifted those axes, chopped off their own hands, and strapped the blades to the stubs. They are fanatics. They are ruthless. They are the only men I fear.*

The Legions fought Requiem's wars—a vast army hundreds of thousands strong. The Axehand Order was smaller, but far more dangerous. Its men were as much priests as warriors; they worshiped Frey as their god, and they spread fear of their lord across the empire.

Shari feared them too.

Seeing these men, shivers ran down her spine. She did not trust the Axehand Order; they were too fanatical. Soldiers in the Legions were broken, molded, and shaped into mindless warriors; all they knew was to serve. Shari had broken enough recruits herself to know that. But these axehands... they were too strong. Their order had gained too much power. Their commander, Lord Herin Blackrose, had grown too mighty.

Shari snarled as she walked past them, heading down into the tower. Someday, she thought, she might find an enemy not only in the Resistance, but here at her very doorstep.

As she descended dark stairs, heading deep into the tower, she left such thoughts behind her. Today she had greater

concerns. Today she might find her greatest challenge not with
the Resistance, not with the Axehand Order, but with her father.

She reached the end of the staircase, opened a door, and
walked down a hallway lined with braziers. Her boots thumped.
Shari snarled and clutched the hilt of her sword, as if that could
save her now.

"You little whore, Kaelyn," she muttered. She drew her
sword and swung it as she walked. "You and your boy will taste
this blade."

Guards lined the walls, saluting their princess, fists
slamming against breastplates.

"Hail the re—" one guard began.

With a snarl, Shari drove her sword into his neck. Blood
flowed down the blade, and Shari growled as she twisted it. The
guard gurgled, hanging upon the sword, blood in his mouth.

"This will happen to you, Kaelyn," Shari hissed. "This will
happen to you, Relesar Aeternum."

She yanked her blade back with a gush of blood. The guard
clattered to the floor. The other guards stood still and pale, fists
still held to their breasts.

After several more halls and staircases, Shari reached tall
iron doors. She paused outside them, for a moment frozen.

Father's chambers.

Frey Cadigus maintained a throne room in the base of the
palace. It was a chamber an army could fill, a paradise of gold,
torchlight, and treasures plundered from around the world. That
grand hall mostly stood empty. For all his glory and might, Frey
Cadigus was at heart a soldier; he entertained guests in his throne
room only several times a year.

Today, Shari knew, she would find him behind these doors
in a humbler, darker place. These were the personal chambers of
Frey Cadigus, far from his servants, his generals, and his gilt and
glory.

Shari took a deep breath, steeled herself, and pushed open the doors.

She entered the wolf's den.

For a moment she blinked, eyes adjusting. Outside in the corridor, torches and braziers crackled, their light shining off the black tiles. In here, nothing but a few candles lit the darkness.

"Father?" Shari kept her sword drawn and bloody at her side. "Are you here, Father?"

She walked a few feet deeper and saw him.

Frey Cadigus, Emperor of Requiem, Slayer of Aeternum, stood with his back toward her. In statues and paintings, he wore fine black armor filigreed with gold. Here before her, he stood in a tan, bloodstained jerkin. His dark hair was thinning, but his shoulders were still wide and strong. Several meat hooks hung from the ceiling before the emperor. Upon one hung a wild boar, still alive and squirming.

Frey spoke without turning toward her; she could not see his face.

"You come to me, my daughter, with fear in your voice. You come to me alone. I smell fresh blood upon you, not the blood of a corpse."

Shari gripped her sword and bared her teeth. "I come alone."

The wild boar kicked and squealed, its cry echoing in the chamber. His back still facing Shari, Frey raised a dagger, grabbed the boar, and sliced its neck. The beast wailed and its blood gushed into a bucket.

"Fresh blood," Frey said and wiped the blade on his pants. "Ahh! Smell it, Shari. It is a wondrous smell, is it not? Tell me, my daughter. How did it smell when you shed the blood of the Aeternum boy?"

Shari lowered her head, jaw clenched. "Father, I..."

Slowly, bloody dagger in hand, Frey Cadigus turned toward her.

Today he perhaps wore no armor, no fine cloak, and no heraldry like in the paintings. In his bloodstained leather, however, he looked to Shari just as regal and cruel. His strength shone not from any armor or finery, but from the hard lines of his face, from the thinness of his lips, and from the cold, hard stare of his eyes, a stare as sharp and bloodthirsty as his blade.

"You let the boy slip away," he said.

Shari could not speak. Her throat constricted and fear pounded through her. There were none she feared more than her father—not the Axehand Order, not Valien the Resistor, and not an army of rebels. She lowered her head and nodded silently. Her blade dipped and its tip hit the floor.

Frey turned away. Muscles rippling, he thrust his dagger into the boar's stomach and pulled down, letting entrails and organs spill.

"I gave my useless son a useless fort," Frey said. He reached into the boar, bare-handed, and scooped out innards. "I gave him a pathetic pile of stones far south where he can't get into his usual trouble." He tossed organs into the bucket with a splash and looked over his shoulder, eyes hard chips. "I gave *you* a chance for eternal glory. And you let it slip between your fingers."

Shari glared and hissed. "I will find the boy, Father! I just need more time, and I need more men. He fled into the forests with Kaelyn. I need more dragons, and I can burn down every tree, and dig up every bolt-hole, and—"

"We used to be weak, you know," Frey said. He wiped his hand on his pants, turned back to the boar, and drove his knife along its flanks. "Not us, not the Cadigus family; we were always strong. But our kingdom. Requiem. We used to grovel before the world, and they would hunt us." He shoved his fingers into the boar and pulled down, peeling its skin; it came free with a tearing hiss. "Yes. They would relish our blood, and they reduced us to a quivering few. They butchered us like I butchered this boar. The Aeternum family did that to us; they had us kneeling in the mud before griffins, phoenixes, and men." He tossed the skin aside and stared at Shari. "I made Requiem strong. The boy, the Aeternum heir; he is a relic of that weakness. He is a drop of poison in the pure blood of dragons. If he meets that Valien, that rat and his rabble, the boy could become a figurehead. Valien will dream that he could place the boy on my throne." Frey snorted a laugh. "The man is a fool. He must be stamped out. Crushed. The boy must be taken from him."

"I will ta—"

"You will do nothing. You had your chance, Shari, and you failed." Frey snorted and began flaying more skin. "Maybe I should have sent your little brother on this task. Maybe—"

It was Shari's turn to interrupt.

"My brother is a fool!" she said and spat onto the floor. "Leresy is as great a fool as his twin sister. The two were always pathetic." She hissed. "But I am strong, Father. I am strong like you. I will make you proud and crush the Resistance, and I will bring you the boy so you can hang him here, gut him, and peel his skin."

Frey gave a choked laugh. "Will you now? You say your sister is weak. You say Kaelyn is a fool. Kaelyn is a traitor, that is true, but weak? Foolish? She found the boy before you did. You had one task—to beat Kaelyn to him. And you failed. So who is weak, Shari? Who is the fool?"

Flames seemed to burst through Shari, even in her human form. She snarled, screamed, and raised her sword as if she would strike her father down. He only stood still, staring at her with those hard eyes like granite.

Shari lowered her head.

Tears filled her eyes.

"I'm sorry, Father," she whispered. "I'm sorry. Please forgive me."

He stood staring, and no compassion or love filled his eyes. No, Shari knew; her father held no love for his children. He loved only Requiem, only the empire he had vowed to forever lead.

He gestured his head to the side. "The meat hook," he said. "That one there."

Shari hissed at him. Her legs trembled.

"I am no longer a child!"

"Today you are barely a worm," he replied. "Remove your armor. Remove this steel and hold that hook. If you let go, I will hang you there and gut you like this boar."

Shari wore steel plates; her father wore bloody leather. She held a longsword forged in dragonfire; her father held only a butcher's knife.

I can kill him now, she thought, snarling. *I can drive my sword into him and take his throne, and this empire will be mine. He will be the one to bleed, not me.*

Shari looked aside, eyes narrowed.

And Leresy would fly against me with his southern garrison. And that whore Nairi would summon her father, and the Axehand Order would descend upon me. The empire would collapse into war, and the Resistance would seize the chance; Valien would fly against me too, and his dragons would surround this palace.

Shari hissed. She hated her father but she knew: He held the empire together. He was the pillar of this realm, at least for now. If he died today, the world would burn. She would replace him someday, yes. But not with blood. Not with war. The time for her to pluck her fruit of power had not yet come.

So I will take his punishment, Shari thought. *I will take his wrath. Every lash will make me stronger. Every blow will stoke my flame.*

She removed her breastplate. She tossed it down with a clang. Eyes cold, Frey lifted his whip. Shari walked to the meat hook, held it, and closed her eyes.

Frey beat her. With every lash, Shari clutched the meat hook harder, grinded her teeth, hissed, but did not scream.

"You have failed me," Frey said and his lashes kept falling, tearing through her tunic, tearing into her skin and flesh. "Feel the pain of your failure."

Shari trembled and smelled more fresh blood, the third spill of the day; this time it was her own.

TILLA

"Move!" Nairi shouted, pointing her punisher at an archway. "Get inside, worms. Move your arses or I'll shove my punisher up them."

The Black Rose Phalanx marched along a portico of columns, moving toward the archway; it led into a shadowy barracks. As she marched among her fellow recruits, Tilla wondered what lay within those shadows. More pain? More officers who'd burn and cut them? What horrors lurked here?

"Move, damn it!" Nairi screamed, marching alongside them. "Into the darkness."

At her side, Mae was already weeping. Silent tears streamed down the young baker's cheeks. Even Erry seemed shaken; her face was pale, lacking its usual smirk, and red rimmed her eyes.

Tilla felt her own eyes sting. She had seen three of Cadport's youths killed already: young Pery back at home, Jem Chandler along the road, and now the red-haired girl—a girl who had only sinned by being one soul too many.

No. Tilla tightened her lips and kept marching. *If I am weak, I am dead. If I cry, I am dead. If I remember home, I am dead. I must be a soldier now, carved of stone, my heart of iron; thus will I survive this nightmare.*

"Move!" Nairi shouted and goaded a recruit with her punisher, making the girl scream and scurry forward.

The phalanx marched in three lines, entering the barracks one flight at a time. When it was Tilla's turn to enter, she clenched her fists and sucked in her breath, prepared for any horror that might lurk inside.

Stifling air, the smell of leather and oil, and shadows awaited her. She blinked and it was a moment before her eyes adjusted. When they did, she breathed a sigh of relief.

"It's an armory," she whispered.

The hall was wide, tiled, and topped with a vaulted ceiling. The recruits gathered here. Behind wooden counters, which reminded Tilla of the Old Wheel's bar, loomed alcoves. One alcove held shelves of helmets. Another held boots. A third brimmed with suits of leather armor studded with iron. The final alcove drew most of Tilla's attention; inside she saw hundreds of swords hanging upon racks.

Outside every alcove, a gruff soldier stood at the counter like a barman. As the recruits streamed into the main hall, these soldiers shouted out their supplies.

"Helms! Get helms here! Move it!"

"Leather armor—grab your armor!"

"Line up for swords, damn you—swords here!"

Tilla wasn't sure where to start. Despite the horrors of the day, she found a smile tingling her lips. It soon widened into a grin.

I'm going to get a sword! she thought. *And armor! What would Rune think of me now?*

Mae sniffed and clung to her arm. "But... Tilla," the baker's daughter said, and her lips trembled. "I don't *want* a sword."

Erry was staring around with wide eyes. "Well I do!" said the ragamuffin. "So watch out, Wobble Lips, because if you cry again, I'm gonna slay you right with it."

"Do you think..." Mae sniffed. "Do you think I can be a baker here too—like I was in Cadport? The Legions need bread too, right? There must be a bakery here somewhere, and maybe I can do that, not fight."

Erry rolled her eyes and snorted so forcefully she blew back locks of her hair. "Oh bloody donkey piss! Burn me, just grab a damn sword. Your days of baking are over."

Leaving the two to bicker, Tilla approached the alcove of armor. A grizzled old armorer stood there, cussing and spitting and shouting at the recruits.

"Here, runt," he said to one short, slim girl and tossed her a suit. "Smallest one I've got. Here, this is for you, pig." He tossed a larger suit at a larger girl. "Merciful stars, but you're going to need a leather sail. You! You—you with the big teats—bloody Abyss, how are you going to fit into a breastplate?"

A few of the girls smirked. Others retreated with their armor in tears. When it was Tilla's turn at the counter, the armorer gave her a shrewd look, scratched his chin, and nodded.

"Aye, you're a tall one," he said. "I like that. How about instead of suiting up, you suit down and slip with me into the shadows at the back?" He spat onto the floor. "I'll do my own slipping into a dark place."

Tilla rolled her eyes. "Well, haven't you just charmed me? Does that line ever work? Fetch me my armor, and maybe I'll forget to visit you again once I get my sword."

Behind her, she heard Erry snicker. Briefly, Tilla wondered if she had crossed a line; would she taste the punisher again for her words? And yet this gruff armorer wore no punisher or blade, and he bore but a single red star upon his armbands; Tilla guessed him too low ranking to threaten her.

All that matters in this place, she thought, *is your rank. Upon her shoulders, Nairi bears the red spirals of an officer; she is death in boots. This man wears the red stars of a lowborn soldier; he is what boots like Nairi's tread upon.*

Her suspicions were confirmed when the armorer grunted, scratched himself, and fetched her a suit of armor.

"Try this," he said. "Tall and slim; should be a bit tight on you, but that's how I like it." He licked his lips and hissed.

Tilla lifted the pack of leather and bolts—it was bundled together with straps—and retreated toward a bench where some recruits were already donning their own armor. After claiming a bit of bench, Tilla unwrapped the bundle.

She found a breastplate studded with iron rings, its boiled leather hard, brown, and tough as wood. This was no fine, steel breastplate like the one Lanse Nairi wore, or like the breastplates Tilla had seen soldiers in Cadport wear—but it was real armor, and it would protect her. Tilla rubbed her chest where Nairi had held a punisher against her, and she wondered if this leather breastplate would protect her from further abuse.

Along with the breastplate, she found tan leggings and a white undershirt, vambraces and greaves for her limbs, thick gloves, and even pauldrons of the same tough, brown leather. She was disappointed to see no armbands bearing insignia; even the armorer wore armbands.

I'll have to earn those ranks, she thought. She wondered how long it took to rise from recruit to soldier. She would not be a real soldier, she knew, until she had armbands with red stars.

"Suit up!" Nairi was shouting across the hall. "Damn it, cockroaches, suit up—fast!"

Tilla nodded, took a deep breath, and removed the woolen tunic and leggings she had worn all the way from Cadport. They were threadbare by now and smelled of mud and sweat and oil. The other recruits were undressing around her; after ten days in a cramped cart, all modesty had left them.

Tilla wriggled into her new leggings, then donned her leather breastplate. Unlike a corset, this breastplate had its straps in the front—three leather belts with iron buckles. When Tilla tightened her armor, she gasped for breath. The damn thing was too tight. Tilla considered returning for a larger suit, but Nairi was screaming that she would slay anyone too slow, and the armorer was shouting while he handed away the last breastplates.

Well, I'll have to lose some weight in this camp, Tilla thought, the armor squeezing her. *I have a feeling that it won't take long in this place. I'm already thinner than I've ever been.*

Mae and Erry approached her, each clad in their own leather armor.

"Merciful stars!" Erry said. She admired Tilla with wide eyes. "You look like a real warrior. That armor is skintight. Burn me, even I'd take you to bed in that suit."

"Don't be disgusting," Mae scolded her. New tears filled her eyes. "She looks *awful.* And I look awful in this suit. And... and... this whole place is awful."

With that, the baker covered her face with her palms and cried silently. Erry only rolled her eyes.

"Come on, girls," Tilla said. "Let's get some boots and helmets."

"And then swords," Erry said and grinned.

Tilla was immensely relieved to find boots her size. She thought that she could handle armor too small, but boots were one thing she needed to have fit well—and these fit beautifully. To be sure, the leather was as hard and unyielding as her armor, but Tilla thought that she could work it in. The boots rose tall above her leggings, ending just below her knees, and their toes were tipped with steel. As Tilla walked around in them, for the first time in her life, she felt powerful—a warrior.

I'm no longer helpless, she thought, and this was a new feeling for her. Back at Cadport, she had always felt lowly, outcast, hopelessly crushed under the weight of the Cadigus Regime. But here, wearing this armor and these boots, Tilla felt strong. She felt like a soldier.

And it feels good, she thought, and the thought surprised her.

At a third alcove, she found a round, steel helmet that fit nicely and left her face exposed; lined with wool, it strapped under her chin with a buckle.

"And now," she said to her flight crew, "we grab swords."

Erry grinned and whooped.

Mae, however, only sniffed. "Why do we even need swords?" she said and her lips trembled. "Aren't we supposed to fight as dragons? Why can't we just use our claws and fire?"

"Because," Erry said with an eye roll, "you're not always going to fight in the sky! Stars, Wobble Lips, but you are slow, aren't you? The Resistance hides in tunnels and caves and such. How are you going to fit in there as a dragon?" She grinned. "But we can get to them with swords. I'm going to stab them real good."

Nairi's shouts flowed over them.

"Back outside!" The lanse stood at the doors, shoving recruits outside, then glared at Tilla and her flight crew. "Grab your swords, you daughters of dogs, or by the red spiral, you'll taste *my* sword."

Tilla nodded, remembering the sight of Nairi's dagger thrusting into the red-haired girl. With her flight crew, she hurried toward the alcove of weapons. Most of the blades were already claimed. A soldier stood at the counter, balding and gaunt and blinking; he reminded Tilla of a giant ferret.

Erry banged her fist against the counter, as if ordering ale.

"Three swords please!" she said. "And make it snappy."

Tilla sighed. "When unarmed, Erry, never order around a man with swords."

The weaselly soldier grumbled under his breath, retreated to the back of the alcove, and returned carrying three blades. He delicately laid them on the counter.

"Take care of these," he said and gave them a longing pat. "Dragonforged, they are. Northern steel." He glared up at the recruits. "If you scratch em, I'll stick em into your guts."

"Well, why don't you just take them to bed with you?" Erry said with another roll of her eyes. When she lifted a sword, those eyes widened, and her lips peeled back into a grin. "Bloody stars, now this is a sword."

The scrawny, dockside orphan drew her blade and swung it, forcing Tilla and Mae to leap back.

"Be careful!" Mae said. She reached for her own sword hesitantly, as if reaching for a venomous snake, and her lips wobbled again.

Tilla lifted the third sword and hefted it. The blade was sheathed in a black, leather scabbard attached to a belt. She slung the belt around her waist, tightened it, and let the sword hang against her left hip. It felt light—lighter than she had expected—but just heavy enough for comfort. She closed her hand around the hilt, squeezing and releasing, but did not draw the blade.

My own sword, she thought.

Since leaving Cadport, Tilla had felt afraid, naked, and alone. But gripping this hilt comforted her. She had a weapon now. She was armed. She was a soldier. For the first time, Tilla felt that maybe the Legions were not a nightmare world. Surely, this was a violent place, and a dangerous one, but there were rules to it. If Tilla played by these rules, she could grow strong here.

Maybe someday I can be strong like Nairi, she thought, *and wear an officer's insignia upon my shoulders. I could command with justice, not cruelty, with pride rather than malice.*

Nairi was shouting again and herding recruits outside. Tilla hurried back out into the sunset. The rest of her phalanx crowded around her, all clad in leather armor and bearing swords.

"Form ranks!" Nairi shouted.

Perhaps it was the pride of armor and blade; this time, the recruits took formation faster than ever. Three lines formed. Boots slammed together.

"Hail the red spiral!" Nairi cried, and hundreds of fists slammed against hundreds of breastplates.

Tilla stood, chin held high. The sun was finally peeking through the clouds. She dared to feel a sliver of hope.

RUNE

They entered the wide, shadowy hall of Valien's crumbling palace.

Limestone pillars rose in palisades, supporting a vaulted ceiling. Dust, grooves, and holes covered the tiled floor and brick walls. Two lines of braziers crackled, forming a corridor of light. At the end of this corridor, a man sat in a chair, his head lowered and his face shadowed. A sword lay upon his lap; the man stared at it, not looking up.

A silent, dark majesty filled the hall, Rune thought. The kings of Osanna had once ruled from this place, presiding over courts of light and life. This man ahead, Rune thought, seemed a different sort of king—a king of death and darkness. He had no golden throne, only an old wooden chair. He wore no armor, only the garb of a forester. And yet Rune thought: He exudes his own regality, as strong as those true kings who had once sat here.

Rune looked at Kaelyn. She stood at his side, still and silent, but a light seemed to fill her eyes—a light of comfort and hope, hearth light shining at the windows for a weary traveler returning home.

She looked at Rune and a smile touched her lips. She held his hand and guided him forward. They walked across the hall, moving down the palisade of braziers and columns, and approached the shadowy man.

"Valien," Kaelyn said softly. "I've returned."

The man did not look up. He was polishing his sword, Rune saw, moving an oiled rag back and forth along the blade. Rune had a feeling that blade had been polished to perfection hours ago. His own father, when troubled, would polish the Old

Wheel's bar over and over for hours, lost in thought. This man was polishing his blade with the same weariness.

Rune could still not see Valien's face, but what he saw of the man spoke of haunting memory, of pain, of a weight too great to bear. Valien's hair was long and untamed, hanging loose about his face; it must have once been a great black mane, but now white streaked it. The man's shoulders, though wide and strong, slumped as if bearing an invisible yoke. Valien's clothes had once been fine, Rune thought; they were made of thick wool and tanned leather. Yet years of age had worn them; the fabrics were now faded into mere memories of lost glory.

Seeing this man, Rune did not know how to feel. Many in Cadport, including his father, would whisper that Valien was a hero, the only man brave enough to stand up to the Cadigus family. Others said that Valien was a ruthless killer, that he had slain many soldiers from Cadport, including Tilla's brother. Standing here today, Rune did not know whether to feel awe, hatred, or fear.

"Lord Valien Eleison," he said softly. "The lost knight of Requiem."

Valien's hands stilled upon the blade. His body tensed. He still did not look up. After what seemed an eternity of silence, Valien snorted.

"Lord Valien Eleison?" he spoke in shadow, and Rune started, for that voice was rough and worn like beaten leather. "I haven't been a lord in many years, boy. And the House Eleison has fallen; I am its last survivor. You may call me Valien now; titles are nothing but a memory of light in darkness."

Rune wasn't sure how to respond to that. The Regime called this man a demon; others call him a hero. Standing here, Rune saw neither. He saw only a tired, broken man, the ghost of somebody who might once have been great.

"Valien," he said. "Just Valien then. And I'm just Rune."

For the first time, Valien looked up... and Rune nearly lost his breath.

He had seen hard faces before. Frey Cadigus, in paintings and statues, bore a face that Rune thought could wilt flowers. Tilla's face, when she was angry, was hard as granite. But this man...

Valien's face seemed carved of beaten leather stretched over iron. Grizzled stubble covered his cheeks. Grooves framed his mouth. But worst of all were his eyes. Those eyes were dark, deep, and haunted as windows in temples of ghosts. They sang of old pain and battles as clearly as tales in books or poems. He couldn't have been much older than forty, Rune thought, but his eyes seemed more ancient than those of old men.

"Just Rune," Valien rasped. "Is that so? Do you think you were brought before me because you are *just Rune*?"

Again, Rune was struck by that gruff voice. Valien spoke like a man being strangled. His voice was but a hiss, a scratch, a deathly gasp.

"Some might think me more than that," Rune said. "I've heard what Kaelyn believes. I come here to tell you: She is wrong." He shook his head. "I'm not the one you seek."

Valien snorted again. "Aren't you now?" He coughed and hissed like a man hanging from a noose. "I smuggled Relesar Aeternum out of the burning palace of his father, slaying Cadigus men as I held the babe. I brought the child, last heir of the dynasty, to an old tavern in an older port. I gave him a new name. I know you better than you know yourself, *Rune Brewer*. I've known you all your life, and so has Kaelyn."

The young woman, hearing her name, walked over to Valien and placed a hand on his shoulder. She leaned down, kissed his cheek, and whispered soft blessings.

When she straightened, she said, "Valien, I barely saved the boy in time. Shari arrived in Lynport the same day. I fought her.

I wounded her. I smuggled Rune out moments before her men stormed the tavern." Kaelyn lowered her head. "She burned that tavern down, and she killed its keeper. I'm sorry, Valien; I did not mean for any blood to spill. I flew too slowly." She raised her head again, and her eyes shone with tears. "But he is here now. The heir to the throne. He will rally the people against Cadigus; he will bring us hope."

A lump filled Rune's throat. His eyes burned. Thinking about the Old Wheel still pained him so much he could barely breathe.

"Wait a moment!" he said, his voice too loud; it echoed in the chamber. "I will not be some figurehead for your Resistance. I hate Frey Cadigus too, but... I'm only a brewer. I'm not who you think I am. I—"

"You," Valien said, "were kept safe. We made damn sure of that. I've been protecting you all your life, Relesar, though you never knew it. I was in the Old Wheel many times, in shadow, watching you grow from a babe, to a boy, to a man. I made sure you never knew your true parentage; not until you were old enough. You were safe in the Old Wheel." He sighed. "At least, safe until you went ahead and started looking like your father."

"Wil Brewer is my father—" Rune began.

"Your father was the last King Aeternum," Valien said. "I should know; I fought for him. And you, Rune, look exactly like him, damn you. The Regime noticed. And so... now you are here. You can no longer hide. The time has come, Rune, for you to accept your true heritage... and to take arms against the man who slew your family." Valien reached out and clutched Rune's arm, digging his fingers like an iron vise. "The throne of Requiem is yours. With your help, we will slay the tyrant and place you upon that throne."

Rune laughed.

He turned away.

He could not stop laughing. His laughter echoed through the hall, and tears stung his eyes, and he clutched his belly but could not stop. Valien and Kaelyn were looking at each other grimly, but that only made Rune laugh harder.

Tilla, his best friend, the woman who had kissed him—gone into the Legions. His father—dead. His tavern—burned. His life—torn apart. And now this! Now this ragged shell of man who ruled over ruins and bones—this disgraced knight—called him the heir of Aeternum. Rune paced the hall, tears streaming down his face as he laughed. As his world burned, as all hope for life faded, as everything he'd ever known crumbled around him, what else could he do but laugh?

"Rune," Kaelyn said slowly. "Rune, I know this is a lot to take in."

He tossed back his head, only laughing harder.

"Do you think so, Kaelyn?" he said. "I only just waded through skeletons to meet your grizzled old friend here—who looks barely better—and was told you want me to dethrone Frey Cadigus. Did I miss anything?"

Kaelyn stepped toward him and took his hands. "You don't have to dethrone him yourself, Rune. It needn't be your hand that slays him. But yes, you will sit upon his throne once we kill him."

He wiped tears from his eyes, chest still shaking with laughter. "Well, there's a relief. And tell me, even if I am this... heir of Aeternum... even if my true father was the king... who cares? Kaelyn, you're Frey's daughter. Kill the bastard and you take the throne." He pointed a shaky finger at Valien. "Or you, old knight. You're supposedly a great warrior. If one soldier could start a new dynasty, why not another? Why not you—"

Valien rose to his feet and roared.

Rune's laughter and voice died.

He had not imagined this weathered man, a wreck who coughed and talked in a wheeze, could roar. And yet Valien now howled, and the cry—the cry of an enraged beast—filled the hall, echoed, and pounded in Rune's ears.

"Silence!"

Valien stomped forward so violently that Rune stepped back, but the man reached him and grabbed his collar. The fallen knight thrust his face close and snarled.

"I've not carried you through fire and blood to hear you mock me," Valien said, voice gruff as old leather cracking under stones. "You know so little. All your life has been sheltered. I made sure of that. You speak of things you do not understand."

Rune's laughter was gone now. Instead he found rage pounding through him, an inferno rising from his belly to sting his throat and eyes. He raged for Tilla leaving, for his father dying, for being taken to this place. He glared back at Valien with burning eyes.

"Is that my fault? You claim to have been watching me all my life. You kept me in the dark! And now you want to use me in your war as some... some figurehead? Look around you, Valien!" He swept his hands around the hall. "Look at this place. A shattered hall. Look at the city you dwell in! A ruin of skeletons. Look at your men! A few hungry souls with chipped swords and no armor. You speak of killing Frey Cadigus? Your war is hopeless."

"Then it is hopeless!" Valien howled. He shoved Rune back, and his eyes burned. "Then we will die! Then we will die like the rest of them—like your parents, like your siblings, like the knights of my order, like my—"

Valien froze.

His face paled.

His lip trembled.

The gruff man stepped back, whispering and staring at Rune.

Then, with a hiss, he spun around and marched into the shadows. He disappeared into the back of the hall, a door slammed shut, and Valien was gone.

Rune's heart pounded, his fingers shook, and his breath rattled his ribs. He turned toward Kaelyn. She stood by the empty chair, eyes sad like birds left to die in an abandoned cage.

"What was that all about?" Rune demanded. "Why did he just... leave like he saw a ghost?"

Kaelyn heaved a sigh. She looked over to the shadows where Valien had vanished.

"Because he did see a ghost," she whispered. "He saw *her* again."

Rune too looked toward those shadows, but Valien was gone and did not return. The room seemed to grow colder, and Rune hugged himself. He had just met the leader of the Resistance, the supposed hope of Requiem, the only man who had ever stood up to Frey Cadigus, raised his head, and said to him: This land is not yours.

And I saw only a broken, haunted wreck, Rune thought.

"Who was she?" he asked. "The woman he lost."

Kaelyn placed a hand on his shoulder. "Come, Rune. Evening falls. Let's go find a meal and a place to sleep. Valien needs to be alone this night."

She took Rune through a doorway, down a flight of stairs, and into a cellar filled with bookshelves, jugs of wine, and a bed. Several candles stood on a table, and Kaelyn lit them with her tinderbox. A painting hung on one wall, showing a woman with golden hair and sad eyes.

"Another gopher hole?" Rune asked.

Kaelyn smiled softly. "No. This one is a Kaelyn hole. My home—if any place can be called my home anymore. You can share it for now." She glared at him and jabbed a finger against his chest. "At least until we figure out what to do with you."

He frowned at the room and his stomach sank. "There's only one bed."

"Of course there's only one bed!" She bristled. "We're not running a tavern here, Rune Brewer. You will be quite comfortable sleeping on the floor. Well, I lied. You'll be cold and stiff, but you'll be *alive*, and that's all I care about."

With that, Kaelyn turned away. She hung her bow, quiver, and sword on pegs. When she doffed her cloak, remaining in only her leggings and tunic, Rune was struck by how fragile she looked. Armed and cloaked, Kaelyn had seemed a warrior. Now he saw only a slim girl, barely half his size. Her golden hair cascaded down her back, and her skin shone orange in the candlelight, and despite himself, and despite all this death and horror, Rune's blood heated.

She's beautiful, he thought. He found himself imagining what her body looked like under her clothes. With how snugly they fit, he didn't have to imagine much. His mouth dried.

She looked over her shoulder and glared.

"What are you looking at?" she said. "Stop standing there like a useless lump and get some food." She nodded at a shelf. "There, you'll find some bread and cheese. Slice us a meal."

Rune shook his head and blinked, banishing those warm, ticklish, disturbing thoughts. Kaelyn was a menace! She was bossy, she had dragged him from his home, and besides—he had Tilla. He had sworn to find her someday; he would stick to that vow.

They sat on her bed and ate a cold dinner. Rune wanted to demand more answers: about Valien, about this shattered palace, about what they planned next. But weariness tugged him so strongly he could barely chew his meal. When they were done eating, Kaelyn nudged him off the bed.

"Go on," she said. "There's a nice comfortable floor for you. I'm not sharing my bed with you yet."

"Yet?" he asked.

She gave him another one of her famous glares. "Not ever, but I thought that, for tonight, I'd give you just a bit of hope to help you sleep." A wan smile touched her lips, and she mussed his hair. "Get some sleep, Rune. Tomorrow we continue the fight."

When he lay on the floor, wrapped in his cloak, he looked up to see Kaelyn lying in the bed. She pulled a blanket over her and wriggled. A moment later, she kicked her leggings and tunic outside the bed, letting them drop to the floor.

Rune swallowed.

She's naked under that blanket, he thought, and again his blood began to boil. Stars, he could imagine her body there, warm and lithe and—

Stop it, he told himself. He turned away from the bed, so that he lay facing the wall. He closed his eyes and thought about Tilla instead. He remembered all those times they had walked along the beach, whispering or just walking silently. He remembered their kiss. He remembered her smooth, black hair that fell to her chin, and her dark eyes, and the rarity of her smile.

We will walk along that beach again, Tilla, he thought.

Sleep found him, and he dreamed of her at his side, sand under his feet, and waves under starlight.

TILLA

Tilla wasn't sure how she ended up being the standard-bearer.

Arriving in Castra Luna that morning—stars, it seemed like ages ago!—she had wanted to keep a low profile. This was hard enough to do with her height; she towered above the other girls. Now, marching ahead of the Black Rose Phalanx, bearing its standard while shouting out time, she stuck out like, well... like a tall, awkward girl in ill-fitting leather, shouting while waving around a huge banner.

It was night, but even that didn't help conceal her; braziers and torches crackled across the fortress grounds, their light falling upon her. Tilla sighed.

"Three, two, one!" she yelled, marching ahead of the other recruits. Their boots thudded behind hers in unison.

She hefted her standard; the damn thing was damn heavy. The pole rose ten feet tall. Upon its crest rose an iron rose inside a ring—sigil of the Black Rose Phalanx.

And of Nairi's house, Tilla thought sourly as she called cadence. Tilla herself was a commoner, her surname merely her trade, and she had no fine sigil of her own. Yet Nairi Blackrose was the daughter of nobles, and she bore the dark rose upon her breastplate, her sword, and now upon her phalanx.

Tilla looked over at Nairi. The young lanse alternated between marching ahead of the phalanx, leading its way around the fort, and falling back to inspect the marching troops. Her narrowed eyes stared at every thudding boot. Whenever a single soldier stepped out of time, Nairi swooped in, lashed her punisher, and a scream rose.

"You will learn to march as one!" Nairi shouted. "Or I will burn it into you."

Tilla kept calling time and marching. The standard was so heavy her arms ached, but she dared not lower it; the one time she had let it dip, Nairi's punisher had driven into her ribs.

I'm nothing but a tool to serve her, Tilla thought, watching the young noblewoman.

She wondered if commoners could ever rise in the Legions' ranks. Upon her shoulders, Nairi wore the red spirals of an officer, but she was nobleborn. Every lowborn soldier Tilla had known—back home and here in Castra Luna—only wore red stars on armbands; they fought and died, but did not command.

Could I become an officer too? Tilla wondered. *Could lowborn wear red spirals, or does my common blood doom me to a life of obeying orders and suffering the burns of punishers?*

She didn't know. Yet as she kept shouting—"Three, two, one!"—Tilla vowed that if commoners *could* rise somehow, she would find the way.

I will not serve as Nairi's standard-bearer forever.

As they marched, Tilla got to see more of Castra Luna. It was a sprawling complex, larger than she had first thought. They passed by the armory, a smithy where hammers rang, kitchens pumping smoke from a dozen chimneys, towering walls where dragons perched, and barracks of mossy bricks.

As they walked, Tilla wondered which building she would live in. They passed many structures, some squat and dank, others rising tall and topped with towers. Soldiers moved behind their windows. How many would share her room, and would her bed be clean, and would she have a little space to herself? Like it or not, this would be her home for several moons of training. Every building they passed, Tilla looked up nervously and wondered: *Will I be living in this one?*

Nairi led them toward a towering wall. Dragons stood upon its battlements between cannons. Oaken doors stood open in an archway, revealing a forest of barren trees and shadows. Patches of snow covered the forest floor, and a lone coyote fled, eyes golden in the night.

We're leaving the fort, Tilla realized and her stomach sank. As bad as Castra Luna was, she did not relish time in that dark forest. Beyond the gates, the trees creaked and swayed like lecherous old men, their branches hoary with snow. It was a place of shadows and whispers.

Nairi stepped through the gates, and Tilla reluctantly followed into the forest.

"Three, two, one!" she kept shouting, her voice hoarse, and heard her fellow troops marching behind her. She kept her standard raised high.

They left the fortress behind and walked down a gravelly road. Torches lined the roadsides, crackling as snow fell. The trees rose around them, reaching out branches to snag at Tilla's arms. Crows circled and cawed above. Cold wind blew, fluttering wisps of snow around her boots.

The road curved ahead. Nairi led them around the bend, and when Tilla followed, her stomach sank even further.

So here is my new home, she realized.

A great clearing lay ahead, nearly as large as the fortress grounds. Dozens of tents rose here, their cloth black and unadorned. A palisade of sharpened logs surrounded the camp, and troops patrolled it. Between the tents, more recruits marched and shouted in reply to barking officers.

It was harder than ever to hold up her standard. Tilla had not hoped for much—a roof over her head, walls around her, and a fireplace for the cold nights. Here, it seemed, she would have none of those.

Nairi led them through the camp, and Tilla looked around. Hundreds—maybe thousands—of recruits marched around her. Tilla recognized some faces from Cadport; other recruits were strangers, probably drafted from other towns. All these faces were pale, their lips blue and shivering, their breath frosting. Finally, after walking across half the camp, Nairi led her phalanx to a long black tent. It was barely larger than the cart that had brought them here.

"Halt!" Nairi barked.

Tilla slammed her standard down and her boots together. Behind her, her fellow recruits froze.

"Form ranks!" Nairi shouted. "Move it, maggots."

Tilla stepped back, still holding her standard. She formed ranks along with her fellow troops. Mae and Erry, her flight crew, fell in line behind her. Boots thumped down, and ninety-nine troops stood still and stiff.

Nairi nodded in satisfaction.

"This will be your home until spring," she said. "You will keep this tent clean. You will keep yourselves neat. You will all partake in guard duty, at least an hour a night—every one of you. Do you understand?"

"Yes, Commander!" they shouted together.

Nairi nodded. "You are my soldiers now. You will make me proud. You will keep your swords oiled. You will keep your boots polished. You will keep your armor neat, your fingernails clipped, your hair tied or braided, your bodies clean and groomed. I will inspect you every morning before dawn. If any of you break these rules..." She drew her punisher and raised its crackling head. "...you will taste this. Do you understand?"

They shouted their understanding.

"Good," Nairi said. She looked them over, one by one. "This is the Black Rose Phalanx. This is *my* phalanx. That means you will become the finest troops in this fortress—in the entire

Legions. If any of you let me down, I will personally slice you open and drink your blood." She snarled. "You will find rations and supplies in your tent. I suggest you get some food and sleep. I will be back before dawn, and your training will begin."

With that, Nairi shifted into a dragon, took flight, and crashed past the forest canopy and into the sky. She disappeared into the night.

Everybody started talking at once.

"Pig's puke, what a royal pain in the arse that Nairi is!" Erry exclaimed and spat.

"Do you mean... we have to live here in the forest?" said Mae and whimpered. "I don't *want* to live here. I'm scared."

Other recruits were talking about seeing the prince, or how older relatives had served in Castra Luna too, or how Nairi was the daughter of Herin Blackrose himself, lord of the Axehand Order. A dozen other conversations rustled like leaves.

Tilla did not feel like talking. This had been the longest day of her life. Her muscles ached and her belly cramped with hunger; she could not remember the last time she'd eaten.

"Come on, girls," she said to Mae and Erry. "You're my flight crew; stay with me and let's find some food."

She stepped into the tent, and one by one, the other Black Rose recruits followed.

At first Tilla wondered if this was the wrong tent. There were no beds here, no chairs or tables, nothing but a great wooden chest and a few blankets on the ground. With a sigh, she realized she'd miss the wooden walls of the cart.

"Tilla," Mae said and sniffed back tears. "Tilla, where are the beds?"

"I don't think there are any," she replied, and surprising herself, she placed an arm around the baker's daughter. "Come on, let's see if there's food at least."

Erry beat them to it. She leaped toward the chest in the center, lifted its lid, and whooped.

"Battle rations!" she said with a grin. She pulled out bundles of leather and began tossing them toward the others.

Mae and Tilla grabbed a bundle each, unwrapped them, and found a wafer, a wheel of cheese, and a strip of dry meat. Tilla had not eaten all day, and this was not nearly enough; it was barely worthy of two bites.

"Not bad!" Erry said, slumped down to the ground, and began chewing on her meat, looking like some wild dog gnawing a bone. "Bit chewy. I've had worse."

Mae glared at the waif through her tears. "Of course you've had worse! You... you just used to live along the docks at Cadport. You probably lived off fishbones and garbage. But I was a baker." She sniffed at her wafer. "I can't eat this." She grimaced at her dried meat. "And I don't eat animals either."

"Well, starve then, Wobble Lips!" Erry said. "We'll be rid of your whining, at least." She stuffed the cheese into her mouth and chewed lustfully.

The rest of the phalanx, ninety-nine of Cadport's young women, sat on the ground and began to eat.

"Make some room," Tilla said to Erry, nudging the urchin aside with her boot.

When Erry had squirmed over, Tilla sat beside her and began to eat too. Even Mae, sniffing tears, finally sat down and nibbled a few bites. With everyone seated, they covered the tent floor; a mouse would've had no room to scurry between them.

"I miss home," Mae said. She leaned her head against Tilla's shoulder. "Tilla, do you remember home?"

Tilla laughed. "We haven't been gone a moon yet. Of course I remember home."

"Do you remember the smell of baking bread from my bakery?" Mae inhaled through her nostrils as if she could smell it.

"I do. And I remember your shop too, Tilla. My father bought a rope there once. Oh—and do you remember the Old Wheel?" Light filled Mae's eyes. "I remember how we used to sing there sometimes—you know, the old songs of Requiem. Jem and I used to sing together, and..." Tears filled her eyes. "Oh Tilla... he just... he just died like that, in the forest, alone."

Tilla felt ice trickle down her spine, and guilt rose through her belly. She had been rolling her eyes at Mae all day, but of course the girl was teary; Beras had butchered her lover not days ago.

"Oh Mae," she whispered, pulled the baker's daughter into an embrace, and smoothed her hair. "Do you know what the old priests used to say?"

Mae sniffed and shook her head. "What did they say?"

Tilla held the girl close. "That when we Vir Requis die, our souls rise to the Draco constellation. A starlit palace rises there, the columns all white and glowing. The souls of our fallen drink, sing, and dine there forever." She kissed Mae's cheek. "Jem is there now, Mae, and he's at peace."

Mae looked up with teary eyes, holding Tilla and trembling. "Really?"

Tilla nodded. "Really. I promise."

"I like that." Mae closed her eyes, leaned against Tilla, and mumbled. "Thank you, Tilla. I'm sorry for crying so much. I'll be a good soldier. I promise. Just don't let me go yet."

Tilla nodded and kept stroking the girl's hair. When she looked to her other side, she saw Erry watching them. For once, the scrawny dock rat had no quip or smirk, and ghosts filled her eyes.

Erry chewed her lip for a moment, looked down, and suddenly blurted out, "My father wasn't really a dockhand."

Tilla turned toward her; the girl was furiously staring at her feet, her face was pale, and her fists were clenched.

"Erry," Tilla said softly, "you don't have t—"

"He was just a sailor!" Erry said, and now her eyes dampened, and she blinked them madly and punched her thighs. "He wasn't even *Vir Requis*. He was some... some soldier from southern Tiranor—my mother didn't even know his name—and... he paid for my mother at the docks. She was a prostitute, Tilla." Erry looked up, tears in her eyes. "I just lied to people. I didn't want them to know. I was ashamed of my mother and my mixed blood. I'm nothing but... but a bastard, halfbreed, whore's daughter!"

Mae gasped, eyes wide.

"Oh, Erry, that's all right..." Tilla said and tried to embrace her, but Erry shoved her off.

"I don't need no hugs!" Erry knuckled her eyes. "And I don't need no stinking pity. I'm strong. I've been strong and fighting all my life on the docks. I'm just... a little less strong here. But like it or not, we're stuck in this damn place now, and three of us already died, and... I just need to be honest here. I need to tell the truth, at least to you and Wobble Lips." A crooked grin managed to creep through her tears. "But just to you two, so don't go telling anyone else, or I'll shove my sword so far up your bottoms, I'll use the blade to clean your teeth."

Mae scrunched up her face. "Oh, Erry, that mouth of yours. It's horrible."

Erry opened that mouth wide and stuck out her tongue at Mae. Then, with a mischievous gleam, she grabbed Tilla's arm.

"Now what about you, Roper?" Erry grinned at her. "While we're all sharing secrets, what's yours?"

Tilla laughed. "My secrets? I have none."

"Everybody has secrets," Mae said. "I can't believe I'm doing this, but I'm agreeing with Erry. Tell us, Tilla!" She tugged at Tilla's other arm. "Tell us your big secret."

"Secret! Secret! Secret!" Erry chanted, bouncing up and down on her bottom.

"All right, all right!" Tilla said, laughing. "Settle down first." The two girls fell silent and stared with eager eyes like puppies awaiting treats. Tilla continued. "Do you remember Rune Brewer?"

Erry gasped. "You... you bedded Rune Brewer!" She began to laugh hysterically. "Did the boy even know where to stick it?"

"Erry, your mouth!" Mae scolded, then turned back toward Tilla. "Oh, Tilla, did you... really?"

"No, no!" Tilla held up her hands. "I just kissed him, that's all." She sighed. "It was the night before we were drafted. On the beach by Ralora Cliffs."

"So..." Erry said slowly, "he didn't know where to stick it."

Tilla roared and shoved her, and Mae squealed, and soon all three were shoving one another and laughing.

In the distance, the clock tower of Castra Luna chimed. Tilla fell silent, cocked her head, and listened. The tower was far, and soldiers still talked around her, but she managed to count twelve chimes.

"Midnight," she said and stretched. "This has, quite officially, been the longest day of my life. What say we get some sleep, girls? I have a feeling tomorrow will be just as long."

Tilla wriggled out of her new armor, breathing in relief as her body was freed from the tight, hard leather. She grabbed a blanket, wrapped it around her, and lay down. The blanket stank, and mold spread across it; at once Tilla's skin and throat began to itch. And yet she was so tired, sleep tugged at her at once. All around, the other soldiers were lying down to sleep too, pressed together like snakes in a pit.

"Goodnight, Erry," Tilla whispered. "Goodnight, Mae."

The two were already sleeping beside her, wrapped in their own moldy, tattered blankets. Ignoring her itching skin, Tilla closed her eyes and slept.

"Wake up, girls!" shouted a voice. "Damn it—guard duty! We ain't staying up all night waiting for you."

Tilla opened her eyes, blinked, and vaguely heard the distant clock tower chime again. Was it morning already? No, it was still dark. She counted only a single chime.

"It's one in the morning!" Erry mumbled beside her, wrapped in her blanket. "Frothy griffin snot, who's making that racket? By the emperor's hairy arse, I'm going to cut out their tongue."

Tilla rose, rubbed her eyes, and saw a young recruit—he wore no insignia upon his leather armor—standing at the tent entrance. She had seen his face in Cadport—he was a grocer's son—but she couldn't remember his name.

"Come on!" the young man called. "You girls going to get up, or do I have to walk around kicking?"

Tilla rose to her feet, realized she was wearing nothing but her underclothes, and wrapped her blanket around her.

"What are you on about?" she demanded. "Get lost before I do my own kicking."

He pointed at her. "Wear your damn armor, not a blanket. This is the Black Rose Phalanx, right? It's your guard-duty shift. You walk around the camp palisade three times, then wake up Red Blade Phalanx." He grumbled. "There are bloody siragis patrolling all over this place, so don't think of weaseling out. They got punishers. Now put on some damn armor!"

With that, the grocer's son turned and left the tent.

Bloody siragis. Tilla cursed. She had heard of these soldiers before; veterans back in Cadport would mutter about them. The sons of commoners, they wore three red stars upon their armbands, denoting several years of service. The siragis didn't have the noble blood for command; they were the officers' pet brutes. Tilla's body still ached from the wounds Nairi, a young woman like herself, had given her. She did not relish a confrontation with the siragis, hardened warriors.

"All right, you heard him!" Tilla said and clapped her hands. "Into your armor, grab your swords—quickly."

A moment later, the Black Roses emerged from their tent, tugging on boots and buckling swords to waists. When Tilla blinked in the night, she saw a men's phalanx outside their tent. Its soldiers were dropping bulging sacks; they thudded onto the ground.

"What the Abyss are those?" Tilla demanded.

The young grocer scowled. "Cannonballs," he said. "You carry them around the palisade."

"We what?"

"Three walkarounds!" he said, then showed her his arm; a welt rose across it. "If you drop your sack, the bloody siragis burn you. The bastards are patrolling all over the place."

His phalanx, ninety-nine young men of Cadport, turned and limped back to their tent, rubbing their shoulders and cursing. Ninety-nine sacks lay on the ground.

"Oh, piss and blood!" Erry said, trying to lift a sack. "Thing weighs more than I do."

Tilla peered into a sack. It held three cannonballs, each one nearly as large as her head. She lifted the sack with both hands. She grunted, slung it across her back, and nearly collapsed. The sack must have indeed weighed more than Erry. The other Black Roses were lifting their own sacks and cursing.

When Tilla stared ahead at the palisade, she saw the siragis standing there, watching. There were three of them, tall and burly men in black steel. Upon their arms, their three red stars gleamed in the torchlight. Their punishers crackled in their hands. Tilla shuddered. These men craved to burn flesh; she felt their bloodlust like heat waves.

"I can't... carry this!" Mae said, wobbling under her sack. Her sword swung between her legs like a tail.

"Oh, come on!" Tilla said and began walking, the sack across her back. "Three loops and we can get back to sleep. Black Rose! Follow me. Three, two, one!"

She began to march, gritting her teeth. Her back screamed under the weight. Her boots drove deep into mud. She reached the palisade that surrounded the camp, hefted the sack, and began her first loop. Her fellow Black Roses groaned and cursed and walked behind her.

"This isn't fair!" Mae said, jaw clenched as she trudged forward. "Why do we have to carry the same weight as the boys? They should make it lighter for the girls."

Erry spat and glared. "Dog dung. I can carry just as much as any boy."

Mae moaned. "Why do we need to carry cannons balls on patrol anyway? It's not like we even have cannons here! What, if an enemy attacks, are we to toss these balls at them?"

"You could just whine them to death," Erry said. The poor slight girl—the smallest one in the Black Rose—was wobbling and barely trudging forward. "Shag-a-dog, these things are heavy."

"Language!" Mae said, then squealed as she slipped.

Tilla could not guess the diameter of the palisade, nor how long it took to complete the first round. All she knew was: By the time they started their second round, her legs howled with agony, her toes felt ready to crack, and her spine creaked. She had to rest. She had to stop for just a moment—to catch her breath, to find some water, to let her heartbeat slow.

She paused for just a moment, let the sack fall, and wiped sweat off her brow.

Shadows leaped.

A siragi, burly and clanking in armor, lunged toward her. His punisher lashed out. Tilla cursed and leaped back, trying to dodge the weapon, but was too slow. The punisher drove into her side, and lightning shot across her. She screamed.

"Keep moving!" the soldier barked and pulled his punisher back, leaving Tilla's armor smoking. "Damn it, you stop again, I'll burn every last inch of skin off your flesh."

Tilla gasped and shook. "I—"

He raised his punisher again.

Heart thudding and fingers trembling, Tilla grabbed the sack of cannons balls, hefted it over her back, and began her second patrol.

Behind her, the other Black Roses trudged along, no longer speaking. Tilla heard only grunting, wheezing, and the odd whimper. She wanted to talk to her friends, but had no breath for words. She kept walking, step by step, inch by inch. All around in the camp, the other troops slept in their tents. Tilla envied them more than she had ever envied anyone else. Sleep—pure, beautiful sleep—was now her greatest lost love, greater than Rune, greater than her father, greater than home.

By the time she finished her second round, she was limping. Her back twisted, and her shoulders felt ready to dislocate. Sweat drenched her, and her throat blazed with thirst; she could not remember the last time she had drunk. It felt like every bone in her feet had cracked. When she looked over her shoulder, she saw the others looking the way she felt; their faces were pale, their hair damp with sweat, their lips tightened.

She wanted to rest, but the siragis raised their punishers. Tilla grunted and began her third round.

Pain.

Pain leaped through her bones and ground her spine.

Pain twisted her feet, clutched at her chest, and burned through her lungs.

Behind her, she heard a soldier fall, then smelled smoke as punishers burned flesh. Tilla turned to help the girl rise; punishers thrust her way too, and Tilla screamed. She kept walking, sack slung over her back. Step by step. Inch by inch.

Think only about every new step, she told herself, sweat blinding her eyes. *Don't think about anything else; just the next step, one after the other, and it'll be over.*

When finally the nightmare ended and the Black Rose completed its third round, Tilla's head spun. She dropped her sack to the ground, doubled over, and felt fire racing through her bones. The other Black Roses gathered around her, bedraggled and drenched in sweat.

"Come on, girls," Tilla said and wiped her brow. "Let's drag these sacks to the next phalanx and get some sleep."

Finally—it must have been close to two in the morning—Tilla lay back in her moldy blanket. She was too tired to even itch now. Everything hurt. Vaguely, she saw the other Black Roses collapse around her.

There are still a few hours until morning, she thought. *If I can only get a good, solid five or six hours of sleep, I...*

Her thoughts trailed off.

Sleep welcomed her into a deep, black embrace.

"On your feet!" The shout pierced the night. "Black Rose Phalanx—inspection! Form ranks!"

Tilla blinked. Her muscles cramped. Her bones ached. Somebody was shouting at the tent entrance. When Tilla rubbed her eyes, she thought that she saw Nairi there, a torch in her hand. Darkness still covered the world.

"Hairy horse dung," Erry cursed at her side, sitting up. The clock tower began to chime in the distance, and Erry counted on her fingers, then cursed. "It's only four in the morning!"

Nairi was still shouting. "Out, Black Roses—morning inspection! Move!"

The recruits stood up and shivered. Tilla's teeth chattered. It felt cold enough to freeze liquor.

"Armor!" Nairi screamed. "Swords! *Move!*"

The Black Roses moved in a daze, strapping on armor with numb fingers. Swords rattled and pale, numbed feet thrust into boots. They stumbled out into the darkness, ninety-nine souls half frozen, eyes blurred and breath fogging. Outside the tent, they formed ranks and stood shivering.

Nairi stared at them in disgust. Her torch crackled in her hand.

"Pathetic," she said and spat. "If we were under attack, you'd be dead by now." She began to pace along the lines, staring at each recruit as if staring at flies upon her dinner plate. "Buckles unstrapped. Boots covered in mud. Half of you are missing your helmets. Not a single sword is oiled." Her voice rose to a howl. "You are a disgrace!"

Standing behind Tilla, Erry muttered under her breath. "That woman needs a few cannonballs dropped onto her head."

Nairi did not hear, but kept pacing along the lines, cursing.

"Not one of you is properly armed and ready. I thought of letting you eat dinner today. I thought of letting you sleep a full five hours next night." She shouted so loudly her face turned red. "You will eat nothing, and I will let you sleep only three hours next night, and this will continue until you can pass morning inspection!"

Erry muttered again. "Next night? Morning? Tonight? I have no idea when's what and who's who. Is it morning or night now? Bloody stars."

"Shh!" Tilla said; Nairi was marching back toward them.

"Back into your tent!" the lanse shouted. "You have one minute. I want to see a proper inspection now—boots shining and swords oiled. Go, go!"

Nairi waved her torch, showering sparks and goading the recruits back into the tent. Outside, the lanse counted down the seconds. Inside, the recruits rummaged through the chest for oil. Finally—it must have been several minutes—they stumbled back outside.

"Second inspection!" Nairi shouted. "You are late. You have failed. You will not sleep for *two* more nights. Go, back inside! One minute. Again!"

Tilla sighed.

With pain and darkness and bitter cold, her second day at Castra Luna began.

KAELYN

She entered his chamber, her fingertips tingling and her throat tight. She took a deep breath, steeled herself, and spoke softly.

"Valien?" Her voice shook. "Valien, it's me."

He sat hunched before a hearth, his back to her. The firelight outlined his form but left him in shadow. He said nothing. He did not move. He could as well have been a statue.

Kaelyn sighed. Valien was in one of his moods again. Lately these dark spells had been coming more frequently. When they hit, Valien could brood here for hours, eating little, drinking much, and try as she might, Kaelyn could shine no light into his darkness.

It was a small room, hardly the chamber of a great warrior. In the stories Kaelyn's father told, the cruel Valien Eleison sat upon a throne of bones, commanded a hall of demons, and drank from goblets of children's blood. But this chamber was no larger than Kaelyn's own. Half the shelves bore books: ancient bestiaries, histories, and epic poems. The other shelves bore jugs of the spirits he drank, overpowering rye that made Kaelyn's eyes water and Valien's memories fade.

In Kaelyn's chamber, she kept a painting of her mother, the dearest woman she had known. Valien too had lost someone, yet no memories of that woman were allowed in this chamber. No paintings. No mementos. Just mentioning Marilion, his fallen wife, was enough to send Valien so deep into darkness he would not emerge for days.

"Valien," she tried again. "We must discuss the boy."

Still facing the fire, Valien grunted. "He is not who I thought he was."

Kaelyn gasped. "Valien! You said he's the spitting image of King Aeternum. You said—"

"I know what I said." His voice was raspier than ever, the death croak of a hanging man. He turned toward her, eyes red in the firelight. "He is the flesh and blood of Aeternum, that much is true. But he's not who I thought he was. He's not strong like his father. He's not brave. He's not wise." Valien grumbled. "The boy is a fool."

Kaelyn sighed. "He is young."

"So are you." Valien reached for a mug and took a swig of rye. "You're eighteen. You're his age, or only a year older." He snorted. "I was eighteen when I first joined the Legions, then the knighthood soon after. Yet this one..." He drank again. "Rune Brewer is nothing but a spoiled, soft city boy."

"He's not yet been hardened," Kaelyn agreed. "But I traveled with him for ten days. He knew where he was going. He stayed with me." She took a step forward and held Valien's shoulder. "That shows some strength. He will learn. Teach him."

Valien leaped to his feet so violently he knocked his chair back. It clanged to the ground, and Kaelyn started.

"The boy will not learn." Valien paced the chamber, teeth bared, face red in the firelight. "The boy brought us death and misery from the first day. I was wrong, Kaelyn. I was wrong to think he could bring the people hope."

He brought his mug to his lips and drank deeply. His cup held strong spirits—Kaelyn had tried a sip once and nearly choked—yet Valien drank down this liquid fire like water.

"Valien!" Kaelyn said. She stepped toward him, held his arm, and lowered the mug from his lips. "Valien, look at me. Please. Listen to me."

He looked at her. His eyes were wild and bloodshot. In them Kaelyn saw his pain, his memories, and his loss.

When he looks at me, she knew, *he sees her. She too was eighteen. She was my age when she died. When he looks at me, he sees his wife. When he looks at Rune, he sees the babe he saved while she died.*

He panted, breath raw, and Kaelyn embraced him.

He needs me now, she thought. *He needs me more than he needs Rune. He needs me more than his memories.*

"It's all right, Valien," she whispered into his ear as she held him. "Don't lose hope now. We have more hope than ever before." She touched his cheek. "And I'm with you, as I've been for two years now. I fly at your side—through fire, light, or blood, whichever will fall upon us."

You are weary, she added silently. *You are broken. And you are drunk. But you are our leader, and you are the greatest man I've known. And you will lead us home.*

He wrapped his arms around her, great arms that even now, even here, made Kaelyn feel safe and small; each of those arms was nearly as wide as her body. She laid her head against his chest and felt his heart beat against her cheek.

"I cannot guarantee that he will live," Valien said. "If once more we face the fire, and I must choose between him and another... I cannot guarantee his life."

Kaelyn looked up at him. Those old ghosts circled in his eyes like crows around a gallows tree.

"I know," she whispered. "He might die. So might the rest of us. For now, let him be a beacon of hope to the people. Let him be a torch in the shadow my father cast upon this land." She gave him a twisted smile. "Am I not the same? I'm the daughter of the emperor, a voice rising in defiance. Am I too not a symbol for your uprising?"

He grabbed her arms so roughly that she gasped.

"You are more than a symbol, Kaelyn." He snarled at her. "You are a bright blade. You are a lioness. You are—"

"—the daughter of Emperor Frey Cadigus," she said. "I am a statement and a banner of rebellion. Rune will be one too. You lead us, Valien Eleison, and you will lead us to victory. But the people... the people will rally around Rune." It was her turn to snarl. "I fly at your right-hand side. Let Rune fly at your left. Together—the last knight of Requiem, the daughter of Cadigus, and the son of Aeternum—we will topple this regime, kill my father, and place Rune on the throne."

Valien turned away from her. He walked to the hearth, placed his great hand—wide as a bear paw—against the mantel. He looked into the flames, head lowered.

"If I have to choose again, Kaelyn... if I..."

His voice died, and Kaelyn felt her eyes water. Valien rarely spoke about that night, but Kaelyn had heard the tales whispered in countless taverns and halls. Seventeen years ago, when Frey Cadigus had stormed the capital and slain the royal family, Valien had fought him; he still bore the scar of Frey's blade across his chest. That night, Kaelyn knew, Frey had given him a choice. Valien had but moments to flee before more of Frey's troops swarmed the palace—just long enough to save the babe, the last heir of Aeternum... or to save Marilion, his young wife.

Valien fled the palace that night with a babe in his arms.

His wife burned.

Tears stung Kaelyn's eyes, and she approached her leader, embraced him from behind, and laid her head against his back.

"You will not have to choose," she whispered.

He spun toward her, teeth bared, cheeks flushed red. He clenched his fists.

"When fire rises, we will all burn!" he said, eyes blazing like a rabid animal's. He clutched Kaelyn's arms, and his voice rose into a torn howl. "I will not lose you! I will not see you burn, Marilion, I—"

Kaelyn gasped and stared silently.

Valien's eyes widened. He shut his mouth. His face whitened. He looked aside and blinked and his fists trembled.

"I've had enough to drink this night," he rasped. "Leave me, Kaelyn. Leave me."

She touched his cheek with trembling fingers, and tears filled her eyes. "Valien—"

"Leave me!" he roared, waved his arms, and tossed his mug across the room. It smashed against a shelf, and more mugs fell and shattered, and Kaelyn turned away. She fled the room, eyes stinging and legs trembling.

RUNE

They flew in the night, a black and green dragon, two shadows under the clouds.

As Rune glided, the cold wind felt heavenly in his nostrils. Whenever he went only a few days without flying, the magic tingled inside him, and he lashed out, grumbled, and felt as if ants were crawling through his bones. He would fly with Tilla many nights above the water.

And now I fly with Kaelyn.

He looked at her. She flew to his right, the hint of fire in her nostrils like two embers. She gave him a sad smile and tapped him with her tail.

"What did you want to show me out here?" he asked.

"Be patient!" she said. "I'm taking you there. And be quiet; imperial dragons still patrol these skies."

They glided silently. Forests and plains streamed below and clouds hid the stars. Dragon eyes were sharp—sharper than his human eyes—but Rune could barely see more than smudges in this darkness. Some distant lights shone—fortified outposts of the Regime—but otherwise the land lay in shadow and mist. A drizzle began to fall, and Rune allowed just a little more fire to fill his belly, crackle in his mouth, and warm him.

He tried to imagine that these forests below, rolling shadows in the night, were the waves back at home, that those distant lights were Cadport waiting on the shore. He missed those waves. He missed the cobbled boardwalk with its shops, rusted cannon, and Tilla walking beside him. He missed the Old Wheel, he missed Scraggles, and he missed his father.

I miss home, he thought. But what was his home now? And who was his father? Rune did not know, and so many questions still burned inside him like the fire. As he glided through shadow and rain, ice filled his belly along with the flames. He looked at Kaelyn, and she met his gaze, and he saw the same sadness in her eyes.

"There," she said and gestured below. "There's an old ruined temple on the hill. Do you see it?"

Rune squinted. He could discern only vague shapes in this darkness. He thought he saw pale columns, some only broken stems, rising upon a hilltop.

"A temple," he said. "An old temple to Requiem's stars."

Kaelyn nodded and began diving toward it. "It *was* a temple. Priests used to worship the Draco constellation here. My father..." Kaleyn sighed. "He didn't like that."

Rune descended beside her. Wind and rain stung his face. A temple of marble columns had once stood in Cadport; Rune had heard the city elders whisper of it in awe. They said priests and healers would play harps there, sing to the Draco stars, and bless the city. Today that temple was a courthouse, its walls draped with banners of the red spiral, its marble columns stained with blood.

But there was no use for a courthouse here in the wilderness, and as Rune descended toward the ruins, he marveled at the columns. Their marble shone like moonlight. Some columns lay shattered upon the hillside, but others still stood, forming a rectangle. The roof they had once supported had fallen; its bricks lay strewn across the grass, pale lumps in the night.

The two dragons landed upon wet grass. Above them loomed the temple columns, two hundred feet tall at least. Rune tried to imagine this temple standing in its glory days—back when the Aeternum Dynasty had ruled. He could almost see priests' white robes fluttering between the columns, almost hear their harps.

When he looked above, Rune gasped to see the clouds part. The Draco constellation shone between them, the holy stars of Requiem.

"Our people used to worship these stars," he said softly. "My father would pray to them at night. He thought I couldn't hear. Many of Cadport's elders would still pray secretly, knowing that if any soldiers heard, they would be broken upon the wheel. Do you think those stars have any real power, Kaelyn?"

She stood at his side, a slim green dragon, and watched the constellation with him. The starlight glimmered on her wet scales.

"I've never doubted it," she said. "My father hates those stars. How he would rail against them! He would shout that these stars had never protected Requiem, that under their light, so many of our people died. He claimed that only he could defend this land, that only he was worthy of being called godly, not some lights in the heavens." Kaelyn blasted smoke from her nostrils. "Anything he hates so much must have power, Rune. And so I believe."

She shifted into human form. The rain dampened her hair, and her clothes clung to her. She smiled, spread out her arms, and twirled in a circle.

"Oh, you're one of those horrible people who loves dancing in the rain, aren't you?" Rune said.

He shifted into human form too, then hugged himself as the rain chilled him. Grinning, Kaelyn grabbed his hand.

"Dance with me," she said. "Join us horrible people for one night."

He tried to tug his hand free. "Bloody stars, Kaelyn, did we fly all the way here for this—to dance in the rain? I'm cold and wet."

"Poor baby." She pouted at him, then grinned again. "The stars shine between the clouds! The old priests would always dance when rain and stars met."

She began to skip around him, tugging his arm.

"You made that up," he said.

Yet she was tugging his hand too powerfully—damn it, the girl was strong for her size!—forcing him to spin around.

"Come on!" she said and danced around him, the rain drenching her. "It's fun."

He sighed and gave a quick, sarcastic jig. "Happy?"

"Not nearly enough." She placed both arms around him and pressed her body against his. "Just... do like this. Sway a bit. That will be an easier dance for your clumsy feet. Now go on! Put your hands on my waist—like this. Don't stand there like a block of wood!"

She grabbed his hands and placed them against her waist. Rune held her awkwardly. Even through her cold, wet tunic, he felt the heat of her body. She placed her arms around him, laid her head against his shoulder, and swayed gently. Her hair smelled of grass and flowers.

Rune rolled his eyes and allowed himself to sway with her.

"This is hardly the time to dance," he said. "Not here in the rain and darkness."

She looked up at him. "It's always time to dance, especially in the darkness."

Fast as a squirrel after a nut, she broke apart from him, grabbed his hand, and tugged him.

"Now come on!" she said. "I want to show you something. Follow me. Come *on!*"

She laughed and tugged him toward the temple columns. With a sigh, he allowed himself to be pulled. They leaped over a fallen column and raced between two standing ones, entering the ruins of the temple. Only the moon and stars, shining between gaps in the clouds, lit their way.

Bricks and shattered columns littered the grass here, lumps of white upon black. Kaelyn scurried around the ruins like a dog seeking a scent. Finally she approached the fallen capital of a column, its marble carved as leaping dragons, and tapped the ground with her boot.

"Here!" she said, leaned down, and pulled a rope from the grass. She tugged open a trapdoor.

"Another gopher hole," Rune said.

Kaelyn smiled. "My favorite one."

They walked down a rough, wooden staircase and into a chamber. Kaelyn scurried around the room, lighting candles that stood upon shelves. Orange light fell upon jars of preserves, jugs of wine, racks of swords and bows, and...

Rune gasped.

"It's... me?"

Upon one wall hung a painting, life-sized, of himself clad like a king. Rune rubbed his eyes and stared. His doppelganger wore a crown, a green cloak embroidered with silver birch leaves, and a golden broach shaped as a two-headed dragon—sigil of House Aeternum. The painted king held a wide longsword, its dragonclaw pommel clutching polished amber the size of a chicken egg.

It's Amerath, Rune realized. *The Amber Sword.* It had been the sword of the Aeternum kings for a hundred years.

Kaelyn came to stand beside him. She placed a hand on his shoulder.

"You look just like him," she said.

Rune tore his eyes away from the painting. He frowned at Kaelyn.

"What kind of joke is this?" he said.

She smiled sadly. "This used to hang in the royal palace. You gaze upon Ardin Aeternum, King of Requiem, the man my father slew." She looked at Rune. "Your father."

Rune could not believe it. Could not! Surely Kaelyn had found some painter to trick him, or used dark magic, or... Rune clutched his head. Wil Brewer was his father! The Old Wheel was his home! He was only a brewer, not a prince, not...

"Oh stars," he whispered.

Kaelyn approached a rack of weapons. A dozen swords hung there, the rough and simple blades of soldiers. Among them hung a bundle of green cloth embroidered with silver dragons. Kaelyn lifted the bundle, brought it toward Rune, and held it out.

"It's yours now," she said solemnly. "It's time you raised your father's sword."

Her eyes shone with tears. She pulled back the green fabric, unveiling Amerath, the Amber Sword of Aeternum.

It was the sword from the painting; every detail was the same. The candlelight danced along the black scabbard. The platinum pommel, shaped as a dragonclaw, clutched the amber stone. It was a large sword, at least four feet long, its hilt built for two hands. It looked heavy enough to chop down trees.

To Rune's surprise, Kaelyn knelt before him, holding the sword upon her upturned palms.

"My prince," she whispered.

Rune wanted to laugh. Her prince? Stars, she was an emperor's daughter! Yet he found no mirth upon his lips. Amerath beckoned to him, and Rune reached for the hilt and wrapped his fingers around it. The black leather was warm, soft, and worked in by many hands.

"The kings of Aeternum have wielded this sword for generations," he whispered.

"Draw the blade," Kaelyn said, still kneeling before him. Her tears shone in the candlelight. "Let its light shine in a temple of Requiem."

Rune took a step back. He drew Amerath, and its blade caught the firelight and shone, golden and red and white—a shard of memory and light. Despite its size, the sword was surprisingly light; it felt lighter than the Old Wheel's broom. Rune raised the blade and saw his reflection within. He held it side by side with the painting before him.

My father and me, he thought. *The same face. The same sword. The same blood.*

"It's true," he whispered. "Stars, it's all true, isn't it Kaelyn?"

She rose to her feet. "You loved Wil; I know it. He was a father to you too, more so than the king. This will not diminish your love for Wil Brewer or cheapen your memories of him. But now you have drawn Amerath, the Amber Sword of Requiem. Now the light of Requiem shines again in the darkness."

Rune sheathed the sword.

"Well," he said. "Lovely blade. Lovely painting. I do think I'll need a better cloak now, and maybe some fancy doublet and jewels, but overall, not bad." He looked around. "There's only one more thing missing."

"What's that?" Kaelyn asked

"A chair. I really need to sit down."

He stumbled to the corner, slumped down onto his backside, and leaned against the wall. His head spun, and he clutched it. Kaelyn sat beside him and patted his shoulder.

"No chairs here, but how about a strong drink?" she asked.

"I would *love* a strong drink."

She nodded, rushed to a shelf, and grabbed a bottle. She yanked the cork out with her teeth, sat back beside Rune, and passed him the drink.

"Here," she said. "It'll help."

Rune drank. It was strong rye—southern brew, he thought, possibly even from Cadport. The spirits burned down his throat and through his head. Stars, it felt good. He passed Kaelyn the bottle.

"I think you deserve a drink too."

She took a swig, then wrinkled her nose. "Horrible stuff. I don't know how Valien can drink it."

"It's *fantastic* stuff," Rune said. "And I reckon it's from my hometown or very near it. We would serve this in the Old Wheel." He sighed. "But the Old Wheel is gone now. And Wil is gone. And this sword is here."

Kaelyn leaned over and kissed his cheek. "And I'm here. I'm here to help you, Rune. You're not alone."

His cheek blazed; her kiss shot through him, stronger than the spirits. Rune drank again and Kaelyn leaned against him. He placed his arm around her and found himself stroking her hair— soft, golden hair like silk. Her breath fluttered warm against his neck, and she placed her hand on his thigh. They huddled in the dark and cold, passing the bottle back and forth.

"I don't like any of this," Rune said. "And I never wanted this war. I hold no love for your father, but I never wanted to pick up a sword and fight him. But yes, my home is gone now. My best friend is a soldier, and my family is dead. Like it or not, this is my life now."

"You have a new family," Kaelyn whispered. "You have me, and Valien, and the rest of us. You will never be alone. Will you fly with us?"

She was looking up at him, her eyes large and her lips parted.

"I will fly with you," he said. "I'm no warrior; I don't know how to wield this sword. But I can fly as a dragon and roar fire, and however I can help you, I will, Kaelyn. I will fly by your side."

She smiled tremulously and touched his cheek, and her tears fell.

Rune kissed her. He did not mean to. He did not want to. Yet he stroked her hair, and he kissed her, and her tears mingled in their kiss. It was warm and soft and wet, and it tasted of spirits, and Rune never wanted it to end. He held Kaelyn in his arms, and she was so small, a delicate doll held against him, and at that moment Rune loved her—loved this woman who had dragged him from his home into shadow and fire.

He pulled away from her, leaving her breathing heavily, her cheeks flushed.

I can't, he thought. *I have Tilla. I can't. This is wrong.*

Kaelyn leaned against him, wrapped in his arms, and smiled softly. She closed her eyes and slept in his embrace.

TILLA

Tilla stood in the square, arms pressed to her sides and chin raised. Her helmet topped her head. Her leather armor still squeezed her, so tight she could barely breathe. She kept her fist around the hilt of her sword.

Nairi stood before the phalanx, face twisted like a woman staring at dung upon her boot.

"Listen up, maggots!" the lanse shouted. "You are now divided into flights of three. These flights are your life! In tunnels and halls, you will swing swords in threes. In the skies, you will roar fire as three dragons. Every flight will have one leader—one attacker!—and two defenders. Do you understand?"

"Yes, Commander!" Tilla shouted along with the others.

It was the only acceptable answer, of course. One recruit, only an hour ago, had dared to ask a question. Nairi had driven her punisher into the girl for so long her flesh had cracked.

Flight commanders, Tilla thought and sucked in her breath. She knew that dragons flew in threes—two defending one attacker—but not how the attacker was determined.

I'm going to find out now.

"First flight!" Nairi shouted. "Forward."

Three recruits—those who formed the left flank of the formation—stepped forward. They glanced around nervously and clutched their swords. They were the daughters of farmers; Tilla vaguely remembered them selling eggs, fruits, and grains in harvest fairs. Today they wore armor and bore blades.

Nairi snarled at the farm girls.

"If you ask me, all three of you are worms. You should be squirming under my boots, not standing before me in armor." The lanse raised her voice. "The last one among you standing will eat and sleep tonight! The two who fall first—you will spend the night cleaning the outhouses. Do you understand?"

"Yes, Commander!" the three answered, faces pale.

"Your swords are blunt," Nairi said, "but they will still bruise flesh. Swing them! Last one standing will lead your flight."

The girls glanced at one another, hesitating.

Stars, oh stars, just swing your blades, Tilla thought.

Yet the girls did not move.

With a snarl, Nairi drew her punisher. She drove the crackling rod into one girl.

The recruit screamed. She fell into the dust. Her body convulsed, and Nairi knelt above her, growling and shoving her punisher against the girl's belly. The girl doubled up, weeping and begging and smoking.

Finally, after what seemed like ages, Nairi withdrew her punisher and rose to her feet. She spat onto the fallen girl.

"This one is out," she said. She looked up at the two recruits who still stood. "Go on—fight each other! Or I'll burn another one."

The two recruits swallowed, drew their blunt blades, and began to swing at one another. Steel clanged.

"Faster!" Nairi screamed. "Harder! Beat her bloody."

The steel kept clashing. Finally one girl disarmed the other, slamming blade onto wrist.

"Finish her!" Nairi ordered. "Beat her down."

The armed girl's eyes were damp, yet she obeyed. She swung her blunt sword against her friend's legs, sending her falling.

Nairi spat in disgust. "Useless cockroaches, you are." She snarled at the last girl standing. "You lead your miserable trio of

worms. Drag the other two back to formation." She turned back
to the ranks. "Next flight—you three, forward!"

The next flight stepped forward.

More blades swung.

As Tilla stood, watching each trio fight for leadership, she
heard wings thudding overhead. She looked up to see a red
dragon descend into the square, fire streaming between his teeth.
Tilla sucked in her breath and her heart thrashed.

Prince Leresy.

The dragon landed before the phalanx, shook his head, and
scattered curtains of smoke. He shifted into human form, placed
his hands on his hips, and smiled. His plate armor shone in the
dawn, black steel bedecked with gold. His golden hair shone just
as bright.

Whispers and gasps flowed across the ranks, and Tilla's
heart thudded. Smiling thinly, Prince Leresy stared directly at
her—into her—and winked.

"Hail Prince Leresy!" Nairi shouted and slammed her fist
against her chest. "Kneel before your prince."

Nairi knelt, fist clutched to heart. The rest of her phalanx,
Tilla among them, repeated the salute and knelt too. Tilla kept
her head lowered, daring not look up, but she could feel Leresy
still staring at her.

Stars, why does he look at me among everyone? she thought. She
only wanted to be a good soldier here, to fit in and fly low. And
yet wherever she went, it seemed, she attracted trouble like
flowers attracted bees.

"Back on your feet!" rose his voice; it was smooth and
melodious and still carried the high pitch of youth. "Carry on,
please. I've only come to watch my troops, not interfere."

Tilla made the mistake of glancing back at the prince—just
a glance—and caught him staring at her. His lips peeled back and

he licked his teeth. She looked back at Nairi... just in time to hear the lanse shout her name.

"Tilla Roper!" Nairi pointed her crackling punisher at her. "You and those two dogs of yours—forward! Let's see who among you will sleep tonight, and who will clean nightsoil from a ditch."

Heart pounding, Tilla stepped forward, leaving the formation of her phalanx. The square seemed to spin around her. She felt hundreds of eyes watching her—her fellow recruits, her commander, and her prince. She glanced over her shoulder to see Mae frozen, her face pale, and Erry trying to shove her forward.

"Roper, bring your two whores forward, or you'll taste my fire!" Nairi screamed.

It took some tugging from Tilla, and more pushing from Erry, to bring the trembling Mae out of formation and into the dust of the square. The three recruits stood together, trapped between the rest of their phalanx, Lanse Nairi, and Prince Leresy.

"Draw your swords," Nairi ordered.

Tilla drew her blade. She gave it a few quick swings. It whistled as it sliced the air.

Whenever Tilla had seen soldiers carrying swords— especially wide longswords like this one, their hilts large enough for two hands—she had thought them crude weapons for hacking and slashing. Yet this sword, even blunted, was light and agile. It felt no heavier than waving a sprig of holly. The blade was long and wide but flexible, and despite herself Tilla smiled. For the first time, she thought of soldiers not as brutes hacking with crude chunks of metal, but as artists mastering an ancient dance. At her side, Erry was waving her sword around, slicing the air. The slim girl seemed just as impressed; her eyes shone, and her lips peeled back in a smile. Mae, however, wasn't even testing her blade; she merely held it before her, and it wobbled like her lip.

I think I'll only have one contender here, Tilla thought.

Nairi took a deep breath, opened her mouth, and seemed ready to order the duel start. Before the lanse could speak, however, the prince interrupted.

"A moment," he said, raising his hand.

Again he was looking straight at Tilla, and her heart thudded. He walked toward her, and Tilla stood frozen before him, sword in hand, not sure if to salute, kneel, or simply stand still.

When Prince Leresy reached her, his lips peeled back in a smile, but it looked hungry, the smile of a wolf. His eyes scanned her from top to bottom; they lingered against her breasts, which pressed against her leather armor. He reached out, fast as a viper, and clutched her wrist.

Tilla gasped.

He's going to kill me, she thought. *Stars, I did something wrong, and he's going to kill me now—just like his sister Shari killed the girl back at Cadport.*

But Leresy only turned her wrist, adjusting her grip on the sword.

"Here," he said. "Like this. Hold your right hand a little higher on the hilt. Now place your left hand beneath it near the pommel—like that. Give the blade a swing—from top to bottom."

The prince stepped back, and Tilla dutifully swung her sword. Leresy's face split into a grin, and he clapped.

"Splendid!" he said. "Now here, move your left hand to the base of the blade—just above the hilt. Don't worry, it's not sharp. This is called half-swording—a different grip. Give it a try."

Leresy stepped back again, and Tilla gave the blade a few more swings. Holding the sword this way, her thrusts were shorter but more powerful.

"Good!" Leresy said. "You use this one for piercing armor. A strong soldier can break steel this way. Shorter range but tougher punch."

He stepped toward her again and reached between her legs. Tilla gasped, but Leresy only winked and moved her thighs apart.

"Don't get all flustered," he said. "I'm just fixing your stance. Here, like this—legs parted, right leg forward. Try again! This time strike my blade."

He drew his sword and Tilla's eyes widened. His was a beautiful blade. Its dark steel shone with ripples like midnight waves. Its golden, dragonclaw pommel clutched an egg-sized ruby. Tilla hated to attack such a beautiful weapon—what if she chipped it?—but Leresy beckoned her, and so Tilla swung her blade.

He parried. The two swords rang.

"Excellent!" Leresy said. He slammed his sword back into its scabbard. "What's your name, soldier?"

"Tilla," she said. "Tilla Roper."

Leresy nodded. "I'll remember you."

But there was no pride or kindness in his voice; there was only lust. Tilla had served tables at Rune's tavern when she could not sell enough ropes; she had seen such lust in the eyes of many drunkards.

He cares less for blades of steel, she thought, *and more for the blade between his legs—one he would thrust into me.*

Leresy clutched her shoulder and looked over at Nairi.

"This one is a warrior!" he announced.

Tilla glanced over at her commander... and what she saw chilled her more than Leresy's lust. Pure, blazing fire filled Nairi's eyes. Her cheeks flushed red. Her teeth grinded. She stared at Tilla with a look of such unadulterated hatred that Tilla felt herself blanch.

But... but it's not my fault! she wanted to shout out. *I didn't ask the prince to speak to me, I...*

For the first time, Nairi did not shout. She spoke in a low, venomous hiss, and it seemed to Tilla more cruel than all the screams in the Abyss.

"Let us see the great warrior in action," she said. "Fight!"

Immediately, Erry roared and launched into a wild attack.

Tilla gasped and raised her sword; Erry was charging like an enraged badger disturbed from its den. Yet Tilla parried only air. Erry wasn't attacking her; the diminutive urchin swung her blade against Mae Baker.

Mae squealed. She raised her sword in a useless attempt to parry. Erry's blunt blade slammed against Mae's chest, thudding against the leather armor.

Tears budded in Mae's eyes. She fell to her knees, and her sword thumped into the dust.

"I yield!" she cried and covered her head with her arms. "I yield!"

Roaring, her face red, Erry turned and came charging toward Tilla. Her sword swung in mad arcs.

"Bloody stars!" Tilla cursed and swung her blade.

She had never parried a sword before; she had to learn fast. Her blade checked Erry's onslaught. The short, brown-haired girl barely seemed fazed. She leaped back, then charged again, thrusting her sword. All around, the other troops gasped and a few cheered.

Tilla parried again. *Stars damn it!* Erry was no taller than her shoulders, yet the little beast seemed unstoppable. Her blows kept flying. It was like a rabid rodent attacking a wolf.

The blades clanged. Erry screamed. Her sword swung. The blade slammed down onto Tilla's shoulder.

Pain exploded. Erry's sword was blunt, and Tilla's leather pauldron stopped the blade, but the damn thing hurt. Agony shot

down to her fingertips. Erry's blade swung again, and this time
Tilla managed to parry, then attack.

Her blade swung. It slammed into Erry's hand.

The dock rat screamed, her fingers opened, and her sword
fell.

Tilla kicked the fallen blade; it flew across the square. She
breathed raggedly. She lowered her own sword, thinking the
battle was over.

She was wrong.

Howling, Erry leaped onto Tilla and clung to her. The little
demon bit Tilla's wrist.

"Erry, stars damn it!" Tilla shouted. Her own sword fell
into the dust. "Get off."

Erry still clung to her, biting and clawing at her armor,
trying to reach her face. Tilla fell to the ground. Erry fell upon
her, scratching and screaming, her eyes wild.

"Fantastic!" Prince Leresy called somewhere in the distance.

"Abyss damn it!" Tilla said.

She lay on her back, Erry atop her. This dockside orphan
was perhaps half her size, but fast and wild and strong. With a
grunt, Tilla kicked and managed to flip herself over. Now Erry
lay on her back, Tilla atop her.

"Damn it, Erry!" Tilla said.

The girl squirmed and screamed below her. Tilla cursed
and finally managed to pin her down.

"Get off me!" Erry shouted, face red.

"Calm yourself," Tilla said. "Stars, Erry, I'm bigger than
you and I have you pinned down. Do you yield?"

Erry stopped struggling. She lay still for a moment and
scrunched her lips. She looked from side to side, as if deep in
thought, and bit her lip. Finally she flashed a toothy grin.

"All right!" she said brightly. "I yield. Good fight. Now get off me, you lumbering mule, before I bite your face off. You're bloody heavy, you are."

Tilla grabbed her sword, rose to her feet, and helped Erry up. She then approached Mae, who still lay mewling in the dust, and helped her stand too. Tilla felt pride well up inside her. She raised her chin and thrust out her chest.

I won! she thought. *I'm flight commander! I've only been a soldier for a few days, and I can already command two others.*

She turned toward Nairi, expecting to see the officer give her a grudging nod. But Nairi was still glaring, hatred blazing in her eyes. That glare was so strong Tilla took a step back and swallowed.

She wanted me to lose, she realized.

"Splendid!" Prince Leresy said. He approached and clasped Tilla on the shoulder. "I must be a good teacher. I'll be keeping an eye out for you, Tilla Roper." He leaned down and whispered into her ear. "Perhaps someday you will visit my chamber, and I can give you some private lessons."

Tilla stood stiff and still. Her knees trembled only the slightest. She looked over at Nairi; rage still flamed in the officer's green eyes, but pain dwelled there too, and Tilla understood.

She loves the prince, Tilla thought. *Oh stars damn it, Nairi and the prince... and me in the middle.* She wanted to shout out. *This isn't my fault! I didn't ask for Leresy's affections!*

"Well!" the prince said. "I've seen enough for one day. Lanse Nairi, keep up the good work. You'll whip these girls into warriors yet."

With that, the prince shifted back into a red dragon, took flight with a cloud of smoke, and disappeared over the walls.

When the smoke and dust settled, Tilla turned back toward Nairi, hesitating. She gasped to see the lanse draw her punisher, snarl, and come marching toward her.

"Lanse Nairi," Tilla began, "I—"

Nairi drew her sword, slammed Tilla's blade aside, and drove her punisher forward.

Pain exploded across Tilla's chest.

She couldn't help it. She screamed and fell to her knees.

"You were to fight with swords," Nairi said through clenched teeth, shoving her punisher against Tilla. "I teach swordplay, not wrestling, you seaside scum."

Tilla gasped for breath. Lightning flowered across her. She screamed again. She tried to clutch at Nairi's wrists, to push the punisher back, but her arms felt rubbery like loose skin.

"Please!" she tried to say, but screams drowned her words.

Tilla fell onto her back and writhed in the dust.

"Please, no!" somebody called behind her.

"Lanse Nairi, please!" cried another soldier.

Tilla could barely hear them. Tears streamed down her cheeks. Nairi knelt above her, snarling, twisting her punisher as if trying to shove the rod through Tilla's chest. Smoke rose from her. Tilla's eyes rolled back. Darkness, pain, and fire flowed over her world.

RUNE

"Again!" Valien barked and thrust his wooden sword.

Cursing, Rune tried to block the attack. His own practice weapon blocked Valien's. A second thrust flew. Rune checked the blow; the two wooden blades clanked. The third thrust slammed into his chest, and Rune gasped and fell back two steps.

"Dead again," Valien said in disgust. "If I were Frey Cadigus, you wouldn't last five heartbeats."

Valien Eleison, leader of the Resistance, stood clad in a steel breastplate, tan breeches, and leather boots. Sweat matted his grizzled hair and clung to his stubble like dew to grass.

"If you were Frey Cadigus," Rune said, "I would shift into a dragon and burn your arse."

Rune wiped sweat off his brow. He wore a breastplate too, but Valien's thrusts—even with a wooden sword—left his chest aching. He imagined that bruises spread beneath the steel.

Valien spat into the dust. "Dragon? Frey Cadigus dwells deep in his fortress; its corridors are too small for dragons. You'd have to fight his guards foot by foot, man by man. I doubt you'd slay one before they captured you."

The ruins of Confutatis sprawled around them, a hodgepodge of fallen columns, the shells of towers, crumbled walls, and countless bricks strewn across dead grass. It was a tapestry all in whites, tans, yellows, and grays. Men and women of the Resistance, clad in robes the colors of these ruins, stood upon what remained of the walls and towers. They bore swords of real steel, and they clutched bows. They said nothing. They only watched.

Rune growled, raised his wooden sword, and swung it at Valien.

The older man scowled, knocked the blow aside, and slammed his wooden blade against Rune's shoulder.

"Stars damn it!" Rune cursed.

Valien snarled and whacked Rune's shoulder again. "Never curse by your stars. Your stars saved your life, boy. That's more than your skill with the sword would do, it seems."

Rune tossed that sword down, spat, and glared at Valien.

"It isn't fair!" he said. "You've been fighting all your life. You were a knight. I was a brewer until a moon ago."

"Pick up your sword," Valien said. His eyes blazed and his face reddened. "It isn't fair? Life's not fair, boy. Was it fair when Frey slew your parents? Was it fair when he toppled this city? Was it fair when my w—" The grizzled warrior stopped himself and gritted his teeth. "Life is cruel and death is crueler. You can cry about how things aren't fair, or you can stand tall and *make* things fair."

Rune stared at the man. Rage flared inside him like dragonfire. *You are why I'm here!* Rune wanted to shout. *You sent Kaelyn to drag me out of my home, to take me here, to...*

As fast as it had flared, his rage dissipated. He thought back to the night with Kaelyn in the rain. That sword—the Amber Sword of Aeternum—stood against a fallen statue only feet away.

Make things fair.

Rune grumbled, reached down to his fallen wooden sword, and lifted it.

"The wooden sword's too heavy," he said. "The Amber Sword is light and fast. I could parry assaults with that one."

Valien's face softened, and he sighed and nodded. "The wooden sword needs to be heavy," he said. "It will strengthen you. When you've trained with thick wood, thin steel will seem lighter than air. You are right, Relesar Aeternum. Until a moon ago, you were only Rune Brewer, not a warrior, and I've been swinging swords for longer than you've lived. But now you are a warrior. Now you too will fight. I will bruise you here, Rune, until your body aches so badly, you will even dream of pain. But it will make you strong." Valien smiled thinly. "When training is hard, the battle is easy."

"I don't want to fight any battle," Rune said.

Valien clasped his shoulder. "Nor do any good men. A brute craves battle. A coward flees from it. The wise man hates war, but will fight to defend what he loves."

"And what do we defend, Valien?" Rune asked. "What do we love?" He swept his arm around. "A pile of ruins? Bricks and broken statues?"

"An idea," Valien said. "A memory. A story as old as starlight. We defend the light of Requiem, even as darkness closes in around us. We defend the heart and soul of our people. And that, Rune, is one battle I am willing to fight."

Rune thought about this for a moment. Valien's words rang true to him. Rune too wanted to fight for light, for the soul of Requiem, and for justice. And yet... he wondered. Valien's men—some said Valien himself—had slain Tilla's brother. The Resistance had slain many legionaries. Those soldiers had not been bloodthirsty worshippers of the red spiral. They had been humble farmers and tradesmen—people like his friends from Cadport—torn from their homes, given swords, and sent to die. Frey was evil and deserved death, but could the same be said for his soldiers, the youths the Resistance killed?

Can light shine in a kingdom so shadowed in death? Rune wondered. *Can we ever light the beacons of justice after shedding so much blood?*

He did not know. But he nodded. Fighting was *something*, he thought—fighting was standing up, flying onward, and making a change. That, Rune thought, was still better than hiding in shadows.

Sweat dripped into his eyes, and he wiped it with his hand, then raised his wooden sword again.

"All right, old man," Rune said. "You're going to slow down soon, and when you do, I'll be the one making bruises."

With a grin that looked almost like a snarl, Valien nodded and lashed his sword, and the wooden blades clattered.

That evening, the Resistance gathered in the fallen hall of old kings, the place where Rune had first met Valien. Candles burned upon the craggy walls. Trestle tables stood topped with bread rolls, smoked meats, dried fruits, cheeses, and nuts. Men and women, their robes and faces dusty, raised mugs of ale and drank deeply. Steam, smoke, and the scents of the feast filled the air.

Hundreds of warriors filled this grand hall. Across the ruins of Confutatis, two thousand others gathered in burrows, abandoned homes, and old cellars. This city had become a place of bones and old blood, but today light and hope shone here again.

"It is the Night of Seven!" Valien announced, standing at the head table of his hall. He raised a goblet of ale. "Tonight is the holiest night of Requiem's stars. Tonight marks a thousand years since the heroes of Requiem, the seven who survived the Great Slaughter, stood and rekindled the light of Requiem." Valien raised the goblet higher, and hundreds of mugs rose across the hall, returning the salute. "We live in a time of darkness. Requiem lies cloaked in shadows—the shadows of the Cadigus Regime." The resistors hissed across the hall, and Valien spoke louder. "Tonight we say: Like the Living Seven, we will fight. We will keep our light blazing. Tonight let us drink for those old heroes, and let us vow to continue their fight."

Valien drank deeply from his goblet. Across the hall, hundreds of warriors drank from their mugs.

Rune drank too. The ale was bitter and dark, but it flowed well down his throat and warmed his belly. This feast, these candles, and these stories warmed him like the ale. Back in Cadport, soldiers never spoke of the Living Seven, the ancient heroes of Requiem. Soldiers never spoke of the stars. They only hailed the red spiral, worshipped Frey Cadigus, and mostly they hated—they hated the Resistance, they hated the old enemies of Requiem, and they hated the fallen Aeternum Dynasty for its weakness.

"Here there is no hate," Rune said softly into his mug. "Here there is memory and camaraderie and hope."

At his side, Kaelyn placed her mug down, wiped suds off her lips, and touched his hand. She smiled softly, and the candlelight glowed in her eyes. Their fingers twined together under the table.

"I'm glad you're here with us, Rune," she said and squeezed his hand.

Rune thought back to how he had kissed Kaelyn; this memory too warmed him. When he looked at her now, he could almost feel her lips again. Kaelyn's hazel eyes shone, her hair cascaded like waves of molten gold, and her smile warmed him more than hearth fire. His hand, which held hers, felt more alive than his entire body.

I want to fly with her again, he thought, *to dance in the night, to hold her body against me, to feel her lips against mine.* She drew him like heat draws a freezing man, so powerfully he could barely breathe.

With a bolt of pain, he tore his eyes away. He stared at the tabletop.

Tilla, he thought. *Tilla Roper. I walked with her on the beach. I kissed her too. I vowed to see her again.* His throat stung. *How will I find you now, Tilla? Do you too have food, friends, and a warm fire? Or are you cold and afraid, and do you need me?*

He felt a hand in his hair. Kaelyn was looking at him, eyes soft with concern.

"Rune," she said, "you look sad."

He forced a smile and drank some more. "Are you going to force me to dance again?"

She laughed. "Of course I am! Many more times. For the rest of your life. But not now—now we do not dance. Now we sing." She stepped onto her chair, raised her mug, and cried out to the hall. "Vir Requis, let us sing the song of our people. Will you rise and sing the Old Words with me?"

They rose across the hall, hundreds of men and women with gaunt faces but bright eyes, with calloused hands but raised heads. Kaelyn stood before them, and she sang, and their voices rang with hers. Rune realized that he knew these words—his grandfather used to sing them on quiet nights—and Rune joined his voice to theirs.

"As the leaves fall upon our marble tiles, as the breeze rustles the birches beyond our columns, as the sun gilds the mountains above our halls—know, young child of the woods, you are home, you are home. Requiem! May our wings forever find your sky."

They all drank again, and when Kaelyn turned toward Rune, her eyes were solemn, her smile gone.

"The song of Requiem," Rune said to her. "It is forbidden now."

She nodded. "My father forbade it, but it is old beyond reckoning; we have been singing this song for thousands of years. We will sing it again in the palace of Nova Vita, and starlight will fall upon us." She raised her mug again and cried to the crowd. "Blessed be Relesar Aeternum, rightful King of Requiem! Blessed be his name!"

The hall erupted with cries.

"Blessed be Aeternum!" they called. "Stars bless the rightful king!"

Their cries echoed all around. Men and women stood waving their mugs and chanting his name. Rune stood up too, uneasy. Maybe it was the ale, but the room spun around him, a sea of faces and voices and eyes.

"Blessed be Relesar Aeternum, the rightful king!" they cried.

Rune looked around, feeling his face flush and stomach clench. He wanted the ruins to collapse and bury him; never had so many eyes stared at him. He wanted to cry out: *But I'm not a king, only a brewer. Not Relesar, only Rune!* Yet he remained silent. He had accepted Amerath, the Amber Sword. He had drunk from these men's brew; if not as a king, then as a brewer, he knew the significance of that. And so he only stood silently. Perhaps it was the best thing he could do now.

They ate, drank, and sang long into the night—a night of light and heat and Kaelyn's hand holding his.

LERESY

He stood above the infirmary bed, looking down at the burnt, wretched girl. A sigh flowed through him.

"By the stars, Nairi," he said. "You didn't have to burn the damn girl half to death."

The young lanse leaned against a wall, arms crossed and face twisted into a scowl.

"Don't you bloody mention the stars," she spat at him. "Your father would beat *you* half to death if he heard you mention them."

Lersey rolled his eyes. "Oh yes—it's red spiral this and red spiral that now. Of course. Only you're forgetting something, my dearest Nairi." He pointed at her. "You are a lowly lanse, a junior officer not worthy to lick my boots, and I am your prince. Granted, a prince you're bedding, but your prince nonetheless. And if I want to mention the bloody old gods..." He raised his voice to a shout. "I will!"

Nairi only glowered at him; he could hear her teeth grind.

With another sigh, Leresy turned back to look at the bed. The soldier lay there, her eyes shut, her bandaged chest rising and falling as she slept. Burn marks stretched out from the bandage like cobwebs; they spread across her shoulders, neck, and arms.

A memory pounded through Leresy, making him wince. How many times had he seen Kaelyn lying wounded like this, all burnt and bloody? So often throughout their childhood, Leresy would stand weeping as Frey, or sometimes Shari, beat and whipped and burned his sister. So many times Leresy would kneel over his wounded twin, trying to comfort her, to heal her.

Just be strong, the boy would whisper to his twin. *Be strong and they won't hurt you.*

But Kaelyn had always been too weak. Leresy had grown strong and survived; Kaelyn had fled.

And now Tilla too lay wounded. Would she grow strong like he had, or would she shatter and flee like Kaelyn?

"Nairi has done a job on you, Tilla Roper," Leresy said with a sad shake of his head. "I'm quite afraid that when you do wake up, you'll be sore for a good moon or two."

Behind him, he heard leather creak and boots stomp toward him. He turned to see Nairi marching his way, her teeth bared. She drew her punisher and held its crackling tip between them.

"How about I finish the job now," she said. "I'll burn that whore into a scarred, twisted freak of melted flesh and sores. But I'll leave her eyes. Yes. I want to leave her eyes so she can see the monster she's become."

"Or," Leresy said, "you can calm yourself before I demote you from lanse to dung shoveler." He pulled her arm down. "For pity's sake, Nairi, put that thing away. You've had your fun. The girl fought well. Your job is to train warriors here, to cull the weak and foster the strong, not disfigure the best in your phalanx."

Nairi snorted a laugh. "So you think her the best in my phalanx? Have you seen them all fight? Or do you simply choose the tall ones with the nice t—"

"Nairi!" he roared. When she fell silent, his voice softened. "Nairi. Are you jealous? Yes, she is tall, and yes, she does have a rather splendid pair of breasts on her. I see them. I like them. I'm the prince of Requiem; I'll stare at as many splendid pairs of breasts as I like. But the only ones I'll touch, Nairi, are these."

He reached for her chest. She glared and slapped his hand away.

"Don't you touch me, Leresy Cadigus," she said. "Your father is far from this land. We are in the south here, and the Black Rose is my phalanx—mine to lead! You are a prince, yes, but you do not serve in the Legions. I do. Within the Black Rose, I am ruler, I am supreme." She hissed. "And if you ever interfere with my command again, and if you ever touch one of my soldiers again, my father will hear of it." She gave him a caustic grin. "You're not the only one with great parentage, Leresy Cadigus."

Leresy opened his mouth to retort, then closed it.

Abyss damn it, he thought. The woman was right. Leresy was perhaps the son of the emperor, but he wasn't heir to the throne—not until he figured out how to kill Shari, at least. But Nairi... Nairi was firstborn daughter of Herin Blackrose, lord of the Axehand Order. If anyone in Requiem approached the emperor in might, it was Lord Herin.

And isn't that why you're here in the first place, Leresy Cadigus? he asked himself. *Do not forget your purpose. You're not here to bed young recruits with large dark eyes—at least, not only. You flew down to this wretched, southern cesspool to woo power. And power means Nairi.*

He had the grace to lower his head.

"Nairi, you are right. What can I say? I am a young, foolish man, and my blood is hot, and I think with my pants more than my head. What young man is different?" He placed an arm around the small of her back. "But the only woman I love is you, Lanse Nairi Blackrose. Not common girls. Not seaside soldiers. Just you, Nairi—my rose of Requiem."

He tried to pull her into an embrace, but she resisted and snapped her teeth at him.

"Do not try to woo me like I'm some common harlot," she said. "I've heard of your conquests in the capital; they say you bedded half the women in Nova Vita. Don't mistake me for another conquest. I am an officer in the Legions, not one of your courtesans."

Though she struggled against him, Leresy pulled her close, pressing her body against his. He hissed into her ear between clenched teeth.

"Oh, but I *will* conquer you." He slid a hand between her legs. "And you *are* but a whore. I know it. You know it. And I know that you love it. You are mine, Nairi Blackrose. I am your prince, and you are mine, and I will do with you as I like." He shoved her toward an infirmary bed, the one beside the cot Tilla lay on. "And I'm going to prove this to you right here."

She stood with her back to the bed, narrowed her eyes, and hissed at him like a cornered animal. He stepped toward her. Her grabbed her clothes, tore at them, and shoved her onto the mattress.

And he conquered her. And he showed her who she was.

"Who am I?" he hissed into her ear as he thrust into her.

"My... prince," she whispered.

"I own you, Nairi Blackrose. Don't you forget it. You do not command me. I am your lord, and I will be your husband."

As he claimed her and she moaned below him, Leresy looked over to the bed beside them where Tilla still slept.

You will be mine too, Tilla Roper, he thought as Nairi screamed and tugged at his hair.

Moments later, as Nairi was collecting her fallen clothes, Leresy approached a bronze mirror that stood behind the beds. He stared at his reflection and passed a hand through his golden hair, fixing an errant strand. He smoothed his doublet and nodded in satisfaction.

"I'm thinking of returning to the capital when the moon is full," he said, speaking to Nairi's reflection in the mirror. "I will announce our betrothal then. We've waited long enough, Nairi.

I'm eighteen now. I'm of age. I'll not wait longer. Let us marry here, in my fort, this winter."

She looked up from tugging on her leggings. Her reflection met his eyes.

"You've only just claimed lordship over this fort," she said. "Already you rush to be wed?"

He turned from the mirror to face her. "I thought you would be glad," he said. "Were you not complaining of my wandering eye? Marriage sticks a dagger into that eye. Knowing you, you'd make sure of that." He stepped toward her and held her. "Nairi, I love you. I want to marry you this winter. Not in the spring. Not next year. Not in the capital. But here—in our fort, in our home, in our passion. I will fly to the capital, and I will ask your father for your hand."

She gave him a sidelong glance. "My father. That would be... my father the commander of the Axehand Order."

Leresy stiffened. "That is his position, yes. A useful servant to my family."

"A powerful servant," Nairi said. "Some would say not a servant at all, but... an ally, maybe even a danger. Sometimes I wonder, Leresy, whose backside you crave more—mine to bed or his to kiss."

"Can't I do both?"

It was a mistake, he knew; he regretted those words at once. And yet they tickled him, and he could not stop a grin from spreading across his lips. To his great, great relief, even Nairi's lips twisted into a small smile.

"My poor, lustful prince," she said and mussed his hair. "Lustful for flesh and for power; which will win?" She placed a hand behind his neck, craned her neck upward, and hissed into his ear. "I too play this game, dearest prince. I too crave power. And yes, you are powerful, Prince Leresy. You are powerful in my bed and in the courts of your father. Fly to the capital. Ask for my hand. We will wed this winter, here in Castra Luna, and someday I will be queen."

He raised an eyebrow. "You do know that Shari is heir to the throne."

She kissed his lips, smiled crookedly, and patted his cheek. "Not for long."

TILLA

She lay abed, wrapped in pain.

When she opened her eyes, firelight seared them. When she breathed, the air sawed at her throat. She tried to wriggle in bed and froze at once; the blankets rubbing against her skin cut her like blades.

What had happened? Tilla could barely remember. Her mind felt foggy. Thoughts floated like clouds, and she could not grasp them. She recalled only training with a sword, and Prince Leresy touching her legs, and...

Nairi.

The memory thudded back into her.

The pain! The pain had pounded through her for so long, so hot, all consuming; it had rattled her teeth, raised welts across her, and twisted her fingers and toes. Tilla had thought her bones would dislocate and her skin shatter.

It's not my fault! Tilla had wanted to cry, but she could only scream, beg, weep, and fall into endless agony and darkness.

"Tilla!" a voice said, muffled and distant and echoing, a voice from another world. "Tilla, can you hear me?"

Tilla blinked. Two shadows stood before her, dark blurs upon orange light. It seemed the shadows were speaking, but the voices sounded so distant Tilla could barely hear.

"Stars, Tilla, can't you hear me?" one shadow said, speaking louder.

"Oh, bloody puke soup, Nairi did a job on her," said the other shadow. "I swear, I'm going to grab that woman's punisher and shove it up her fat arse!"

"Language, Erry!" said the first shadow. "I told you to watch your language. You're not living on the docks anymore."

"As if this place is any damn better! How about you go eat hairy donkey bollocks, Wobble Lips. Get your mouth dirty for once."

The two shadows began to shove each other. Groaning in pain, Tilla forced herself onto her elbows and blinked vigorously. Slowly the shadows came into focus, becoming two young women. One was pale and doll-like, her golden hair braided— Mae! The other was scrawny, her short brown hair rising in tangles—Erry! Her two friends didn't even notice her sit up; they were busy hitting and scolding each other. Oil lanterns lined the wall behind them, lighting a stone chamber with several empty beds.

"Will you two stop it?" Tilla demanded, voice raspy.

"Now don't you butt in!" Erry said. "This is between me and Wobble Lips, and—" Erry froze and her eyes widened. "Tilla! Sweaty codpieces, you're awake and talking!"

Tilla fell back into bed and groaned. "Barely."

At once, the two girls leaped onto her bed and began to bounce and cheer.

"You're alive!" Mae said and hugged her. "Oh stars, Tilla, I was sure she *killed* you."

Erry was bouncing up and down. "I knew our flight commander would live! We're going to make you strong enough to *kill* that rat Nairi someday."

Every bounce of the bed sent pain thudding through Tilla, and she moaned.

"Ow, ow!" she said. "Stop it. Please."

The two soldiers froze.

"Sorry!" Mae said and gasped. "I... did I hurt you?"

Tilla waved weakly. "Never mind that. Just... sit still and speak quietly. Where am I? How long have been sleeping?"

"You're in the fortress infirmary," Erry said and gestured around at several empty beds. "You're the only one here now. Usually when somebody upsets the lanses that bad, they end up buried, not bedridden. You were damn lucky, Roper. You've been here for..." She counted on her fingers. "This is the second night."

"You need to count on your fingers for only two nights?" Mae said. "Stars, Erry, you are a dumb one."

"You're the one who thought the infirmary was the barracks for ground troops!" Erry retorted. "That's *infantry*. I told you that a million times, barnacle brain, Tilla was wounded, not drafted into the ground forces."

Mae sniffed and tears filled her eyes. "Well it's not my fault. I don't know all these soldier things. At least I can count properly!"

The two girls began to hit each other again, and the bouncing shot more pain through Tilla.

"Stop!" Tilla said. "Please." She rubbed her eyes. "How bad is it?"

The girls fell silent and Mae began to weep. Tilla dared to lift the blanket and look down at her body. She closed her eyes.

Stars.

Nairi had indeed done a job on her, as Erry had said. Below the blanket, bruises and welts covered Tilla's naked body. Her leather armor had perhaps protected her from dulled swords, but not from Nairi's punisher. She wondered if she'd forever carry these scars.

"It's... not that bad," Erry said. "Really, Till. Stars, I got beat up worse on the docks a few times, and I'm still standing." The waif snarled. "You're going to keep fighting, Roper, or I'm going to beat you up even worse."

Sniffing back tears, Mae reached into a pack she carried and pulled out a bundle of cloth. When she unwrapped the fabric, the scents of honey and bread filled Tilla's nostrils so powerfully her mouth watered, and she couldn't help but moan. Inside the bundle lay three plump pastries still steaming from the oven.

"Honey cakes!" Mae said. "With raisins in them. We, uhm... kind of... stole them."

Erry nodded. "It was a daring heist: sneaking out of our tent at night, breaking into the kitchens, grabbing honey cakes, and finally climbing the wall into this place. Forget being soldiers. We should become thieves."

"Oh, you were always a thief," Mae said to the girl. "She has a lock pick set, Tilla! Stars, a real one, with a bunch of little skeleton keys and wires and stuff. I bet she stole from at least half the houses in Cadport."

Erry raised her chin. "More than half! By the way, Mae, nice little doll collection you've got in your old bedroom. How old are you again—one?"

The two girls lifted their hands again, ready for more blows.

"Stop!" Tilla had to say. "Fight later. Now we eat."

"They're all for you," Mae said. "All three honey cakes. Erry and I already ate ours."

Tilla looked at the cakes. Each steaming pastry was larger than her hand. She did not imagine she could eat one, let alone all three. Yet when she bit into the first pastry, it melted in her mouth, rich with butter and raisins and honey. She closed her eyes and let out a sigh. She had not eaten a proper meal since leaving Cadport; she thought this was the best food she'd ever tasted.

"It's what the officers eat," Erry said. "Stars, Till, you should see their kitchen! Roast chicken, cakes, fresh fruits, wines..." Erry smacked her lips. "And all they give us is stale wafers, moldy cheese, and slop that's probably full of rat droppings. I need to be a lanse too someday."

Tilla finished the first honeycake. Her stomach still rumbled, and she was tempted to eat the remaining two. Instead, she wrapped them back into the cloth and placed them under the blankets. She didn't know how much longer she'd be here, or how scarce food would be.

"How are things back at the Black Rose?" Tilla asked, trying to keep her mind off her wounds.

"Awful!" Mae said. "We only got three hours of sleep last night too, and we failed the morning inspection. Erry's boots weren't polished."

"And your sword wasn't oiled!" Erry said, eyes flashing.

"Well, I don't know how to oil a sword!" Mae sighed. "Nairi said we can only sleep for three hours this night too, and we have to carry the cannonballs again soon. Erry, when did she say we have to—"

The clock tower chimed outside, cutting her off. Four chimes. Four in the morning.

"Wormy dragon vomit!" Erry said and leaped off the bed. "It's our night patrol time. If we're not there..." She made a beeline to the window, placed one foot upon the ledge, then looked back at Tilla. "Get better soon, Till. We need our flight leader back."

With a wink and a grin, Erry leaped outside into the darkness. Sniffing back tears, Mae followed; Tilla heard the baker's daughter thump against the ground outside and wail. Then their boots thudded and disappeared into the distance.

Weariness tugged on Tilla. She closed her eyes and slept.

It was another two days before the infirmary nurse, a severe woman with muscles like the ropes Tilla would weave, deemed Tilla healed. Tilla did not feel healed; bruises and welts still covered her, and when she tried to walk every step hurt.

"If you can walk, you can train," the nurse said, a scowl twisting her wrinkly face. "Now out! Return to your phalanx, soldier, and by the red spiral, stay out of trouble this time."

Tilla left the infirmary clad in her leather armor, which rubbed against her welts so powerfully every movement made her wince. Her sword hung upon her hip, her helmet topped her head, and fear gripped her heart.

What if Nairi hurts me again? she wondered as she stepped into the courtyard. Snow dusted the cobblestones and glided before her. *What if Leresy speaks to me, and Nairi gets jealous, and...*

Suddenly Tilla wanted to flee. She stood alone in this courtyard, the nurse still in the infirmary, her phalanx in the forest.

I can shift into a dragon, Tilla thought. *I can fly away from this place—back to Cadport, back to Rune.*

She stood alone in the snow and looked at the southern wall. No, she could not fly back home, she knew. If she fled the Legions, she would be an outlaw; the Cadigus Regime would hunt her down and slay her.

I can join the Resistance, she thought, *if I can find them.* Yet the stories she had heard returned to her: stories of the Resistance slaughtering babes, snatching children and forcing them to fight, burning farms and killing peasants simply to punish the emperor. As bad as Nairi was, surely the Resistance was worse. Even if Tilla could find the resistors, would she only stumble into a den of monsters? Would they kill her like they had killed her brother?

She sighed. No. There was nothing over those walls— Cadport was now banned to her, the Resistance frightened her, and Tilla did not fancy a life on the run, hiding in caves and forests.

All she could do now, she decided, was survive this training. Nairi would not command her forever. If Tilla completed her training, she would advance in the ranks. She would be assigned to a better fortress. She would become a warrior, a proud legionary of the empire, clad in steel and glory. Surely that was better than living as a filthy, frightened outlaw.

I'm going to show Nairi. She clenched her fists, and marched across the courtyard. *I'm going to be the best damn soldier in Castra Luna.*

She marched out the gates, took a deep breath, and headed back to her tent.

The clock chimed.

The snow fell.

Day and night molded into a blur of pain and weariness.

Every night, as the clock chimed one, the Black Roses emerged from their tent to carry their cannonballs around the camp. Every morning, as the clock chimed four, Nairi woke them with screams, threats, and thrusts of her punisher.

They fought with blunted swords, then sharpened ones.

They ran through the forest for hours, tasting the punisher when they fell.

They ate scraps. They slept shivering in moldy blankets. They drank melted snow when they could steal it. They were always hungry, always thirsty; they would fight for the last slice of stale bread.

Castra Luna brought them to the edge of humanity. The Black Roses did not bathe; they stole snow, melted it in their tent, and shivered as they rinsed their grime. They had no outhouses or chamber pots; when Nairi looked aside, they sneaked into the forest and dug holes, praying that Nairi would not shout and order them back into formation. Whenever the young lanse slept or ate, she left with them the hulking siragis, and they were worse; they thrust their punishers with glee, and once they whipped a recruit until she passed out.

More than the hunger and thirst, and more than the pain, Tilla longed for sleep.

I can live without food, she thought during the endless runs, marches, and swordplay. *I can live without water to drink or bathe in. But sleep... sleep I long for with every aching fiber in my body.*

And yet sleep, this most precious of lovers, was only allowed brief visits. An hour here, two hours there; that was all.

"Whenever they march us," Tilla whispered to her fellow soldiers, "I want to sit down. Whenever they sit us down, I want to stand and march."

Marching was agony—it was blisters upon her feet, cramping muscles, aching breath, and her spine twisting under the sacks of cannonballs. Whenever she marched, she prayed for it to end. She prayed only for rest—to sit, to rub her feet, to breathe again.

Yet whenever Nairi ordered them to sit—while they ate, while they listened to her speeches, while she demonstrated new sword thrusts—Tilla prayed to please, please stars, only to stand up, only to walk. Sitting down meant a visit from her greatest foe: weariness.

Whenever she sat, sleep leaped onto her at once, tugging more powerfully than all the ropes Tilla had ever woven. Blackness began to spread across her. Invisible demons tugged at her eyelids, forcing them down.

Sleep, Tilla, voices whispered. *Sleep, sleep...*

One time, sitting with her fellow Black Roses to hear Nairi praise the emperor, Tilla could not help it. Her eyes closed—just for an instant, barely more than a blink.

At once, Nairi pounced upon her. The punisher drove into her chest. Lightning crackled.

"You will not sleep as I speak, dog!" the lanse shouted and pulled her punisher back, leaving Tilla gasping. "Anyone who closes her eyes, I'll cut off her eyelids!"

And so whenever they sat—or even stood—Tilla bit her cheek, dug her fingernails into her palms, and used every bit of strength to stay awake, to keep her eyes opened.

Every time they sat or stood, a few eyes closed. A few recruits screamed under the punisher. Twice recruits fell asleep while marching, a feat Tilla had thought impossible; Nairi's punisher burned them.

How long had it been? A moon now? Two moons? Three?

Whenever we marched, we wanted to sit. Whenever we sat, we prayed to march.

That was how, Tilla knew, she would remember her training for the rest of her life—marching in pain and hunger, sitting through the agony of forbidden sleep, one or the other, again and again, day after day. A dreamscape. A blur. A nightmare of weariness, hunger, thirst, dirt, chiming hours, and endless pain.

During these moons, Tilla found comfort only one hour a day—her favorite hour of the day, the hour that kept her going, that made this agony bearable.

The morning hour right after dawn.

The hour they trained as dragons.

All her life in Cadport, shifting into dragons was forbidden. Dragons were not docile citizens. Dragons could blow fire, slash claws, and rise up against the Cadigus family. Dragons were outlawed.

It was one law that Tilla, all her life, could not obey. Since she was old enough to shift, she had craved Requiem's ancient magic, the magic that flowed from the Draco stars. And so she and Rune would walk upon the beach at night, shift into dragons in darkness, and fly over the water. She knew that many others in town shifted too; she had seen other youths above the waters at night, even some older souls.

But this—this was new. This was flying in daylight, in the open, not concealing her fire behind her teeth, but roaring it in great pillars of fury.

This was life in death, light in darkness, the beacon of her soul.

"Warriors of the Black Rose!" Nairi shouted, pacing along the courtyard before her troops. She drew her sword and raised it high. "Shift and fly!"

With that, Nairi shifted into a gray dragon, beat her wings, and took flight. Across the courtyard, her ninety-nine soldiers shifted and followed.

Tilla inhaled deeply and let the magic flow across her. For the first few days of training, her armor and sword would constrict her; she had ripped one breastplate trying to shift. Today her armor and blade were like parts of her, as familiar as her own skin. They shifted with her, melting into her body. Her wings sprouted from her back. Her white scales clanked across her. She soared and blew a pillar of fire.

All around her, the other dragons ascended too. Her flight crew flew around her, one defender at each side. Erry flew to her right, a slim copper dragon with blazing eyes. Mae flew to her left, a lavender dragon with white horns.

"Flight one!" Nairi shouted. "Flight two—charge!"

Three dragons swooped in from the east. Three more charged from the west. They crashed together with beating wings and blasts of smoke.

"Flight three, four—charge!"

When it was Tilla's turn to fly, she led her flight in assault. She screamed and blew streams of smoke, charging toward another flight of three dragons. Sparks and smoke flew. Their claws and horns, tipped with cork, slammed against scales.

In real battle, Tilla knew, she would breathe fire, not just smoke, and slash bare claws. Day by day, she practiced with cork and smoke, and she grew faster. Her defenders whisked around her, holding back the enemies, letting Tilla charge into battle.

Every day her flight won more rounds. Within a moon, Tilla's Three, as they called them, was ranked top flight in their phalanx.

Some days, Nairi cracked open cages of doves and sent hundreds of birds flying. The Black Rose dragons chased, blew jets of fire, and roasted the birds; for every dove that escaped, Nairi docked them a meal. Other days, they flew for hours over the forests, shifting from attack formation to defense and back again a hundred times—changing shape in the sky from arrows, to rings, to great V's like skeins of geese.

In the long days of impossible pain, it was freedom.

It was joy.

It was the song and light of dragons.

It's why I stayed, Tilla thought, flying over the forest with her phalanx, roaring fire and howling the might of the Legions. *It's why I never ran away when I had a hundred chances to. It was for this— wind in my wings, smoke in my nostrils, and fire in my heart.*

As the dragons of Requiem flew, Tilla thought: *I wish you were here with me, Rune. I wish we could fly together again—one more flight like those above the sea.*

That night, when she lay in her tent, Tilla thought of him. Her fellow soldiers slept around her, a great mass pressed together. Tilla closed her eyes and tried to remember Rune: his dark hair, his somber eyes, and his hand holding hers. Yet hard as she tried, every night his face seemed more blurred to her, and he seemed farther away.

"I miss you, Rune," she whispered.

But I also have a new home now. And I have new friends and a new purpose to my life. I have Erry and Mae and all the others—and an hour a day of wings and fire.

He faded into the shadows. She slept.

RUNE

"So I suppose you want to know about that night," Valien rasped, took a swing of spirits, and slammed down his mug. "The night I saved your life. Don't deny it, boy; you've been burning to ask. I've seen it in your eyes since Kaelyn dragged you into this place."

Rune stood at the entrance to Valien's dark, dusty chamber. Candles, bottles, and books covered the shelves. A spider wove a web in the corner. A log crackled in the hearth. Valien sat at an oaken table, his scruff thickening into a beard, and drank from his mug. His grizzled hair hung wild around his face—a face as rough and leathery as the ancient codices around them.

"Did you summon me here," Rune asked from the doorway, "to tell me the tale?"

Valien grumbled and snorted something that sounded like a laugh. He drank again, swishing the spirits before swallowing, then wiped his lips with the back of his hand.

"Ah!" he said. "Seemed as good a night as any to remember. I've had a bit... to drink. In with spirits, out with secrets, they say." He slapped his palm against the table. "If I didn't summon you, you'd be coming here soon enough to ask. I reckoned we'd talk when I'm nice and ready, with a hearth fire warming my bones and rye warming my belly. Come on. Step in. Sit down. Make yourself at home and all that, as you innkeepers say."

Rune hesitated. He had seen Valien gruff before. Stars, the man was always scowling and rasping and cursing. But this—this was worse. Valien's voice was slurred and scratchier than ever, and something about that invitation seemed less than welcoming.

"Come on, boy!" Valien said again. "Aye, I'm a bit drunk, but I won't hurt you. Sit down. I have some memories to spill, and well... you're the one to listen."

Rune did not want to enter this room. He wanted to return to the main hall, walk outside and look at the stars, or seek Kaelyn in her chambers; he had begun to teach her mancala, using a board he'd carved himself. At the same time... Valien was right. Rune had wanted to ask these questions, to learn more about that night. He knew the story, of course—everyone in Requiem did. He too had heard of Valien Eleison battling Frey Cadigus, snatching the last heir, and smuggling the babe out of the palace. Yet all those stories had been told in taverns, or at military rallies, or in dark caverns. Here before him stood the man himself, the great outlaw, the rebel leader; here was the story of Rune's life.

Rune entered the room, pulled back a chair, and sat at the table. Valien leaned forward and fixed him with a red-rimmed glare.

"They say you battled a hundred men with a broken sword," Rune said, "all the while holding the Aeternum babe—me—in one hand."

"Aye," Valien agreed. "They also say that Frey Cadigus stands eight feet tall and the sun waits for him to piss every morning before it rises. What do you believe, Rune?"

He thought about this for a moment. He answered carefully.

"I think," he said, "that I would very much like a bit of whatever you're drinking."

When Rune too held a mug and the warmth spread through him, he allowed himself to lean back. Valien seemed less frightening through the glaze of spirits, and after all, Rune had seen many drunken warriors at the Old Wheel.

"You're eighteen now, are you?" Valien asked after another gulp of the rye.

Rune nodded. "Almost—a moon away. If I were eighteen already, I'd have been drafted last recruitment with my friends."

He had almost said: *with Tilla.* He had stopped himself just in time. Valien did not need to know about Tilla Roper. Nobody did. That memory was pure, and Rune would not stain it with this war.

Valien sighed and leaned back. "Aye, still a youth. I was only a squire when I was your age. It was another few years before I was knighted—I was twenty-one and still too young for wisdom." The grizzled man's eyes seemed to be looking back upon better days. "Had my proper armor and all and a good sword; I still carry it. I served your father, and he was good man. And those were good days."

"Until Frey Cadigus flew with his troops into the capital," Rune said. "We've heard the story countless times in Cadport. They always tell us how Frey Cadigus, the hero, saved Requiem from its weakness, from the old corrupt blood."

Valien raised his eyebrows. "Cadport? No, we don't call it that here. Lynport is the name of your city. It was named after the great Queen Lyana Aeternum, an ancestor of yours. She fought a battle upon Ralora Cliffs outside the city. Cadport!" Valien snorted. "Frey Cadigus renamed half the cities in this kingdom after his miserable self. But it's still known as Lynport here, Rune, and you should call it that."

"My father did," Rune said. "My stepfather, that is, but I still think of him as Father. He would whisper 'Lynport' sometimes late at night after our tavern closed, but... it was a forbidden name. Once a man was caught saying 'Lynport' in our tavern. The soldiers dragged him outside, and..." Rune had to drink again. "Nobody's called it Lynport since, not even in a whisper."

"It's a good town," Valien said softly. He stared at the wall as if lost in memory. "A good town. Good, honest folk. It's why

I took you there, Rune, why I placed you in the Old Wheel with your stepfather. And Wil Brewer kept you safe for seventeen years. Aye, a good town, and good folk."

"How did you know Wil?" Rune asked. "Why did he agree to raise me as his own, to place himself in danger, to protect me?"

Valien said nothing for a long moment, only stared at the wall. Finally he took a gulp of spirits, grimaced as he swallowed, and slammed the mug down.

"My wife, Rune," he said and clenched the mug so tightly, it trembled. "My wife. Frey Cadigus slew her the night I saved you. He stuck his blade into her as she screamed for me. I couldn't save her, but I could save you, Rune. So I took you to my wife's hometown. And I took you to her brother." He grumbled and sighed. "Yes, Rune. I took you to the only family I still had, to Wil Brewer. He lost his sister that night, but he gained a son."

Rune's head spun, and it wasn't from the drink.

"Stars," he whispered. "My father—I mean, Wil—spoke of losing a sister. I never imagined..."

"Of course you didn't." Valien scowled into his mug. "I told Wil not to speak of it. You were never to know who you were—not until you were old enough, until you were ready to fight with us."

Rune lowered his head, and his belly felt cold. Guilt and sorrow swirled inside him. He tried to imagine losing the woman he loved, losing Tilla. Of course, Tilla wasn't his wife, and he had only kissed her once, but he loved her. She was his best friend, his companion all his life. If Frey killed her, Rune would become a ruin of a man.

I would become like Valien, he thought. *Hurting. Mourning. Seeking solace in my cups.*

"Valien," he said and looked up at the man. "I'm sorry for your loss. For Marilion dying. I know it must hurt, and—"

"Oh do you now?" Valien hissed and leaned forward, and suddenly fire filled his eyes, and rage twisted his face. "Do you know what it's like, boy? Are you sorry? What do you know of loss, of—"

Valien sucked in his breath, grimaced, and growled. He swallowed his words, then pushed himself back. He seemed to wilt. His shoulders slumped, and all the fire left his body.

Rune watched, heart thrashing.

"I..." he began.

Valien waved him silent. "It's not your fault, boy. I know you mean well. And... thank you." He heaved a rattling sigh and drank again. "I don't talk about her much, as you can imagine. She looked like Kaelyn, do you know?" He laughed bitterly. "Same age when she died. Same golden, wavy hair. Same eyes. When I look at Kaelyn sometimes, I... Well, never mind that."

"She was very pretty," Rune said softly.

Valien laughed. "Marilion was, and Kaelyn is."

"I'm sorry." Rune was surprised to find his eyes stinging, and his voice shook. He clenched his fists in his lap. "They say that you saved me while Frey killed her. If... if you weren't saving me, maybe you could have... you could stopped Frey from..."

"Maybe," Valien agreed. "But you were only a babe. What did you know? It was a bad night, Rune. It was a bad night for me, for you, for the land. Frey Cadigus and his battalions flew into the capital as heroes; we welcomed him, the great general returning home from the wars. He entered the palace unopposed. He was in the throne room before he drew his sword. I was there, and I fought him. I fought him well, and I suffered the wounds of his sword, and still I fought. But his men were too many; he slew your father, your mother, your older siblings. But you... you were a babe. You were in a nursery upstairs. I ran. I burst into your room. And I saw a soldier above your crib, a blade in his hand."

Rune leaned forward, clutching his mug like a sword. "And you killed him," he whispered.

"Well... I tried to," Valien said. "Thrust my sword at him, but he saw me in a mirror, and I was too weak, too wounded. He blocked my blade, and our swords shattered in a rain of steel. We fought with fists upon the floor. He grabbed my throat. He squeezed and squeezed and squeezed. I saw stars. I thought he would snap my neck. I kicked. I punched him. Still he squeezed. Finally—stars, I must have been seconds from death—I kicked down the mirror, shattering it. I grabbed a shard the size of my fist. I drove it so deep into his eye it scraped the back of his skull." He gave a gruff laugh. "He released me then. I wheezed and coughed on the floor like a wretch, every breath like a saw of fire working at my throat. He couldn't kill me, but he did ruin my voice; left it all gravelly and scratched, the bastard. Since that day, I've sounded like a man dying of consumption." He gave Rune a squinted, sidelong look and spat. "If you ask me, you weren't worth it, boy."

"Maybe I will prove you wrong someday," Rune said. "You kept me alive for a reason. You need me now. We're going to kill that bastard Frey Cadigus, and we're going to rename my city, and stars, Valien—we're going to get you a bath. You stink."

And I'm going to see Tilla again, he thought. *I'm going to save her from whatever fort they dragged her to. We're going to return to Cadport—to Lynport!—and rebuild the Old Wheel, and Tilla and I will live there together.*

"Aye!" Valien said, leaned back, and slammed his boots against the tabletop. "You know what they say. Good men stink of soil, oil, and other toil; villains smell of roses."

Rune was about to reply when the door slammed open behind them.

Kaelyn burst into the room. Her eyes were wide, her hair wild, and her fingers clutched her bow like a drowning woman. Her chest rose and fell as she panted.

Both Rune and Valien leaped to their feet and gripped their swords.

"What is it, Kaelyn?" Valien demanded.

"It's Beras," she said, panting. "He's back with news. He claims this one's worth gold. Oh bloody stars. He's waiting in the main hall."

They rushed down the corridor, boots thudding. As they moved, Rune frowned. *Beras.* Surely she didn't mean Beras the Brute, the infamous enforcer of the Cadigus Regime, the man Rune had seen deliver a trembling girl to her death in Lynport?

As they burst into the main hall, Rune's stomach sank.

It was him.

Rune cursed and drew a foot of steel.

The burly man stood in the crumbling hall, facing them. Circles hung under his eyes, black rings upon an ashen face. His armor was a tattered jumble of buckles, scraps of chainmail, rusted plates, and beaten leather. In his fists, he clutched his axe—not the axe of a soldier, but a great thing of wood and steel built for felling trees. Rune had seen this man in Lynport before, but only from a distance. Facing him in the hall, Rune felt a chill; Beras stood nearly seven feet tall, his shoulders wide as a wagon. Even before Frey Cadigus had taken power, Beras the Brute was feared across the kingdom, the most bloodthirsty outlaw in Requiem, a thief and murderer and rapist.

He raped a child once, Rune remembered and snarled. *He strangled her and buried her body in the woods.*

Frey Cadigus had been so impressed, the stories whispered, he had hired Beras at once, elevating him from outlaw to bodyguard.

"So this is the boy," Beras said, fixing Rune with a dead gaze. His lips peeled back, revealing rotted teeth. "So here is the so-called Whelp of Aeternum."

Rune growled and drew his sword. He doubted he could defeat Beras in battle—the man was twice his size, and his axe was larger than the Amber Sword—but rage pounded through Rune, drowning his discretion.

"You've stumbled into the wrong lair, Beras," he said. "I saw you in Lynport hiding behind the skirts of Shari, your mistress. You will find no such protection here."

Beras grinned—the grin of a feral beast. "The pup's got some spunk. You're a feisty one, aye. Normally I like me a nice girl to warm my bed, but you'd do fine. Come here, boy—let me take that sword from you."

Valien marched forward and stood between them.

"Enough!" the fallen knight said. "Rune, sheathe your sword. Beras, tell me your news."

Rune fumed. He wanted to leap toward Beras and stick his sword in the man's neck. Yet Kaelyn took his arm and pulled him back.

"Let them talk, Rune," she whispered. "Sheathe your sword. It's all right. Beras works for us."

Rune's head spun. He took a few steps back with Kaelyn until they stood in a shadowy corner.

"What?" he said and shook his head wildly. "Beras the Brute—the outlaw, Shari's henchman, the murderer and rapist—fights for the Resistance?"

Kaelyn sighed and kept her hand on his arm. "I wouldn't say he fights for us, no. And I wouldn't say he holds much love for us either, or for anyone. Beras is a mercenary, that is all. My father was a fool to hire him. Beras loves his wine, his women, and his blood, but one thing he loves more than all—his coin.

Frey pays him to murder and torture. We pay him for information."

Rune growled, and it took Kaelyn's hand to guide his sword back into its sheathe.

"How could you employ scum like that?" he demanded. "Folk whisper about the Resistance being a rabble of outlaws and killers. When you pay Beras, you are only—"

"—gaining information we need," Kaelyn finished his sentence. "Rune. Listen to me. I have no love for Beras. I hate the man, and he knows it. But I hate my father more. What is Beras? Nothing but muscle. Frey Cadigus is the heart of the Regime; with Beras taking our coin, we can learn what we need to stab that heart. The wise work with small devils to slay the big ones."

"You cannot trust anything Beras says," he told her. "The man is a rabid beast. Anything he tells you will be tainted with lies."

Kaelyn raised an eyebrow. "Is that so? It was Beras who told us Shari was flying toward Lynport to kill you. His information saved your life that day. Beras is a rabid beast, it's true, but you owe him your life. And so do many others among the Resistance." She sighed. "War is rarely black and white, rarely goodness fighting evil; we are all different shades of gray. There are no pure means, only pure ends."

Rage still bloomed in Rune, and he wanted to retort, but more than that, he wanted to hear what Beras was saying. The brute was smirking and reaching out his hand to Valien.

"This one's a real gem," Beras said and spat. "Pay up! Gold this one's worth. No more of your silver. One gold coin now, another once I deliver your news. Go on! Still less than what you pay for your booze, I wager."

Rune's rage crackled with new vigor. He didn't know how Valien managed to stay calm. Yet the leader of the Resistance only nodded, fished through his pocket, and produced a golden coin. He slammed it into Beras's outreached, craggy palm.

"Talk to me, Beras," Valien said. "Share your tidings and I'll toss you another treat."

Beras chuckled, spat again, then bit the golden coin. "Aye, this is good gold, it is. All right. I'll share my tale." He leered at the shadows where Rune and Kaelyn stood. "You want your pups here while I speak?"

Valien nodded, and it seemed like all the drunkenness had drained from his eyes; those eyes now burned with an intensity Rune had never seen.

"I have no secrets from the emperor's daughter," Valien said, "nor from our king's son. Speak freely, Beras. Tell me all you know."

"A wedding," Beras said and barked a laugh. "The boy Leresy is making a grab for power—and for some young arse. Got his eye on Nairi Blackrose, daughter of Lord Herin, the bald bastard."

Valien nodded slowly. "It's a smart move for him. Leresy is second in line for the throne. Nairi's father could threaten Shari, if push comes to shove between the siblings. But this news is hardly worth gold, Beras. These rumors of Leresy courting Nairi have been flowing since the boy took command of Castra Luna."

Beras was chuckling—a horrible, bubbly sound like grime rising in a sewer. "Ahh, but you haven't heard the best part yet, my grizzled old friend. The wedding, you see! Ah, the wedding. The pup insisted on it."

"Insisted on what?" Valien demanded. His shoulders had lost their stoop, and he stood tall and proud as a knight. "Tell me your news, Beras, if you want your second coin."

"Oh, I'll have my second coin," said the brute. "Leresy Cadigus, that whore of a pup, demanded to have his wedding in his new home—Castra Luna itself. The whole clan will be attending—Frey Cadigus, Shari Cadigus, and Herin Blackrose. The whole bloody echelon of Requiem. They'll be there in ten days at noon—the first day of spring."

Valien stood silent for a long time. His face hardened into a blank mask. Finally he reached into his pocket, pulled out three more golden coins, and placed them into Beras's palm.

The brute grinned, barked a laugh, then turned to leave. He trundled out of the hall, gurgling his chuckle. The sounds of wings beat outside, and through the windows, Rune saw the bronze dragon take flight and vanish into the distance.

Rune stood still, fingers tingling around his sword's hilt.

Frey Cadigus. His children. Herin Blackrose. In one fort.

"Castra Luna is a training fort," Valien whispered. "It lies in the middle of nowhere, leagues away from any other fortress or town. The entire high command of Requiem... in an isolated fort full of young, green recruits."

Kaelyn shook her head mightily, her wavy hair swaying. "No. I know what you're thinking, and no. I know my father; he will suspect an attack. He will bring the Axehand Order with him, hundreds of his finest warriors, fanatical priests who worship him as a god. Valien!" She glared at the knight. "You can't seriously be considering this. We're *not ready.*"

Valien stared at the wall as if he hadn't heard her. His leather glove creaked as he gripped his sword. His jaw too creaked, tightening under his salt-and-pepper beard.

"Valien!" Kaelyn said again. "We've talked of attacking in force. We agreed that we must first enlist more warriors. With Rune here, we can rally hearts. We can bring more men to our side. We can—"

Valien turned toward her, his eyes haunted.

"This is the best chance we've had in years," he rasped. "The echelon of Requiem—together, isolated. We've not seen such a thing since Frey Cadigus seized the throne seventeen years ago. We might never see it again."

Kaelyn's chest rose and fell as she panted. Her eyes flashed and she bared her teeth.

"Will you have us crash against the walls of Castra Luna now? Will you dash our hopes so soon after Rune joined us? Will you douse our flame just when it begins to burn? Valien." She held his hands. "Valien, listen to me, please. We need more time. We need to send men to every city, to spread the news of Relesar Aeternum fighting on our side. Many remember him. They will flock to his banner. They will fight with us. But we *need time.*"

"Time is what we do not have." Valien grunted, gripped Kaelyn's shoulders, and stared into her eyes. "If we don't attack now, we might lose this chance forever. I've been fighting Frey Cadigus for seventeen years, and now is our chance to strike. To kill him. To reclaim our kingdom." He snarled and flames burned in his eyes; his face turned demonic. "Blood must now be shed. We will fly out in force. Kaelyn, you've been flying at my side for two years; fly with me now."

She pulled herself free and glared at him. "No, Valien! No, I will not. I will not let you just... just fly out and die. We had a plan. We've had a plan for years. Bring Rune here. Rally the people around him. Raise the kingdom in rebellion. Not this— not flying to face Frey in open battle." She looked away, eyes damp. "You don't know him. Not like I do. You haven't seen the Axehand Order, how they train... Oh stars. They murder babes for sport. I saw it. In their training, they... they snatch babes from mothers and use them for crossbow practice. They complete their training by severing their own hands; they do this with glee. We cannot face these men head on—not with the forces we have now, weary men of these ruins. My father would kill us, Valien. He would kill you."

Tears filled her eyes, and she embraced Valien and clung to him.

Rune watched from the side, feeling somewhat like a third wheel. He was not sure who he agreed with. He had seen the cruelty of the Cadigus Regime—Pery beheaded in Lynport Square, men broken upon the wheel simply for speaking the wrong word, and his friends carted out of the city like cattle. Rune did not relish flying to battle these people; the mere idea churned his belly with so much fear he almost gagged.

And yet... was Valien right? Was this a chance they had to seize?

If we kill Cadigus now, he thought, *I'll have my city back. I'll have Tilla back. The entire kingdom will be freed. No more breaking wheels, troops patrolling every street, or statues of Frey in every square. No more youths carted off and broken into killers.*

Valien turned to look at him, Kaelyn wrapped in his arms, a pale and fragile doll in his bear-like grip.

"It seems to me," the haggard knight said, "that it should be Relesar Aeternum, our future king, who decides."

Rune couldn't help it; he barked a laugh. The room swam around him.

"You want... *me* to decide?" he said, eyebrows firmly raised. "Only last moon you were calling me a green boy who knows nothing of the sword. Now you want me to choose whether we fly to battle?"

Valien raised his own eyebrows. "You are our king, or will be. And you know a bit of swordplay; I taught you. So what say you? Do we do as Kaelyn says—bide our time, rally the people around you, and eventually, years down the line, strike at the capital with greater forces? Or do we fly to uncertain battle now—seize this chance to end the war in ten days and crown you?"

Rune clutched his head and laughed again—a mirthless laugh that sounded almost like a sob. Valien's voice sounded far too casual to him.

"But..." he said, "but... stars, Valien! Don't ask me. You're the knight. You're the leader of this Resistance. And you, Kaelyn." He turned to look at her. "Kaelyn, you know your father better than anyone here. And you've been fighting this war for two years now. How can *I* decide this?"

He raised his hands to the ceiling, and his legs shook. Stars! Thousands of warriors hid in these ruins. Thousands of warriors would be waiting at Castra Luna, guarding the emperor. Millions of souls suffered throughout Requiem, and their only hope for salvation was the Resistance.

All these people, Rune thought, *all their lives... depending on my decision.*

"Oh stars," he whispered.

"It's true, Rune," Valien said. "I've been fighting this for a while now. So has Kaelyn. We're both experienced, seasoned warriors, and we both know exactly what to do. Only problem is... we want to do exact opposite things." He gave a rare smile. "It seems fair that you, who will be our king, give your first decree."

Kaelyn looked at Rune too, her eyes damp but solemn. She tightened her lips and nodded.

"Let us hear," she said, "what the heir of Aeternum decides." She stepped toward him, clutched his hand, and squeezed it. Her eyes softened. "Choose, Rune. I will respect your choice. Do we rally more men to our cause, or do we strike the snake as he leaves his lair?"

They were both looking at him, waiting.

How could he decide? How could he possibly know what to do? The fate of the empire—hinging on his word!

I am the child of great kings, he thought, but today he felt like only a boy, alone and afraid. Even Amerath, which hung at his waist, did not comfort him. It still felt like a foreign object, the weapon of greater men. He had accepted his dynasty but still felt like only a brewer, only Rune of Cadport, not King Relesar.

I miss you, Tilla, he thought. Whenever troubles had found him at home, he would talk to Tilla, and they would find a solution together. So many times they would walk along the beach, discussing their problems—a bad brew of ale, not enough customers buying ropes, or a hinge needing repairs.

But this... this was the world itself awaiting his word, and Tilla was far away.

What do I do, Tilla? What would you tell me?

He closed his eyes and tried to imagine her beside him. They were walking on the beach again in darkness. They flew over the water as two dragons, him black and she white. He held her hand, kissed her lips, and looked into her dark eyes. Tilla—pillar of his childhood, light of his life, the beat of his heart.

"You are in danger now, Tilla," he whispered in his dream. "You are in pain. You are a soldier of Frey Cadigus, the man I must kill. I have to save the world, but I also have to save you."

He stood in silence, eyes shut, and closed his fists at his sides. All his life, he had hidden in shadow. Walking in the night. Flying in the dark. Withering in his tavern as the Regime crushed his city under its heel. But now—now he stood among the Resistance. Now he had Valien, a great leader, and Kaelyn, a great light, to guide his way, to fight at his side.

"It is time," he said softly, "to rise from ruin. It is time to light the darkness with fire." He opened his eyes and stared at his companions. "It is time for war."

LERESY

He stood upon the northern wall, hand on the pommel of his
sword, and watched his father's procession fly toward Castra
Luna.

"Bastard always knew how to fly in style," Leresy muttered.

The dragons—five hundred or more—still flew a league
away. Most were dragons of the Axehand Order; they wore black
dragonhelms topped with blades, the steel engraved with the red
spiral. They were missing their front left paws; great axeheads
were strapped to the stumps, mimicking their human deformity.
They flew in five phalanxes—four framed the procession, while
the fifth brought up the rear.

Between these elite guards flew the emperor and his
contingent. Frey Cadigus led the formation, a burly golden
dragon, the largest among them. The emperor wore no royal
raiment like the old kings of Aeternum, only the armor of a
soldier; a steel helm topped his head, engraved with the red spiral,
and a great breastplate—large as a boat—covered his belly where
no scales grew. And yet none would mistake him for a mere
soldier, for his horns were gilded, his eyes commanding, and his
bearing noble. Every flap of his wings, creak of his scales, and
snort of his flames spoke of his dominion.

At his right side flew his heir, the Princess Shari. Her scales
were blue, her armor black, and she roared and blew flames.

The Blue Bitch, they call her, Leresy thought and snarled. *An
apt title.*

He clenched his sword's hilt, hungering to spill his sister's
blood. Shari would learn, he swore. After his wedding this night,

she would learn that he, Leresy, was the strongest sibling, that he—the only son—would inherit the throne. When he was done with Shari, she would envy the miserable outcast Kaelyn.

He looked at the dragon who flew at his father's left side. *Here is my power.*

Leresy's scowl twisted into a grin. Lord Herin Blackrose, lord of the Axehand Order, flew as proudly as an emperor. The old dragon had no scales, the result of some disease no priest or healer could name. The dragon's flesh rippled, naked and raw, covered in boils instead of scales, a pale yellow that reminded Leresy of pus. Lord Herin was a foul, twisted freak, a beast that belonged in a menagerie, not in command. But he was strong. Leresy would swallow his disgust for a taste of Herin's might.

"He will be my father-in-law tonight, Shari," Leresy whispered as he watched the dragons fly. "Are you afraid yet? You should be, Blue Bitch. You should be."

Wings flapped behind him. An iron dragon landed upon the wall at his side, smoke pluming between her teeth. The dragon shifted, then stood as a woman with short yellow hair, mocking green eyes, and black armor engraved with a rose.

"The guests arrive," Nairi said, placed her hands upon a merlon, and nodded. "Soon I will be a princess."

"And I the heir," he said. "With your father's help, Shari won't last long." He placed his arm around Nairi, pulled her toward him, and kissed her cheek. "You will be my queen someday, Nairi. Today we rule Castra Luna—tomorrow, the empire."

Leresy looked around him, giving his fortress a last inspection. He had made sure to whip this outpost into proper shape for his father. His recruits, all three thousand of them, stood upon the walls or in the courtyard. Leresy had dressed them in black, steel breastplates bearing the red spiral; he would not have them wearing sweaty leather for the emperor's visit.

Each soldier stood stiff and still in perfect discipline; beneath their armor, their bodies bore the scars of punishers.

"You will make me proud today," Leresy hissed, inspecting their lines.

His eyes fell upon Tilla Roper and his pulse quickened. The young woman stood upon the eastern wall, a good head taller than the troops at her sides. Her face was pale, nearly pure white, but strong; her cheekbones were high, her nose straight, her eyes dark and proud. Leresy remembered reaching between her legs to correct her stance, and he sucked in air and hissed. He craved to reach there again, to touch her, own her, break her, to beat that pride out of her eyes. Tilla stood here a tall, proud soldier; Leresy ached to drag her into his bed, to make her scream, to shatter this shell of her strength and make her weep, to claim her.

Don't think you are safe, he thought, staring at her. *Don't think because I'm marrying Nairi that you won't be mine. I will break you, Tilla Roper. You think you are my soldier, but I will make you my whore.*

The imperial dragons roared their cry, and Leresy turned back toward them. Five hundred beasts of the Axehand Order howled together, announcing the emperor's arrival. It was the first day of spring, but the trees were still bare; they bent and creaked under the wind of a thousand wings. Blasts of fire rose to paint the sky red. The castle walls themselves shook. Only Frey Cadigus did not roar or blow fire; the great golden dragon merely flew with narrowed eyes, fangs bared.

"Welcome, you old bastard," Leresy said softly.

The old scars across his body flared, and Leresy clenched his fist around his sword, narrowed his eyes, and grinded his teeth. Frey had given him those scars, beating him throughout his childhood. Leresy knew every scar across him: those dealt by the rod, the whip, and the blade.

I will not have suffered for nothing, he thought. *Your cruelty made me strong, Father. I did not flee in weakness like Kaelyn. Your empire will be mine.*

He grabbed his banner, which stood in a ring upon the wall, and lifted it high. The banner unfurled, revealing the red spiral, sigil of his house.

"Welcome to Castra Luna!" he shouted to the approaching force. "I am Leresy Cadigus, Prince of Requiem! Welcome to my domain!"

The dragons approached, Frey at their lead, a great host of shimmering scales and fire. Leresy raised his banner as high as he could.

"Welcome, Father!" he shouted. "Welcome to Castra Luna!"

The emperor flew with narrowed eyes toward the wall... then overshot Leresy, not sparing him a glance. The rest of the procession did the same, the flapping of their wings nearly tearing the banner from Leresy's hands. His hair and cloak billowed madly. The dragons didn't even seem to see him, only flew above him, then began to descend toward the fortress courtyard.

Only Shari even spared him a glance, but her eyes were mocking, and she smirked and blasted smoke his way. Then she, too, overshot him and landed in the courtyard below.

Leresy spun around, fuming, to stare down at the courtyard. The five hundred dragons were landing and shifting into human forms. The axehands formed ranks, silent figures robed in black like ghosts. Their hoods and masks hid their faces. The sunlight gleamed on the axeheads strapped to the stubs of their left arms.

Between them, Frey Cadigus and Shari shifted into human forms too. They wore black steel, the plates filigreed with gold, and their cloaks were woven of rich crimson fabric. At once, they two began marching toward the fortress's main hall, not even turning back to glance at Leresy.

"Father!" Leresy cried from the wall.

Frey ignored him. The emperor snapped his fingers, and the gatekeepers—burly men in chainmail—pulled open the hall doors. Crimson capes billowing, Frey and Shari entered the hall and vanished into its shadows.

Leresy snarled.

Still a bastard.

He grabbed Nairi's arm.

"Come on," he said and began pulling Nairi down the stairs into the courtyard.

He entered the main hall of Castra Luna. The hall was wide, but its vaulted ceiling was low, and columns rose every few feet. This place, like every chamber in Castra Luna, was built with no space for dragons. Should the Resistance ever reach this hall, they'd have to fight here in human forms.

Frey Cadigus was already sitting at the high table, occupying Leresy's seat. Shari sat to his right, Lord Hiran Blackrose to his left. Several recruits, whom Leresy had stationed to guard the hall, were pouring wine as if they were servants.

"Make yourself at home, why don't you?" Leresy called out, marching toward his father. "Would you care for a seat? Perhaps some wine?"

Frey Cadigus finally acknowledged his son. He stared at Leresy, eyes narrowed and cold. The lines on his face deepened. He held his cup near his lips, but did not yet drink.

"Spare me your failed attempts at wit," the emperor said; his every word sounded like he was spitting. "And for pity's sake, what's that bauble on your head?"

Leresy touched the golden ringlet he wore in his hair. He had paid a small fortune for it; its golden wires twisted to form dragons aflight, their eyes made of diamonds, their scales rubies and sapphires.

"A symbol of my lordship," Leresy said, chin held high.

Frey grunted, rose to his feet, and marched forward. He grabbed the ringlet off Leresy's head, glowered, then snapped the priceless work of art in half. He tossed the pieces aside, and jewels spilled across the floor.

"I've seen finer trinkets on whores," Frey said, staring at Leresy. It was his old, withering stare, eyes hard and sharp as daggers. "You lead soldiers. Start behaving like one yourself."

Leresy squared his jaw. "I will—"

But Frey turned away, ignoring him. The emperor looked at Nairi, who stood at Leresy's side, and his eyes softened.

"Nairi Blackmore!" Frey reached out his arms. "Come to me, darling, and give an old man a kiss. You are looking more beautiful than ever. The south agrees with you, which is more than I can say for my son."

"My Commander," Nairi said, embraced the emperor, and kissed his cheek. "I am so pleased to see you, my lord. Welcome to our home."

Frey clasped her pauldron. "Ah! You wear good steel and speak well. Learn from her, Leresy! She is a real soldier; she cares for steel and fire, not tiaras. Come, Nairi! Sit with me at my table. Tell me all about these new troops you've been training for me."

With a wink at Leresy, she followed the emperor to the table, sat beside him, and began to share the bread and wine.

Leresy stood fuming. His fists trembled at his sides.

He's trying to enrage me, he thought, jaw clenched. *He wants me to scream. He wants me to embarrass myself before his men. I will not give him that satisfaction.*

He spoke loudly, letting his voice fill the hall.

"These recruits I've trained—yes, Father, *I* trained them— will receive their rank as the sun hits its zenith. Eat your bread and drink your wine! Soon the clock strikes noon, and you will see my gift to you. Three thousand soldiers will receive their rank, a new host for the Legions. They will watch me wed this night!"

Frey was chewing his bread and still speaking with Nairi. He looked back at his son and snorted.

"*You* trained them? Did you march with them in the mud, or blow your fire with theirs, or teach them the values of our empire—strength, honor, and eternal glory?" The emperor snorted again. "Or were you busy staring into a mirror, admiring your fine jewels, as Nairi broke in the troops? Yes, Leresy, I will most gladly watch three thousand recruits receive their rank. And I will gladly watch the woman who trained them—Nairi Blackrose—wed into our family. Now leave us! Go and cut your hair; it's longer than a woman's. Return to me looking like a soldier yourself before you present me with three thousand of them."

With that, Frey returned to his meal and conversation with Nairi.

As Leresy fumed, almost shaking with rage, he saw his sister looking at him from the table. Shari Cadigus, heir to the empire, was stabbing grapes with her dagger and eating them. She wore no helm; her curly dark hair cascaded across her armored shoulders. She swallowed a grape, winked at Leresy, and gave him a crooked smile. Then she slammed her dagger down, piercing another grape, and her grin widened—a wolf's grin.

Soon, Leresy, her eyes said. *Soon this dagger will thrust into your back.*

Leresy spun, fists clenched, and marched out of the hall. In the courtyard, he shifted into a dragon and took flight. He soared toward his tower, flames spilling from his maw.

You will die, Shari, he swore and blasted flame at the sky. *You will die, Father. Do not think you are safe. You mock me now, but you don't know my strength. I will crush you both in my jaws, and Requiem will be mine.*

He landed upon his tower, shifted into human form, and entered his chamber. He walked to his mirror and drew his dagger. With clenched teeth, he began shearing his hair, tearing nearly as much as he cut.

"I will play your game for now, Father," he said. "But when I'm done, this dagger will enter your heart."

His beautiful, golden hair fell around his boots, and his eyes stung.

TILLA

She stood in the courtyard, clad in steel, on the most frightening day of her life.

Today I will watch the prince wed, she thought. *Today I will receive my rank. Today I will become a soldier, ready for war.*

The tower rose above her, a shard of obsidian scratching the sky. Its great black-and-red clock chimed noon, and Tilla sucked in her breath, raised her chin, and struggled to calm her thrashing heart.

Her fellow recruits stood across the walls and courtyards, three thousand in all. Many were from Cadport, youths she had grown up with; the rest were from towns and villages across the south. They stood in their phalanxes, a hundred each. Tilla clutched the standard of her own phalanx, a black rose within an iron ring.

Nairi Blackrose herself, her commander and soon her princess, stood before her. She wore her finest armor this day, polished black plates engraved with roses. Her insignia—the single red spiral of a lanse—shone upon her shoulders.

Tilla herself wore metal for the first time. The prince had equipped all his recruits with real steel for this day. The armorer had forged Tilla's breastplate only days ago. It fit snugly, polished black and engraved with a red spiral upon the chest. Soon she would receive armbands, and each one would display a single red star.

I will be a periva, she thought. *A low rank, yes. But I will be a true warrior of the Legions, no longer merely a recruit.*

Her fingers tingled to think of it. After all this time—three moons of pain and dirt and sweat and blood—she would become a true soldier.

I made it, she thought. *I survived Castra Luna.*

Wings thudded, and Tilla looked up to see the emperor, the princess, and the prince—three dragons in armor—descend into the courtyard. Once they landed, they shifted into human forms.

Frey Cadigus stood in the center, the tallest among them. His dark, thinning hair was slicked back. His eyes, shards of stone, stared upon the troops that stood before him. His thin lips twisted, deepening the grooves around his mouth. His face was almost cadaverous, Tilla thought, but his armor shone, and his shoulders were wide and strong.

Frey raised his fist.

"Hail the red spiral!" he shouted, then pounded that fist against his breastplate.

Across the courtyard, the soldiers repeated the cry.

"Hail the red spiral!"

Fists rose, then pounded against chests. Tilla sucked in her breath, and her body tingled.

This is power, she thought. Thousands of warriors shouting together, united under one banner—this was glory.

She was no longer afraid, she realized. It was the first time in moons, maybe in years, that she felt no fear. She had come to Castra Luna a timid, terrified girl. Now she stood as a warrior, clad in steel, a sword at her side, shouting for the glory of her kingdom.

"Today you become soldiers!" Frey Cadigus cried to them. "You have trained for long moons. You have grown strong. You learned to fight with swords, to fly as dragons, to kill our enemies. But more importantly, you learned our moral code." He clenched his fist. "You learned of strength. You learned of honor. You learned that pity, compassion, and cowardice lead to decline and death. Requiem is strong! Requiem is a great blade and a pillar of flame. Requiem will never more fall. Hail the red spiral!"

"Hail the red spiral!" Tilla shouted with the others, fist raised.

The cry echoed across the fortress, across the forest, across the empire itself. Tilla held her head high, allowing the power to flow through her.

"Speak your vows," Frey called out, "and join the might of Requiem."

Across the courtyard, the ranks of troops held fists to chests and chanted together. Tilla spoke with a loud, clear voice.

"I hail the red spiral. I hail Emperor Cadigus. I vow to fight for Requiem. I will crush her enemies. With fire and steel, I will slay all who threaten her. I am strong. I am proud. I will allow no weakness, fear, or mercy in my heart. I am the fist, blade, and flame of Requiem. The fatherland will never fall! Hail Requiem—today I am her champion."

As Tilla chanted her vows with thousands of others, she felt that strength rise through her. She had always been so afraid, so weak; for the first time in her life, she felt pride.

Is this not better than fear? she thought. *Is this not better than the woman I was—crushed under the emperor's boot, timid, alone? I was so afraid then, but now I am strong.*

The lanses, commanders of the phalanxes, marched forward. They carried boxes full of black leather armbands.

Nairi stood before her phalanx, hands on her hips, and nodded.

"Today I am proud of you," she said. "I broke your bodies. I broke your souls. I molded you into warriors. Today you are soldiers of Requiem."

Tilla stared at the box. Each armband gleamed with a single red star; it was the lowest rank in the Legions, but by the stars, it meant she was a real legionary now. She felt her eyes dampen. All her life, she had lived in hunger, poverty, and fear. Now she had achieved something—a bit of honor. She would wear her insignia proudly and know: *I survived and I have a purpose.*

Nairi began to call out names. Across the courtyard, other lanses were doing the same.

"Erry Docker!" Nairi shouted, and the slim urchin stepped forward.

"Yes, Commander!" Erry said, the shortest among them but today standing tall.

"I promote you to Periva Erry Docker," Nairi said, reached into the box, and produced two armbands. She buckled them around Erry's thin arms; they gleamed with the new rank. "Hail the red spiral!"

Erry saluted. "Hail the red spiral!"

The young orphan, now a warrior, returned to her formation. Her face beamed.

"Mae Baker!" Nairi cried next, and soon Mae too wore insignia upon her arms.

When it was Tilla's turn to walk forth, her knees shook, and she clenched her fists to hide her trembling fingers.

"Yes, Commander," she said, standing before Nairi.

Nairi stared at her, eyes narrowed and shrewd. The lanse paused.

She's not going to promote me, Tilla suddenly thought, and fear washed her. *She still remembers how Leresy touched me. She's still jealous. She's going to pull out her punisher and hurt me—right here before the emperor. Oh stars...*

"Tilla Roper," Nairi said slowly, nodding.

Tilla's belly clenched with fear; Nairi was among the most powerful women in Requiem, and after tonight's wedding, she would only rise in status.

She could kill me here in this courtyard, Tilla knew, *and nobody would bat an eyelash.*

"Yes, Commander!" Tilla replied.

Nairi tilted her head, examining her quizzically. "You think you are a soldier, Roper?"

Tilla raised her chin high. "I will fight for the red spiral, Commander."

"Will you now?" Nairi leaned close and whispered. "Or will you just spread your legs for my husband?"

Tilla's heart thrashed. Sweat trickled down her back.

"I..." She stiffened and whispered back, "No, Commander! He is yours. You are a great leader, a woman of nobility and strength. I am but a lowly servant of the empire."

"You are *my* servant," Nairi said, teeth bared. "Do not think—not for an instant—that you are free of me today, Tilla Roper. You will remain in my phalanx. I commanded you in training; I will command you in battle. You will be mine for the rest of your service." She clutched her punisher and its tip flared. "If I see you near him, Roper, your last punishment will seem merciful. I will drive this punisher against you all night until you beg for death. Do you understand me?"

Tilla felt herself blanch. She took a shuddering breath.

"Yes, Commander," she whispered.

Nairi all but slammed the bands onto Tilla's arms, tightening them so hard it hurt.

"I promote you to Periva Tilla Roper!" she shouted, teeth still bared. "Hail the red spiral!"

"Hail the red spiral!" Tilla shouted in return, then stepped back into her formation.

Bloody stars, she thought. Her breath shuddered. She had thought that, after the wedding, she would be rid of Nairi. Wouldn't a princess of Requiem command entire battalions, not a humble phalanx of only a hundred troops? When Tilla had heard of the wedding, she had rejoiced, thinking that Nairi would leave her.

256

How will I fight under her heel? Tilla thought. *Is there any hope for me to ever leave the Black Rose?*

When all the troops had received their rank, Frey Cadigus raised his fist and shouted for the red spiral. The troops returned his call, three thousand new warriors of the empire.

Prince Leresy paced the courtyard and cried to the troops.

"Today you are warriors! I have trained you well. As my gift to you, you may stay to celebrate my wedding. You will feast with me! Today you will dine upon fresh meat and wine." Leresy raised his fist in salute. "Tomorrow you will fly to war, soldiers of Requiem. Hail the red spiral!"

LERESY

"Everything changes today," he whispered, perched upon the fortress walls in dragon form. "Today Leresy Cadigus rises."

He snorted fire from his nostrils. Below him in the courtyard, tables were set out in the open air. Winter was ending; the day was crisp but sunny. Smoke was pumping from the kitchen chimneys, and when Leresy sniffed, he could smell his wedding feast cooking. There would be roasted fowl, wild boar, lambs cooked in mint, and hundreds of pies and loaves.

It was a small feast, of course, compared to the splendor of the capital. Had he chosen to wed in Nova Vita, the Fire of the North, the entire city—a million souls—would feast with him. Banners of gold and crimson would flap from every roof. Ten thousand dragons would fly overhead, roaring for him. Troops would march down hundreds of streets, blowing horns and chanting his name.

Here in the south there would be none of that. Here in Castra Luna there would be some food, some drink, but mostly power. And power was what Leresy craved even more than splendor.

This is my domain, he thought and blasted smoke from his nostrils. *Here is my fortress, my rule, my home. Here I will form this great alliance, and from here my wrath will descend upon the capital.*

His troops stood upon the walls around him, all in human forms. Some faced the forests, keeping watch upon the horizons. Others faced the courtyard below; they would witness the glory of his wedding.

Again Leresy's eyes sought out Tilla. He saw her upon the eastern wall. She stood with her back to him, keeping vigil upon the woods. She held the banner of the Black Rose, a ring of iron upon a wooden pole—Nairi's sigil.

Strangely, seeing Tilla holding the sigil of his betrothed only made her more intoxicating. Tilla's hair blew in the wind, revealing her pale neck. She was a tall, noble warrior, yet so fragile, so afraid, so weak compared to his might. Leresy had always wanted to break her, to hurt her, to hear her scream, yet now he felt a strange need to comfort her.

What if he flew toward her, grabbed her, and carried her into the wilderness? What if they found some distant land to dwell in, just him and her? No more Shari plotting to kill him. No more Frey belittling him. No more Nairi craving his power and planning her ascent.

I could protect you from all that, Tilla, he thought. *I could shield you from all the pain in the world. I would hold you in the dark and we would feel warm.*

He looked away, grimacing.

No, he thought. He had worked too hard for this. He could not give up his ambitions, not so close to seizing his prize. He would have to play this game a little longer, to tolerate his family for a few more moons or years. But then... then he would strike. Then the throne would be his—and so would Tilla Roper.

Below in the courtyard, Frey Cadigus waited, clad in a burgundy robe and holding his scepter of power. Shari stood at his right side, Lord Herin Blackrose at his left. Before them, all across the cobblestones, five hundred axehands stood in formation—the men whom Leresy would soon rule.

"It's time," he whispered.

He took flight and dived toward the courtyard.

From the clock tower above, an iron dragon flew—Nairi Blackrose—and landed beside him. The two dragons, red and gray, stood in the courtyard before the emperor. Plumes of smoke rose between their teeth. They shifted together and stood in human forms, clad in black steel, awaiting their union.

Leresy looked at his father. He looked at the grooved face, the cold eyes, the thin lips. He looked upon this man and he hated him.

He looked aside at Lord Herin Blackrose, soon to be his father-in-law, and shivered.

Like all men of his order, Lord Herin wore black robes, and his left arm ended with an axehead instead of a hand. But unlike the others, Herin Blackrose—as their commander—wore no iron mask. Leresy thought it a pity; if anyone needed to hide his face, it was Herin. The man looked like a dying, furless cat. Herin was completely hairless; not merely bald, but lacking eyebrows and eyelashes too. He had no more teeth than hair; when his lips parted, they revealed bare gums. Wrinkles and boils covered his skin. Leresy could barely believe such a monster had fathered the beautiful Nairi. Lord Herin was a diseased freak, Leresy thought, but he was strong. His eyes blazed like steel in smelters. After the emperor, he was the strongest man in Requiem.

Finally Leresy looked at Shari, his older sister. She smirked at him, her eyes mocking, and gave him the slightest of winks. He knew what that wink meant. *I will kill you, Leresy,* she was saying, and he clenched his jaw.

Not if I kill you first, he thought.

He wondered where his twin lurked on this day. Was Kaelyn hiding in some tunnel, filthy and stinking? Did she run through some forest, dreaming of the day she could strike the capital? Was she bedding that vagabond Valien, the disgraced knight?

One day I will kill you too, Kaelyn, he swore. *One day I will kill you all—everyone in this damn, foul world.*

Emperor Frey raised his scepter, a rod of gold topped with a red spiral. He called out to the crowd.

"Today we join two great houses!" he said. "Today House Cadigus and House Blackrose become one. Today Requiem grows strong!"

The wedding began.

TILLA

She stood on the walls, her insignia upon her arms and her banner in hand—a soldier defending her emperor.

The forests rolled into the east, trees still bare, but spring began this day in Requiem, and spring had come to her life. She had arrived in Castra Luna in winter's cold, shivering and pale in a cart, no better than cattle. She had been frightened, weak, and lonely, yet now she stood in steel, armed with her sword.

I'm no longer that old Tilla, the one who was always so afraid, she thought. *I am a periva now. I am a soldier. And I am strong.*

Behind her in the courtyard the wedding began. Tilla could hear Emperor Cadigus speak of the union, joining two mighty houses. Tilla had been ordered to defend the walls and watch the eastern sky; she could not view the wedding, which pleased her. She had no wish to see Nairi's power grow. Watching the forest, defending these walls, was the task of a true soldier.

"Bloody Abyss," Erry muttered at her side. The girl clutched the hilt of her sword. "I was sure we were rid of that gutter stain Nairi. Is she really going to keep commanding us now in battle?"

Mae stood at Tilla's other side, her pale cheeks pinched pink in the cold. Her lips quivered, and she nervously tugged her golden braid.

"But I don't *want* to fight battles," she said. "Now that we're real soldiers, can't we just... guard walls? Standing here isn't so bad. I want to be a guard, not a fighter."

Erry snorted. "Wobble Lips, you want to spend your five years of service standing on a wall? Not me. I'm going to *fight.*

I'm going straight to the front line to kill those bloody resistors."
She snarled. "I'm going to burn them good."

"Hush!" Tilla whispered; the conversation was growing too
loud, and she worried the sound would carry to the courtyard. If
it did, they wouldn't have to worry about any battles; they'd be
hanged after the wedding.

She returned her eyes to the east. The forests rolled into
distant mist. Many called Castra Luna the most isolated fort in
the empire, a single light shining in the wilderness. Tilla
wondered where the next five years would take her, and whether
she would see Cadport again before her service ended.

*And will I see you again, Rune? And if I do see you, will you
recognize the woman I've become?*

Movement on the horizon caught her eyes.

Her thoughts died and Tilla squinted.

Thousands of shapes fluttered in the distant mist like a
flock of birds.

"Nairi Blackrose!" the emperor's voice rose below. "Step
forward and hail the red spiral."

Tilla squinted and leaned forward. Those were no birds.
They were too large, too many. She could barely see them
through the mist.

"Erry, you'd last maybe five minutes in battle!" Mae was
saying, incurring curses from the shorter girl.

Tilla clutched her sword. Fear washed her belly. Whatever
was flying ahead was moving fast. She thought she saw orange
sparks rise among them. A few of the shapes glinted as if clad in
armor.

"Leresy Cadigus!" The emperor's voice rose from the
courtyard. "Step forward, hail the red spiral, and turn toward
Nairi."

Tilla's fingers trembled around her hilt.

Stars no, stars, it can't be.

"Wobble Lips, maybe you'll die," Erry was saying, "but I'm a warrior. I'm going to *kill*."

We're all alone here, Tilla thought. *Alone in the wilderness. The emperor. The prince and princess. And us upon the wall.*

The horde flew from the east, and Tilla heard their distant cries.

"Dragons," she whispered, voice shaking. "Thousands of them. The Resistance."

"Exactly!" Erry said. "Tilla understands. I'm going to kill thousands of Resistance dragons, and—" The young woman gasped. "Stars, Tilla, what the Abyss is that in the east?"

"Your chance for battle," Tilla whispered.

The eastern dragons roared, and vaguely upon the wind, Tilla thought she could hear their words, just a hint of sound: *For Aeternum! Death to Cadigus!*

"Join hands!" Frey announced below. "Nairi Blackrose and Leresy Cadigus, I now—"

Tilla spun around toward the courtyard, raised her standard high, and shouted over the emperor's words.

"Dragons! Dragons fly from the east!" She waved her standard. "The Resistance attacks!"

LERESY

Leresy stood frozen, holding his new wife's hands.

"The Resistance!" Tilla was shouting from the walls, waving her arms. "We're under attack!"

Leresy blinked. He could not move.

He looked up. His father met his eyes, then shifted into a golden dragon and flew. Shari too took flight, a blue dragon blowing fire. The axehands shifted as well, and hundreds of dragons rose. Roars and thuds of wings filled the air.

Leresy could not move. He only stood, clutching Nairi's hands.

"Are we... married yet?" he said.

Nairi snarled and pulled her hands free.

"Damn it, Leresy!" she shouted, shifted into a dragon, and took flight.

"The Resistance attacks!" Lord Herin Blackrose was shrieking, circling above the courtyard, a wrinkled dragon with no scales. "Axehand—battle formations, surround the emperor!"

Leresy looked to his right. Nairi was flying above the walls, shouting for her phalanx.

"Black Rose—behind me! Assault formation, shift, fly!"

The hundred soldiers of her phalanx, Tilla among them, took flight as dragons. Thousands of the other legionaries were doing the same, grouping around their own commanders.

Leresy cursed, shifted too, and flew.

He had no phalanx of his own. He was not sure where to go. He soared higher than the others, so high that the thin air spun his head, and stared east. He saw the enemy there, and he snarled.

"The Resistance," he hissed.

Thousands of them flew from the east, roaring and blasting fire. They wore no dragonhelms or armor. They were feral beasts, unwashed and wild. They flew in no formations, but as a single rabble, howling and wreathed in flame.

Fear—stabbing, pulsing, all-consuming—washed over Leresy.

"Death to Cadigus!" the resistors were howling. "Slay the emperor and his children!"

They're coming to kill me, Leresy thought, staring at the horde. His wings shook. His smoke blasted uncontrollably. *Oh stars, they're coming to slay me upon the walls of my fort.*

Tears stung his eyes, and fire flared inside him, and Leresy soared higher.

"Into the barracks!" he howled at his troops. "Retreat! Retreat into the halls, lock the doors, man the walls! Defend this cast—"

His father roared, soared from below, and slammed into him.

The blow knocked the breath out of Leresy. He tumbled, and his father cudgeled him with his tail. Lersey spun in the air, fell a hundred feet, and barely righted himself.

"Assault formations!" Frey Cadigus shouted to the troops around him, his voice deep and steady. "Axehand—man the walls and await my orders. Dragon Legions—prepare for aerial battle. I will lead the charge."

The phalanxes began to take formation. These dragons had been soldiers for only several hours, but had trained well enough to form ranks quickly. Frey flew to their lead, then looked over his shoulder at Leresy. Disgust filled the emperor's eyes.

"Go defend your castle," he said, then turned and began flying east. "To war! To glory! Dragon Legions, fly!"

Thousands of dragons howled and flew behind the emperor. Shari flew at her father's side, roaring flames. Nairi flew ahead of her phalanx, shouting orders. They charged over the forests toward the Resistance.

Leresy hovered in midair, panting and trembling.

Before him in the east, the two armies crashed with exploding fire and blood.

Leresy stared, jaw open.

He had never seen so much blood.

One of the resistors, a burly beast of chipped scales, flamed a young periva. The dragon screamed and returned to human form, flesh peeling. Another resistor, a black demon with flaming eyes, lashed his claws at another dragon; this dragon too returned to human form, clutched spilling entrails, and tumbled to the forest below.

Do you fly here too, Kaelyn? Twin sister, do you howl with this mob? Leresy's eyes stung. *I always protected you, Kaelyn! When Father beat you, I always comforted you! Now you come to kill me?*

Leresy could not breathe. He could barely flap his wings. He let out a howl—he meant it to be a battle cry, but it sounded more like a wail.

"The prince!" roared a burly, silver dragon missing his left horn. "Leresy Cadigus, there! Slay the prince!"

Hundreds of resistors looked up, eyes blazing and fire burning, and began to fly his way.

Leresy screamed, spun around, and began to flee.

"Axehand!" he shouted as he flew. "Into the barracks! Into the hall! Defend the gates—defend your prince!"

The sky burned. Howls shook the walls. Leresy screamed and panted and landed in the courtyard. He shifted into human form and ran, arms pumping, into the grand hall of Castra Luna.

"Axehand! Into the hall—defend your prince!" His voice cracked. "That is an order!"

Outside the doors, fires blazed, and thousands of wings hid the sky.

Leresy panted, fell backward, and felt warm liquid trickle down his leg.

TILLA

Blood, smoke, and fire raged around her.

Thousands of dragons, soldiers and rebels of Requiem, covered the sky. Claws slashed. Fangs bit. Jets of fire howled. Dragons burned and bled all around. In death, their magic left them; they tumbled to the forest as humans, armor shattered, flesh charred, and limbs torn.

Terror. Terror clutched Tilla like claws. Her head spun. Ice filled her belly. Her wings could barely flap.

How could this be? I've only just received my rank! I can't—

"Assault formation, damn it!" Nairi howled, streaming before them, her gray scales caked with ash. The lanse roared fire, burning a resistor who swooped toward her. "Black Roses, form ranks—rally here! Charge!"

Tilla bared her fangs and growled.

No fear now. Just fire.

"Erry, to my right!" she cried. "Mae, my left! Soar!"

Roaring, Tilla beat her wings and flew after Nairi. She blew her flames. She howled her rage. Her flight crew flew at her sides, their horns at her shoulders in defensive positions. Around them, the other flights of the Black Rose flew, roaring and blowing flames. Above them, hundreds of resistors swooped, fire raining and claws stretched out.

"Hail the emperor!" Nairi shouted above... and the sky exploded.

Fire rained onto Tilla. She shut her eyes, screamed, and blew her own flames. A great weight slammed into her. She peeked to see scales and claws slashing. She howled. She thrust her horns. She bit into flesh and tasted blood.

"Soar!" Nairi shouted above. "Break through their lines—arrow formation, after me, fight!"

Tilla howled and rose through flame. Fire swirled around her. A dragon's head burst through the inferno, fangs biting, and Tilla slashed her claws. Blood rained and she kept soaring. Her flight crew screamed at her sides, blowing fire over her shoulders, clearing a path for her. A triangle of dragons, they rose after Nairi. Behind and around them, the rest of the Black Rose flew, a spearhead driving upward.

They burst through the rebel assault. Clear skies opened ahead. Tilla looked around, panting. The battle covered the sky. Bodies lay strewn over the trees. All around, dragons were battling. The Legions flew in phalanxes, lanses leading perivas. The Resistance flew as a mob, a wild mass of howling beasts; they seemed to have no ranks or formations, only their rage. Flames and blood showered. Tilla could barely even see the fortress, though it lay only a league away; smoke and blood curtained the sky.

"Swarm!" Nairi cried above. She flew toward the sun, turned, and dived. "Follow, Black Rose—rain fire!"

Tilla howled, spun, and swooped. Her phalanx followed. They crashed down, spewing fire. Dragons of the Resistance soared toward them.

The two forces slammed together.

The thud of crashing bodies shook the sky.

Flames burst and claws slashed at scales. Tilla screamed and lashed her tail, clubbing a dragon's head until its neck snapped; the resistor fell as a man, his skull caved in. Flames rose. A dragon at Tilla's side, once a seamstress from Cadport and now a soldier, screamed and burned. She lost her magic and tumbled, a human girl aflame.

In an instant of respite, Tilla looked around her. Her heart pounded and her chest heaved. The battle was moving closer to the fortress; the Resistance was still howling in berserk rage and pushing forward. The emperor was leading a charge against their northern flank, roaring flames.

Where is Valien Eleison? Tilla thought, tongue lolling as she panted. *Where is the leader of this rabble? I will slay him.*

She looked across the Resistance, seeking him. She had only seen him in paintings and drawings—a scarred, silver dragon, one of his horns chipped off. He was said to be the largest among them, a demon of bloodlust and fire. Where—

Tilla's breath died.

No.

Her head spun.

No, please, no, this can't be.

"Charge, break their lines!" Nairi was shouting hoarsely, her wings beating. A gash ran down her face, and blood splashed her scales. "Black Rose Phalanx, charge! Assault formation, go!"

The Black Roses began to charge. Tilla could barely move. She shook.

Oh, stars, it can't be him...

"Come on, Tilla!" Erry screamed at her side. The young copper dragon slapped Tilla with her tail. "Fly!"

Tilla looked over her shoulder to the east, and she saw him again. Tears filled her eyes.

A young black dragon.

"Rune," she whispered.

"Attack!" Nairi shouted.

Fire rained and dragons crashed against them.

Heart thrashing, Tilla joined the charge. She screamed. A claw slashed her shoulder, her blood spurted, and she blew her flames. She clawed a resistor and sent the beast tumbling.

"Break their lines!" Nairi was howling. "Hail the red spiral! Attack—for Requiem!"

Tilla looked over her shoulder again, seeking him. Yet the black dragon was gone.

No. No! It couldn't have been him. Tilla shook her head wildly. There were many black young dragons. How could this have been Rune?

And yet... the dragon had dived just like him. Tilla had flown alongside Rune so many nights. She would recognize his dragon form anywhere.

How could he—

"Death to Cadigus!"

The howl rose below.

Tilla whipped her head down, and she gasped.

A burly beast rose from flames. He was the largest dragon Tilla had ever seen, perhaps even larger than Emperor Frey. His left horn was missing; he had only a chipped stub. Scratches and dents covered his scales. And yet he ascended with the fury and might of a demon, blowing his flame and lashing his claws.

Valien Eleison, leader of the Resistance.

"Charge!" Nairi screamed and dived.

The Black Rose Phalanx roared and blew their flames.

KAELYN

She flew on the wind, roaring fire.

The battle raged around her, thousands of dragons crashing through flame and blood.

Her father's troops flew with horrible precision. Their phalanxes changed formation at a single order. They charged as arrowheads, breaking through the Resistance lines. They swooped in the shape of great claws, trapping resistors amongst them. They flew toward the sun, then dived, the light at their backs, blinding the Resistance before raining flame.

The Resistance fought like wildfire; the Legions were clockwork killers.

We can't beat them, Kaelyn thought, heart pounding against her ribs. She beat her wings mightily, rose higher, and blazed her fire. *They're too well trained. They wear armor. They fight like machines. We can't defeat them.*

"Kaelyn, you harlot!" rose a shriek ahead. "Come die in my flames!"

Kaelyn gasped.

She looked up.

"Nairi," she whispered. "Nairi Blackrose."

She had known the young woman all her life; they'd been born only days apart and raised together in the palace. Nairi's father was Lord Herin himself, the most powerful man in the empire aside from Frey. Nairi's house ruled the Axehand Order, enforcers and torturers.

Nairi herself tortured me in my childhood, Kaelyn remembered. The cruel young girl, with her mocking green eyes, would strut around the palace, spreading rumors about Kaelyn bedding common soldiers.

She always saw me as a rival, Kaelyn thought, teeth grinding. *She is the firstborn daughter of the Axehand; I'm the lastborn of the emperor. She is the prince's lover; I'm his twin. Two girls, of an age, equal in power: one cruel, the other hurt.*

"Kaelyn Cadigus!" Nairi was screaming, an iron dragon wreathed in fire; a hundred soldiers flew behind her. "The Whore of the Resistance! The traitor of the empire! Come to me, Kaelyn, and burn!"

Kaelyn snarled.

"Fly with me, Rune!" she said. "Keep to my right and blow your fire with mine."

The young black dragon flew beside her. Fear filled his eyes. Smoke burst from his nostrils, trembling with his breath. Flames charred his scales. And yet he reared, clawed the sky, and bared his fangs.

"We fly!" he howled.

"We charge!" Kaelyn shouted. "Resistance, fly! Slay the iron dragon."

Kaelyn roared and they shot forward. Around them, a hundred other resistors howled and blew flame.

The two forces streamed toward each other: a hundred dragons of the Legions, clad in black helms and breastplates, and a hundred dragons of the Resistance, howling wild and bare.

Streams of fire blazed and crashed together.

An instant later, the dragons shot through the flames and slammed together.

Kaelyn screamed. Flames showered her. Claws lashed her back, ripping off scales. Blood flowed.

"Scream for me, sow!" Nairi shouted somewhere above. "Scream like a pig as I gore you!"

Kaelyn roared flames and lashed claws. The Legions' dragons mobbed her. Blades topped their helms; one scratched along her leg, and more blood poured. Kaelyn howled and clawed the beast. It screamed, lost its magic, and fell as a young woman.

"Kaelyn!" Nairi cried above and laughed. "Come die, Kaelyn."

The iron dragon shot down, a shard of fangs and fire.

Kaelyn screamed, bucked, and raised her claws.

The two dragons, green and gray, thudded together. Flames engulfed them.

Nairi laughed and bit.

Fangs drove into Kaelyn's shoulder.

She screamed.

The gray dragon drove her fangs deeper, and her claws lashed, and Kaelyn writhed but could not tear her off. Pain exploded through her. She dipped in the sky. Nairi clung to her like a scaled leech, biting deeper, tasting her blood, *drinking* it.

"Rune!" Kaelyn cried, looking around for him, but could not see him. She could not see any of her dragons. The legionaries surrounded her, horns drove into her, and fire bathed her. Kaelyn screamed and the flames covered her. She bucked and clawed, but couldn't dislodge Nairi, and the beast's fangs drove deeper. Nairi's throat bobbed as she guzzled the blood.

Goodbye, Requiem, Kaelyn thought, eyes rolling back. *Goodbye, Rune.*

But no. No! She could not give up, not now, not so close to the end. Kaelyn growled. There was only one thing she could do now, one maneuver Valien had taught her. If she failed, she'd die at once. She would have to take that risk.

Screaming, Kaelyn released her magic.

She returned to human form.

She expected Nairi's fangs to tear through her. But Kaelyn wriggled, pushed back, and tumbled from the gray dragon's jaws.

She fell through fire and blood.

Above her, Nairi screamed and reared, then began to dive.

Kaelyn fell, cloak billowing, and drew an arrow from her quiver. She thudded against a dragon's back, tumbled over the beast, and kept falling.

Nairi swooped above, a dragon wreathed in flames.

Falling backward toward the forest, Kaelyn nocked her arrow and fired.

The arrow slammed into Nairi's eye.

The gray dragon screeched.

Kaelyn's back grazed the trees below. At once she shifted back into a dragon, soared, and roared fire.

Her flames crashed into Nairi. The iron beast screamed, blinded, an arrow in her eye and fire engulfing her.

"You will be the one to die!" Kaelyn screamed.

She flew higher, howling, and slammed her horns into Nairi's neck.

Pain exploded. Kaelyn's horns punched through scale and skin like blades through boiled leather. Blood showered Kaelyn.

She knew nothing but fire and blood.

Above her, Nairi returned to human form.

Kaelyn flew higher, the human Nairi skewered upon her horns. Dragons battled and screamed around her. Kaelyn shook her head wildly, tossing Nairi off.

The young lanse fell through the sky, pierced with holes, her eyes wide and mouth crying silently. She was still alive.

"Please," her lips seemed to whisper as she fell. "Please..."

Kaelyn snarled, dived, and blew a jet of fire.

The flames engulfed Nairi.

A burning corpse crashed through trees below, thudded into the snow, and lay crackling.

Kaelyn landed above the body, still in dragon form. Blood and ash stained her scales. She panted, and her tongue lolled, and her wounds bled. She snarled down at Nairi's body.

"You fell today, servant of evil," she hissed. "Your emperor dies today too. I killed you, Nairi Blackrose, and I will kill my father."

Kaelyn gritted her teeth, flapped her wings, and soared. She crashed back into a sea of dragons and death.

RUNE

"Tilla!" he cried. "Tilla!"

He had seen her! Stars, she flew here in the battle!

"Tilla!" he shouted again, seeking her. He had only glimpsed her white scales, and she was gone, drowned in this sea of fire and blood.

Was it even her? Did he truly fly in battle against Tilla, his best friend, the woman he loved?

"We have to turn back," he whispered. "Stars, we can't kill Tilla." He raised his voice to a howl. "We have to fly back!"

But it was too late. Nobody heard him. The battle raged. Dragons fell all around, returning in death to human form. Three legionaries charged and flamed a resistor; when the dragon became human again, the legionaries bit and tore the body apart. Two other dragons slammed into each other, and claws ripped down one's belly, spilling blood and organs. The trees below turned red. Smoke hid the sky.

This was slaughter. This was carnage. And Tilla was somewhere here in this sky... or lying upon the forest below.

"Tilla!" Rune shouted again and whisked between the battling dragons, seeking her.

"Rune, get back here!" Kaelyn shouted somewhere below. "Rune, fly among us..."

Her voice faded. Rune ignored her. He snarled and darted between the battling dragons, seeking Tilla. He crashed between legionaries, barely dodging their claws. He dived under a falling body; it thudded against his back, then rolled off and kept tumbling. Rune rose higher.

"Tilla!" he shouted.

Shadows hid the sun. Blue wings unfurled. A great dragon cackled above, spraying drool and blood from her jaws.

Shari Cadigus.

Two smaller, metallic dragons flew at her sides, wearing helms topped with blades.

"The pup!" Shari said and laughed. "The vermin child! Slay him."

The two metallic dragons bared fangs, plunged down, and spewed fire.

Rune snarled and soared toward them.

He swerved right, dodging one stream of fire. The other jet crashed against his shoulder. Rune screamed, his scales cracking in the heat.

Shari—the woman who'd murdered a girl in his hometown, who'd taken Tilla from him, who'd crushed the empire under her heel. Rage filled Rune.

I will kill you, Shari.

Screaming, he rose higher and slashed his claws. Blood showered from one metallic dragon's face. Rune howled and blew flames, bathing the other with fire. He drove forward, shouting, and clawed madly. Scales rained like coins from a cut purse. Rune blew his flames, lashed his tail, and the two metallic dragons screamed.

They lost their magic.

They tumbled, two men in cracked armor, and crashed into the forest below.

Rune looked up, panting.

Shari still flew there, a hundred yards above, her blue wings wider than his own. She laughed, mocking him. Her eyes burned. Bits of flesh dangled from her maw, the remnants of men she'd killed.

"Relesar!" she called down to him. "Tell me, has my sister spread her legs for you yet? How much did you pay her? Or was it the other way around?"

Rune snarled and soared, roaring fire.

Laughing, Shari swerved and dodged his flames. The blue dragon snapped her teeth at him, forcing him back.

"Who was the man who adopted you again?" Shari asked, eyes shining with amusement. "Wil Brewer, was it not? Was he close to you? I enjoyed burning his flesh."

Rune snarled. "Now *you* will burn, Shari."

He blew his flames.

Shari laughed, flapped her wings, and rose higher. She spewed her own fire.

The inferno crashed against Rune.

He screamed.

He fell.

His scales cracked in the heat, Shari laughed above, and Rune tumbled. He righted himself just in time to see Shari swoop. He raised his claws but was too slow. She crashed atop him, her fangs bit his neck, and his blood spilled.

"Yes, scream, whore!" Shari said and laughed. "Your father screamed the same way when we killed him."

He fell through the sky. More of her fire rained upon him.

I can't win this, he thought in a haze. *I was wrong, Kaelyn. I was wrong. I should have listened to you. I've led us to death.*

He blinked, gazed through the fire, and saw Shari charge toward him. No more amusement filled her eyes. She opened her maw wide, and her claws lashed.

"And now, Rune," she said, "it's time to die."

No, Rune thought. *No.* He could not die today. He could not let Kaelyn fall here, and Valien, and all the others. He had to save them, and he had to save Tilla.

Her flames crashed down.

Rune beat his wings, drove forward, and dodged the blaze. He soared. He flew past her. He spun and swooped, the sun at his back, and rained fire.

The blaze crashed against Shari and she screamed. Welts rose across her wings.

Rune slammed into her, lashed his claws, and tore through her wing. It ripped like leather under a blade. Air whistled through it.

Shari shrieked. She bucked. She lashed her tail, and its spikes drove into Rune, but he ignored the pain. He kept tearing at her wing, widening the rent.

"You will die!" Shari screamed and blew flame over her shoulder.

Rune shut his eyes. The flames roared across his back. The pain nearly broke him. He felt more scales crack across him. He clawed and bit madly. Blinded with smoke and fire, he felt the joint where her wing met her back.

He bit down hard.

He tore through cartilage.

He pulled back, ripping her wing off, and spat.

She tumbled below him, screaming, a dragon with one wing. The severed appendage caught the wind and flew away like a sail torn from a ship. Shari roared. She flapped her one wing uselessly.

Rune rained his fire. The flames crashed against her.

With a howl that sounded far too young and afraid—the cry of a hurting girl—the blue dragon returned to human form. Shari Cadigus fell screaming, a woman with blood on her shoulder, her armor shattered.

Rune dived after her.

"Shari!" he screamed.

Dragons flowed between them. Rune crashed into one, shoved the beast aside, and kept diving. Shari tumbled. Rune reached out his claws. He had to catch her, to kill her before she could escape. Another dragon shot between them. Rune cursed and slammed against scales. He leaped off, pulled his wings close, and roared fire. He kept swooping. He saw Shari below. He could almost catch her. He reached out his claws—

A white dragon streaked below.

Rune howled.

The white dragon caught the tumbling Shari, flapped wings, and flew westward over the forest.

Rune stared, heart freezing.

Stars no.

"Tilla," he whispered.

He hovered in the sky. His eyes burned. His wounds blazed. Then a dozen dragons charged toward him, roaring fire.

TILLA

She flew, the wounded princess of Requiem in her claws Her eyes burned and her belly roiled.

I saved her. Oh stars, I saved her. I could have let her die. But I stopped Rune. I chose Shari over him. Oh stars.

She flew through smoke and fire, tears in her eyes. She looked down at Shari; the princess was writhing, and her eyes rolled back, and her lips mumbled. Blood poured from her shoulder blade. The forests streamed below them; half the trees were blazing and raising smoke that nearly blinded Tilla.

"I'm taking you to safety, Commander," Tilla said.

The fortress of Castra Luna rose ahead from the inferno. Cannons were firing from its walls. Smoke unfurled and the fortress shook. Dragons flew above it in defense; the Resistance had not yet broken through to the walls themselves. There would be safety inside those stone halls.

Why did I save her? Tilla thought as she flew over the walls. Stars, she could have let Shari fall! She could have tried to escape with Rune. She...

She was a soldier of Requiem.

Tilla nodded and blinked tears from her eyes.

She had sworn a vow when receiving her rank. She has sworn to fight for Requiem, to defend her lands, to protect her commanders.

I will keep an eye on you, Tilla the ropemaker, Shari had said that first day in Cadport. Tilla had sworn to prove her worth to the princess. She would prove it now.

She shot over the walls. The cannons fired beneath her, shaking the fort. Tilla dived toward the grand hall; its doors stood closed. Corpses of resistors, those brazen enough to have flown this far, lay strewn outside the gates.

Tilla hovered above the courtyard, her wings scattering dust, bits of armor, and a severed leg. She placed Shari down upon the cobblestones, then shifted into human form too.

"Princess Shari," Tilla whispered, kneeling above her. "You're safe."

Shari moaned and her eyes fluttered open. Blood filled her mouth.

"Tilla Roper," the princess whispered, voice hoarse, and spat out blood. "Tilla of Cadport."

She remembers me!

Despite the blood, terror, and pain, Tilla felt pride well up inside her. Hundreds of thousands served in the Legions—and Princess Shari remembered her.

If I save her life, Tilla thought, *she will reward me. I can rise above the Black Roses. She will promote me. She will grant me power.*

Tilla tightened her lips. She had sworn to survive in the Legions; this was the greatest thing she could do now.

"I'm going to save you, my princess," she said. "Can you stand? I'll get you inside. There is safety behind the walls. The enemy still fights above the forest."

She helped the princess to her feet. Shari slung her arms across Tilla's shoulders, and the two began to limp toward the doors. Tilla was the tallest woman in her phalanx, possibly the entire fort, yet Shari stood even taller, her body lithe but heavy with muscle and steel. Tilla struggled to support her; her knees ached and nearly buckled.

When she reached the doors, Tilla pounded against them.

"Shari Cadigus is here! Open the doors!"

Arrowslits lined the walls and turrets. Behind them, shadows stirred and men called out.

"Shari Cadigus!" The cry echoed behind the doors. "Open the gates!"

The doors creaked open, and Tilla entered, supporting Shari. The princess limped, most of her weight pressed against Tilla's shoulders. Once they were inside, the doors slammed shut again.

Axehands stood in the hall, arranged in battle formations, their namesake blades raised. The low, vaulted ceiling and crowded columns left no room for dragons; if the battle reached these halls, it would be a battle of blades.

Prince Leresy stood behind the Axehand formations. His eyes widened and he gasped.

"Shari!" he said. He ran between the axehands, shoving them aside. "Move. Move! Let me through." He reached Shari and stared at her, eyes narrowed. "You're wounded."

Still leaning on Tilla, the princess snarled. "Go back and hide behind your thugs, brother. The battle still rages."

Confirming her words, howls sounded outside. The archers at the walls cried out and began firing through the arrowslits. Thuds shook the doors, and fire burst around their frames.

"Break down the doors!" howled a voice outside. "Kill the prince and princess. Kill them all! Break inside!"

Tilla laid her princess on the floor, drew her sword, and stood above her.

She bared her teeth, sucked in her breath, and watched as the doors cracked.

VALIEN

The sky darkened into night, clouds brewed into a storm, and Valien flew through dream and memory.

Rain fell in sheets, thunder boomed, and lightning flared. Dragonfire reflected in every raindrop. Smoke rose like demons and blood spilled. All around, through ash and rain, the shadows of dragons spun, rose, fell, and crashed together with bursts of light. Valien flew through a nightmare, a single dragon in a sea of ghosts.

"Marilion," he whispered as he flew, still seeking her. "Do you fly among these ghosts?"

Cannons boomed ahead. A cannonball cut through the clouds and slammed into a dragon beside Valien. The dragon collapsed into human form. The cannonball kept flying; the man fell, limbs torn and tumbling.

Valien snarled.

I've come here to save the living, he thought. *And to avenge the dead.*

"Resistance!" he howled. "Follow my fire—to the fort! We break through."

He blew a pillar of flame skyward, a beacon for his warriors. Behind him, he heard them answer his call. Thousands of flaming pillars pierced the clouds, spinning and roaring. The rain steamed.

"Claim this fort!" Valien roared and flew forward. "Death to Cadigus!"

He beat his wings madly. He could still see little of the battle; all around, the smoke, fire, and blood curtained the forest.

The battling dragons were nothing but shadows and firelight upon scales. Yet Valien drove onward. He could hear the enemy ahead: their cannons firing, their dragons calling, their emperor shouting for the red spiral.

Yes, you await me here, old friend, Valien thought. *You who killed my king, who killed my wife. I hear your call, Frey. I come to answer.*

He blew more fire, clawed an imperial dragon who charged his way, and kept flying. From smoke and fire, he saw them rising: the black walls of Castra Luna.

Years ago, Valien himself had served in this fort. Back then, the Aeternum dynasty had ruled here. Ivy had covered pale walls. The sons and daughters of Requiem had studied swordplay, dragonfire, and justice. Today no ivy covered the walls, only black tiles draped with banners of the red spiral. Today the youths studied no justice, only cruelty and murder.

Today, Valien vowed, *we cleanse this fortress.*

Cannons boomed.

Balls of iron flew through the smoke and clouds.

Valien howled, rose higher, and dodged a missile. Behind him, dragons screamed and blood sprayed him. Dark shadows leaped from the walls below, and pillars of fire blazed his way.

"Break down the walls!" Valien cried. "Resistance, follow—take this fortress!"

He swooped, claws outstretched. More dragons flew toward him, their bladed helms engraved with spirals. Valien bathed them with fire, then clawed their blazing bodies. He dived. A cannon fired toward him. He dodged the missile, landed on the gun, and roared his fire. Men burned and fell screaming from the walls. Casks of gunpowder blazed, and Valien soared, the flames licking his feet.

"Slay the enemy!" he howled. "Show Cadigus no mercy."

The Resistance descended from the sky, a rain of scales and claws. Hundreds of dragons landed upon the walls, towers, and courtyards, roaring their flames. Arrows shot from inside the halls and towers. Dragons clad in armor—frightened youths only moons into their service—fought and died.

Valien stood in the courtyard, tail lashing, breath blazing. Arrows clattered against his scales. A dragon shot toward him, and he flamed it; it crashed down in human form, a charred young man crying for his mother.

"Break down the doors!" Valien howled, pointing a claw at the main hall. "Slay all who lurk inside."

The main hall of Castra Luna rose from the fire, its columns wreathed in smoke; the Regime's echelon would be lurking inside. Arrows flew from slits. One slammed into Valien's shoulder, and he roared.

We end this tonight, Valien swore and let flames fill his maw. He flapped his wings, prepared to charge at the doors and smash into the hall.

A cackle from above froze him.

Old pain flared in dark shadows.

Valien knew that cackle. He had heard that cackle the night his wife died. He heard that cackle every night since in his dreams. It was a rumble like thunder, like demons in the deep, like the death of all Valien had ever loved.

He looked up.

Through the rain and fire, he saw him there, a great golden dragon upon the clock tower—burly, demonic, wreathed in fire.

Frey Cadigus. Emperor of Requiem.

The man who killed you, Marilion.

"Valien!" the beast cried from above. "Valien, come to me! You have flown here slaying youths. Now face an emperor. Or will you run again, coward?"

Valien snarled, beat his wings, and took flight.

The clock tower rose before him, the tallest spire in Castra Luna—in all southern Requiem. As Valien flew past the great dials, the bells chimed midnight. Each chime clanged across the palace, as loud as the cannons. Valien kept ascending until he reached the tower's top. Black crenellations rose here like jagged claws reaching skyward.

Atop this dark steeple, the emperor waited.

"Valien!" shouted Frey Cadigus. "You've at last come to join your wife."

Frey's wings beat, churning cloud, smoke, and fire. Lightning blazed against the emperor's golden scales. His teeth shone. Flames crackled in his maw like a smelter. He seemed less a dragon than a primordial beast, a demon of the Abyss.

"*You* will die this night!" Valien called, hovering before the beast. "Your stronghold falls, Frey. Your reign ends here. Aeternum has returned; you cannot survive."

Frey cackled again, the sound of tar bubbling from the deep, and blasted his fire.

Valien howled and blew his own flames.

The two streams crashed together and exploded, showering sparks across the sky. Valien drove through the inferno, opened his maw, and slammed into the emperor.

The two dragons thudded together. They fell. They crashed against the tower, and its obsidian cracked. Lightning slammed into a jagged crenellation; its light revealed thousands of dragons still battling around the fort. Thunder pealed.

"You cannot defeat the power of the red spiral," Frey said. The gold dragon lashed his tail, shoving Valien aside. "The pup you brought here won't save you, Valien. Nothing can save you now."

Valien slid across the roof. The knob of a trapdoor drove into his flesh and snapped off, remaining inside him. Valien roared and Frey's fire blasted him.

Agony flared. Frey's tail cudgeled him again, and a spike pierced his scales. Valien howled, slid another few feet, and dangled over the tower's edge. Below him, hundreds of dragons battled across the walls and barracks.

"Now you can only die, Valien," said the emperor. The golden dragon loomed above him, a god of scale and flame. "Only die."

Frey's fire blasted down.

Howling, Valien leaped up.

The dragons crashed together in a shower of fire.

"You have already failed, Frey!" Valien howled, driving the golden dragon back. He clawed and bit at the beast. "Your daughter left you; she fights at my side. The heir of Aeternum flies with me too; the people rally around him. Your reign ends tonight. You—"

"Your wife, Valien!" Frey said, biting and clawing. "What was her name? Marilion, was it not?"

Rage flared in Valien, blinding him, spinning his head. He howled and blew flames.

"You will not speak her name here! You will—"

"I bedded her that night, Valien!" the emperor shouted, still laughing maniacally. "Did you not know? She spread her legs for me, and I thrust into her, and she loved it. She moaned with pleasure. I gave her a taste of a true man before I stuck my blade in her gut."

Claws lashed Valien. His scales fell like jewels. His blood poured. Frey roared his fire, and heat blasted Valien, and he howled. In the flames, he saw her again: His Marilion, his wife, his love. He saw her smile—that smile that always seemed so hesitant, trembling, a ray of joy breaking through her sadness. He saw her eyes again, kind eyes that carried so much old pain, yet which shone whenever he held her, whenever he kissed her cheek, whenever she sang to the birds they kept in a golden cage.

Marilion. Scarred and afraid, pure and loving, a moonbeam caught in a storm.

And he saw her dead. He saw the blood soaking her gown. He saw Frey's sword stuck inside her. The cage had fallen; the birds had fled. Her eyes had stared. Her smile had died.

Marilion. Timid and strong. Hurt and beautiful.

I will join you now, Marilion, Valien thought as the fire washed him, as the emperor's claws cut him, as his blood spilled. *I fly to you now, and we will meet in the starlit halls of the fallen. I will never let you go again, and your eyes will never know more pain.*

"Valien!" cried a distant voice, high and afraid. "Valien!"

Was it Marilion calling? Did his beloved shine down from the starlit halls?

"Father, no!" cried the voice.

Valien opened his eyes. Through the blood and fire, he thought he could see her—a green dragon in the storm.

Kaelyn.

Above him, the emperor chortled and turned his flames away.

"My daughter!" Frey called. "You've returned to me, traitor of Requiem! Come die too in my fire."

Welts and blood covered Valien. He wheezed and gagged for breath. He flapped his wings weakly and struggled to stand. Frey held his claws against his chest, pinning him down; Valien struggled and lashed his tail, but was too weak to rise.

"Kaelyn," he whispered.

The emperor was still laughing. "Fly to me, Kaelyn! You've betrayed your empire and your family. Come die in my fire."

Valien drew flame into his maw.

Kaelyn—a new light in his life. Kaelyn—daughter of his enemy, beacon of his soul. Kaelyn—the woman who looked so much like Marilion, the woman who stirred memories he feared, the woman Valien had vowed to defend.

I will not let you die too, Kaelyn.

She came flying toward them, a green dragon caught in the wind. Frey roared and blasted fire her way.

Valien howled, shoved himself up, and crashed against Frey.

The two dragons fell against the tower, cracking stones and shattering the trapdoor. Valien bit down hard. His fangs drove into Frey's shoulder, tore through scales, sank into flesh, and drew blood.

Frey screamed.

Valien lashed his claws. He pulled his head back, blasted Frey with fire, and thrust his horns. He pierced the emperor's chest, and blood spurted, and Valien kept clawing, kept biting, kept blasting his fire.

With crackling heat and shimmering scales, Kaelyn landed upon the tower and joined her flame to his.

Frey Cadigus burned.

His scales cracked.

His skin peeled.

And yet he laughed. He kept cackling. He spread his wings wide; they rose in flame like burning sails, spreading smoke. And still he laughed.

"Your fire makes me strong!" he called. "You are like me, Valien. You are like the thing you hate. You too are a killer. You too lead hordes to blood. You fight to slay a monster; you've become one yourself!"

With that, Frey Cadigus fell.

The golden dragon slammed against the tower top... and lost his magic.

Frey's smaller, human form—charred and clad in armor—crashed through the shattered trapdoor and vanished into shadows.

Valien leaped, shifted into human form, and jumped after him into the darkness.

He crashed down against a ladder, reached out, and grabbed a rung.

"Frey!" he shouted. "Face me, Frey! Does the great emperor run like a coward?"

He could not see the emperor; darkness cloaked the chamber. Lightning blazed outside the windows, illuminating tapestries stained with blood. Valien descended the ladder, placed his boots upon the floor, and drew his sword.

Located above the tower clocks, this was the chamber of Castra Luna's lord—once a benevolent princess of Aeternum, today the foul Leresy Cadigus. The prince was away now. A mirror stood against one wall, framed in gold, and firelight glowed behind a stained-glass window. A bed stood by a table topped with wine jugs. A trail of blood led across the floor toward a shadowy corner; groaning rose from those shadows.

Valien grunted, clutched his sword, and marched across the floor.

His torchlight fell upon a charred, bloody Frey Cadigus.

It ends now.

Valien raised his sword and kept marching, only feet away from the emperor.

A dagger gleamed.

Frey snarled and tossed the blade.

Pain burst across Valien. The dagger pierced his chest beneath the shoulder.

Valien's breath left him. Stars swam across his eyes. He howled and raised his sword again, prepared to land the killing blow, even if he died with it.

"Marilion lives, Valien!" Frey called and cackled, blood on his lips. "She lives in my dungeon, you fool!"

Valien faltered.

Horror thudded into him, sharper than the dagger.

Frey dragged himself up, ran toward the window, and crashed through the stained glass. Multicolored shards flew. Frey tumbled outside into the rain.

"Frey!" Valien howled, blood washing his eyes, blood soaking his shirt. He ran toward the window. He fell to his knees. "Frey!"

Outside in the storm, a golden dragon beat wings, spun toward the tower, and blasted fire.

"Valien!"

Hands grabbed his shoulders and pulled him back.

Kaelyn dragged him aside, and they pushed themselves against the wall, and flames bathed the room.

"Dragons of Requiem!" Frey shouted outside, voice ragged. "Fall back! Fall back to the capital."

Valien could hear no more. Was Frey dying? Did his injuries silence him? Had Valien himself died?

He held onto Kaelyn, and tears streamed down his cheeks.

"She lives," he whispered, trembling and clutching her. "She lives, stars, she lives."

The tower shook. Flames crackled outside. Thousands of dragons roared in a storm of sound and fury.

LERESY

Thuds shook the door. Chips of wood flew. Around the doorframes, dragonfire roared and blasted into the hall.

"Break down the doors!" cried voices outside, and again the doors shook. Splinters flew. "Slay everyone inside!"

Leresy stood trembling. His hand was so sweaty he could barely grip his sword. His head spun and his breath shook in his lungs.

"Do something!" he screamed. "Soldiers—slay them! Drive them back!"

He whipped his head from side to side madly. His trousers, soaked with his own urine, clung to him. The doors kept shaking—again and again. Every time the dragons outside slammed against them, more chips of wood flew, and more fire raced around the frames.

"Go on, kill them!" Leresy screamed, voice hoarse. His sword shook madly in his hand. "I order you! Are you disobeying your prince?"

And yet his soldiers—a mix of the Axehand and the Legions—only stood still, weapons raised, facing the door and waiting. Waiting! How could they just stand and wait like this?

"I order you to kill them!" Leresy cried, and his voice cracked. "You took vows. You swore to defend your price— now kill the enemy!"

He looked around madly, seeking an exit. There were no windows here, only arrowslits, and men stood there firing their bows. Who had designed this damn fortress? How could they not have built windows for escape? The enemy kept slamming at the doors, and outside the arrowslits, Leresy glimpsed thousands of the flying beasts.

Barbarians! A horde of unwashed outlaws! And his own men—soldiers trained for honor and strength—did nothing?

"Why don't you kill them?" he demanded, pacing among his troops. They only stood like damn statues, frozen and watching the doors. He screamed so loudly, his voice became but a shrill rasp. "I order you to get out there and kill them all!"

"They can't, you fool," Shari said. The princess sat slumped in the corner, bandaged and bloody. Her face was ashen, but scorn still filled her eyes. "They know war. *You* know how to fluff up your hair, choose the finest embroidery, and kiss our father's arse. Stand back and let them do their job, little brother."

Leresy spun toward her, baring his teeth. "Look at you! Look at you, sister, the great warrior. You lie wounded and dying. What do you know of war?"

Sitting in the shadows, she smirked. "Enough to fly out and fight one, not cower in a hall."

"And yet now you too cower," he said. He raised his sword; it wavered in his palm. "I should end your life now, Shari. I—"

A thud echoed across the room.

Leresy spun back toward the doors. A great crack had appeared, showering splinters. Flames burst into the hall, forcing his soldiers back.

Tilla stood among the troops, Leresy saw. Sweat drenched her face, blood stained her armor, and yet she stood tall. She clenched her jaw and held her sword before her, ready to fight.

"Do not let them break the doors!" Leresy shouted at the soldiers. "If you let the enemy in, I will butcher you myself!"

He spun away, marched across the hall, and approached an arrowslit. A soldier stood there, firing his bow. Leresy grabbed the man and shoved him aside.

"Let me see!" Leresy said. "I must view the battle to lead you."

He stared outside, and he felt the blood leave his face. Sweat drenched him.

By the red spiral...

Their defenses had crumbled. Dragons of the Resistance covered Castra Luna's walls. Their tails slammed at the cannons, sending the great iron guns tumbling. Bodies of legionaries lay across the courtyard, torn apart. Leresy saw strewn limbs and severed heads and everywhere blood. The horde approached from all sides; they covered the sky.

Leresy gasped for breath. His heart blazed with pain. This hall, with its low ceiling and many columns, was too cramped for dragons to enter, but the Resistance could still swarm in here as men, screaming and bloodthirsty and armed with steel.

I'm going to die, Leresy realized, and tears filled his eyes. Kaelyn was going to kill him. *Why, sister? I always comforted you. I was a good brother to you...*

"Fall back!" roared a voice outside, and great wings stirred the smoke. "Fall back to the capital! Dragons of Requiem—rally behind me. Follow!"

Leresy squinted through the arrowslit, peered up, and saw his father flying north. The golden dragon was badly wounded; his scales were cracked and charred, and gashes bled across his flesh. A few survivors rallied behind him and began fleeing north, breaking through the Resistance.

"He's leaving without me," Leresy whispered, and his fists trembled. His voice rose to a howl. "He's betrayed me! My father's betrayed me!"

He pulled back from the arrowslit, looked around wildly, and saw the doors shaking. More cracks raced across them. Fire blazed through.

I have to get out. I have to get out!

Leresy sucked in his breath. *Of course. The tower top!*

He began racing across the hall, shoving soldiers aside.

"Move. Move it! Out of my way!" He ran toward the staircase at the back. "Defend these doors. Defend these stairs!" Saliva flew from his mouth as he screamed. "Do not let the enemy in, or I'll hang you from Requiem's palace!"

He leaped onto the staircase, glanced back at the hall doors, and saw them shatter open.

A hundred dragons of the Resistance, beasts of fire and scale, shifted into human forms and raced into the hall.

Leresy ran.

He left the hall. He ran up the spiraling, stone staircase, heart thudding. Below, he heard the screams—so many screams. Steel clashed. Fire blazed. Shouts of "Requiem!" and "Death to Cadigus" rang across the fort.

Leresy shrieked, pumped his fists, and kept racing upstairs.

"Hold them back!" he shouted over his shoulder. "Soldiers of Requiem, I order you! Defend this fortress!"

He raced around and around. His breath rattled. He slipped, banged his hip, then leaped up and kept running. The fire blazed and the screams rose behind him. When he looked over his shoulder, he saw shadows racing upstairs; he didn't know if they were his troops fleeing too, or the enemy pursuing.

The stone staircase ended in a chamber of gears, springs, and bells. Upon the four walls, Leresy saw the inner faces of four clocks. A hundred gears, some taller than him, moved and clanged together. The clocks ticked. Ropes creaked and weights shifted. Instead of stone stairs, an iron stairwell coiled up toward a small door near the ceiling.

"Grab the prince!" rose shouts below. "Slay him!"

Leresy leaped onto the iron stairwell. He raced up, the gears and springs all creaking around him. He shoved the door open and burst into his chambers.

Blood soaked the room; men had fought here too. One window was smashed open, and outside, Leresy saw the battle raging. Thousands of dragons still flew, roaring fire; most were beasts of the Resistance, too barbaric to even wear armor. His father was leading legionaries through the encircling enemy, cleaving a way north.

"Leresy!" cried a voice below from the staircase. "Damn it, Leresy!"

It was Shari.

Leresy snarled.

"No, sister," he hissed. "You will not flee this place with me. This will be your tomb."

He spun toward the doorway and saw her limping up the iron staircase, pale and bleeding and screaming for him.

Leresy slammed the chamber door shut, grabbed the keys from his belt, and locked it.

Shari slammed against the door.

"Brother!" she screamed from behind. "Damn you, Leresy, open this door!"

He cackled. "No, Shari! You were too late to flee. Go fight with your troops, Shari! I thought you were a great warrior. So die like one!"

He ran toward his heavy bureau and shoved with all his strength. The bureau scratched across the floor, and Leresy pushed it against the door. Panting, he placed himself behind his bed next, gritted his teeth, and shoved. The bed slammed against the bureau. Nobody would be breaking through this door now.

"Leresy!" his sister screamed from the stairway. "Damn it, Leresy, open this door, or I'm going to butcher you like the pig you are!"

He laughed, spraying sweat and spittle. "Goodbye, sister! Enjoy your death!"

With that, Leresy ran toward the window, leaped outside into the night, and shifted.

Wind whipped him. Fire blazed below and smoke blinded him. Rain crashed down and lightning rent the sky, and everywhere the dragons flew. Below in the courtyard, Leresy saw more resistors pouring into the fort.

"Father!" Leresy cried; he spotted the emperor and his troops ahead, cleaving a way out. "Wait for me, Father!"

Dragons dived toward him, blowing fire. Leresy soared higher and rained flame upon them. He flew madly, tail lashing, and joined the retreat.

"Goodbye, Shari!" Leresy screamed over his shoulder, and delight filled him; he had perhaps lost this fort, but he had gained his inheritance. "Goodbye, you wretched pile of rocks!"

They broke through the ring of beasts. They streamed over the forests, bloody and charred and howling. A hundred dragons—the emperor, a cluster of survivors, and Leresy— howled and beat their wings and fled into the night.

TILLA

The hall had fallen.

Tilla screamed through flame, swung her sword, and cut a man. A column cracked beside her. A bearded warrior howled, charged her way, and their swords clanged. The walls shook. Fire burned.

The hall had fallen.

"Fall back!" somebody screamed behind her. "Up the stairs—into the tower!"

Tilla could not even turn around to seek the stairs. Warriors rushed all around her. Axehands fought at her sides, axes swinging and black robes fluttering. She had lost Erry and Mae; had they died? Bodies lay across the hall. Blood flowed around boots. Men screamed and blades swung.

I'm going to die here, Tilla thought. *The hall has fallen. I'm going to die.*

One soldier, a tanner from Cadport, tried to shift into a dragon. He ballooned in size, only crushing himself between the columns, floor, and low ceiling. Swords slammed into his flesh, and the dragon screamed, then returned to human form—a butchered boy, belly slashed open. The legionaries fell all around, their insignia only hours old on their armbands, and their blood washed the floor.

And I will fall with them.

The clock chimed above her five times. Dawn was near, a last light before the darkness.

We die at dawn, Tilla thought. She held her sword before her. *A new day rises; an empire falls.*

"Fall back!" the voice shouted behind. "Tilla, with me!"

Swords swung at Tilla. She parried blow after blow. She could not turn around, not without letting the enemy slay her. She walked backward, blocking attacks. Axehands screamed around her, clashing against the resistors, swinging the axes strapped to their stumps. Tilla kept retreating. Her boots slammed into a corpse; she stepped upon the dead man and kept moving.

"Tilla!"

Somebody grabbed Tilla's arm, and she spun around and raised her sword. Her heart thrashed and she screamed in rage, prepared to kill. But the hand grabbing her belonged to Erry.

"Erry!" she said. "Bloody stars, you're alive!"

The scrawny urchin looked half dead. Blood matted her short brown hair. Her face, normally tanned bronze, was ashen. Welts rose across her left temple.

"To the stairs!" Erry said. "Come with me, Tilla."

"Where's Mae?" Tilla shouted.

"I don't know! I think she fled with the others. The emperor is leading us north. Come on!"

Erry tugged and Tilla ran with her. Soldiers and resistors fought all around. The two Black Roses—if they still belonged to a phalanx at all now—leaped over bodies and onto the staircase. Blood stained the steps. The two young women ran, and behind them resistors screamed, and boots thudded.

"Take the stairs!" howled a voice below—the rough voice of the enemy. "Don't let them escape. Up the stairs! Death to Cadigus!"

"Dirty dog bottoms!" Erry cursed as she raced upstairs. "Stars, Tilla, did you think it would end like this?"

"We're not dead yet!" she shouted back. "Run!"

They raced up the spiraling steps. The battle cries echoed behind them. Swords clanged.

Pain flared on her calf. Tilla yelped and spun to see a resistor; his blade had nicked her. With a scream, Tilla swung her sword down, cleaving his hand. She kicked, and the resistor tumbled backward, crashing into men behind him.

"Tilla!" Erry cried.

"Keep running!"

They raced upstairs, breath ragged, boots slipping in the blood. Finally they emerged into the great clock room. Gears, larger than the greatest wagon wheels, turned and clanged all around. Ropes and weights rose and fell, and on each wall, a great dial ticked. An iron staircase coiled up between the gears like a giant spring, leading toward a door.

Tilla gasped.

Princess Shari stood at that door, ashen and bleeding. Blood filled her hair and stained her face. She was driving her shoulder into the door, again and again, but could not break it.

"He blocked the door!" the princess cried from above. "Leresy—he left us to die. Help me break it open."

Erry leaped onto the iron stairwell and raced up toward the princess. Tilla ran close behind. They reached the locked doorway near the ceiling. Below them, all across the chamber, the gears turned and ticked.

"Death to Cadigus!"

Resistors burst into the clock chamber from below, a dozen warriors in armor, their swords bloody. They ran between the gears, leaped onto the iron staircase, and began racing up.

"Erry!" Tilla shouted. "Help the princess break the door. I'll hold them back!"

Standing upon the staircase, Tilla swung her sword. It clanged against an enemy blade. She swung down, cleaving the man's helmet. He fell, blood gushing from his head, and crashed into the men behind him. Another resistor replaced him. His blade met Tilla's. She screamed and kicked, knocking the man over the staircase banister. He crashed into the gears below; they kept spinning, crushing the man between them.

"Break the door!" Tilla shouted. "Get out of here!"

She glanced behind her. Erry and Shari were both slamming against the door, cracking it. It opened an inch; something was blocking it.

Tilla spun back toward the enemy. She swung her sword again, parrying a blow. A red-haired woman was attacking her, screaming wildly. Tilla screamed too, blocked the mad attack, and thrust her sword. She pierced the woman's belly, sending her tumbling down; the gears crushed and swallowed her. Tilla glanced over her shoulder to see the door opened another inch.

"It's almost open!" Erry cried from above. "Hold them back just a little longer."

Another resistor charged toward Tilla. Another sword swung. Tilla parried and the blades clanged.

No.

Shock flooded her. Her eyes stung. Her heart froze, then leaped.

"Rune," she whispered.

The resistor below her, covered in sweat and blood, was him.

"Rune!" she cried.

"The door's almost open!" Erry screamed behind. "Almost there!"

He stared at her, face bloody and blade raised. He was thinner than Tilla had ever seen him. His eyes were colder than she'd ever known.

But it was him. It was her Rune.

"Tilla," he whispered.

His voice raised memories in her like waves over rocks. In the shadows of the chamber, she saw the sea again, the cliffs at night, the stars above. She felt the wind beneath her wings as they flew together. She felt his kiss again, lips warm against hers in the cold. She saw Cadport, two lost youths, and soft lights in the dark.

"Rune," she said, and tears stung her eyes. "You are here. How can this be?"

"Got it!" Erry cried above. "The door's open. Come on, Tilla!"

Yet Tilla only stood still, staring at Rune. He craned his neck up, peered over her shoulder, and snarled. Tilla had never seen him snarl.

"Tilla, I have to get through!" he said. "Shari Cadigus is escaping."

He took a step up. He made to run around her.

What do I do? Stars, what do I do?

She moved and blocked his climb.

"Tilla!" he shouted. "Tilla, she's getting away."

Tears streamed down Tilla's cheeks. She placed a hand against Rune's shoulder.

"I can't, Rune," she whispered. "I can't. I made a vow. I can't."

He shook his head in amazement. He tried to shove past her. She stopped him.

"Tilla, let me through!"

He grabbed her arms. She pushed him back.

"Rune!" Her tears fell. "Please, Rune, listen to me. I made a vow. I vowed to defend Requiem. You can't—"

"Shari is getting away!"

Rune grabbed her and tried to pull her back.

She wrenched herself free.

She raised her arms—only to block his climb—but he mistook her gesture for a sword's thrust. He raised his own sword. Their blades crashed together.

"Tilla," he whispered, and surprise and pain filled his eyes. "Tilla, how can you do this? How can you protect her? Stars! We can end this tonight. Fight with me—with us. Not with... not with these murderers!" His eyes burned red. "I don't know what they taught you. What did they do to you? Oh stars, Tilla—"

"I am Periva Tilla!" she shouted.

Her pain pounded through her. Her chest shook. Their swords swung and clanged again. All around them, the clock gears moved and clanged too, locked in their own duel.

"You are Tilla Roper!" Rune shouted back. "You are a ropemaker from Cadport, Tilla! Don't you remember? Can't you remember who you are?"

He tried to push by her. She blocked him again. Their swords rang.

"That girl is dead," she said, barely able to see through her tears. "I am a soldier now, Rune. I made a vow. I vowed to fight for my kingdom. I cannot let you pass. I cannot let the enemy through—"

"The enemy?" Rune said, voice torn. "Stars, Tilla, I'm not your enemy! The Cadigus Regime—the ones you protect—are the enemy. Tilla, can't you see?"

Her body shook. Her throat tightened.

"I see outlaws!" she shouted, weeping now. "I see a horde that burned my fort, that killed my friends, that slaughtered youths from Cadport. Stars, Rune! Six hundred youths from Cadport trained here! How many of your own townsfolk did you murder? How many of your own friends did you kill?" Her tears fell. "My brother served in this fort. He died serving two years ago—this Valien you follow murdered him! Now you murder too!"

Rune froze. He stared up at her, panting, his eyes wide with horror.

"I..." His sword trembled. "I didn't know. I didn't know the Cadport recruits were here. I—"

"You flew with monsters!" Tilla was panting now, barely able to breathe. "And now they're dead. Now hundreds of boys and girls—the people we grew up with—lie butchered across this fort. And you want me to let you through? I am Periva Tilla! I am a legionary of Requiem!" She slammed her fist against her chest. "I hail the red spiral!"

He stared up at her, frozen. A tear rolled down his cheek, trailing through blood.

"No," he whispered. "No, Tilla. You don't mean that. You can't—"

"Goodbye, Rune," she whispered, and a sob racked her body. "Goodbye."

She spun around.

She leaped through the broken door.

She raced across the prince's chamber, jumped out the window, and shifted.

Wind and lightning and dragons flurried around her. Thunder boomed. The fortress and forests burned below, and smoke shrouded the world.

"Tilla!" he cried behind her. "Tilla!"

She looked over her shoulder and saw Rune standing in the broken window of the tower, calling to her, a shadow in the night.

Goodbye Rune, she thought. *I love you. I love you always. But now you are my enemy.*

She turned her head north, roared a pillar of fire, and flew into the blazing horizon.

SHARI

She stood in her chambers, hand against the fireplace mantel, and stared down into the embers. The fire crackled and danced, a small battle whose light fell upon her. In the flames and shadows, she saw dragons aflight. She saw the Aeternum heir land upon her, claw at her flesh, and tear off her wing. She saw the deaths of thousands.

Shari Cadigus clenched her fists.

"You crippled me, Relesar," she whispered. "You stole my wing. You will suffer. You will scream like none have screamed before."

Her eyes burned. Her fists shook. The flames danced in the hearth, an endless war, their light red like blood, and in their crackle, she thought she heard screams again: the screams of men dying, of her own body tearing, the rip of leather, and—

A knock sounded on her door.

Shari turned from the flame.

She loosened her fists, took a shuddering breath, and raised her chin.

"I will not succumb to the night," she whispered. "I will not allow those flames to claim me."

She walked across her chamber, boots clacking against the tiled floor. Tapestries hung around her, depicting dragons aflight in war. Golden vases engraved with the red spiral stood upon her tables, and swords hung upon the walls. When Shari reached the door, she froze and took a deep breath.

Do not show her your pain, she thought. *No one must know. Here in the capital, weakness is death. Weakness is a stab in the back.*

She opened the door.

Guards lined the hall, faces hidden behind their visors. Tilla Roper stood between them, dressed in a steel breastplate, her new insignia upon her arms. Her sheathed sword hung at her belt. Her black, chin-length hair peeked from under her helmet.

"Commander," the girl said and saluted, slamming her gloved fist against her chest. "You summoned me."

Shari nodded. "Come inside, Roper," she said softly. "Close the door behind you."

She young periva entered. Shari led her across the chamber toward her table, poured two glasses of wine, and handed one to Tilla.

"Drink," Shari said. "Southern wine from your hometown."

Tilla opened her mouth as if about to speak, then closed it and nodded. She sipped.

"Thank you, Commander," she said.

Shari looked upon this young woman.

She's only eighteen, Shari thought. *A decade younger than I am, and frightened, and confused. But there is strength in this one. There is so much cruelty here for the red spiral.*

"I have a gift for you, Tilla Roper," she said.

She stepped into the corner and pulled back a silken veil, revealing a shield. Carved of oak and banded in iron, its surface was painted crimson. It sported a new sigil: a black cannon overlooking the sea.

"Is this... mine?" Tilla asked, narrowing her eyes.

Shari nodded. "Cadport has the oldest cannon in the empire, did you know? I visited it once; it stands upon the boardwalk, overlooking the sea. It no longer works. It rusted years ago. But it's a great symbol of Requiem." She looked at Tilla. "It will be a great symbol for you."

"For me?" Tilla asked and placed her glass down.
"Commander, I'm but a commoner. I cannot have a coat of arms.
I was not noble born."

"That is true," Shari said. "But neither was my father."

Tilla's eyes widened. "Frey Cadigus, the emperor... a
commoner?"

Shari laughed. "The poor son of a logger. He excelled in
the Legions. He began as a humble periva—like you. He rose to
power." Shari lifted the shield and handed it to Tilla. "You will
rise to power too. I vowed to you in Cadport, Tilla, that I will
watch you closely. I have watched you, and I am pleased. Take
this shield, Tilla of Cadport, and bear your sigil proudly. Hail the
red spiral."

Tilla took the shield, lifted her chin, and blinked. She held
the shield tight against her.

"Hail the red spiral," she whispered.

Shari smiled softly. She touched the young woman's cheek
where a tear trailed.

"You are overcome with joy," she said. "That is good. You
are a noble warrior and strong, but you must remember: Never
shed tears. Never show weakness. If you shed a tear again, I
cannot protect you."

Tilla nodded and blinked. "Yes, Commander. I vow to
you: I will be strong. I will serve the Legions well."

Shari sipped her wine and looked back into the flames.
They danced there, the old battle of light and darkness, of heat
and endless winter.

"You will *command*," Shari said and looked back at the
young soldier. "Tilla, you were meant for more than servitude.
You are noble now. You were meant to lead dragons in battle,
not *serve*. Would you like to train in Castra Academia here in the
capital, to become an officer someday like Nairi was? The
training is grueling. You will have to train there for long moons,

and they will break you. But if you survive, Tilla—and I believe you will—you will wear red spirals upon your shoulders. You will become a lanse like Nairi, a young officer. You will lead your own phalanx in war."

Tilla's jaw shook, but she tightened it.

"Castra Academia," she whispered. "Commander! It is a fortress of legend. I would be honored. I vow to you: I will succeed. I will fight for Requiem."

They will break her there, Shari thought, looking upon this young girl. *She will miss the southern Castra Luna. In the academy, they train no cannon fodder like they do in the south. They train killers.*

"Good," Shari said and smiled. She lifted a scroll from her table and handed it to Tilla. "Only a Cadigus can appoint a cadet to Castra Academia. Take this scroll; it bears my seal. Fly there tonight. This scroll assigns you a chamber and commander. Your training begins tomorrow."

Tilla saluted, chin raised and lips tightened. She spun on her heels and marched away.

"Goodbye, Tilla Roper," Shari whispered, then winced.

Pain flared across her shoulder where Rune had torn off her wing. Even when she stood in human form, the wound ached, and Shari rubbed it.

"I will capture you, Rune," she whispered through the pain. "And you, Tilla, will kill him. I heard you speak with him. I will have the boy die at the sword of his beloved."

Shari snarled, gulped down her wine, then tossed the cup into the fireplace. It shattered, and the wine burned like dragons ablaze.

RUNE

Dawn rose over death.

A light snow fell upon Castra Luna, a lingering whisper of winter. A shroud of white clung to the bodies as if preparing them for burial. Hands rose frozen, fingers reaching toward the snowflakes. Dead eyes stared. Mouths screamed silently. Everywhere the ice and frost glittered in the morning, a blanket of stars.

Rune walked among the dead. The battle had ended.

"We claimed this fort," he whispered. "But we lost this battle."

He looked up at Kaelyn. She stood solemn at his side, snow in her long golden hair. The flakes covered her blue cloak and frost coated her armor, yet when she reached out and held Rune's hand, her grip was warm.

She whispered to him, "Battles are always lost. Where youths fall dead, the wise do not rejoice."

Rune lowered his head. "Castra Luna is ours. We claimed this fort. And yet... the emperor fled." His eyes stung. "I killed so many. For nothing."

He walked across the courtyard. Dragons of the Resistance stood upon the walls around him, watching silently. The bodies of legionaries lay upon the cobblestones, some torn apart, others still whole and peaceful like children playing in snow. Rune walked among them, holding Kaelyn's hand.

"I know so many of these faces, Kaelyn," he said. "This boy here—he was a weaver. I knew this girl—she used to sell eggs at the summer fairs."

"I'm sorry, Rune," she whispered.

He walked toward a fallen cannon and knelt by a body. It was a young woman, her strawberry hair braided. Her face was soft, doll-like, and her blue eyes stared.

"I know this one," Rune whispered. "Her name was Mae. She was the daughter of bakers. I used to buy bread from her." His breath frosted and shook, and Rune lowered his head. His tears fell into the snow. "I'm sorry, Mae Baker. I'm sorry."

He closed Mae's blue eyes, the eyes of a friend.

"It wasn't your fault, Rune," Kaelyn said, kneeling beside him. "We couldn't have known."

He looked up at her. "I killed them, Kaelyn. I killed my friends. I killed... oh stars. Tilla was right."

Kaelyn's lips quivered, and she pulled Rune into an embrace so tight he could barely breathe.

"You didn't kill them," she whispered. "My father armed them. My father sent them to battle. We could not have known. Please, Rune. Please."

He held her for long moments, then rose to his feet. He looked around him at the dead, hundreds of them youths from his home.

"We will bury them," he said. "We will bury them with honor—every one."

He shifted into a dragon, filled his wings with air, and flew toward the clock tower.

Valien waited upon the roof, a silver dragon coated in snow, his left horn chipped away. The leader of the Resistance was staring north, his breath frosting. Rune landed beside him, and the two dragons—one burly and silver, the other slim and black—stared north together, silent.

Finally Valien spoke.

"Rune," he said in his deep, raspy voice. "Rune, listen to me."

Rune wanted to speak, but did not trust his voice to remain steady. He nodded silently.

"Rune," said Valien, "what we've begun cannot end here. We cannot let these deaths be in vain. You hurt. You rage. You know loss." He turned to stare at Rune, his eyes burning. "Do not let this be for nothing."

Fire filled Rune's mouth. He wanted to burn the old dragon, to rage, to break down the tower, to fly into the forests and hide forever in their depths.

"They're all dead," he said. "All the youths of my home. My best friend lived, but she serves the red spiral. What do I fight for now, Valien?"

The silver dragon snarled. Fire flared between his teeth.

"You fight for Requiem!" he hissed. "You fight for your father. You fight for your friends who lie dead below—yes, even if they fought for the enemy. We failed here in this fort, but we will fight on." That raspy voice shook now, and the dragon's claws gripped the tower so tightly they chipped the stone. "We will send word to every corner of the empire. We will drop scrolls upon every town and village. We will let them know: Relesar Aeternum has returned, and he rules the south, and he is king. Requiem will be freed."

Rune shook his head. "A king? Valien, my hands are stained in blood. How can I ever hope to rule Requiem?"

The silver dragon's rage seeped away. The smoke from his nostrils died. He sighed, scales clanking, and moved closer to Rune.

"Have you ever seen the capital?" he asked, voice soft.

Rune shook his head.

Valien took a deep breath that rippled his scales. He closed his eyes and a smile revealed his fangs.

"It's not much to look at now," the silver dragon said. "Now it's all banners of the red spiral, and marching soldiers, and towers of obsidian, and statues of Frey." Valien snorted. "Ha! But back then, Rune... back in the days of your father... you should have seen it! Whenever we'd fly toward the city, the guards would greet us from the walls, blowing silver trumpets. When we'd march through the streets, children would throw flowers at us, and people would smile. So many flowers, wine, pretty women..." Valien opened his eyes and winked. "You'd have liked that part, I think."

Rune lowered his head. "I've never seen a city like that."

"You will," Valien said. "You will, Rune. That is why we fight. Not for strength, glory, or any of that rubbish Frey spews. We fight for flowers, for wine, and for silver trumpets upon white walls."

"And for pretty women?" Rune asked.

Valien snorted a laugh; Rune did not think he'd ever heard him laugh before.

"Especially for pretty women," he answered. He nudged Rune with his wing. "Come on, Rune. Let's fly back to Kaelyn. The dead wait below, and we will bury them. And we won't forget the living. You are king of the south now. You have returned." Valien's eyes gleamed. "You will see the capital. I vow this to you. We will fly toward the walls of Nova Vita. Silver trumpets will call you home."

They took flight and Kaelyn joined them. They soared high above the fortress, three dragons in the snow, and roared their song.

Rune looked north. Beyond forest and mountain lay the capital, too distant to see. The throne of Requiem awaited him there; so did the emperor.

"And you wait there too, Tilla," he whispered.

The snow fell and Rune blew his fire. The flaming pillar rose, a pyre for the dead, a beacon for the living... and a light for a lost friend.

THE END

NOVELS BY DANIEL ARENSON

Standalones:
Firefly Island (2007)
The Gods of Dream (2010)
Flaming Dove (2010)

Misfit Heroes:
Eye of the Wizard (2011)
Wand of the Witch (2012)

Song of Dragons:
Blood of Requiem (2011)
Tears of Requiem (2011)
Light of Requiem (2011)

Dragonlore:
A Dawn of Dragonfire (2012)
A Day of Dragon Blood (2012)
A Night of Dragon Wings (2013)

The Dragon War
A Legacy of Light (2013)
A Birthright of Blood (2013)
A Memory of Fire (2013)

KEEP IN TOUCH

www.DanielArenson.com
Daniel@DanielArenson.com
Facebook.com/DanielArenson
Twitter.com/DanielArenson

www.ingramcontent.com/pod-product-compliance
Lightning Source LLC
Chambersburg PA
CBHW031657170626
46808CB00005B/1491